THE TRAI

D0485916

"An assured and complex debu[...]
nist of questionable loyalty and ...ᴜᵣᴀᵢₛ ᴛʜᴀᴛ, despite yourself,
you can't help but love. It's not often you come across a fresh
voice and a fresh take on magic, but *The Traitor God* gives
both. Moments of absolute horror sit cheek by jowl with humour of the blackest kind and some of the monstrous cre-
ations in this book are nauseatingly wonderful."

Anna Stephens, author of Godblind

"Cameron Johnston is an exciting new voice in fantasy. His
writing has a dark sense of humour and his debut is bursting
with imagination and wonders. Fantastic stuff!"

Stephen Aryan, author of the Age of Darkness trilogy

"High magic and low lives collide in *The Traitor God*, one part
street-level procedural and two parts an urban magic apoc-
alypse, this is fantasy walking tall and carrying a big stick."

Gavin G Smith, author of Age of Scorpio *and* The Bastard
Legion

"*The Traitor God* by Cameron Johnston is part murder mystery,
part detective story, and all fantasy that's full of magic, shady
villains and even shadier heroes. A hugely enjoyable tale
and definitely a 2018 debut to look out for. Marvellous stuff."

Edward Cox, author of the Relic Guild Trilogy

"From the frantic opening page, *The Traitor God* grabs you and
doesn't let go. Facing gods, monsters, and a magic elite that
wants him dead, Edrin Walker's return to Setharis is a noir-
ish romp packed with action and laced with black humour,
and marks Cameron Johnston as a real name to watch in the
epic fantasy genre."

Neil Williamson, author of The Moon King

CAMERON JOHNSTON

The Traitor God

ANGRY
ROBOT

ANGRY ROBOT
An imprint of Watkins Media Ltd

20 Fletcher Gate,
Nottingham,
NG1 2FZ • UK

angryrobotbooks.com
twitter.com/angryrobotbooks
A gift for trouble

An Angry Robot paperback original 2018

Cover by Jan Weßbecher
Set in Meridien by Argh! Nottingham

Distributed in the United States by Penguin Random House, Inc.,
New York.

ISBN 978 0 85766 779 3
Ebook ISBN 978 0 85766 780 9

Printed in the United States of America

9 8 7 6 5 4 3 2 1

To the readers and the dreamers,
who in my experience tend to be
one and the same.

CHAPTER 1

Ten years.

Ten wretched years spent fleeing daemons and debt, reduced to a vagabond with little more than the clothes on my back and a set of loaded dice. Every week brought different taverns, different faces, and none that cared if I died in a ditch. The same old scams day after day, blurring into a dreary endless mass as I kept two steps ahead of the unnatural beasts that stalked me. I was a hollow man clinging to existence for a single purpose. It was a price I was more than willing to pay.

I stared into my ale-cup and wondered what had become of my old friends, the very reason for my exile. Concentrating on Lynas' presence in the back of my mind, I felt his comforting warmth pulsing through the Gift-bond that irrevocably linked the two of us. We were more than friends, and more than family; we were part of each other. He was still alive, though a hundred leagues between us had reduced our magical bond to a single thread of sensation that offered no further insight. The deal still held – my exile kept Lynas, Charra and their daughter Layla safe and healthy. It was all that kept me going.

As I did on every anniversary of my flight from home, the great city of Setharis, I lifted a cup in their honour. I drained dregs as sour as my mood and thumped it down on the rough table, a splinter jabbing my finger. The wood was battered and scarred, every bit as worn down as I felt. Come the morning I'd be glad to finally see the back of this dingy tavern and tedious town of Ironport. I teased the sliver of wood from my skin and sucked at the bright bead of blood, the fiery savour of magic bursting on my tongue, expanding my senses.

A hint of burning reached my nostrils: pitch, woodsmoke, and something more unpleasant that tickled the back of my throat. It wasn't coming from the tavern's kitchen. The docks perhaps? I squinted at the door to the street and wondered if I should step out into the night air and take a look, but then the serving girl drew my full attention, weaving towards me through a clamouring crowd of dusty and drink-starved miners just off the last shift in the iron mines.

"Here you are, m'lord," she said, setting a steaming bowl of stew down in front of me. She flashed a coquettish smile and batted her eyelashes in what I could only assume was meant to be an alluring manner; or perhaps she had something stuck in her eye. Her gaze lingered over the ragged scars that cut from the corner of my right eye to my jaw and trailed off down my neck, intrigued by their unspoken tale – which was how it would remain. Some stories are dangerous.

"Thank you, lass," I said, already feeling the fuzzy warmth of alcohol spreading from my belly. I was pleasantly tipsy rather than drunk, but the night was young yet and I wasn't here for anything so insipid as pleasant – no, I was trying to drown the thought of yet another year bled out in the gutters. I slid my cup towards her. "More ale. Keep it coming."

The high and mighty magi of the Arcanum had beaten it into us that no magus should ever get drunk, but I never had given a rat's arse about their stupid rules. They might rule Setharis but they did not rule me. Once those arrogant bastards got their claws into a magically Gifted mind like mine they never, ever, let go, and they would be hounding me still if I hadn't taken great pains to fake my death. A bucket of my blood, a lot of magic, and a masterwork of deception was a small price to pay to get them off my back. If only my daemons were as easy to fool.

From the other side of the tavern, old Sleazy glared at the serving girl with his one remaining eye, bald and scarred pate beading with sweat as he hefted a barrel of ruby ale into place behind the bar. She hastily collected my empty cup, favouring me with another smile before scurrying off back to the kitchen.

She wasn't dissuaded by my scars, overlooking the ugliness because of my fine clothes and a pouch fat with coin. I was ostensibly a good catch, and she was still young and pretty enough to think herself destined for something more exciting than a life of drudgery in a grimy little mining town like Ironport. She wasn't to know that I was a liar and a killer, or that my pouch held mostly copper bits. She couldn't know that in Setharis the name Edrin Walker would cause folk to slam doors and trace symbols in the air to ward off evil.

I shuddered. Best avoid thinking about home, of deals, dead gods and daemons, and force myself to ponder better things. Safer things. I watched the bloodied sliver of wood burn in the flame of my table candle – it really wouldn't do to leave any trace of my magic here. My pursuers could track me by such things, which is why I used it so rarely.

The girl hurried back with another cup of ale – a better brew than I'd paid for – before moving on to serve a table of rowdy, drunken sailors bandying rumours of missing ships and Skallgrim sea-raiders pillaging villages up and down the coast. Sailors were wont to exaggerate, and their fanciful tales devolved into wild rumours of kidnapped children and blood sacrifice, nothing I hadn't heard a hundred times before about the tribal savages from across the Sea of Storms.

I ignored their wagging tongues and watched the girl. I wasn't about to disabuse her of any fanciful notions on my last night in town, to ruin my only chance for a little fun; with my itinerant lifestyle it was in short supply. Sleazy turned his gimlet glare on me and I looked away. That sour bastard's single eye held as much malice as any ten normal men could muster. The tavernkeep was not so easily fooled. He must have been pleased when a couple of overdue ships finally docked, ready to carry me away from his shitty little tavern in the morning.

I was sat in a corner of the rundown shack, eponymously titled Sleazy's Tavern, swilling ale and chowing down on the special stew, trying to figure out what the slimy grey lumps of surprise meat actually were, when somebody kicked open the door and hurled in a lantern. It exploded against the wall, flaming oil showering drinkers and setting the rush floor-mats ablaze. People screamed, tearing at burning clothes and hair. Wood that had soaked up untold years of spilt alcohol eagerly took light, black smoke billowing through the tavern.

Coughing and spluttering, smoke stinging my eyes and burning my throat, I snatched up my pack and shoved a dirt-smeared miner out of my way as I bolted for the door. I got out a split-second before the panicked and heaving mob behind me blocked the only exit to the street in a frantic attempt to claw their way out of the inferno all at the same time. Those at the back would die choking if they were lucky, burning if not.

I sensed the attack a moment before blackened steel came

swinging through the smoke towards my face. I ducked and an axe crunched through the skull of the unlucky sap behind me. A bearded Skallgrim raider in chain and furs, his shaven head tattooed with angular runes, snarled and yanked at the weapon embedded in the corpse blocking the doorway. Head still down, I charged, ramming my shoulder into his belly. He lost grip of his weapon and stumbled, falling to one knee. I wasn't a great fighter, but even I knew that only fools gave their foes time to think. I booted his raised knee and it crunched inwards. He fell onto all fours and I stamped on his weapon-hand, grinding down. He howled in pain as small bones popped beneath my heel.

I thought he was done and tried to make my escape, but he had other ideas. He grabbed hold of my belt with his uninjured hand and hauled me closer. I tried to pull away but the press of bodies behind me made that impossible. He launched himself forward, jaw clamping down on my crotch. *Shitshitshitshit* – it wasn't the first time somebody had swung an axe at my face, but nobody had tried to bite my cock off before! In drunken panic a trickle of magic squirted through my flesh, strengthening muscles. I smashed my fist into the raider's face and his teeth lost their grip. My knee snapped up to break his nose with a crunch of bone and cartilage. He went down hard, shaved head cracking off the cobbles. The protective runes inked into his scalp didn't seem to help much as my boot rammed into his face, once, twice, then again for good measure, leaving it a toothless cavern – that biting bastard was finished now.

I frantically checked my crotch. I was all there. Fortunately he had just eaten linen. These Skallgrim were cracked in the head – I was all for fighting dirty, but trying to bite a man's cock off was just plain *wrong*.

A half-dozen people scrambled out behind me, wheezing

for air and hissing in pain, their legs and backs blackened and blistered. A handful more crawled out into the muddy street, hair and clothes smouldering. The rest were dead or dying. The sulphurous reek of burnt hair was vile enough, but the fetor of burning human flesh made me gag: that sweetly putrid coppery stench is so thick and cloying that it is more like taste, and not something you ever got used to, or forgot.

The Worm of Magic had uncoiled inside my mind and was begging to be unleashed, promising to extinguish my panic. Magi had never determined if the Worm was real – the urgings of a living magic wanting to be used – or an imaginary personification invented to explain magic's effects on the human body, but in any case the seduction to use magic was a palpable need, and the more you used it, the more holes the Worm ate through a magus' self-control. Like a leaky bucket riddled with woodworm, sooner or later most of us gave in and let the magic flow. That was the beginning of the end – there was no patching over holes in self-control if the entire bottom of the bucket fell out. I fought down its urgings to open my Gift wide and let the sea of magic beyond flood through unchecked – when you've had magic-sniffing daemons snapping at your heels for ten years it tends to make you wary about advertising your presence, and I'd already been stuck in this dunghill town too long for comfort thanks to those missing ships.

Even lying low, traces of my magic lingered in bodily excretions and the shadow cats would scent it sooner or later, when they eventually got close enough. Their nose for magic was far more sensitive than any human, even the vaunted Arcanum sniffers. The daemons had been hunting me ever since I fled Setharis, were still stalking me long after everybody else thought me dead, forcing me to constantly move from place to place to ensure the damned things *didn't* get close enough. By cart, boat and constant subterfuge I had mostly managed to stay two steps ahead. Now I needed to find somewhere well-lit, somewhere safe from prowling shadow cats. Despite the dangerous delay, thanks to the many streams around Ironport I *should* still be safe – the things couldn't abide running water – but paranoia had kept me alive thus far.

The serving girl lay face down in the mud, sobbing, her dress burnt onto her back. I stepped over her and squinted into the night, trying to figure out what was happening, which way to run.

It was chaos. Smoke and running battles filled the street. Fire had spread from Sleazy's Tavern to the adjoining houses but the smelters and smithies had been left intact. Screams and the clash of steel pierced the night as Ironport militia leapt from their beds to repel the raiders. In the smoke and darkness it proved impossible to tell how many were attacking the town. I'd been due to embark on the first ship out in the morning and it was bloody typical they'd chosen to attack the night before I sailed.

I looked out to sea. Ah, cockrot. By the light of the broken moon I glimpsed a dozen more Skallgrim wolf-ships pulling up onto the wide shingle beach, red crystals set into snarling, bestial prows catching the firelight and flaring bright like daemonic eyes. They disgorged bellyfuls of hairy axemen, who charged straight towards the centre of town. Towards me. They were desperate to join the battle before others claimed the best loot. They were accompanied by a shaman in an antlered deer-skull mask. I was no Arcanum sniffer but even I could sense the unfocused magic leaking from him, marking him as strongly Gifted but untrained. He was one of the halrúna, the spiritual leaders of the Skallgrim tribes that ranked above war leaders and tribal chiefs.

The shaman began wailing, harsh voice undulating as he slit his palm with a knife and shed blood in a circle across the pebbled shore, the beginnings of some vile heathen ritual. Drums beat in the night as yet more ships approached the beach, the heavy, primal booming infecting the townsfolk with fear.

Somebody limped up beside me. It was old Sleazy, an iron-bound club held in his scarred hands. He stared at the Skallgrim, jaw working but no sound emerging. Then he spat at his feet and hefted the club, looking as if he expected me to fight by his side.

"Sod that," I said. "You're on your own, pal." With that limp, there was no way Sleazy would be able to escape and I wasn't about to tangle with any Gifted heathen, however weak his magic. This town was already doomed and I wasn't going down with it. Heroism could get a man killed.

I raced for the docks. With any luck the sailors were preparing to make a run for it. I rounded a corner and caught sight of the ships. Sailors swarmed over the rigging of a decrepit Setharii caravel and our sleek Ahramish merchantman, readying both to set sail. For once my luck had held. I was glad that I wouldn't have to lay low in the sodden bowels of that rotting caravel, hugging the coast of Kaladon south to Setharis; me, I was heading out across the Sea of Storms to the librocracy of Ahram in the distant lands of Taranai. I loathed the sea, but any destination that wouldn't get me killed was better than home.

Shouts and screams rose over Ironport as the raiders overwhelmed the militia and began wholesale butchery. I could sense the tiny sparks of magic that were carrion and plague spirits flocking to the town, invisible mindless mouths drawn to feed and breed on the magic released by spilt blood and death.

The greasy, rancid reek of blood magic filled the air, and with it the wince-inducing shriek of the Shroud tearing, like the metallic screech of a knife across a plate to the magically sensitive. The world cried out in pain as its protective magical skin was punctured by the power of human sacrifice. The Skallgrim's corrupt shaman opened a portal to alien realms far from this one and ravening daemons crawled through the wound, ripped from their lairs in the Far Realms, other worlds distant and wildly different from ours but every bit as real. Most did not have a Shroud to guard their unfortunate and deadly inhabitants from abduction and domination by blood sorcery.

The burning debris of another wolf-ship floated nearby, the handiwork of an Arcanum pyromancer standing on the deck of the caravel, flames crawling up his bare arms. I grinned, glad that the magus was heading the other way – there was always a small chance the magus might know a name and face as reviled as Edrin Walker's. Hah, I was safe.

And then the vision pierced my skull. Lynas' terror surged in through the Gift-bond and I saw through his eyes:

"Help!" Lynas scrambles over the rain-slick cobbles, pounds on another crude door, the stench of blood and smoke all around him. "I need help!" Splinters from the rough wood prick his flesh but he ignores the pain, pounds all the harder. "Let me in, curse you!" He slams his shoulder into the door, but it barely shakes.

No answer, just a dog barking in reply. But then nobody in the slums of Docklands is going to open their door to a stranger at night, not if they know what's good for them. He's all too aware of that, but it's not like he has any other choice. He keeps trying to reach his old friend Walker through the Gift-bond, to somehow warn him in case he doesn't make it, but with his stunted Gift he knows it's likely impossible. He's no magus and has no way to even know if it works.

Clickclick, clickclick, clickclick...

Lynas spins, heart thudding. A daemon glitters in the moonlight, crystalline, many-eyed, scuttling towards him down the alley like a spider made of knives, its limbs all straight lines and jagged cutting edges. With just enough of the Gift to sense the otherness of the creature, Lynas can tell it's not native to Setharis, not even to this world. And he knows it's been sent to tear him to pieces.

They've found him.

CHAPTER 2

I fell to my knees screaming. I was frantic, stuck in this shithole town and unable to come to Lynas' aid. A pair of young spearmen of the Ironport militia ran over to check on me, looking panicked. Blackest dread filled me as I realized my Gift had opened wide to receive the vision and that my magic was bleeding out into the world unchecked, advertising my presence like a blazing beacon in the night.

The shadow cat came from the direction of the Skallgrim shaman, a writhing mass of deepest dark the size of a horse leaping through a tenebrous doorway. *They've found me.* My eyes wanted to slide over it and I had to concentrate to see it at all. Obsidian fangs and claws glistened, wisps of black breath misting the air, green eyes fixed on me burning with recognition, with hatred.

Lynas' terror eclipses my own–

He runs as fast as his bulk will allow, slipping and sliding across cobbles slick with the bouncing rain, splashes through a pool of street filth, the rotting refuse and sewage coating his boots. Puffing and panting, he staggers up to a crossroads, skids to a stop, backs away. Another daemon squats straight ahead. A whisper of memory, something Walker once said, names it: shard beast. He lurches right, down a dark winding alley. His only chance is to head for the open space of Fisherman's Way.

17

His legs burn with the effort. He's too old and too fat for this. Why couldn't he just have met Charra and Layla for dinner and wine, as they did at the end of every week? Oh no, instead he had to go snooping! All this because he is trying to grow his business so his daughter is set for life. He crushes all pointless thought: ignorance means death. A pile of garbage trips him and he stumbles, almost falls, flails to a stop against the alley wall, breathing in ragged heaving gulps, his legs shivering beneath him.

But he can't stop; he refuses to. Charra and Layla's smiling faces flash through his mind. He has too much to lose.

Pushing himself off the wall, he forces leaden legs back into motion. He's bought the city some time, but now he has to get out into a main street, to call for the wardens, the street gangs, anybody. He has to warn them all or thousands will perish. His family will die.

"Come on – you – fat – fool," he pants, focusing on keeping his feet moving, trying to ignore the sweat pouring down his face and the salt stinging his eyes. He wipes them with the back of his hand, blinks his vision clear.

A hooded man in dark and sodden robes blocks the exit from the alley, loitering in deepest shadow. He prays it is a magus here to help.

"There are daemons back there," Lynas shouts. As he tries to run past, the man hooks his arm out, slams it into his throat. Lynas' feet fly out from beneath him.

"I know," says the man.

His back crashing to the cobbles leaves Lynas gulping for air that his stunned body can't provide. The shadows close in around them.

"I should know," says the hooded man, pulling a scalpel from a voluminous sleeve. "I am their master, after all."

I hissed in pain. Magic thudded through blood and muscle whilst my mind shuddered, the vision stabbing into my head in fits and starts. Burn all daemons!

For ten long years I'd had no inkling of who hated or feared me enough to set daemons hunting me. I had assumed it had something to do my part in the death of a god. And yet, perhaps I'd been wrong all those years, for I recognized this particular shadow cat's badly burned muzzle from where I'd dropped a blazing house on her and her mate years ago. This daemon cat I called Burn had been summoned by the Skallgrim shaman in the skull-mask, but no untrained Gifted reliant on blood sorcery could compel the allegiance of a whole pack of such powerful daemons. Whoever their real master was, they were either one of those tribal savages, or allied. But who was it, and why me?

Now that the daemons had found me I didn't have to hold back, reduced to relying on my paltry skill with two other – and to my thoughts lesser – magics dealing with air and manipulation of the human body. Every Gift processed the flow of magic differently, offering certain innate talents, and my accursed Gift to control the human mind was powerful when used subtly, and far more dangerous when used without restraint. It was the oldest and rarest of all human magics and these particular daemons could smell it from a league away.

The minds of the two militiamen were snarls of fear. If they caught sight of the shadow cat they would flee and leave me to die. One of them put a reassuring hand on my shoulder. I grabbed it and my magic surged into him, breaking into his thoughts. It was always easier with skin contact, and with all his panic and confusion it was a simple task to order him to defend me. The man spun and levelled his spear at the daemon. His confused companion followed suit.

I left them to delay the thing while I lurched towards the ships. They'd be dead anyway when the Skallgrim caught up with them. "I'm coming, Lynas. Hold on!" I tried to reach out to him through the Gift-bond but–

A warm wetness blooms over Lynas' crotch: he's pissed himself. "Please. Please, no," he wheezes. "I won't tell anybody."

"No, you will not," the man replies, a grin flashing inside the hood. "I have need of your flesh, mageborn. The magic it contains will be put to good use." He kneels down to straddle Lynas, pinning his body to the cold cobbles, arm held skyward in a vice-like grip. A single deft slice and he opens Lynas' arm from wrist to elbow.

Lynas screams, knows he's about to die. "Gods save me!"

The hooded man chuckles. "The so-called gods of Setharis have been blinded and chained, Lynas. They are too consumed by their own struggle for survival to notice what happens here. You will get no help from them."

He knows he has to keep trying to send a message through the Gift-bond. Others would claim it's an abomination – an invitation to his enslavement by Walker's stronger Gift – but that trust had already been repaid a thousandfold. Wherever Walker is in the world now, he has to reach him, to tell him of the threat to Setharis, to warn him that Layla and Charra are in danger. If he's still alive, then maybe...

"I feel you, Lynas. Run! Get out of there. I'm coming. Please..."

It's too late.

He gathers the power of his stunted Gift, lets it fill him until he's almost bursting, hoping it will prove enough to bring his friend home. He imagines Walker: that cynical smile, those exhausted and haunted eyes as he walked out of Lynas' door for the last time.

The scalpel cuts deep. Bright arterial blood spurts across the silvery face of the broken moon.

Lynas feels his power building, eager to surge through the Gift-bond, but then the knife twists and he screams instead.

The hooded man's grin widens, white teeth gleaming in the moonlight. He shakes his head and tuts. "Nobody will be coming to the rescue, you pathetic waste of the Gift. To think you once thought to become a magus." He starts to cut the skin from Lynas' flesh, the scalpel shining red and silver.

Lynas screams as hot sticky rain drips onto his face. He yearns to be home with his family in front of a crackling fireplace, merry with food and wine. All he's ever really wanted is for everybody to be happy and healthy. And he's failed them. He closes his eyes and wills the pain to stop, prays for death.

"Death won't save you either, Lynas," the man says. "I have something far more useful planned for you."

A memory surfaces, Walker's words: unbalance the bastards; kick them in the balls and do what needs doing while they're busy puking. He can't give up yet. He has no idea what he's doing, but if he can somehow distract the hooded man then he has one last chance to bring Walker home.

He fastens his eyes on an imaginary saviour behind the hooded man's back, starts laughing – mocking laughter that reverberates down the alley.

The man's eyes widen. "What are you...?"

As the hooded man jerks back, spins to look behind him, Lynas fires off another message, fuelled with every last ounce of his life-force, hoping it's just enough, that at least part of the message might make it through and speed off into the night, to reach...

Agony exploded inside my skull. I clutched my head as blood gushed from my nose. It felt like something inside my brain had burst. *Gods no! Lynas! Lynas!* There is no answer. The constant and comforting presence in the back of my head that had kept me sane for ten wretched years began to fade. Then, nothing.

I was truly alone.

Pyromancer or not, I knew what I had to do. Instead of

boarding the Ahramish merchantman I staggered onto the battered old caravel, collapsing to the deck just as the sailors cast off ropes and began pushing us away from the dock with long poles. I was going home and wouldn't allow anything or anybody to stop me.

Memories forgotten for ten years had been torn loose, were bleeding back into my conscious mind, mixed with something from Lynas. The scent of smoke and blood filled my nostrils as one memory surged to the fore, summoned by the vision: a steel gate slamming shut. As if I were floating outside my body I saw our horrified expressions as that bastard Harailt locked Lynas and I in the catacombs of the Boneyards. Oh how he laughed! The darkness, the harrowing darkness...

The details of the vision drained away like sour wine from a burst skin, leaving behind a fearful mass of muddled imagery and a sudden certainty that by going home I wouldn't have long to live. So be it.

Canvas snapped taut as sails caught the wind. We slid from the docks, leaving the two militiamen to be torn to pieces by the claws and fangs of my personal daemons. Out of frustration Burn took her time with them, tearing off their arms and legs one by one before finally burying obsidian fangs in their throats. She watched me leave, gaze dripping with malevolence – I *had* killed her mate.

As the caravel surged out to sea we stared at the forest of masts and sails filling the horizon, an enormous fleet of wolf-ships bearing the emblems of dozens of tribes: rearing bears, wolves, dragons and various runic emblems. Ironport's sheltered bay was the largest and safest on the east coast, making it the perfect place to anchor a fleet, and with the town's abundance of mines and smithies they would have a plentiful supply of weapons. Nobody brought a fleet eight hundred leagues across the Sea of Storms just to see the sights and indulge in a spot of raiding – this was an invasion of all Kaladon. The savages had always been numerous, but riven by tribal blood feuds, religious warfare, and hobbled by a strict and somewhat fatal code of honour. Something of huge import must have occurred to see blood-sworn enemies travel halfway across the known world to fight side by side on our shores. Bile rose up my throat. Those sailors' rumours of stolen children and human sacrifice had not been as wild as I'd thought.

And then my guts heaved as it hit me – Lynas was dead, really dead. He was supposed to have been protected! I had made a deal with somebody too dangerous and powerful to refuse; the reward was the lives of my friends at the cost my exile. There was a secret buried deep inside my mind, locked away by powers far beyond my own, one so dire that even I couldn't be allowed to know what it was. All I knew was that it had something to do with the death of a god. Every time I tried to remember it only brought back paralysing panic and blackest terror, but now the deal was off and I had to find a way to recover those memories.

The details of the deal itself were fragmented, most of it locked away with that dire secret in my head. I couldn't remember who, but still knew some of the why: it had been the only way to keep Lynas and Charra safe, their daughter Layla too. They had made some kind of deadly mistake, and Charra had taken dangerously ill. I had been promised that mistake would be rectified, Charra healed, and all three kept from harm if I completed their task and then left Setharis, forgetting everything. Whoever they were, they had broken our deal. And that would not, and could not, be forgiven. I held my head in my hands, throat seized up, eyes gone tight and watery. The sorrow didn't last. It drowned in a flood of anger. That hooded man would burn for this. Charra and Layla must be protected at all costs.

It was time to go home to a city that feared and despised me. It was time to kill, and I didn't care how many or how powerful they thought they were. Lynas had always been my conscience, urging me to use my power wisely and well, but now my friend was dead and that "wisely and well" could go fuck itself. I would rip his murderer apart and then I would deal with these Skallgrim that thought they could hunt me with impunity.

The deal was off, and so was my leash.

CHAPTER 3

We spent five days hugging the Dragon Coast south, battered by huge waves and howling winds. Racked by hunger and constant vomiting, huddled up with the other refugees in that sodden and cramped cargo hold, I was desperate to be back on dry land. Only one more day confined in darkness.

I shuddered and tried not to think of the walls closing in on me, the darkness swallowing me once again – it was only a ship. Only a ship. I could escape into the open air above deck if I really wanted, and I only had to keep out of sight of the pyromancer and pretend to be nothing more than a meek little merchant for one more day, for Lynas. Haunted by feverish dreams of his murder, I endured the waking claustrophobia and dwelled on happier days, to when I'd last had hope.

The previous Archmagus of the Arcanum, Byzant, had taken me under his wing and helped me come to terms with the trauma of being buried alive beneath tons of stone and left for dead, thanks to that arrogant vermin Harailt of High House Grasske who had thought himself so much nobler than a poverty-stricken Docklands pup like myself. He trapped Lynas and I in the Boneyards below the city and left us to rot, sniggering into silken sleeves all the while. Lynas managed to get out. I did not. I'd have died there in the crushing darkness if Lynas hadn't fetched help, if he'd

not found Byzant to haul me back out into the light. They
had both saved me in more ways than one.

Byzant had been the head of the entire Setharii empire,
with hundreds of magi and noble High Houses under his
command and a thousand tasks needing done every day,
and yet somehow he'd made the time to mentor me when
I'd needed it most.

Those had been the happiest years of my life, running
the streets with Lynas and Charra. So many wild nights of
drunken truths and raucous laughter with the very best
company the world had to offer, touring the disreputable
taverns of the city and drinking them dry, dreaming those
golden days would never end. I had felt fulfilled doing
tasks for Byzant to earn my Arcanum stipend and I'd had
friends, a life, and a purpose. The old magus had been like
a second father to me, and now he too was dead, reported
missing only days after I'd fled the city.

The happier days turned to ash and all I was left with
was trying to recall everything about the deal I'd made.
As much as I had tried to remember during the voyage,
all magic and mental trickery had failed. The locks on my
mind remained solid. I would need levers to help crack
them open, reminders from the old days. I swallowed,
fearful of the atrocity I had been involved in all those
years ago.

An age passed in that darkness, worrying at the holes
in my memory, until rattling chains announced our ship
had dropped anchor. The human cargo crawled up onto
the deck, blinking against the burning dawn light.

Pauper's Docks, the arse-end of Setharis. The air reeked,
every sewer and stream in the city spewing out into the
harbour our decrepit old coast-hugger was anchored in,
almost a million bowels emptied daily. That thought forced
me to lean over the side and retch, adding my vomit to the

grey scum of shite, rubbish, and fish guts; if anything, it felt like I'd just made the sea a bit cleaner. Bloody ships. If I'd sailed for Ahram I might have died! My Clansmen cousins had the right idea in sticking to their hills and mountains in the rugged north. No mountain had ever rocked and pitched underfoot and made me empty my guts onto the ground... well, not while I'd been sober anyway. I tried to ignore my nausea, to focus instead on the familiar sooty stench of humanity crowded together inside the black granite walls of the ancient city. It smelled like home.

Autumn was waning and the broken moon, Elunnai, was swollen in the sky, every wound on her shattered face visible to the naked eye. One of her tears fell streaking across the sky, then another. It was an omen of bad luck for the tears to fall before winter had even begun, an occurrence that agitated water spirits in the Sea of Storms and caused the unusually vicious waves that had threatened to batter our ship to kindling against the rocks of the Dragon Coast and the hidden reefs around Lepers' Isle. It heralded a harsh winter and the seas would soon grow far worse, not long left before the storms blew in and all sea travel ceased until late spring for anything other than great Setharii carracks protected by coteries of hydromancers.

Dusty memories woke and stirred. Ten years! It felt like another life. A part of me felt pleased to be home, despite the reason. A murderous grin slid across my face. Somebody had killed Lynas, and now they would burn for it.

Setharis hadn't changed one bit. Looking bored and miserable in the rain, wardens in rusty chain hauberks and burgundy tabards patrolled city walls slick with slime and moss, while beyond the smog-wreathed slums of the lower city the high and mighty swanned about in the lofty gothic palaces of the Old Town, high on its volcanic crag. The gleaming golden spires of the Templarum Magestus and the

Collegiate, centres of Arcanum power, reared above every other building – well, those built by human hands anyway. From amongst the gargoyle-flocked buttresses and steeples of the merely rich and powerful, the five unearthly towers of the gods – slick black, almost organic-looking – jutted from the heart of the rock, twisting around each other like enormous snakes, so high they seemed to pierce the sky. Coronas of raw magic usually crackled from their spires, but now the gods' towers stood as lifeless as any other lump of stone. The air felt subtly different, the heavy magical presence of the gods was missing. Another bad omen.

I grabbed the burly arm of a passing deckhand. "The towers – when did they go quiet?"

He refused to look up, "Few months back. Same day the earth tremors began." He pulled his arm free and scurried off to avoid the topic, fingers tracing symbols to ward off evil.

I stared at the towers and recalled a fragment of the vision: Lynas' murderer had said our gods were blind and chained. But what could do that to beings who could incinerate entire towns with the flick of a finger? Not that these towers were the homes of what other peoples would consider actual gods, mind – primitive worship of natural spirits that gained power from devout worship wasn't tolerated in Setharis – but assuming a powerful magus survives that long, assuming they don't burn out or give in to the Worm's seductions and get put down like a rabid dog, then when they grow old and addicted enough you might as well call them a god for all the humanity left in them. Our gods had been human once.

The elder magi of the Arcanum stood far above the rank and file in power and skill, even as a magus like me stood above the lesser Gifted: the sniffers, hedge witches and street illusionists, unable to ever wield true power without burning their minds to a crisp. Then there were mageborn like Lynas, those whose Gifts never matured and opened up to the magic; mostly all those poor bastards got was good health, or some extra strength and speed as magic slowly dripped into them like water leaking through a cracked pipe. If their Gifts allowed them a drip of magic, I was a stream and the elders a swollen waterfall. And as the elders were to the lowly mageborn, so were our gods to the elders.

Our legends claim that long before the rise of ancient Escharr, the five Setharii gods had been mighty elder magi before they ascended. There was more to it than mere age and skill however, there was a secret to their ascension – I was sure of it; and just as sure that the answer was firmly locked away deep inside my head. My exile had begun the night a god died and that was no coincidence.

Any elder magi I'd ever met were obscenely powerful, deeply knowledgeable, and they always had to be right. They were much like inveterate drunks, their tolerance of magic increasing as the years went by to match their inflating egos. I didn't think our gods any different. Derrish, Lady Night, The Lord of Bones, Artha the dead god of war, and even my patron Nathair, the Thief of Life – arrogant and self-centred pricks the lot of them, a veritable treachery of gods, though Nathair was better than all the rest. I shuddered at this line of thought. It was an unsettling subject for me, given what was locked away inside my head. Whatever happened back then, I was sure I was in the right. But for a magus certainty always merited scrutiny.

That's the thing with magic: it erases your doubts and replaces it with a sense of your own magnificence. It seems to me that the more powerful you get, the more certain you are that your opinion is the only one that really matters. Almost every powerful magus I'd ever met had disappeared up their own arse long ago. Bugger that for a game of soldiers. Me, I was content to be a nobody.

A hand thumped down onto my shoulder. "All passengers off," the captain said, his breath reeking of cheapest dockhouse rum. My grin dissolved back into a mask of queasy suffering as he spun me round and shoved me towards the gangplank where the rest of the refugees were massing.

I bobbed my head like a meek little merchant, then held a hand to my mouth as my stomach gave another lurch. "Thank you, Captain, thank you," I said, my voice cloying with false humility as I shuffled over to join the others standing in the rain, as far away from the pyromancer as I could manage. Acting was all about the look in the eyes and the body language: most people didn't realize how much they picked up, or just how much they gave away. It wasn't magic but it could bloody well seem like it.

We clustered together at the gap in the rails, swaying on that nauseating, pitching deck while dockhands grabbed flung ropes and tied them to iron rings set into huge stone blocks. The wait was aggravating. I itched to get inside those walls and hunt down the man who murdered Lynas.

Our captain had been subtly persuaded not to pay good coin to berth his leaky old boat at the secure and guarded quays of Westford Docks, instead dropping anchor on the east of the city, amidst fishing boats and single-masted cogs offloading untreated wool, raw hides and other low-profit goods. This side of the city was more suitable for my needs: the guards cheaper to bribe and the sniffers a lot less competent. Back in my day, it was seen as a punishment posting, and I doubted much had changed in my absence.

An aura of utter disbelief still hung about the refugees. Only five days ago they had watched Ironport burn, seen their livelihoods destroyed and their family and friends slaughtered. In the space of an hour they had lost everything but their lives. Some whispered horrific stories of witnessing the Skallgrim shaman summoning daemons and allowing them to gorge on living human flesh.

Strictly speaking Ironport was a member of the Free Towns alliance and no longer part of the crumbling Setharii empire, but blood sorcery was an abomination, and I wondered if even the eternally bickering magi of the Arcanum political elite would be forced into taking action. After all, it was the lust for that vile power that caused the fall of the ancient empire of Escharr – the mightiest empire the world had ever known – and plunged humanity into a dark age of slaughter. Sorcerers had sacrificed untold thousands to sate their addiction to magic. The Arcanum had to recognize the danger the Skallgrim now posed.

Still, in my experience the councillors of the Arcanum would probably debate such hefty and urgent matters for years while the bureaucrats of the Administratum, the heads of the High Houses, and the high priests of the gods quietly ran the lesser affairs of the city: the likes of road and well maintenance, trade fees, crime and fire and plague prevention. A mageocracy like the Setharii Empire was probably not the most efficient of governments, but nobody else could ever dream of controlling the hundreds of Gifted throughout the empire. Without the Arcanum we would still be living in muddy huts and small villages like the Skallgrim, a mass of squabbling tribes loosely controlled by Gifted shaman wearing bits of dead animals on their heads and shouting at spirits. The Arcanum was a necessary evil. Now if only a god would show up and kick their arses into action, as they did on rare occasions when they deemed it important enough – even the mighty Arcanum dared not disobey the gods.

A yellow-robed priest of Derrish, the Gilded God claimed as the figurehead of Setharii commerce for obscure historical reasons I couldn't care less about, shuffled into line behind the pimple-faced pompous prick of a nobleman I'd taken to thinking of as Lord Arse due to the amount of absolute shite he talked. I watched the priest look back over the sea towards Ironport, his haggard face tightening as this jumped-up lordling of some minor house began spouting more crap about his family's extensive holdings in Setharis, of how Ironport's fall wasn't a total loss for him.

As the gangplank thudded down onto the rain-slick jetty Lord Arse strode to the front of the queue, his two retainers pushing the riffraff out of his way. He began whining at a leather-faced sailor, demanding to be let off immediately. Nobility and all that. Then the Arcanum magus walked straight past him to the front of the queue. Lord Arse ground his teeth but gave way. He wasn't brave or stupid enough to risk igniting the volatile temperament of a pyromancer. After five days of my baiting and mental conditioning this brat was taut as a bow-string and ready to snap. Perfect timing. I shuffled up behind him and smiled at his belt. The idiot had left his purse tied there in full view of any would-be thief; he would need to learn quickly in Setharis. I slipped a nasty little present into it.

There was no way of totally avoiding detection by the sniffer on guard duty, but I could direct their sight elsewhere. My poncy tailored clothes were all well and good, but even after ten years some of the sniffers on gate duty might still recognize the unique scent of my magic if we came face to face. Better to keep my head down and hide amongst the herd while they focused on some other well-deserving git.

Lord Arse glanced back, frowning, but his eyes slid right over me. To him I was a nobody, just another hollow-eyed and newly-paupered merchant from Ironport bewildered by recent events. Under that perfectly boring mask though, I smiled on the inside.

At a nod from the captain, the sailor began ushering us down the gangplank. The rain died off as we hustled along the jetty in a disorganized mass and slogged along the muddy track leading to Pauper's Gate. It was a huge relief to have solid ground underfoot but my stomach still felt like it was pitching up and down. Weathered old men and women busy gutting fish paused to eye us dully as we passed their small shacks clustered around the warehouses. Drunken sailors crowded into makeshift drinking dens waved cups of grog and called us over for games of dice and the exchange of news. Some of the refugees drifted towards them; I suspected they'd wake up in the gutter the next morning, naked, penniless and feeling rough as a badger's arse.

It was hard to imagine how this once-great city had looked when it had been the heart of an actual empire. All we had left was the southern half of Kaladon and a few far-flung colonies that drained coffers and barracks alike. The Free Towns had seceded before I'd been born, but some old folk still remembered, and lamented, that last gasp of imperial rule. Ancient gods of Setharis aside, the Arcanum's elder magi were the only ones who remembered the city at the height of its power, before it became this lice-infested midden-heap.

Gulls wheeled above the docks, trailing in the wake of fishing boats offloading their hauls, screeching and cackling, diving down to fight over stinking piles of guts heaped outside the shacks. Unlike other ports, the gulls didn't infest Setharis itself – the corvun saw to that. Akin to a cross between a sea eagle and giant crow, the corvun were the colour of deepest night, as vicious as debt collectors, and as cunning as any street urchin. They were found nowhere else in the world. One of the evil-eyed birds perched atop the fortified gatehouse we were making for, busy tearing chunks from a gull's splayed belly. I glowered at a message daubed across the wall below it in bold red paint, barely legible: "Skinner's gonna get you."

Through the open gatehouse doorway, I glimpsed the wardens on guard duty yawning and rising from their benches, grabbing halberds to block the path. An Arcanum sniffer joined them, looking very grand in robes emblazoned with arcane symbols. That was half the battle with the subtle arts of suggestion: if somebody believed your power would work on them then self-suggestion dictated that it usually did. It was the difference between being confronted by a child waving a carrot and somebody dressed like an Arcanum magus pointing a sparking wand of glowing crystal at your face. One was far more likely to fuck you over than the other.

It took some blocking and shoving through the crowd to get ahead of Lord Arse. I ended up third in the queue for the gate, seeing no point attracting attention by being the first to be questioned and processed, and in any case that honour always belonged to magi. The pyromancer waved a parchment stamped with the wax seal of the Arcanum and walked straight past the guards to converse with the sniffer. They exchanged pleasantries while his papers were verified. The sniffer scrutinized him for traces of unfamiliar or dangerous magic and then waved him past. Ostensibly, nobody escaped their checks, not even the Archmagus himself, the head of the empire. It was far too dangerous to allow blood sorcerers or the magically-corrupted into the city, and any unregistered Gifted would be arrested and tried by the Arcanum unless they carried diplomatic papers from other lands. I could well imagine what they would do if they discovered a rogue magus like me standing before them.

The ragged young man next in line became irate as he argued about paying the gate tax. The guards were having none of it, told him to bugger off back to the docks and beg for work if he didn't have the coin.

Just then the ground began to tremble, buildings creaking, the gatehouse doors and portcullis rattling their fixings. The guards glanced up at the wall as dust and stone chips rained down. It was over in a moment, but the ragged young man ahead of me took advantage of their distraction to make a run for Pauper's Gate.

I winced as the ignorant fool darted past the sniffer towards the gatehouse. The guards didn't even bother trying to stop him. The sniffer sighed and pressed the activation crystal set into the ring adorning his index finger. Ward glyphs carved into the stone archway sparked into life as magic fed into their patterns, flaring red as the man sprinted through.

The scream was brief and a smoking corpse dropped to the dirt, rags and hair burnt away. A grumbling, hungover guard dragged the blackened remains back out and booted it to one side, spitting on it for good measure. The corvun on the gatehouse ceased eating the gull and cocked its head, eying up fresh meat.

And then it was my turn to stand in front of the wardens on guard duty. I wrung my hands and did my best to look nervous and pathetic. "It is so good to be back on dry land again, sirs," I said, sniffling and wiping at my nose. I reached out and shook the guard's hand vigorously, pressing my last remaining silver coin into his palm. The coin disappeared into his pocket with a deftness equalling that of any thief or street magician I'd ever seen.

"I am here to meet my kin," I said. "I am hoping they

will have a job for me at the smithy after... after..." I made my eyes go glassy and distant.

"Which family?" the warden said, narrowing his eyes and studying my expensive green coat. "Might be I know them. That be Steffan's smithy?"

I shook my head. There was no Steffan's smithy in Setharis as far as I knew. It was an age-old trick. "I'm kin to Old Carthy living in an area called... Carrbridge, I think it was."

The warden grunted. "Good luck with that then. Old Carthy is one mean old bastard."

A nod and a smile for him, doing my best to look reassuringly bland. There wasn't much I could do to hide the ragged scars marring my face, but I was doing my best to play the part of the spineless, boring merchant, and plenty other refugees bore scars and wounds of their own, albeit fresher. In many ways my scars were a better disguise than the fine coat I wore – for those in the city who had known my face ten years ago anyway. I'd ditched my tattered pack days ago to avoid any possible suspicion of smuggling, only keeping my coin pouch, loaded dice stuffed down the front of my trousers, and a set of lockpicks in my boot – just the essentials.

I paid the gate tax, scrawled "Reklaw" on the admittance scroll, and was waved onwards. "If you want Carrbridge," the guard said, "take a right at Sailor's Spire and head on up Fisherman's Way. I'd avoid the alleyways just after the spire, friend, what with you dressed so fine. The scum have recently taken to loitering thereabouts – they will have you marked in no time."

"Thank you, warden," I said. It always helped to slip them a little something. How very useful for my purposes.

The sniffer was young, and not the ageless youth retained by some magi either but with a trace of puppy fat still on his bones, so I wasn't worried about him recognising me. He was entirely disinterested in his job, which is what I'd been counting on. Their peculiar talent for scenting the unique flavours of magic aside, sniffers were only a little better than street magicians and hedge witches. Their main tasks were to identify Gifted children, detect a variety of magical corruptions, and most importantly, to sniff out any and all traces of vile blood sorcery. A sniffer would burn their Gift out or go insane if they tried to open themselves up to the amount of power a full magus could channel, and their magical dexterity – akin to a toddler playing a musical instrument next to a master bard – was distinctly lacking. Even if they'd had the raw power, they failed to feel the rhythms in the magic and thus were unable to twist it into the forms needed to carry out their will with precision. They were blunt tools of the Arcanum, but effective.

It was far from glorious work for a sniffer to be stuck on guard duty at Pauper's Gate, where nothing interesting ever happened. I didn't dare use my Gift to try to manipulate the sniffer's mind into letting me pass through – even if I managed to stop him raising the alarm the moment he sensed my magic slipping into his head, in Setharis you could never be sure who, or what, else might be watching.

The sniffer was just about to raise his hands to sweep me for traces of magic when I sent the mental command that set off my little present inside Lord Arse's coin pouch. Magic burst into the air behind me, thick and potent, and undetectable by the mundanes around us. The sniffer's eyes went wide, flicking from me to Lord Arse. He waved me off and barrelled past, dismissing my cringing form as that of any other mundane merchant, exactly as I'd intended. "By the Night Bitch, beware! Gifted!" he shouted. Lord Arse reeked of my magic more than I did at the moment, making it an easy mistake to assume he was the source, at least for the next few minutes until the miasma dissipated. No harm done beyond broken bones, bruises, and a few hours of painfully invasive questioning.

Taut by my days of constant baiting, the foolish nobleman snapped and ordered his retainers to draw swords. The refugees scattered, shrieking as the wardens piled into the fight and the sniffer began running through his repertoire of disabling arts.

While they were distracted subduing the idiot I slipped through the gatehouse, fearful that – even here – my daemons might show up at any moment. I paused on the other side and took a deep breath.

I was home.

CHAPTER 4

The noise and odour of the city hit me like I'd walked into a wall. I lost myself among the smell of roasting meat and fried onions, mixed with dozens of other nostalgic scents. A hundred accents and a dozen languages merged into a constant babble, broken here and there by street traders hawking their wares at the top of their lungs. A dozen languages, and I was proud to say I could curse in every one. It wasn't hard to pick up foreign tongues when you could peek into people's minds to find out what they were gibbering on about.

Gaunt refugees from the coastal areas of the Free Towns huddled in small groups, begging for scraps of food from anybody that passed by. There was a suspicious lack of corvun, cats, and dogs in the area. I suspected they were now wary of the starving packs of refugees. I often felt that animals had more sense than humans.

Rickety stalls and spread blankets surrounded the inside of Pauper's Gate, selling everything from baskets of bruised fruit and "bags o'mystery" sausage made from, well, something, to gaudy and supposedly enchanted trinkets, secondhand clothes, and skins of homebrewed ale.

Everything was for sale in the dark underbelly of Setharis, if you knew where to look. Every possible vice catered for, from rare and expensive alchemics and nubile younglings sold in the flesh markets of the Scabs, to serial debtors bought for darker purposes, likely destined to die in brutal cavern fights. Life could often be exchanged for a loaf of bread in the slums of Docklands, where coin was rare and corpses common. Whores of both sexes plied their trade openly and the wise dared not antagonize the lords and ladies of sheets, as the polite called them. In the Free Towns they'd have been driven into the shadows out of sight of so-called righteous folk, but not here where most Docklanders were a step away from starvation, a mere crust away from selling themselves.

The empire of Setharis might be almost dead and gone, swallowed up by apathy, corruption, and perpetual political deadlock, but as an artefact of history the city was a melting pot of peoples from all over the world. Pasty-skinned locals like myself rubbed shoulders with pale Clansmen from the mountainous north, while olive-skinned sailors from Esban bargained with darker local traders whose ancestors had come from our island colonies amongst the Thousand Kingdoms south of the desert of Escharr. To my great surprise I even spotted an exotic duo of snowlanders passing through, their ice-blue flesh beaded with sweat. It was said that the sea itself was frozen solid around their homelands, and that they made their homes from snow and sculpted ice much as we made ours with earth, wood and stone.

A throng of barefoot and muddy children swarmed me, begging for coin. I liked cheeky wee pups like them; their thoughts tended to be far more hopeful than adults, less tarnished than the minds I usually touched. I distracted them with a few coppers and made my escape heading north, towards where Lynas was murdered. I tried and failed to make sense of his muddled vision, to figure out where he'd encountered the shard beast and the hooded man, where my friend had died.

The slums of East Docklands consisted of random formations of five- and six-storey tenements, no two alike, leaning drunkenly out over twisting alleyways. The luckier people lived along Fisherman's Way in solid stone buildings built during the height of the empire, but here most had one or two storeys of stonework before extending upwards in wood. Every few years a dry summer hit Setharis and entire areas of the slums were razed by outbreaks of fire, only to be rebuilt in new configurations that looked like the scribblings of a mad cartographer.

In the centre of the lower city, the Warrens boasted the worst streets, ones that squelched with ankle-deep shite and piss that autumn rains washed down from higher ground. Folk with decent professions and skills clawed their way upwind to West Docklands to avoid the stinking smog that prevailing winds blew southeast, and where sewage ran downstream into the Warrens instead of pooling at your doorsteps on rainy days.

A sonorous *DOOOOOOMMMMMM* of a great bell tolling out mid-afternoon made me look up at the looming basalt rock that the Old Town was perched on, a place most low-born would never set foot in if they wanted to keep it attached. They couldn't have the nobility and the magi rubbing shoulders with the poor – after all, that would be vulgar. On the far side of Docklands, over the river Seth and uphill towards the Old Town, the fine dressed stone abodes of the middle-classes fawned in a wide crescent of higher ground around the base of the rock. A peasant would be lucky to cross those bridges into the Crescent, never mind dream of setting foot in the Old Town.

A pockmarked old whore sidled up to me and gave me a toothless smile. An overpowering floral scent followed her, probably intended to hide her rotten breath. She was no high-class lady of sheets, that was certain.

"Not today, love," I said, pushing past her and plodding on towards Sailor's Spire. I had a man to find and kill.

"Eunuch!" she spat at my back.

Ah, it was good to be home.

The black needle of Sailor's Spire loomed ahead, a memorial paid for by the Docklanders' own hard toil. Fresh flowers garlanded the stained stone edifice and a widow was on her knees before it, wailing as she offered two straw-woven likenesses of her dead. People paused in passing to lay down a parcel of food, a coin, or just to offer a respectful nod. In a place like Docklands every family had lost somebody to the sea.

At the spire I turned up onto Fisherman's Way, heading north towards Carrbridge. A short time later I felt eyes watching me from the alleyways. I wrung my hands and looked left and right, peering at the wooden signage of workshops and shop fronts in apparent confusion. Then, remembering the guard's warning about where the thieves frequented, I turned off the Way and wandered down a side street, then into a darkened alley away from bustling open streets. The buildings above creaked and groaned as I penetrated deeper into the warren of narrow passages.

I passed a group of torch-wielding women at the mouth of a vegetation-choked lane, all clad in thick leathers, busy beating back snapping green mouths of thorny witherweed and searing its roots with fire. The venomous weed was tenacious, hibernating for years in the mud before bursting up overnight to catch the unwary. A single bite could kill a child in seconds, and then it sucked them dry of all fluids before digesting their withered flesh. Witherweed was but one of the many twisted wonders of Setharis, some occurring naturally and others escaped experiments. I kept my head down and continued on through winding alleyways.

Nothing looked familiar. My recollection of Lynas' message

was garbled, the images almost unintelligible and these alleys were all of a muchness. All I could see with certainty were those glittering daemons, a shadowed hood and a red-stained scalpel. I'd need Charra to help me decipher it.

I heard soft footfalls behind me, as expected. I turned to see a rake-thin youth brandish a rusty knife. My heart sank. The pup couldn't have seen fourteen summers, if that. A tarnished earring of twisted silver wire adorned his left ear.

"Gimme your money," he snarled, thrusting his weapon towards me.

Staring at the knife, I made a show of cringing back against the alley wall with my coin pouch clutched to my chest. He swept closer and snatched it from my hand. Unseen, my other hand flicked out to his belt and pocketed his own pouch. The thief peered in at my few remaining copper bits and scowled. He'd been expecting more. He eyed my fine coat. It was all going exactly as planned.

I stripped off my coat and thrust it at him. "Here, take this. It has to be worth something."

He grabbed it and appraised the cloth; it would be worth a few silvers to a fence. He looked me up and down and saw that I had nothing else of worth. His intentions were obvious in his eyes, muscles tensing ready to plunge the knife into my chest. He didn't want any witnesses left to raise a cry of *Thief!* He stepped in close, knife poised.

I let my mien of meekness slip, a sudden change in posture to radiate killing intent. My eyes hardened, fixed on his own. I'd kill him if I had to, and then find another thief. He flinched back. Street rats needed a strong survival instinct if they wanted to live for long. He had second thoughts, turned and fled down the street with my coat and almost-empty pouch.

The pathetic merchant mask slipped back onto my face. Wringing my hands, I stumbled towards Fisherman's Way after taking a quick peek into the youth's own money pouch. I whistled at the sight of silver; seemed the boy had already robbed a few others today. Now I had enough coin for a few nights at an inn, and to my delight I found two tabac roll-ups in there. It was the good stuff too, not the usual choke-throat I found in far-flung villages and towns.

The boy had tried to steal from a bigger and nastier thief than he was. The main thing was that my fine coat was into other hands and onto other backs. The shadow cats shouldn't be able to survive in the daemon-toxic air of Setharis, but only fools left survival to assumption. If they still hunted me then they should instead pick up the scent of my magic in the wool. I'd been sleeping in it for days, letting it soak up my sweat. No amount of washing would be getting that out soon, not beyond the noses of those damn cats. It might buy me more time. Pity it'd been a barely-weaned pup that robbed me. Even if he'd been about to stick me with a knife, I would still have it on my conscience if the daemons caught up with him before he could shift it on to some nastier, hardened scumbag. Lucky my conscience was a withered husk of a thing. I wouldn't shed any tears for the likes of him, and I had more urgent things to concentrate on: Lynas had been trying to warn me that far more that his own life was at stake. I owed it to him to finish what he'd started.

The Gift-bond to Lynas was no longer a constant presence, his innate goodness helping to steer my wayward morality. When I'd been a Docklands street rat, that selfish mentality had been a boon to survival, but now that I wielded terrifying power it made me dangerous. I wasn't one to shy away from abusing power if somebody deserved it, and if I could get away with it. Without his comforting guidance in the back of my mind all I could do was keep asking myself: *What would Lynas do?* I would try not to disappoint him.

I had no intention of going to Carrbridge. Instead I searched for a suitable inn, some middling place with a bath where I could scrub off the ship-stink. I spotted one down a side street, the sun-bleached sign proclaimed it The Throne and Fire.

Heading down the street I passed a scrawny girl at that awkward age somewhere between child and adult, a purple wine-stain birthmark covering her bruised cheek. As I approached she looked up at me without any trace of fear, just a dull acceptance, and held up a bowl. Too many Docklands girls had that same look. But for the grace of Gift I might have shared a similarly unsavoury fate. I had escaped thanks to my mother's foreign bloodline, with all my father's kin being about as magical as bricks; all gone thanks to the Grey Pox. I sighed. It had been a very long time indeed since I last thought of my parents, and I found the pangs of loss little dulled.

I fished out a handful of coins; I was a sucker for underdogs and second chances, and had been given more than a few of the latter myself. After a moment's reluctance I added two silvers. It was what Lynas would have done. Easy come, easy go. The girl's eyes went wide as the coins clinked into her bowl. She stared up at me with fearful hope, probably thinking I wanted something especially foul from her.

"It's not payment, girl," I said. "Get some food in your belly and a new dress. Clean yourself up and go see if any of the inns are hiring. And don't let anybody see you have silver if you want to keep it."

She swallowed and opened her mouth to reply but I didn't want thanks, just waved her off and entered the inn. I hoped she wouldn't spend it on drink and alchemics but didn't care enough to stick around. I'd been disappointed far too many times for that, but everybody deserved a chance. What they made of it was up to them.

The innkeep overcharged me but I didn't argue and allowed a young boy to show me to my first floor room. He brought up stones heated on the downstairs hearth and dropped them into a huge old ale barrel that served as a bath. Once it was hot enough I dismissed him and made sure the door was locked and barred before slipping in.

It would be sheer bliss to soak and let the heat relax cramped muscles, but I wasn't here to enjoy myself. I sank down, the hot water enveloping my head, scrubbing grease from my hair and washing myself thoroughly to get rid of the weeks of sweat caking my skin. Any daemons would have a harder time tracking me down now. I could have used a little trick of aeromancy to rid myself of the filth but with my horrid luck a sniffer or shadow cat would have been passing by at exactly the wrong moment. It wasn't as risky as using my innate talent with mind magic but wasn't worth the added danger.

I scrubbed myself raw, then rose from the bath and dripped my way over to the bed. As it dried, my hair gradually lifted and spiked back into its usual unruly mess. It felt good to be able to sense movement again, like a blindfold had been removed. Every magus that had survived as long as I had inevitably suffered changes to their body in one way or another, alterations induced by the torrent of magic flowing through them. In some manner I didn't understand, the black spikes of hair helped me to sense movement and vibration in the air currents. No whoreson would be sneaking up behind me in the dark. Maybe that said a lot about me.

Examining myself in a copper mirror nailed to the wall, I checked to make sure all the ship-filth was gone. Grey flecked my stubble now; funny how that had crept up on me. Not that a single new hair had gone grey in years though – my aging had ceased. It happened to most magi sooner or later, and unlike some I hadn't withered away to a wrinkled husk.

I looked every bit as tired as I felt, but then I never had turned heads on entering a room – not for good reasons anyway – though I did like to imagine my scars lent me a sort of roguish charm. I shed the rest of my disguise, all the submissive mannerisms of a meek merchant, the slouching stance, and let my usual sneer creep back onto my face. It felt much like trying on an old pair of trousers and finding the fit a little too tight.

I stuffed a roll-up into my mouth and lit it from a lantern, drawing the smoke deep into my lungs and blowing it out like dragon's breath.

"Welcome home, Edrin Walker," I said to my reflection. For the first time in years I wasn't running from place to place, adrift with nothing to live for but the next cup of ale. Lynas was dead, and suddenly I felt alive again, a monster roused from deep slumber for a single deadly purpose.

"Now, my old pal," I said to mirror-me. "Let's go find out who we have to burn."

CHAPTER 5

It was a short drop from the window to the cobbles, and then I was off through the warren of alleys in the opposite direction to Fisherman's Way. My eyes darted to everyone I encountered, taking their measure. Paranoia had served me well over the years.

I knew that I looked like an idiot in the oversized tunic and patched trousers I'd stolen from the inn, but beggars couldn't be choosers. The inn's locks had been a joke for my picks and the clothes newly laundered and laid out in some poor sod's room. They'd have to repay the man. Served them right for overcharging me.

My head snapped up as a shadow moved beneath a broken cart. I sighed in relief as the hairy black head of a hound peeked out to snuffle along the ground. Ha, I wished those shadow cats luck trying to find my scent – magical or otherwise – through the alleys of the Warrens. Any nose that sensitive would suffer in streets awash with raw sewage.

First stop was Charra. If anybody knew the details of what happened to Lynas it would be her. I also hoped to pick up all my old gear I'd hidden away before boarding the first ship leaving Setharis ten years ago. I would need every weapon I could get. They had hopefully sat undisturbed in a chest at Charra's Place all this time. I really hoped that she hadn't let curiosity get the better of her. I didn't fancy mourning two friends today. The twists and turns of the streets were unfamiliar to me now, and it would take time to find my way there. It gave me the opportunity to think, and that was never good. Lynas died over and over again in my mind, driving me to the edge of impotent fury. My hands curled into fists, nails cutting into my palms. If only I'd been here.

The local thieves didn't bother me this time. They could tell that I belonged here from my jaunty walk, the flash of a feral grin and the aura of imminent violence that said I'd as soon smash their head in as look at them. Of course, in these borrowed clothes I also didn't look like I had two copper bits to my name either. Might have helped.

I was glad I didn't have to risk using my magic on such lowlifes. I tried not to use magic to mess with people's heads if I could avoid it – it was a sickening violation of privacy and it hadn't been terribly difficult to swindle a living out in the hinterlands of the Free Towns, where people were more naive and trusted far more readily than properly civilized Setharii folk like myself. Unlike pyromancers, burning bright and burning out quickly, I was subtler and canny enough not to let the magic run riot through my body long enough to risk more changes, rationing it until needed instead of putting on flashy shows. A magus is too fragile a channel to let the sea of magic roar through unchecked for long, and the more you used it the more you wanted to; no, the more you needed to. *Want* was far too weak a word.

Affinity for one of the elements was by far the most common Gift, but I was different, classing myself as a right manipulative bastard, or a peoplemancer if I wanted to be polite about it. Most people had worse names for those with my rare sort of Gift: tyrant if they were being polite, mindfucker if not. The Arcanum kept an eye on all magi and made sure we didn't abuse our powers too much, and they'd known I had the potential to enslave people to my will and become a true tyrant. They had always watched me with an extra level of vigilance, one hand on a knife ready to plunge into my back. Happy times.

As it turned out, Charra's old premises were long-gone, burnt down and replaced by a creaking block of slum housing. A copper in a beggar's bowl gained me the information that Charra was still very much alive, much to my relief. She had shifted her business all the way over to West Docklands, which was impressively upmarket for a brothel. The new Charra's Place was as close to the luxury of the Crescent and the Old Town as such an establishment could get without the wardens and the Arcanum taking exception to such undesirables getting above their station.

It took a good half day to make my way west through the maze of narrow streets, and as I walked I gradually became aware that something was not right below the surface of the city. An atmosphere of fear and uncertainty pervaded the seemingly cheerful chats and greetings of friends and neighbours. It wasn't what they said, it was what they didn't. I witnessed an old woman ask how a carpenter's sister was doing. He didn't answer and just looked away, focusing on repairing a door. Her face paled and she didn't enquire further. I eavesdropped on other conversations and asked people a few leading questions on my way, and it seemed a worrying number of people had gone missing over the last few months, especially those with a touch of magic in their blood. "The Skinner", the same name daubed on the gatehouse wall, seemed to be on everybody's lips; a deranged madman some said, while others called him a daemon from the Far Realms.

By the time I found the right area dusk had fallen and the great bell up in Old Town was tolling its last until dawn. A few travellers new to the city paused in the middle of the street to gawp up at the great houses and gothic spires as illusionary faerie flames flickered into life all along their walls and rooftops, painting them with hues of light that swirled through red, pink, green and blue at the artistic whims of the lords of the High Houses. It was beautiful, but I had seen it countless times and knew just how much gold the noble families wasted on maintaining such magical frivolities.

Charra's new place of business was a large building of fine grey stone decorated with fluted columns and delicate ornamentation, all set within small but meticulously maintained gardens. Elunnai was almost full tonight, her tears diamond-bright and scattered across the sky. The silvery light lent an ethereal beauty to the garden as hundreds of delicate moonflowers rose from the earth, translucent buds blooming, petals glowing gently as they bathed in Elunnai's radiance. It must have cost a fortune to build this small oasis of tranquility and for me it was far more magical than the illusionary artifice adorning the manses of the High Houses on the rock above.

Charra had gone up in the world.

Two bullish red-haired clansmen – twins, all looming muscle and whorling blue tattoos, short necks and bristling beards – stood flanking the main entrance. Their hairy arms crossed over leather vests as they watched my approach. I noted the wooden hilts of clubs peeking out from the square-sheared low hedges on either side of them. These two were as well-armed and armoured as the wardens would accept in the lower city. I could tell from a glance that they were seasoned warriors: the knife scars on the arms, the solid stance, the way their eyes sized me up. They had smashed more than a few heads in their time.

I wouldn't have expected anything less from Charra; she had always boasted a good eye for talent. Hah, and if I knew Charra, then guarding this door wasn't all the twins would be doing on a regular basis.

Neither of them looked impressed at the sight of me in my oversized patched clothing. I probably did look like some soft southern twat to them, more at home in the gutters than in a high class brothel. Still, I reckoned I knew just how to deal with Clansmen, being half of one myself.

Straightening up to try and look vaguely imposing, I sauntered over and stopped just out of arm's reach, nodded to them. "How's it goin', pal? I'm here to see Charra."

Both looked me up and down, well, mostly down. The one on the right sneered at me. "Oh aye?" he said, the scent of whisky on his breath. "And why would she want to see you then, wee man?"

The Clan tattoo running up the side of his neck identified him as hailing from one of the northeastern clans. I grinned up at him as the name came to me. "Have some respect, you little Clachan prick."

He blinked, exchanged glances with his brother. That was the way to deal with clansmen – a bit of banter and a lot of front. I shook my head and tutted. "Why, I–"

His fist ploughed into my stomach, lifting me off my feet. Air whuffed from my mouth and I collapsed, shocked lungs refusing to suck in air, my belly a mass of pain like I'd been kicked by a horse. The bastards. They'd spent too long in Setharis, gone native; and as for me – I'd been too cocky.

Staggering over to the hedge, I doubled over and vomited all over the handle of his club, just to spite the prick.

"Ugh, you dirty wee bawbag!" he cried, hauling me round by the scruff of the neck. I gasped, struggling to speak as his other fist drew back to pound on my face, managing to force out a few words.

"The rabbits are fast here."

His face screwed up in confusion. "Eh?"

"Purple snow?"

"What are–"

It was just enough to set his mind off-balance, enough confusion to make it easier to slip into his head. I wouldn't get out of this in one piece without using a tiny bit of magic and I refused to allow the likes of them to get in my way. I opened my Gift, just a sliver. Skin contact made working magic so much safer and easier. I reached into his mind and rummaged his memories for the big fat bag of gold at the centre. It wasn't difficult: a haze of alcohol-induced malleability overlaid his every thought.

Ah, there it was. Dirty bastard.

I made the hand clamped round the back of my neck spasm with pain like it had just been stabbed. He snatched his hand back, hissing. The iron band squeezing my chest eased off slightly. I clutched my throbbing stomach.

"I know your secrets, Nevin," I sneered back at him, raising an eyebrow. "How was Fenella? Enjoy it, did you? Wet for you, was she?" I tutted again. "Wasn't your brother here madly in love with her for years?"

Nevin's face went pale. Both men's eyes widened in horror. My arrow had struck home. Grant stared at him in disbelief. Which turned to rage.

"You lying cunt!" his twin snarled, launching himself at Nevin, meaty fist smashing into his brother's face.

As the twins set to rolling about the ground beating the crap out of each other, I staggered over to the entrance and shouldered the heavy oaken door open. A tiny bell tinkled as I slipped inside and let it swing shut behind me.

Inside, the air in the reception hall was fragrant with exotic spices and expensive oils, the carpets and furnishings all in the best possible taste. I closed my eyes for a second and concentrated on blocking away the pain, telling my body that it belonged to somebody else. It receded to a dull ache.

A lady of sheets carrying a silver tray and cup sashayed down the hallway towards me, nipples almost visible beneath her silken halter, the slit on her long skirt revealing a glimpse of bronzed thigh. No toothless old whores with rotten breath here. And I was certainly no eunuch, that was entirely evident.

Her eyes took in my ill-fitting and now puke-stained clothes. Her brow creased.

I winked at her. "Ah, so good to be back!" I plucked at my baggy tunic. "Urgh, I really must arrange a better disguise next time. Is that wine, my sweet?" Not one to turn down free drink, and keen to wash the foul taste from my mouth, I snatched the cup from the tray and took a gulp before she could protest. It was far from my usual pig-swill. Not even a hint of vinegar. "Is your mistress at home this evening?"

She was having none of it. "Mistress Charra is indeed, m'lord, but she is otherwise occupied."

The front door shuddered as something heavy slammed into it. Muffled cries of pain and cursing came from the other side. Those brothers were really going at it.

A weary sigh escaped my mouth. "Alas, work before pleasure then. I am here on Arcanum business."

She stared at me sceptically for a moment before bobbing her head. "Yes, m'lord. I shall inform the management immediately." She refused to meet my eyes as she backed down the hallway.

I stood, hands clasped behind my back, studying the paintings on the walls and the fresco on the ceiling until the sound of boots on stone gave cause to make me turn. A young woman of serious mien approached, tall and brown skinned with cropped black hair. She couldn't have seen much more than eighteen summers, but those dark eyes held a composure far beyond her years that seemed oddly familiar. She wore a sombre outfit of black tunic and trousers with a thigh-length tailored coat over it, which on closer inspection appeared weighted in places. I had no problem imagining the knives secreted in there, or any illusions as to her competency with them.

This was Charra's personal attendant most likely. She reminded me of her mistress in many ways, completely self-assured, her movement precise, smooth as a dancer. An edge of danger clung to her, and that made the woman far more appealing to me than any giggling lady of sheets with a fake smile. Never one to shy away from illicit pleasure, I let my eyes linger.

She took in my patched clothes, then bowed formally, her eyes never leaving mine. "Good evening, Master…?"

"Reklaw," I said, with full-on pomp. "I am here to see the mistress of the house." Faced with a member of the Arcanum, even the lowliest full magus, most people tended to react like they'd been dropped into a nest of vipers. Not this girl.

"I see," she said. "The mistress of the house is not currently seeing visitors. If you would care to return whe–"

"Not a chance. She will want to see me."

"You sheep-shagging craven little bitch!" a Clansman bellowed outside. Another heavy thump rattled the door.

The girl's eyes were cold enough to kill. "If you would excuse me for one moment, Master Reklaw."

She opened the front door and stepped out, sniffed the air. "Is that whisky I smell?" As it swung closed behind her the racket outside cut off mid-swear. I couldn't hear the bollocking she gave them, but when she opened the door again Grant and Nevin stared at me with seething hatred, all torn clothes and bloody noses. She slammed the door in faces as bruised as their egos and favoured me with an unamused smile.

"Now, where were we? If you insist on forcing a meeting then I must warn you that she does not suffer fools and she has friends in high places."

I smiled; Charra had suffered my particular style of foolishness for years. "As I said, she will want to see me."

"On your head be it then." She beckoned me down the reception hall, "This way please."

We passed through a curtain into a long hallway with a dozen doors each side. Clearly there was a whole lot of fucking going on here and I pitied whoever had to launder all that linen. Halfway down, she pulled out an intricate black iron key and slotted it into the lock of a door identical to any other. A series of clicks and it swung open to reveal a stone staircase spiralling up, narrow enough that a few men could hold back a small army. I followed her in and pulled the door closed behind me, surprised at a weight more like iron than wood. Reinforced, by the feel of it. The entire building was a small but luxurious fortress.

We emerged from the stairs into a guard room where four men blocked the far door. Armed and ready, three had unsheathed swords, and the fourth held one of those new-fangled Esbanian crossbows aimed straight at my heart. I'd never seen one of the things before: like a normal bow but on its side with some sort of mechanical crank and trigger. It looked all wrong to me, but the things were said to be stupidly simple to use, not requiring the years of practice it took to become a competent bowman. I bet the Arcanum didn't like that one bit. Now any disgruntled peasant could have the power to kill at a distance.

Weapons in the hands of the low-born didn't sit well with the High Houses and it was borderline illegal for a Docklands household to be armed like this, unless the law had changed while I'd been away. Fat chance of that.

"Evening, gents," I said.

At a nod from Herself, they swung the door open. The guard's hard glares warned me to behave as I passed, stepping out of the smoky torchlight of the guard room into the warmth of a lavish suite more subtly lit by ornate candelabra and shutters on barred windows edged with the sunset. Thick rugs, soft underfoot, covered a dark hardwood floor, and on either side of an archway ahead, black marble columns soared to a vaulted ceiling painted with scenes of writhing naked bodies. Some of those positions... I was fairly sure that most people couldn't bend like that. And why had somebody painted horses like... I tore my eyes away from the ceiling. Some things were better left a mystery.

The setup was classic Charra; it was all about the psychology of power. The self-proclaimed respectable classes of Setharis would be suckered in by the opulence only to be flustered by the depraved art. The seedy underbelly, meanwhile, would take the riches as a show of power, but the art as a sign that she was still one of them. She still knew what she was, or at least what she claimed to be – she was suspiciously deadly with fists and knifes, and over the years I'd never actually come across a single client who had enjoyed her services, but I wasn't one to pry into a friend's secrets. Whatever she really was, with her public reputation no amount of money would buy acceptance among the high-born and no point in pretending otherwise. But in her own way she was rubbing her success in their faces every time they stepped into her domain.

I liked her style. Liked to flatter myself that she'd learnt from the worst.

Voices emerged from a side room where a handful of men and women sat in rows at benches, quills scratching while a tutor inspected and corrected their letters and numbers. Charra had always helped people lift themselves out of the gutters to find other work if they wished, and before I fled the city she had started providing funds for several to start up their own businesses in exchange for a small cut of future profit. Judging from this new place that generosity had paid off handsomely.

The room beyond the archway was deep in shadow. I was led through to a plush ebony chair and small ornate table on which an oil lantern had been shuttered to cast its light in my eyes so that I couldn't see much of anything. I felt the attendant's hand on my shoulder, helpfully steering me down into the seat with a grip that told me standing wasn't an option. A surprising strength too; I couldn't help but wonder if she was mageborn.

While waiting I peered into the dark, just making out a lacquered wicker screen and alcoves lining either side of the room. My less orthodox senses filled in the gaps: the soft scuff of leather; the creak of floorboards; eddies and whirls of hot breath in cool air brushing my hair – guards in the alcoves. I drummed an uneven beat on the arm of the chair. Waited some more. Pondered asking for snacks.

Finally, a servant emerged from behind the screen and began folding it back. She wore a head-to-foot Ahramish dress, layers of fine black lace and thread of gold that left only ink-stained hands and kohl-lined eyes uncovered – the traditional dress worn by librarians of the Great Archive at Sumart if I wasn't mistaken. If genuine, it was an impressive feat for Charra to have acquired the services of one of their ilk; they were said to be unwaveringly honest, intelligent, and better read than most magi who had lived twice as long.

My heart thudded like a drum, throat closing up as a woman with the dark skin tones of the Thousand Kingdoms came into view – Charra. She lounged on a plush chair with a silver goblet in her hand, swilling a fragrant, spiced red wine. She had put on a bit of weight over the years, acquired a shock of grey in her short spiked hair, and crow's feet now clustered at the corners of her eyes, but she was still a fine-looking woman. Her smoky hazel eyes were dull and disinterested, bloodshot from wine and weariness. Her black tunic and trousers were a match to her attendant's, but rumpled and unwashed. A cloud of grief surrounded her, causing my own heart to twinge in response. *Oh Lynas...*

The attendant cleared her throat behind me, hot breath caressing the back of my neck. "This is Master Reklaw." I imagined her hand resting on the hilt of a dagger, ready to plunge it deep into my back.

Her mistress only glanced at me briefly, nodded and took a sip of wine, staining her lips purple. "You claim to be from the Arcanum, Master Reklaw. What do you want?"

I stroked my jaw. Sure, I'd acquired a mass of scars and got rid of that ridiculous pointy goatee that had been all the fashion back then, but still... I pulled a bent roll-up from my pocket, lit it from the lantern and clamped it between my lips. I took a deep draw and exhaled, smoke writhing in the lamplight as it drifted towards the hidden guards. "That bunch of whiny, self-important pricks? I suppose I can claim some past involvement, Cheriam."

She jerked upright, shocked somebody had used her birth name, the one only a handful of people from the old days would know. It took her a moment. Then the goblet clanged to the floor and wine gurgled out in a spreading purple pool as she stared at me in shocked pleasure, then anger, that familiar expression seeming more like the old Charra I knew.

"Reklaw? You stinking bastard." She rose and clapped her hands, "All of you, out!" She didn't take her eyes off me as lantern shutters were opened and armed guards shuffled out. Her attendant and her knives remained in place behind me.

Charra stalked over and grabbed me by the collar, hauling me to my feet and into her arms, crushing herself to my chest. "I knew you couldn't be dead, you slippery scoundrel."

I couldn't hide the joy welling up inside me. It was the happiest I'd been in years, even tainted as it was by recent events. We held each other for a long moment until she finally pulled away. Her gaze stroked my scars. "What happened to your face?"

I cleared my throat. "Cut it shaving."

"Shaving?" She raised an eyebrow. "What with? A bear?" Suddenly fury flashed in her eyes. "Ten years! You could've at least sent a letter." Her slap rattled teeth, snapped my head to one side, eye to eye with the attendant. The girl arched an eyebrow, a canny expression that seemed strangely familiar.

I looked from her to Charra, then back again. Then it dawned on me. She had Lynas' eyes. It clicked in my mind and the mix of Lynas and Charra in their daughter's face became heart wrenchingly obvious.

I swallowed the lump in my throat. "No! This is little Layla?" Suddenly I felt horrendously awkward for letting my eyes linger on her earlier.

Layla looked hopelessly confused, that icy control cracked and leaking.

"My darling," Charra said. "Do you remember Uncle Walker?"

She frowned, absently reached over and tugged at my chin, then realized what she was doing and snatched her hand back, cheeks reddening. Seemed she remembered tugging on my beard when she was little.

Charra gave her a hug, "Give us some time alone please, my darling."

"If you are sure..." Layla said, looking none too pleased. Charra squeezed her arm and shooed her away, but not before Layla gave me a meaningful look, promising knives in my eyeballs if I laid a hand on her mother.

Once we were alone Charra kicked me in the ankle, just

hard enough to be annoying. "You grumpy old git. I haven't laid eyes on your sorry hide ever since you came running up my door carrying that old box. I just thought you were in yet another spot of trouble and hadn't expected you to flee the godsdamned city without even a goodbye. Why did you leave? A god died that night – I was worried sick something had got you too."

I swallowed and decided the truth was better than lies. "I, uh, suspect that I might have had something to do with that. I made some very bad enemies that night. Sorry, I'd tell you more if I knew it myself. There is a hole in my memory."

She stared at me, flat and sceptical.

"I made a deal with somebody incredibly dangerous, and most of what happened that night is locked away inside my head."

She scrutinized every change in my face, the scars, lines and greying hair, and then frowned, my appearance not quite matching the age it should have shown in mundanes: one of the benefits of magic. "Very well, I have more than enough to worry about at the moment. You did a good job faking your death to get the Arcanum off your back. Everybody believed your charred corpse was found near Port Hellisen. Well, almost everybody; Lynas didn't seem terribly upset about it, and knowing the special bond you two have... He is–" She grimaced "–was, a terrible liar. I assume you made him promise to keep me in the dark?"

"Sorry about that," I said, raking a hand through my unruly hair. "They would never have stopped if they had any suspicion I still lived. That body belonged to an old farmer called Rob Tillane, dead of the bloody flux judging from the smell. I just covered his corpse in my blood and magic to fool the sniffers. The fire and, ah, a few convenient witnesses to my death disguised the rest." I tapped my temple and grinned.

She shook her head, the ghost of a smile on her lips, "Always the conniving snake, and I am very glad you are. Where have you been holed all these years?"

"Where haven't I been," I said, sighing. "Traipsed through every town and village in Kaladon most likely, from Port Elsewere in the south west, through the Free Cities to the north and the Clanholds in the mountainous hinterlands beyond that. I never stayed long in one place. The Arcanum were not the only ones hunting me, and I couldn't fool all of them."

"That doesn't sound like much of a life," she said.

"It was an existence," I replied, and it had been one that had kept them safe thanks to my deal. I hadn't realized how lonely and pitiful it had been until I'd seen Charra once more. "What about you? Have you been well?"

She smiled briefly and waved a hand at the sumptuous surroundings. "It's been a good life for the most part. Lynas and I got back together a handful of times, but that kind of relationship was not meant to be." She coughed and cleared her throat, then took a deep shuddering breath and gazed longing at her spilt wine. "I assume you returned because you know what happened."

"I'm going to burn the bastard," I snarled.

She nodded, "I don't know who or why or I'd have done it myself."

"I can help with that," I said tapping my head. "I have ways of finding out."

"Good. You'll be wanting to collect your old belongings before we get down to business."

I swallowed, not exactly happy at the thought of being reunited with Dissever.

Fuck, this was going to hurt.

CHAPTER 6

No words could fully convey how good it was to see Charra again. Memories of the old days had carried me through my exile and I couldn't help but think back to when we first met. Those were better times, or at least they had been for me. For Charra, up until then her life had been filled with pain and starvation.

When we first met Charra she had been a skinny little wretch sprinting down an alley, bare feet ankle-deep in slush and snow and wearing not much of anything, her lips an unhealthy shade of blue. She had seen us running towards her and slid to a precarious stop. With her escape route blocked she'd started to panic, a rusty knife brandished in shivering hands. Lynas and I had not fared quite so well: startled, we slipped on the ice, ending up in a crumpled heap atop a pile of yellow snow, but miracle of miracles, we managed to keep the jar of rum and the hot joint of roast pork safely cradled in our arms. We'd much preferred scrapes and bruises to fouling our food. As usual I'd cajoled Lynas into being the lookout, but it hadn't been one of my better planned heists.

Angry shouts of "thieves" and "get the bitch" came from opposite directions of the alley. We all looked at each other incredulously.

"Well, shite," I said.

"Of all the poor luck," Lynas added. "I told you I had a bad feeling about this one."

Charra's eyes flicked to the steaming joint of meat and then back again. An unspoken agreement flowed between the three of us. "Through here," the girl said, darting through the open door to the child's house. Right from the start Charra had proven herself to be the most quick-witted of our trio.

We darted through a mouldering room choked with children and swept through the curtain into the next home, ran past a yelling old man and dodged an angry woman with a bloodied butcher's knife in hand, and then we were out into the adjoining alley. Our feet pounded the icy cobbles as we sped away, laughing as our pursuers got snarled up in the angry mess we left in our wake.

The girl took a sharp left and drew up to a ruined area of tumbled stone and charred wood that had been claimed by a blaze the year before. It stank of rotten eggs. A drove of swine snuffled across the area, grunting and munching on scraps of waste food people had dumped. Nothing went to waste in Docklands and it made for fat, juicy pigs. The drunken swineherder was taking a piss and paying us no notice.

She squeezed into a hollow between stone foundation blocks and disappeared down into a dark cellar space. Lynas and I exchanged glances and I dived into the hole after her, back scraping across stone. Lynas, running to fat even then, got himself wedged and it took both the girl and me to dislodge him, mere moments before the angry voices caught up with us.

They harassed the oblivious swineherder then searched the whole area while we hid in that dark hollow, hardly daring to breathe until a blizzard forced them to give up the hunt.

We waited there for a good few hours until the blizzard blew itself out, crude but strong dockhouse rum warming our bellies, scoffing down chunks of juicy roast pork. For us it was a fine meal, but for that starving waif, on the run for who knows how long, it was a feast. To pass the time Lynas and I ended up exchanging stories with that half-frozen little street rat who said her name was Charra. At first she hadn't believed two such raggedy urchins were Collegiate initiates, and then she had been scared of our magic, but we were far from typical Old Town slicks. She quickly warmed to us, especially Lynas for some reason. Which had irked me at the time. Oh, sure, he had thought to give her his warm cloak, but I'm positive I would have thought of that too.

One thing we had quickly learned about Charra was that while she was a thieving little scoundrel, to friends her word was as iron. It was as if friendship was a novel concept to her, and a thing to be cherished.

Charra's hacking cough shook me from my reverie. It was worryingly reminiscent of her lingering illness all those years ago when I'd made my deal, but the cellar was dusty and stale and irritated my own nose and throat.

She pulled back an oil-cloth from a pile of junk and I began removing old chairs, sacks of skimpy costumes and an assortment of mops, buckets and brooms. I tried not to think about Charra in costume as I delved deeper in the pile.

There it was: the accumulated detritus of thirty years of my life fitted into a single small heartwood chest hidden away in a forgotten corner of a dusty cellar. I was glad she had kept it safe, even after the fire that had gutted her old property.

I ran my hands over the smooth, dark wood. It bore a few blackened scars but was otherwise intact. I sighed in relief, hadn't realized how much it actually meant to me until right then. It was the only thing I had left from my father, a gift given to me on the first day of my entrance to the Arcanum. That dour man hadn't really been able to afford such finery on a dockhand's pay, but hadn't let that stop him. Never one to talk about his emotions, this had been his way of showing how proud he was of his son the magus. He was the sort of man that wouldn't let sleep or food get in the way of something he deemed important. He had worked his fingers to the bone to buy it for me. I hadn't appreciated it back then, brat that I was. My heart was heavy; I missed my old man.

The fuzzy warmth gave way to bitterness. Life as an Arcanum initiate had been harsh for a Docklands boy. I was not one of the old guard of High Houses, old money and political "scratch my back" and the others had made sure to remind me of my place at every opportunity. As a magus I hadn't been better than them, but I proved much, much, nastier.

My wards were still in place, still potent and lethal. In the Collegiate you bloody well learned to protect your belongings early on.

I felt Charra behind me, peering over my shoulder. "So what do you have in there?" she said. "All these years I've been wondering…"

"Thanks for keeping it safe," I said. "But be very glad you didn't try to open it."

Charra shrugged. "I'm no fool. When a magus tells me never to open something, not ever, I listen."

That raised a ghost of a smile. My hand hesitated over the lid, reluctant to open it. It would bring back bad memories and pain, so much pain. When I finally pressed my palm to the lid there was a series of clicks and then a soft hissing. It creaked open without assistance.

On top I had carelessly piled scraps of paper and scrolls covered in my shaky scrawl, artefacts of my Collegiate years.

I scooped them out and dumped them onto the floor.

Charra picked up some furled parchment and studied it. Her eyebrows climbed. "Really, Walker, poetry? You?" She chuckled. "Eyes blue as deepest sea, hair curled like the waves, wanton lips ripe for–"

I flushed and snatched it from her hands. "It was a horrible mistake I didn't repeat."

Under the papers lay my old greatcoat. I lifted it out and shook decade-old creases loose from the grey cloth, studying it with a critical eye. With great effort, master artificers of the Arcanum could make ensorcelled armour proof against arrows, or courtly attire designed to enhance allure – unusual items of all kinds. Normally you had to do some great service for the Arcanum to acquire such rarities, unless, say, a master artificer had certain nasty and illegal habits, unless one were to, say, make a huge mistake and require certain witnesses to forget his face. The item I'd requested as a payoff was something far more practical than armour and allure: the greatcoat was waterproof and self-cleaning, and since those awful ragged tears were all gone it was now apparently self-repairing. That was odd, but I wasn't one to check a gift horse's teeth.

I slipped on the soft wool, fastening black leather and brass buckles across my chest. It felt like donning a second skin, and a little like coming home. I spun to face Charra. "Well, how do I–"

Wait. Ragged tears in my coat? Yes! I used the old memory to ram a lever into the locked doors in my mind. The taste of blood flooded my mouth. I doubled over, clutching my head as the dire secret held inside slammed into its gaol doors.

Tower on fire. Drenched in gore, soaked to the skin through my tattered coat, Artha's blood sizzling against my skin.

I saunter out through the shattered door to the god's tower and light a soggy blood-stained roll-up from the flaming wreckage. I taste his blood on my lips as I inhale. A god's death cry echoes through the city as my plume of smoke twists into the air.

A voice: "Is it done? Is his madness ended?"

Flashing a grin at the only other being present, a woman, perhaps. Whoever or whatever it was, she was blacked out, fuzzy, a gaping hole in my memory.

"I'm gasping for a drink. You buying?"

Panic paralysed me until the horrific memory retreated back into its prison. Oh gods, oh sweet fuck, I'd been in Artha's tower when he died. I'd been right there! I could still taste his blood burning against my lips. Sweet Lady Night, did I kill him? How? He was a god – it would be like trying to murder a mountain.

I'd made a deal to keep the details secret, even from me, in exchange for my friends' safety and I'd kept it for ten long years. But what if that knowledge had something to do with Lynas' murder? I had to uncover every detail of the horrific crime I'd committed, if crime it was. Even this much involvement, if it were to be known, would have had the entire city baying for my head on a spike atop the walls.

"What's going on, Walker?" Charra asked. "You are not well."

I focused on Charra. Only on Charra. I straightened up and scrubbed blood from my face with the sleeve of my coat. The red stain dissipated into the weave, absorbed or eaten. "I'm fine, for now, but being back is going to get me killed. Daemons are hunting me by the scent of my magic and if they don't get me the Arcanum will, sooner or later."

Her lips thinned. "Then you need to leave again. Right away."

"No," I said, shaking my head. "I can't do that. Lynas fought to tell me something as he lay dying. Something important enough for him to sacrifice his life." *And mine.* The shattered details of the vision hinted at something far larger than ourselves. "I need to find the bastard that murdered him."

"A pox on that," she said. "Nothing you can do will bring him back. You have to live." She tried to keep it from her face, gods bless her, but I could tell that she badly wanted me to stay and help.

This was Charra – she had survived everything the streets of Setharis had thrown at her, and not only survived, but thrived. Nobody hauled themselves up out of the gutter without getting their hands dirty. She was hard. Far harder than me when she had to be. She deserved to know what they did to Lynas.

"Charra, they skinned him. The only reason they would do that is to use his flesh for blood sorcery. Our skin and Gift grows more resistant to magic as we age and grow in power, so it's not something they can use. Mageblood is extortionate on the black market, but if they'd just wanted that then there are easier and safer ways." In the past I'd thought little of selling my blood so a few addicts with very expensive tastes could get high on a touch of magic. It was wildly dangerous to the unGifted, who lacked the capacity to control such raw power. It was one of the few things I truly regretted, a foul secret I would never share.

Grave-robbing had been rife in the distant past, magus bones looted for elixirs and sorcerous rituals, which is why cremation was now the ultimate destiny of all Gifted. Every living thing contained a small amount of magic in blood and bone, but every bit of a magus' body was so filled with magic that even our shite was a potent resource, the chamber pots and privies in Arcanum buildings emptied out into special slurry pits whose reeking gunk was spread over the farmlands surrounding Setharis. The magic seeped into the land and fed the spirits of growth and plenty, producing crops resistant to drought, plague-spirits and insects, with yields so enormous that we were almost able to feed this ravenous dark city of ours without relying on imports.

Blood sorcery was entirely different to using the Gift: it tore magic from living flesh and corrupted anybody who sought to use it.

"I already know it wasn't just for mageblood," Charra said. "I'm not without my own resources. As far as we know Lynas was the seventh known mageborn victim of the Skinner, and the latest was a full blown magus. He's stepping up his game, and nobody normal would risk attacking a magus for his blood."

My voice shook with fury. *"Seventh."* It explained the city's heavy atmosphere of fear only too well, and that would only be the surface of the pond. How many more people had the bastard killed? "And the Arcanum did nothing?"

She scowled. "The Old Town scum didn't seem to take much notice until the magus was murdered."

My fists shook, denied any Arcanum throats to tear out with my bare hands.

Charra continued, her voice calm and businesslike, "Also, nobody has seen hide nor hair of any mageblood dealers for the last six months or so."

I ground my teeth. "It has been traded in Setharis for centuries, always has been, always will be." I knew that from personal experience.

She glanced sideways at me. "Not anymore. Good riddance if you ask me. Even for alchemics that stuff is dangerous. But with these Skinner murders I find their disappearance beyond suspicious."

I forced my hands to relax as I mulled over this news. There would be a reckoning with the Arcanum later. One enemy at a time. "The dealers ended up dead?"

She shrugged. "They too went missing. Not a single vial of mageblood can be bought on the black market for gold or threats. Perhaps the supply has run dry."

Not likely, there would always be some magi with debts to pay, me for example.

"I had thought that somebody might have eliminated the competition," she continued, "to hold back the supply and inflate the price. But that appears not to be the case."

I chewed on my lip. "Somebody must be stockpiling it then. But why? And how is that linked to the murders?" I took a deep breath before broaching the next subject. "Charra, blood sorcery is said to be more powerful if you use the blood and flesh of close kin in the same ritual. About Layla…"

She coughed, then noisily cleared her throat. "Somebody already tried to abduct her. Coincidence perhaps. They failed, of course; I had her trained by the best weapon masters gold can buy. More people than usual have gone missing in the last few years."

It was as I'd suspected, and explained all her guards. Coincidence be damned, Charra was taking no chances.

She looked me straight in the eyes, trying hard not to cry. I couldn't remember Charra ever seeming this vulnerable before, but when I first met her she hadn't had much to lose. "Walker, you can't help us. You are a swindler and a trickster. If the Arcanum can't do anything to stop it, then what help can you be? I lost Lynas. I refuse to lose you too."

I had never given Charra an honest idea of the horrors I could unleash if I really let myself go, and even I didn't know the full extent of my power. Nobody would feel comfortable around somebody who could rearrange their mental furniture at will, and I'd always felt the fearful eyes of other magi on me, waiting and watching for me to slip up and reveal the corrupt nature they all thought I had. I had always kept my Gift reined in, refusing to give them a reason to destroy me.

"You think I haven't learned anything these last ten years?" I said. "I'm not the same man I was back then." New hope kindled in her eyes. Sadly, I'd barely used any magic in my exile, just a few subtle suggestions and adjustments when absolutely necessary. Still, Charra didn't need to know that, and in any case she really did not need to worry about me. The deal was off and I was done holding back, done pretending I was weaker than I really was. I hoped for the Arcanum's sake they stayed out of my way.

I sniffed and swallowed, cleared my throat. "I'll need to see where Lynas' body was found," I said. It was too unsettling to say "skin". A twinge of pain burned up my arm, right where the knife cut into him.

"I'll take you there myself," she replied.

"Don't suppose the Arcanum and the wardens have found any clues yet?" I asked, already knowing the answer.

"The lying wardens tried to claim that the Skinner strikes at random," Charra replied, kicking an old bucket clear across the floor. "As if he wasn't purposely targeting people with magic in their blood. And Lynas' three assistants just happened to go missing the next day?" She scowled. "They didn't get off their fat arses to investigate his death properly. The Arcanum is supposed to regulate magic and punish its abuse, and yet they sent along a sniffer and a magus just graduated from the Collegiate. Mewling children with fuzz on their cheeks! I pulled some strings and called in a favour to get Old Gerthan himself down there to take a look."

I nodded. "Old Gerthan is skilled." Not the best, mind, but a well-respected mid-level magus in the hierarchy of the Arcanum. It was a higher rank than they would ever have allowed a political cesspit like me to reach even if I had the might. He was old right enough, both in looks and actual age, but unless things had changed in my absence then he wasn't yet an elder or an adept who had mastered multiple paths of magic like most of the Inner Circle.

"He found little," Charra said. "No evidence or any identifiable traces of magic, just a general feeling that blood sorcery had been used nearby."

Looking back to the open chest I licked my lips and stared down, hand poised to reach in deeper. A few bits of junk, a stack of leather-wrapped journals and a wicked knife of what looked like black iron, but was nothing so innocuous. Dissever was a torturer's wet dream, a thing of black twisted barbs and serrated edges, and somehow it had escaped its leather sheath. There had been times during my exile when having such a dangerous weapon would have saved me a lot of pain, but I hadn't known if the Arcanum sniffers could track down the magical signatures of such a unique weapon, and I couldn't take the risk of being found and dragged back. My hand still hovered over the chest, part of me torn, wanting to leave it be.

I felt sick, but I would need every weapon I could lay my hands on to avenge Lynas. I wrapped my fingers around the hilt. Pain stabbed through my hand, bloody welts and cuts bursting across the skin. It felt strangely familiar, almost like... I grabbed a hold of the slippery memory, another missing fragment of my deal, and ripped it from its prison:

The blade jars against bone and I have to brutally wrench it up and down to saw my way through, working the cut down the centre of the god's chest until a ragged red trench splits it in two...

The mounting agony drove it back into the secret places inside my skull. I gritted my teeth and lifted out the squirming knife, feeling like the skin was being flayed from my hand. I supposed I deserved a little pain after locking it away in a box for ten years. Charra gasped, but again wisely kept her distance.

"Nice to see you too, Dissever," I growled, as rivulets of blood wound down my fingers and seeped into the hungry hilt.

The pain receded, leaving my hand stinging from a multitude of abrasions and shallow cuts. It was a strange feeling to be chastised by a knife, but then Dissever was not any kind of normal blade. It didn't even behave like any other spirit-bound object I had heard of. Powerful enough, perhaps, to kill a god?

Forging spirits into objects was on the level of godly powers and the oldest and greatest of spirits. Oh sure, with objects like my old coat, certain supremely skilled magi artificers could, with almost-prohibitive effort, give it a sort of crude mechanical reaction, but not actual life. Spirit-bound objects required a pact with the spirit involved and that bargain usually expired with their human owners, freeing the spirit once more. But not with Dissever, oh no! My thoughts drifted back to childhood, to two terrified boys exploring bone-crusted catacombs and a knife that had been buried hilt-deep in a corpse for ages unknown. A shiver rippled up my spine as my mind veered away from the darkness below. It was not something I wished to dwell on. Whoever created Dissever clearly had brutal murder in mind.

"Hope you enjoyed your rest," I said to it. "Because we're going to kill somebody."

A wordless hunger answered me, followed by actual words: *Feed me, you odious cretin.* Dissever always had been an exciting conversationalist. Which was another interesting discrepancy: I'd never heard of spirit-bound objects talking to their owners.

I very carefully sheathed the knife and looped it onto my belt, mentally urging it to behave. Then I retrieved the loaded dice from the front of my trousers and the lock picks from my boot, squirreling them away into the much more comfortable hidden pockets of my coat.

"Now I'm ready to go," I said to Charra. But I wasn't, and the thought of walking those streets where Lynas had fled in terror from daemons and then died brought me out in a cold sweat.

CHAPTER 7

The Warrens was not a place to venture at night, not unless you were suicidal or had a full gang at your back. Charra led the way, a lantern illuminating the narrow winding paths between buildings. Normally this would be the height of idiocy, something that would end up with you being bundled into a doorway with a knife at your throat. Not tonight. Not for us. The closer we came to where Lynas was murdered, the hotter my anger burned. I wanted somebody to step out and try something, to give me an excuse. My head was thumping and Lynas' death was an unbearable itch deep in my blood and bones, one I couldn't scratch. If any would-be thieves got in my way tonight then they would end up smeared across the walls of their mouldering homes.

Lynas and I had shared a Gift-bond, something that would have had me imprisoned if the Arcanum ever discovered we'd broken that age-old taboo. Nobody liked their heads being messed with, magi least of all, and in the dawn days of human history those with my rare Gift had carried the darker name of tyrant, and enslaved magi and mageborn through an enforced Gift-bond, a permanent linking of magical Gifts that allowed the tyrant unfettered access to their minds. But I wasn't them, hadn't enslaved people, and didn't deserve the black looks other magi aimed my way – well, not for that reason anyway. As a full blown magus I could have mentally forced Lynas to do as I wished, but I never had, and never would. Lynas and I had been true friends and it had been no burden to bear, nor a thing to fear between the two of us. Instead it was something beautiful. We could always find each other in a crowd or come to the other's aid when they were hurting. He shared my confidence and resilience and I his hope and conscience, while still respecting the privacy of his deeper thoughts. There was nothing we wouldn't have done for each other.

Charra spent the time telling me all she knew of the Skinner murders, and bringing me up to date with notable events of the last ten years. I already knew that Krandus had become the new Archmagus after my mentor Byzant's disappearance – him being the most powerful person in the world made that sort of knowledge widespread – but it was difficult to get specific details way out in the hinterlands. I was in mixed minds about Krandus' ascension. I'd never warmed to the man: far too cold and controlled, too inhuman to be likable, not like Byzant at all.

I actually stumbled over my own feet when Charra told me that Cillian Hastorum had recently joined the Inner Circle of the Arcanum and was now one of the seven most powerful people in all Setharis, and the world.

Charra savoured my reaction. "Probably shouldn't have been such a rotten cur to her, huh?"

You couldn't argue with that. We'd had a "thing" once, Cillian and I, back when we had both been lowly initiates. She'd been slumming it so far beneath her lofty station when by rights I should have only been visible with an eyeglass. It never would have worked out between us. At least, that's what I told myself. After we went through the final rite of the Forging and were acknowledged as proper magi, it had quickly become clear that she was better off without a wretch like me dragging her down. People had a bad habit of getting hurt around me.

"You two fought like cat and corvun," Charra added. "And as I recall, she usually won." All that earned was a grunt from me.

We approached a group of grubby youths, mostly girls from what I could tell, huddled in a doorway that stank of the heady aroma of sour wine and piss. Scarified smiles running up their cheeks marked them as Smilers, a street gang that had been in Setharis as long as anybody could remember, and with magi that was a very long time indeed. Their initiation ritual was to stick a blade into a supplicant's mouth and cut up at either side to give them a permanent smile. Nobody ever left the Smilers breathing, not unless they could find their way out of Setharis to some godsforsaken hole that didn't know what the scar-sign meant.

It would have been nice to think that my glower was enough to scare them off but they barely looked at me, their predator eyes fastening on Charra. The girls ceased lounging against the walls and slunk forward to meet us. Damn the Night Bitch, if they wanted a fight I was happy to oblige.

My hand slipped beneath my coat, wrapped around Dissever's hilt. Its hunger was infectious. Bloodlust bubbled up inside me and I felt a manic grin growing.

Their demeanours changed as we drew closer. They smiled – a disturbing sight – in genuine pleasure.

"Hey Charra-doll," the oldest girl said, a tall youth with bone hoops through her ears, eyebrow, and nostril. "What you two be doin' down the Warrens tonight?"

A stocky girl with greasy hair and a pockmarked face favoured me with a lewd grin. "You lookin' for a little somethin'-somethin'?" She flicked her cut-throat razor open and closed. "I likes 'em rough." She took a pull from a jug of wine, belched, and then looked me up and down in such a filthy, lecherous way that it made my skin crawl. Was this how women felt when drunken arses like me leered at them?

Charra rolled her eyes. "Not tonight, Tubbs, him is with me." Her accent dipped back into the rough patois of the Warrens. I was sure the girl's sort of "play" would not be my idea of fun. Charra turned to bone-face. "Hey, Rosha, good to see ya. Me and him got business down Bootmaker's Wynd."

Smiles died and hands dropped to hidden weapons. They shuffled a little closer together. "Bad business that," Rosha bone-face said. "Not the Blinders or the Scuttlers either. That was magic, that was." She shrugged, then looked me up and down, sneering. "Sure this piece o' shit enough fer you, Charra-doll? Doesn't seem like much of a man. He couldn't make ye scream, so how's about we make him a woman fer'ye? With that arse he'd look good in a dress. Shame about the face." The Smilers broke out in raucous laugher.

The urge to ram Dissever into her guts flooded through me, to plunge it into soft flesh and slowly work my way up. I prised my fingers off the hilt. The desire to kill faded. Mostly.

Instead of gutting her I smirked, prodding her in the chest, skin to skin. "You shut your flapping fish-hole," I said. "You'll never be half the man your mother was."

Her instant of confusion was all I needed to slip magic into her through the skin contact, minimising the danger of detection by any sniffer who might be passing, as vanishingly unlikely as that was in the Warrens at night. Her mind opened up to my Gift like a ripe corpse swollen with gas. It wasn't all rot though. Far from it.

She slapped my hand away and squared up to me, thrusting her chest out and her shoulders back as she stared me straight in the eye and stepped in close, knife in hand, preening in front of her gang.

I leaned in so nobody else could hear. "Haven't told them where you get the coin for all that extra food, have you? Working side jobs with bent wardens is bad for the reputation. And my, my, rutting with him too. How do you think that will go down?"

She went still for a second and then backed off with a flicker of fear blooming in her eyes. "Who are you, man?"

"I'm nobody worth knowing," I said with a shrug.

Charra snorted. "We don't have time to spend jawing with you lot." She grabbed my sleeve and pulled me onwards past the gang. "Be seeing you later, girls."

As we neared our destination, that nagging, throbbing itch in blood and bones progressed into a full-blown body-ache, my head pain into piercing agony. My hands shook as I trailed fingers down the grimy wooden walls of the buildings lining Bootmaker's Way. The smell of leather lingered in the air even though the dozens of small workshops had closed their shutters hours ago.

Finally she stopped. "This is the place." Her eyes glistened, but I knew she wouldn't cry. Charra had used up a lifetime's worth of tears long ago. She once said that an ocean of tears had never solved anything for her, and that a stolen knife in the dark of a grubby backroom had. Over the years she had hunted down everybody that had once harmed her. She had blood on her hands, but then so did I.

We were two blocks away from the main thoroughfare of Fisherman's Way. Lynas had been so near to safety.

The psychic pain coming through the Gift-bond was like a red hot nail driven into my brain. Lynas' fear and agony was still imprinted on the very stones all around me. As I moved down the narrow street the muscles in my arm abruptly spasmed, a line of searing pain shooting down it. "This is the spot. Lynas was murdered here." She nodded. This long after the event, there was nothing physical to show that a good man had died here, his hopes and dreams of a life full of love shattered.

I knelt on the cobbles and pressed my forehead to cold stone. The vision tore through me again. *Panic. Burning need to warn people. Crystalline daemons. A hooded man in black shadow. The gods blinded and chained. I couldn't breathe. Oh gods – the scalpel!* I think I screamed as the scalpel cut skin from my flesh, then delved deeper to sever ligament and crunch through cartilage, and not because the murderer had to, but because they were enjoying it. The garbled details of the message Lynas had sent sharpened into brutal clarity. In incredible agony and terror he had tried to tell me something specific by sending the image of Harailt slamming a steel gate in our faces, locking us in the Boneyards. It was something more than merely bringing me home.

His last panicked gasp rattled in my chest, heart slowing.

I felt him die.

Panic tore me from the vision and sent me hurtling back into the present. I awoke face down and drooling, curled up on the ground and shaking uncontrollably. So this was the other reason that magi didn't form Gift-bonds. The pain had relented but the mental scarring caused by Lynas' death remained. Charra's hands were holding me tight. "Hush," she said softly. "It's over. It's over now. You're safe." I don't know how long I lay there in her arms, recovering what wits I had left. Eventually, inevitably, the fear left and anger flooded in to replace it. I growled and forced myself up.

With a cry of rage I stormed up the alley, stopping every so often to run my hands over the walls and ground, sensing the faint residue of Lynas' terror through the Gift-bond. I paused, eyes closed, sniffing for the psychic spoor of his fear. Charra followed in silence, holding the lantern aloft to light my path. My eyes opened again and I could picture it all in my mind. A crossroads. There – an *otherness*. Gouges in the cobbles. My fingers pressed into sharp indentations.

"What have you found?" Charra said.

"A shard beast was here."

She looked at me blankly.

"Crystalline daemons from one of the Far Realms."

She looked worried, "How can these things be here without anybody noticing? I thought the thick Shroud in Setharis made that impossible. What kind of magus could circumvent that?"

I felt sick talking about it, the memory of Lynas' terror still too fresh, but she deserved answers. "No magus would resort to such a thing. We have more than enough power to kill already. No, I suspect a mageborn did this. Blood magic offers a torrent of power their own stunted Gift could never provide. I just don't know how they managed it."

Only a few magi had the talent, knowledge, and enough power to try to replicate such black rituals, and I had only ever seen the great Archmagus Byzant call up such things, under controlled conditions in an Arcanum enclave far from the city. In Setharis the Shroud was preternaturally resistant to such meddling so this blood sorcerer had to wield immense power. Daemons and spirits did not survive for long in Setharis: the very air of the place ate into them like acid. Many credited our gods with this protective boon, but not even the greatest of Arcanum scholars had ever gleaned the truth of the matter. Tiny, mindless plague-spirits were the only exception, breeding in the teeming masses of humanity faster than they died off. With so many people crammed inside the city walls the diseases those spirits caused were everywhere. Lucky for Magi that our Gift made us all but immune.

Like most people, Charra only understood about half of it. The unGifted couldn't sense the magic all around and I pitied them for it, but I envied them too – they would never suffer that gnawing need to use it.

She followed as I retraced Lynas' panicked flight through the slums, until, finally, I lost his trail. I skidded to a stop, snarled, pounded my fist against a wall so hard the old wood crunched inwards. Even with the Gift-bond his trail had faded beyond my ability to track, merging with other people's thoughts into a hiss of emotion.

I spun to face her. "Where did he come from that night? His murderer said that the gods had been blinded and chained – how was it even possible that gods and sniffers both didn't sense the foul corruption of daemons roaming Setharis that night? Unless what he said was true, or somebody or something was able to hide them."

Charra shook her head. "We couldn't find out. Nobody saw a thing. A few people heard shouts for help, but who in their right mind would go outside to see what was happening in the Warrens at night? Nobody knows anything about his murder, or if they do, they won't talk, not even to me."

I returned to where the hooded man had flung Lynas to the cobbles and examined the scratches on the wall. Lynas had thought the magus was alone loitering in the shadows, but then Lynas hadn't known what to look for. I knew the unnatural nature of that darkness only too well, the obsidian fangs and hidden slits of green eyes. Lynas had been murdered by the very same man that had hunted me for years. And after running into one of his pets in Ironport I now had no doubt he was in league with the Skallgrim.

"When I find that hooded man," I said, "however powerful he is, however rich and influential, he will die slow and he will die hard. I'll take my time with him." I paused, a dreadful suspicion bubbling up inside me. "Charra, tell me about the gods."

Her face had gone ashen. "There are rumours amongst the priests that all their gods are missing." She looked up at the soaring towers of the gods, to where magic should have been lighting up the night sky, to where there was only darkness. "The fifth god. The new one that took residence in the vacant tower after you left. It's said that he wears dark robes with a hood always pulled over his face. People have taken to calling him the Hooded God. You don't think..." She shook her head. "But no, it could be anybody wearing robes. Couldn't it?"

My hand was on Dissever's hilt. It was hungry. *More! More!* it howled in my mind.

I grinned a death-head's grin. *You'll get your fill, Dissever. If it's this new god then I'll destroy him. I don't know how, but I will find a way. And if it's not this Hooded God, then I promise to bury you in somebody else's guts.*

"Maybe," I said to Charra. "But what else could possibly explain the other gods being blinded and chained? God or not, I'll find this hooded walking corpse and make him pay."

"*We*, Walker," she said coldly. "*We* will."

Yes, it was better to follow Charra's example and calm down. I let go of Dissever and felt that boiling bloodlust diminish not one bit, because this time it was all my own emotions. I took a deep breath and forged my red hot anger into a cold and deadly fury.

"What do you need?" she asked, face calm and collected. That was the old Charra all right, all business. She would mourn in private later, but first she would do what needed doing.

"He had been snooping around somewhere, I'm sure of it, and then something made him flee for his life. The question is: what was he up to that night, and where?" And what had Lynas been trying to tell me? I had a horrible feeling it involved the labyrinthine Boneyards, the deep darkness below the city streets.

Our eyes met and I held Charra's gaze. "Lynas was terrified of him beyond reason, but he had discovered something he feared far more, something he deemed worth spending his life to expose."

Charra looked away, not wanting to show how distraught she was. "If he discovered something he shouldn't, then perhaps the hooded man decided to clean house by killing Lynas' assistants. I'll trawl through my reports and find details of everybody else who went missing around the same time. If I mark them all on a map then perhaps that will give us some clue. Lynas wasn't involved in anything terribly illegal. Oh, he wasn't exactly whiter-than-white; he dabbled in some grey trading and a little smuggling, but he mostly kept to the spirit of the law. He was doing well and had been talking about buying new premises over in Westford to be closer to us."

My mouth was dry. I felt a shiver ripple up my spine. "Smuggling?" I said, a nagging feeling at the back of my mind. "What sort of goods?"

Charra's eyes narrowed. "Nothing too unusual. He had official permits to import expensive foreign alcohols, but he also dabbled in small shipments of luxury goods from the continent: spices, silks, tapestries, carvings, furniture, herbs, some from less than official sources. Why?"

I rubbed a hand across my jaw, the bristles rasping. "Not sure. After that vision, when you said smuggling it just felt right. A hunch perhaps." Or a feeling he'd left me.

"I did look into it," she said. "But I couldn't find anything to connect the murder to his business. Perhaps you can convince others to talk, the sort that would never willingly help me. You have unique talents."

I nodded. "First, I need to pay a visit to his home, his offices and warehouse, whatever property he has... sorry, that he had. I need to do it alone, I can't afford distractions." And I had to keep her away from me, for her own safety.

"The place is all locked up under Arcanum wards, but with your weird ways perhaps you can get in where I failed. Lynas lived above his warehouse in Carrbridge. Head up Fisherman's Way and head over the bridge, take the left fork onto Coppergate Road and it's the second warehouse on the left. I'm not sure what more you can find though, the wardens already carted off all his papers for investigation."

So, Carrbridge, was it? As it turned out I hadn't been entirely lying to that gate guard.

I tsked. "You are probably correct. Can you arrange to sneak me into the Old Town, and into the Templarum Magestus tomorrow? I expect they will have taken all of Lynas' ledgers and scrolls to the Courts of Justice."

"Will that be safe?" she said.

"Probably not. But I'll manage. You know how sneaky I can be." She looked dubious. Actually I was almost pissing myself just thinking about it. The tunnels of the Boneyards aside, the Old Town was the last place I wanted to be.

"Very well," she said. "I had Old Gerthan look them over already but perhaps you can see something he did not. I'll call in another favour and get you in tomorrow, around noon most likely. There's an inn down by Pauper's Gate that opens late, you might remember it as a pub called the Bitter Nag. If you lodge there I'll send a message when it's arranged."

"Good, I'm just hoping that Lynas was still using his old cipher." She quirked an eyebrow so I elaborated: "We used to exchange secret notes as initiates. There is a small chance that he might have left a message before he headed out that night, just in case the worst happened." I shook my head, trying to clear some of Lynas' confusion and terror still lingering after the vision. "I don't think he had any idea it would be that dangerous, but I still have to check."

My dried drool and blood crusted the sleeve of her coat. I was one suave and sexy man alright. I held out a hand. "Sorry, but I'll need to take your coat. Just in case anything out there comes across my scent on you." Some things I was not willing to risk. It was unlikely that shadow cats could survive in Setharis, but with shard beasts on the loose and their master prowling the streets she was better cold than cold and stiff and dead.

She set her lantern down and slipped off the coat, handed it over without complaint. "I'll grab something off one of the Smilers."

"Will you be safe out on your own?" I said, worried. "This is the Warrens after all."

She snorted and picked up the lantern. "Walker, we girls stick together. Too many men think they can own us, and sometimes they'll only take a rusty blade to the balls for an answer. In any case, my girls keep their ears to the ground, their lips sealed, and their blades handy."

She reached out to touch my face, stopped, slowly drew her hand back. "I'm more worried about you." She didn't want more of my scent on her but the gesture was still touching. The only other affection I'd seen in the past ten years had been bought and paid for, or from fleeting drunken fumbles.

"I have always held myself back," I said, looking up at the strip of stars visible between looming buildings and banks of thick cloud. "Never really felt the need to stretch my limits. I didn't have any cause to take such risks, you know?" Apart from my mastery of mind magic I could also grant myself a little extra strength and speed and manipulate the air currents in small ways. It was difficult and gruelling, but doable. Would it prove enough? I scowled. "No more holding back."

My eyes fell back to Setharis, back to Charra's dark eyes.

I drew Dissever and the black iron blade squirmed in my hand, eager to kill.

"You don't need to worry about me, Charra. Not tonight. It's everybody else that needs to be worried." After reliving Lynas' agony I needed to be alone with my grief. It went far deeper than mourning for a friend. He was a part of me torn away, leaving only a gaping wound. I was dangerously unbalanced, so what did I do? What I always did: I went looking for trouble.

CHAPTER 8

Even the unnatural vitality of a magus' body had limits: I was mentally drained by the vision, and physically from five days of seasickness. I needed to sleep and regain my strength – oh, to sleep on solid ground again! I found the inn and haggled with a sour-faced woman for three nights' lodging, paying extra for no questions asked. It was strange to be back in a building I once drank in with Lynas.

Sadly I couldn't spare the time to sleep, only taking a few minutes of rest before heaving my sorry arse back up off the bed. I had some small affinity with both body magic and aeromancy, nothing much to speak of really, but occasionally useful. I tweaked my body functions a little, stimulating a few fleshy inside bits I'd discovered as a Collegiate initiate studying for examinations – last minute, naturally. False freshness cleared away the cobwebs and I felt like I had emerged dripping from a mountain stream, but I would pay for it later; the comedown was a bitch.

I slipped back out into the night and headed for Lynas' warehouse. Before long I would sight the titanic black armoured statues flanking Carr's Bridge, looming chest and shoulders over even the tallest of tenements. Cowardice and Greed, two of five titans wrought from enchanted black iron and forgotten magic in ancient days, bearing enormous swords that only god-like strength could lift without rope and pulleys and two dozen cart horses hitched up. They fascinated and terrified me in equal measure.

I turned a corner and missed my step. Their features were visible in the darkness, emitting an eerie green phosphorescence. What. The. Fuck?

I approached with a degree of superstitious dread, studying Greed's heavy jowls and tiny piggish eyes for any hint of movement, then Cowardice's hollow-cheeked cringing expression. There had always been an indefinable something about them that perturbed me, even before I knew what they really were – and now this. The glow was a new aspect, and I should know since I'd once tried to climb the heights of Cowardice on a drunken dare. I think I managed to reach the knee before getting stuck, not that I received any sympathy whatsoever from Lynas. New occurrences were never to be trusted in Setharis, because it usually meant magic gone awry.

I wondered if the titans guarding the other two bridges over the Seth also glowed. Each had been named after one of the cardinal disgraces; their real names, if they ever had any, were consigned to the same desert sands that buried their creators. At the centre of the Crescent, Wrath and Pride guarded the approach to Sethgate Bridge. At Westford Bridge Lust stood lone vigil. The titans were Escharric relics the Arcanum had excavated from half-buried ruins over two hundred and fifty years ago. Crusted in bird droppings and layers of soot, it was hard to imagine that they were in truth arcane war engines. The Escharric empire had fallen before the war engines could be used, and I wasn't sure that was a bad thing, given the disaster caused when the Arcanum used them for the first and hopefully last time during the shockingly brief war against the Vanda city states.

There had once been a sixth and unfinished titan, later named after the final disgrace of Ignorance. In their lust for knowledge Arcanum artificers had tried to take it apart to study the construction. Texts record Ignorance exploded in a lightning storm that incinerated thirty magi and fused the desert sands to glass for leagues around. In our classes at the Collegiate I had been the only one to note that those same texts hadn't bothered to record the number of servants and labourers killed. Hundreds more dead, and yet not worthy of mention.

Finally Carr's Bridge itself came into sight, ancient pitted stone arcing over the turgid and infested waters guarding the Crescent from the undesirables of Docklands. The human features of statues lining the bridge and either side of the stone-walled riverbank were long since worn away by wind and rain.

I slipped into the shadow of a statue as a warden left the bridge tollbooth. Only rogues were abroad in Docklands at this time of night and I didn't want to be remembered. He didn't see me as he wandered over to Greed and dropped his trousers, whistling tunelessly as his piss splashed across the titan's metal heel. I winced. He was pissing on a bloody monster! The lower classes thought them mere statues with a few fanciful tales attached, which was exactly how the Arcanum wanted it.

There were two things to note about the history of the titans: firstly, they had only been used once. History records that during the war with the Vanda city states two hundred years ago, the enemy's mage-priests had conducted a mass human sacrifice of their own people to gain power. The ignorant savages ripped a gaping ragged hole through the Shroud and mistakenly opened doorways to dozens of other worlds. An army of daemons had poured through the breach, destroying their cities and beginning what came to be called the Daemonwar. The Arcanum had been forced to unleash the titans against the teeming hordes of inhuman creatures, and with the heroic sacrifice of half the entire Arcanum they ultimately thwarted that daemonic invasion from the Far Realms. The lush lands of the Vanda were reduced to a barren, cursed wasteland where nothing would ever live again.

The second thing was that the first was a big fat stinking lie. Many years ago in the Collegiate library I'd happened across pages torn from a diary – an eye-witness account of what had really happened: the Vanda city states neighbouring the desert of Escharr had joined in federation, and under the leadership of their mage-priests formed a collegiate of their own with the intention of rivalling the magical might of the Arcanum. The Setharii empire had been at its height, swallowing up the island nations of the Thousand Kingdoms one by one and forming colonies to exploit and export abundant natural resources. The Arcanum could not abide the birth of a magical rival, especially not one that threatened their monopoly on Escharric ruins and ancient artefacts buried beneath the sands.

And so the ignorant magi of Arcanum manufactured an excuse to wage war, and in order to learn more about the workings of their recently discovered titans they gleefully unleashed the ancient war engines upon the Vanda. The official histories were lies, and this horrific act was before the Daemonwar had even begun. The lands of the Vanda burned while the Arcanum looked on in impotent horror, unable to stop the titans slaughtering everything: men, women, children and even animals. It was a mass death of our own devising. We rent the Shroud that protected our world from the depredations of daemonic invaders. The greatest disaster in all Setharii history had been caused by the Arcanum's morbid curiosity, by arrogant children playing with Escharric toys they didn't fully understand. It wasn't the first time dabbling with that fallen empire's artefacts had exploded in our faces and it wouldn't be the last.

It was ancient history to me, but those torn pages showed the Arcanum for the self-serving political entity it truly was and I'd never forgotten the lesson. It is so much easier to blame crimes on the voiceless dead.

In any case, the titans were too dangerous to re-bury and attempt to forget, too massive to hide, and much too valuable to destroy; instead they were deactivated and had spent the last two centuries where the Arcanum could keep close watch over them.

The guard fumbled his cock back inside his trousers, wiped his fingers on his tabard and then joined his colleague in warming their hands over a glowing brazier outside the tollbooth. They were ostensibly stationed here to maintain the peace and keep traffic moving, but in reality their role was to dissuade thieving little Docklands toerags swarming over the bridge at night. If the poor wanted in and out for a spot of thieving they would have to swim the Seth, and I didn't fancy the odds of them making it across in one piece. A thousand years of Arcanum experimentation had let all sorts of abominations escape into the river.

With shard beasts on the loose I dared not rely overmuch on the fabled daemon-devouring air of Setharis. Nobody else was out this late, and the running water should confound the magical senses of any shadow cats and sniffers nearby, so I reluctantly accepted the risk and eased open my Gift.

I eavesdropped on the wardens: just the usual moans about drink, gambling debts and women. Guards proved much the same in whatever city or town I passed through. It was simple to fog their minds and walk straight down the middle of the bridge. As I passed the tollbooth they glanced up, but I was just part of the furniture, entirely expected and effectively invisible.

Unlike the shifting sands of the Docklands slums, Carrbridge looked exactly how I remembered it. Cosily nestled between the massive cliff walls of the Old Town rock on one side and the Seth on the other, the old, stone buildings were plain but solid, and the signs above shop fronts bright with new paint. The Crescent was the domain of the richer merchants and the poorer nobility and Carrbridge was the least of these areas, the furthest east and consequently the recipient of more smoke and foul odours blown in by prevailing winds.

Before long I was passing the mouth of East Temple Street leading into the district's square of worship. The temples here were smaller and less ostentatious than the grand square up in the Old Town, but then Carrbridge was a more practical sort of place, less given to garish displays of wealth and magic when compared to Westford, Sethgate, or the Old Town itself.

The emblems of the gods of Setharis looked down upon the square. Facing me was the ossified throne of the Lord of Bones and the broken moon of Lady Night, both gods' original names long since lost to the mists of time. On my right were the gleaming golden scales of Derrish, the Gilded God and Lynas' patron deity, and next to it a smaller temple bearing the blood-filled hourglass of Nathair, the Thief of Life. On my left was the grim temple of this new god, marble statues of a faceless hooded figure standing sentinel either side of its entrance. Over the door the emblem of the Hooded God had been painted over the axe of Artha the Warlord. The dead god. I ground my teeth and had to force myself to look away. Now was not the time to pick at that scabbed-over wound in my memory.

I'd never seen any hint the gods paid a blind bit of notice unless they wanted something in exchange, and I doubted they would even bother to piss on their worshippers if they were on fire. Charra and I were agreed that it was folly to worship the Setharii gods, but Lynas had felt very differently. It was not a thing we discussed often, mostly because I tended to end up ranting like a drunken oaf. In this very square Lynas had once slugged me in the stomach and hadn't talked to me for a week. I'd probably deserved it.

The street split and I went left down Coppergate Road. A grinning copper lion reared over the entrance to an inn that beckoned me with buttery light, scent of roasting meat, merry music and laughter.

My stomach growled, tightening as I stomped past. I began noticing signs of the same rot that riddled the lower city: refuse piled up in side alleys, broken shutters, buildings with cracked and peeling facades. If the blight had penetrated the Crescent then trade was much worse than I had realized.

Lynas' warehouse was locked up tighter than a gnat's arsehole: every door and window had been chained or boarded over and inscribed with magical ward-glyphs, glowing balefully. A pair of wardens patrolled the exterior, hooded lanterns raised to peer into every shadow where Elunnai's silver light didn't reach. This one was going to be tricky.

I mulled over my options. I could fog the wardens' minds while I broke into the building, but any loud noise would shatter their obliviousness, and more importantly I didn't fancy using so much magic in a place the Arcanum had their eyes on as part of an ongoing investigation unless I had to. So I decided to try the straightforward and honest approach first, an unusual choice for me it has to be said.

I walked towards the wardens, fully visible in the moonlight, giving them the time to see that my hands were empty.

They drew swords. "This area is off limits," the older man with a drooping ginger moustache said. The other warden was younger, with a short dark beard that hadn't yet crept up his cheeks, but his eyes were wary. I was reasonably certain I could take both with ease if necessary.

"The owner was a friend," I replied. "I've been away and just found out about his murder. Would you be willing to discuss it?"

I felt a tremor of movement on the wind brush the back of my hair. It took a moment for my enhanced senses to locate a third warden at a second-floor window in the building behind me. I turned my head slightly, glimpsing a bowman with an arrow nocked drawing a bead between my shoulder blades. Unfortunate.

Ginger moustache was about to tell me to piss off, then checked himself as his eyes grazed my fine greatcoat. You didn't have to be a magus to see the wheels turning in his head: I could be somebody important. "Sorry. I can't tell you anything," he said. "And no, you cannot bribe us to let you snoop about. If you want to know anything, take it up with our captain."

That was my second line of attack wiped out then. I had just been slapped with the gauntlet of bureaucracy and I didn't have nearly enough time or patience to work around it. Their disciplined minds would have proved too difficult for small-time magical dabblers in deception, but I was something else entirely. If there had been only one warden then I could have smashed straight through into his mind, two I could manage with some difficulty, but three at the same time, and with one out of physical reach... well, I supposed life would be dreary without taking risks.

This was blatant tyranny, but they left me no other option. After ten years of hiding what I was and scraping by on meagre trickery I opened my Gift wide, letting the magic surge into me. All tiredness washed away. The street flared brighter as my eyesight sharpened until I could see every pore in their skins. My heart thundered, straining at the cage of my ribs. I took a deep breath, the air filling my body with energy. Sweet Lady Night, I had not felt what it was to be a real magus for so long – it was glorious! I wanted to let it all in, to bathe in the bottomless sea of magic.

I had almost forgotten how sweet the temptation could be. I bit my lip and drew back from the edge. I had a murderer to burn. If I was careful I'd be able to keep the magic within our bodies and minimize any detectable leakage or risk of detection.

I strengthened my muscles with a touch of body magic then shot forward, hands clamping around their throats before they could blink. My magic slammed into their minds with all my might. Their wills shattered like eggshells and they slumped to the ground glassy-eyed.

The swiftness of breaking two such strong-willed men stunned me. I was off balance and reeling. How had it been so easy?

In my shock I hesitated too long. An arrow loosed at my back. I spun, grunting with the sudden effort of using my paltry skill in aeromancy to throw up a meagre wall of wind between us. The arrow veered right, missed me by a few fingerspans and skittered down the road. The bowman nocked another and drew the string back.

I panicked, and instinctively struck out mentally. A surge of power stabbed into the bowman. He collapsed backwards, his mind shredded and his heart stopped. With the might and right of magic surging through me this unknown man's death was insignificant.

Heart pounding, I stood listening and waiting, feeling the vibrations on the air. The street remained empty save for the seductive whispers of magic stroking my mind. No shadow cats and no Arcanum sniffers with guards. I'd gotten away with it.

CHAPTER 9

With reluctance I reduced the torrent of magic running through my muscles to a trickle. A crushing and cramping weariness descended, and an almost overpowering urge to puke. Magi without any talent in body magics had killed themselves trying to learn to manipulate their flesh: bodies giving out, muscles tearing, organs rupturing, heart bursting. I knew a few tricks but couldn't even think of approaching the sort of physical juggernauts that those knights with the true Gift for body-magic could become.

I stared up at the now-vacant window. Where had all that newfound strength come from? I looked at my hands like they belonged to somebody else. I should have needed to touch him to do something that quick and brutal; certainly I had not possessed such power ten years ago. I felt sick. Accident or no, I had killed a man just doing his job. I felt the ghost of Lynas' disapproval. Damn it, I needed to be more careful. Whatever Lynas had uncovered was bigger than any single life, bigger than Lynas', bigger than mine, and certainly this poor fool's. I didn't have time for guilt.

I didn't let my guard down, still scouring the darkest shadows for shadow cats. I only had a short space of time to ransack the wardens' minds, break through the wards and search the warehouse for clues. The Arcanum would have set wards that alerted them if broken.

I focused my Gift on the dazed wardens, fighting back a thrill of power, of mastery. "What do you know about the murder of Lynas Granton?" I asked, sifting through the sluggish tides of their thoughts. Their answer was bugger-all, just that all his papers had been taken from the warehouse to the Courts of Justice up in the Old Town. I would have to go up there myself if I wanted to learn more. "Sit down and go to sleep." The two wardens did as they were ordered.

I extricated my mind from theirs, erasing my tracks and planting false memories of all three of them buying sweetmeats from a saleswoman on her way home for the evening. They would recall an amalgam of several people I'd seen recently, part toothless old woman, part street girl, and part serving girl, and of feeling suddenly sleepy. I shivered, disgusted at the thrill of control this gave me. Other magi didn't know how this felt – how could they? I was the only magus alive with this accursed Gift – but I could well understand how those tyrants of old came to be. Power over others had a seduction all of its own, but I had no burning desire to rule. It was far too much work. Besides, one of the reasons I didn't get on well with the Arcanum was that I didn't like people telling me what to do and I refused to be as bad as them.

That was probably why I thought Nathair, the Thief of Life, was the only god worth acknowledging. Lucky me to get him as my patron. In Setharis it was tradition for all new mothers to gather in the temple squares at the first dawn of each month to beseech a god's blessing on their newborns, to ask one of the gods to watch over and protect the child. A dunk in a basin of holy water drawn from the deepest well in Setharis, a chorus of prayer and then one by one the gods would choose, their temples shifting as if alive to give sign of approval.

Me, when the priest held me up in the air, apparently I pissed all over his face and fancy robes – a proper little waterfall my mother claimed, trying not to laugh. I think Nathair had a good chuckle at that himself, since it was one of the swiftest godly approvals ever known in Docklands according to her. At least Nathair had a sense of humour and didn't try to tell you how to live your life. He was stubbornly independent and freedom-loving, just like me, and refused to squabble with the other gods for a greater share of Setharis' sycophantic worshippers. Nor was he judgmental like the Arcanum.

It would go badly if the magi ever discovered that I had been manipulating the minds of anybody who wasn't "worthless" Docklands scum. The fear was rooted deep in the psyche of all magi, which was why I had carefully cultivated my persona as a drunken wastrel, never allowing them to catch any hint of what I was truly capable of. But that didn't matter now, what with Lynas dead and the Skallgrim invading Kaladon.

I took the dead warden's gloves and tugged them on. It wasn't like he'd be needing them. The fine leather would make it more difficult for any Arcanum sniffers to detect my presence for a short while, until my sweat and magical essence seeped into them. Every touch of skin left a trace of magic behind, which is how those damn shadow cats would always, eventually, track me down. There was a limit to how careful you could possibly be, and a man did have to piss now and again.

I examined a side door, finding thick chains had been looped through the door handles and welded closed by a pyromancer. I wasn't getting in without a prybar, and I didn't want to use Dissever – I needed to stay calm and logical to investigate, not thirsting for blood and slaughter or leaving behind strangely severed ends of steel.

I circled the building looking for another way in, and focused on a shuttered window – chained and locked, but my picks made quick work of that. The visible wards stood out stark red against whitewashed wood. They were too obvious, designed to keep out casual thieves. I explored with my Gift, trying to sense the vibrations of power running through the glyphs. The visible wards were petty things that would shriek and fire sparks into the air, relatively easy to disarm or avoid. What worried me was a cunning creation they'd buried inside those obvious weaves, a thing of killing power hidden inside patterns of petty magic.

I carefully picked the weaves apart and bled off all their stored power. Another once-over revealed no trace of any other dangerous magic. I reached for the shutters, but something pricked my attention, a scratch marring the white paint. I paused to take a closer look at the hinges. Hidden in the metal was something of deadly genius I'd never seen before – two inactive fragments of a lightning ward. It stored no power, meaning there was nothing magical to detect; instead it would draw power directly from its creator when it was triggered. If I opened the shutters the hinge would revolve to complete and activate the ward. This was a trap designed to kill magi. Just as well I'd spent the last ten years not relying on my Gift.

The interweaving skeins of warding were breathtaking in their complexity, comprised of several different flavours of magic. This had been created by somebody with knowledge and skill far in excess of my own. I had more experience than most at breaking and entering warded areas and I wouldn't even know where to begin. It stank of elder. I studied it intently, memorising the structure – you never knew when you might have to kill another magus.

Had the ward been active I would have been out of luck, but as that was not the case the problem was easily solved.

I hit it with a rock. Wood broke and the hinge dropped free. That sort of ward was too clever for its own good, really.

I grabbed one of the wardens' lanterns and climbed through the window, sawdust puffing up around my boots as they thumped onto the floorboards. The warehouse was practically empty. It didn't look like business had been going well. I walked past racks of wooden shelving, examining the goods: a few boxes of scrimshaw walrus ivory carved with ship-borne scenes and Skallgrim runes, a grand Ahramish-styled tapestry of lush red and thread of gold depicting some sort of king bestowing blessings on his subjects, then crates containing a mishmash of dusty and weird-looking foreign sculptures with grotesquely enlarged genitalia. Then I came to the booze. From the quantity and quality it looked like Lynas had got himself a niche market on foreign imports: amphorae of fine Esbanian wine, barrels of Ironport ruby ale and Port Hellisen cider, even a half-dozen expensive fluted glass bottles that shone a lurid green in the moonlight spilling through the open window. I suspected those last originated in one of the Thousand Kingdoms. There were three small casks of Clanholds whisky, old, rare and hideously expensive.

In one corner sat an assortment of imported Esbanian furniture, all carved from rich mahogany: a heavy desk with dozens of small drawers, a series of tables that fit snugly one under the other, and a large ornate merchant's chair that could almost have been a throne. It was high-backed, gilt-edged, and the glossy wood held a hint of blood-red in the grain. It looked uncomfortable, but I supposed it was more for show. Instead of individual chair legs the velvet seat rested on a box platform, the panels all carved with lordly scenes. The seat of the chair was slightly lifted, revealing enough space for a small lockbox. Perhaps used for smuggling if Charra was correct. Questing fingers tapped on the bottom of the space. A hollow sound. There was a tiny hole in one corner and with the help of a stray nail I was able to pry open a false bottom. It was empty, but I bet it hadn't been when it arrived in Setharis. I moved on, aware that the sands of time were draining quickly.

As I walked past a rack of bare shelves a shiver ran up my spine, with no obvious cause. I felt a jumble of faded emotions, and a vague sense of wrongness. The harder I looked for a cause, the less I felt it. It took me a moment to realize that some shelves had less dust than others and a few fresh-looking scrapes in the old wood. I squatted down and examined the floor. Scuff marks in the sawdust, as if people had been moving something heavy from these shelves in the not-too-distant past. A few cracked bits of forest-green wax and some tiny chips of pottery lay on the floor, brushed under the bottom shelf. I squatted down to study them and caught the sharp scent of vinegar. Somebody had scrubbed the floor clean, likely after dropping a jar of wine.

I scanned the rest of the warehouse, finding nothing else of note. If there had once been more evidence, then the boots of the wardens had obliterated any trace. I climbed the creaking steps to his personal rooms and peered into the study and bedroom – all empty; drawers torn out and left broken on the floor, furnishings gutted and abandoned, even the floorboards had been ripped up. Anything that might have proven useful had already been carted off for investigation.

I gritted my teeth in frustration and stomped back downstairs. There was something of Lynas lingering by those bare shelves, an undecipherable hint of strained emotion ticking the back of my mind that would have been undetectable if we hadn't been Gift-bonded. I didn't have the faintest clue what it meant, but a foul metallic tang now lingered at the back of my throat.

Had somebody wanted what was on those shelves? Or was it whatever had been stored in that chair? They were possibilities at least, and more than I had to go on before.

I climbed out the window and carefully closed the shutters behind me, making my escape back over Carr's Bridge and past the oblivious mind-fogged guards, tossing the dead warden's gloves into the river as I went – they were an unpleasant reminder, and already tainted with my scent.

The warehouse had given me no answers, only more questions, but it felt like I was on a trail now. Lynas had made his coin from imports, and I couldn't imagine he'd made much in the way of any enemies while I'd been away – he was the nicest person I'd ever met. Sure, he'd been a bit cracked in the head after going through the Forging rite and failing – which meant the Arcanum booted him out onto the street – but then who wasn't a little broken in one way or another? I was sure he wouldn't have been involved in anything particularly illegal, not knowingly anyway. What goods had those shelves held? Had they been removed before or after his murder, and were they connected to Lynas' presence in the slums that night? Meeting a buyer perhaps.

I had hoped to find something more solid to go on but now I was forced to head up into the Old Town for information, and if I was recognized they would hunt me without mercy. Legend had it that in the dark days before the rise of Escharr, my sort of magus had dominated the tribes of man and made endless war on one another until the sanctors appeared, immune to the tyrants' powers, their Gifts solely used to close down other magi and kill them. No wonder the Arcanum took precautions when a dangerous throwback like me appeared, even if nominally every magus was welcome within their ranks. Not that my sort ever lived long enough to become anywhere near as powerful as the tyrants of old. Once the nature of my Gift became apparent I had researched all my accursed predecessors in the Arcanum records: suicide, street stabbings, tavern brawls, drunken accidents. We were not a lucky lot. And with me fleeing Setharis without leave, I'd been listed as gone rogue. A rogue tyrant was the stuff of nightmares, which is why I'd been forced to fake my death years ago.

In my current state there wasn't much else I could do this evening. Tomorrow I would get in and out of the Old Town in one piece, everything going to plan. After that I planned to kick over some anthills and shake down some local scumbags until all the information I wanted dropped out of their heads. I just needed Charra to tell me which particular vermin I needed to talk to and where they holed up.

With my mental tweaking slipping into crushing comedown, I made my way back to the inn, hammering on the door until the sour-faced woman unbarred it to curse me. I swept past without a word, up the stairs and into the windowless room, making sure the door was barricaded before crawling onto the straw pallet. Sleep proved elusive, the dead warden's face plaguing my attempts, staring with accusing eyes. Eventually, exhaustion brought welcome blackness.

CHAPTER 10

A door slammed, waking me at an unnatural hour of the morning, hanging half-off the bed. Groaning, I hauled myself off the old straw and scratched my many itches. I ran a hand across my bristly chin. The last thing I needed was to look unkempt in the Old Town, and in any case the last few years I'd spent in Setharis I'd sported a ridiculous Ahramish-styled philosopher look with pointy goatee, so in the interest of not being recognized I would need a clean shave and new clothes. Between that, time, and the scars marring my face, if I was careful I should be able to slip into the Old Town without notice.

A quick scrub of face and armpits with a wet rag and then it was time to appease my grumbling stomach. The innkeeper provided some hard bread and a chunk of tangy cheese that was surprisingly good considering the midden I was staying in. Seemed she took more care over her kitchen than her cleanliness. I washed it all down with watery morning ale. Sometimes I missed the crisp mountain streams of the mountainous north, but drinking water in Docklands was asking for your breakfast puked up in a corner somewhere. I dipped a rag into the ale and used it to give my teeth a polish, then chewed on a wilted sprig of parsley to freshen my breath. Most nobles and magi wore expensive perfumes to mask their odour, but this was the best I could do given the circumstances.

A runner arrived with a package from Charra. It was on: Old Gerthan would meet me at the top of Sethgate, and the next morning she would meet me in Carrbridge temple square at three bells before noon with all the information she was compiling. She ended the brief note with: "Buy yourself something pretty". I opened the included coin pouch and smiled at the gleam of silver inside. Outside a soft drizzle was falling, perfect weather for a man to buy himself a cloak and keep the hood up.

Just before crossing into Carrbridge I noticed a blood and bandage barber's sign down a side street. Barbers and chirurgeons had an unsavoury reputation, the shedding of blood and body parts seen as fearfully close to sorcerous practices by superstitious peasants. However much people dreaded going to barbers, their sort were necessary for those without access to Arcanum healers.

A man exited the shop, reeking of rum and holding a swollen jaw. I peered inside. A young man with cropped dark hair was washing his bloody hands in a ceramic bowl by a crackling fireplace, steaming rags hanging above it. A set of pliers on the workbench next to him still clutched a cracked yellow molar.

"Be right with you, friend," he said, cleaning up after that poor sod's adventure into dentistry. He corked a bottle of dockhouse rum and stowed it away in a cupboard before picking up the tooth and adding it to a large pickling jar on the sideboard. The jar was full of human teeth: a week's extractions later to be handed over to the priests of the Lord of Bones for safe disposal. It was a little unsettling to see his collection, but vinegar did render them useless for any sort of sorcery. Even if he did wish to trade body parts in Setharis, the Lord of Bones took a dim view of that sort of thing and tended to nail such people to walls, through their eyeballs if they were lucky.

He looked at my unruly mass of hair. "A shearing, is it?"

"No, a clean shave, thank you." Due to my peculiar magical adaptions a haircut felt akin to somebody pulling off my fingernails.

He opened a leather case and took out a straight razor of fine steel and a small blue bottle of oil. I settled into the chair and he placed a steaming cloth over my face to soften the hair. He stropped his blade up and down a strip of thick leather and when he was ready he removed the towel and poured a small amount of perfumed oil onto his fingers, massaging it into my neck and jaw.

I was grateful he didn't plague me with inane chatter as he carefully scraped the blade across my skin. Acutely aware of the knife at my throat, I fought down a rising paranoia. He was young, and I'd been gone ten years so he couldn't know me. Still, I sat there sweating until he had finished, then watched him clean his tools and pour the gunk of oil and hair into the fireplace. Only then did I pay – a magus had to be careful with their cast-offs. My face felt newly-born as I stepped out and the breeze played over bare skin.

I blended in with the merchant traffic heading into Carrbridge, paid the toll, and then followed the path along the riverbank west to Sethgate at the very centre of the Crescent. All traces of rot disappeared and signs of true wealth were displayed in the finery of every shop front, in the mouth-watering aroma of roast suckling pig and capon from classy eateries, and in the brightly coloured clothing and fur-trimmed cloaks of passersby. Illusionists and acrobats plied their trade on street corners, breathing fire and juggling knives, entertaining with daring tricks and clever artistry. A puppeteer made her painted dragon dance and snap at three giggling children each time they tossed a coin into its wooden maw.

One of the illusionists was Gifted in a minor way; her

glowing balls of faerie fire danced around the audience's heads while shadowy daemon-shapes writhed across the walls. People gasped and stepped back as the shadowy claws reached for them. I kept a hand on Dissever and gave her a wide berth. Daylight or not, I didn't trust shadows that moved on their own.

A pair of grizzled wardens watched me stroll by, noted my patched trousers, and took to following me down the street at a discreet distance. My coat was a fine piece of work, but that could have been stolen. Time to get some new clothing. I went into a store and spent Charra's coin on new trousers and a dark tunic trimmed with vermillion, then fastened a waxed cloak around my shoulders. The shopkeep's apprentice polished and buffed my boots as best he could – the leather was nicely worn-in and I wasn't breaking in new boots if I didn't have to.

When I emerged from the shop I looked less out of place. The wardens lost interest and wandered off to scan the crowd for cutpurses. I pulled the hood of my cloak up and began the long walk up the path to the Old Town. Ornate gilt-and-lacquer carriages bearing seals of noble houses trundled past, the scent of horseflesh and sweet perfumes wafting in their wake. Me, I had to slog my way uphill on foot, puffing and panting.

A gust of chill autumnal wind tore at my clothes. It was raining red, leaves stripped from the ornamental crimson maples so prevalent in the Old Town. Those and the venerable oaks were the only trees that didn't grow twisted and foul in that magic-saturated soil. In another time and place I would have called the leaf fall beautiful, but all it did was remind me of Lynas' skinning, the colours the shade of his blood. By the time I got to the top of the ramp I was in a foul mood, sweating profusely and wheezing for breath, making me realize just how indolent I had become.

Old Gerthan was there waiting for me. He looked unchanged: gaunt face framed by an unruly white beard, watery eyes, that same polished heartwood cane in his liver-spotted hand. Some magi were fortunate that their aging stopped in the prime of youth, while others like Old Gerthan and that hard-nosed bitch Shadea had to suffer the ills of a permanent old age. Some didn't stop at all, slowly withering away year by year, life stubbornly clinging to their crumbling bones until even the magical resilience of a magus' body finally failed.

I was surprised by one new addition: Old Gerthan was wearing the white robes of the Halcyon Order, healers that knew no rank and asked for no coin. So he had discarded the trappings of wealth and power to devote himself to healing the world? A laudable goal, but not one that I could ever follow: I was by nature more egoistic than altruistic. Although all Halcyons I'd ever met had seemed content, so perhaps there was something to it all.

He nodded to me as I hauled my sorry carcass up onto the flat before the gatehouse. "Good day, 'Master Reklaw'," he said. "Still among the living, I see."

Ah, right, that. "Good day, Magus... er... Gerthan," I said, desperately trying to remember his House name. Had I ever known it?

He chuckled. "Only ever called me Old Gerthan, eh? I take no offence." His eyes hardened. "However, before I offer my assistance you will answer these questions: ten years ago, did you kill anybody before you left this city? Did you harm any other magi in any way?"

I frowned. "I haven't the faintest clue what you are talking about." He said nothing. I cleared my throat and clarified. "Not to my knowledge, no." It was the truth as I knew it.

Old Gerthan's gaze scoured my face for a long moment before his expression softened. "I believe you. More importantly, I believe Charra, and she does not give her trust lightly." He plucked his white robes. "I owe this new and higher calling to her. Five years ago plague ravaged the lower city. She came to us, and on her knees before a small council of magi she begged for more aid." He shook his head. "Charra is a proud woman and she does not beg, at least not for herself."

"That does sound like her," I said.

"I was struck by her sincerity and agreed. What I saw on Docklands streets that day, the poverty, overcrowding and sickness... I had no inkling it was so terrible. I put my Gift for healing at her disposal and in so doing I discovered my life's calling. I owe her a great debt."

He was a good man, one of the few who had treated me fairly even after the Arcanum found out what my awakened Gift was. "So how do you plan to get me in?" I said.

"Why, we go straight through the main gate, you scallywag. Luck mysteriously has it that today nobody is on duty that could possibly know you, but keep your hood up to be doubly certain." He strode off, cane clacking, walking quicker than his aged frame should allow. "Come along now, no dallying."

We walked past a dozen guards clad in battle plate and chain, and right on through the massive doors of enchanted oak and steel. The air vibrated with barely restrained magic, deadly ward-glyphs glimmering overhead. On the other side of the doors half a dozen combat-ready magi and two sniffers awaited us, all fresh from the Collegiate. Some magi looked young, but their old eyes and aura of power always gave them away. Old Gerthan nodded to one of the sniffers, a friend, and vouched for me. They frowned but bowed to the wishes of an older and well-respected member of the Arcanum.

We wound between the worshippers thronging the grand temple square, passing marble columns and archways carved with scenes glorifying the gods. The temples had been grown by the gods themselves, their black bones lifted from the living rock beneath us before being clothed in exquisite marbles, bronze and gold. It made the temples of the lower city seem like dirty fishing shacks. The temples changed shape yearly, each god trying to outdo the others, all except for the Thief of Life, whose many-columned classical Escharric edifice at least looked like he had made a vague attempt to rein it in. This new Hooded God looked like he had dived head first into the games of the others, and his many-columned temple was by far the gaudiest, gloating in its aggrandizement. The gods all schemed against one another in petty ways, bidding for mortal influence and prestige. As immortals they were probably bored and used us as playthings and pawns in an endless game of oneupmanship. Nathair generally remained aloof from that sort of nonsense – my kind of god really.

Behind the temples squatted a cluster of sinister step pyramids. The Tombs of the Mysteries were reputed to be shrines of deities forgotten long before Setharis was founded, grown from the same slick black, almost organic-looking stone as the towers of the gods. Their sealed doorways were overlarge and oddly-cut, protected by ancient enchantments no magus had ever deciphered never mind penetrated. Many had tried, and many had died.

The deep *DOOOOOOMMMMMM* rang out across the city. The black-iron tower in the centre of the square seemed crude and out of place next to the majestic temples, but it contained something of incalculable value – the Clock of All Hours. The great bell rang again. The verdigris-crusted spire vibrated and shook off corvun-crap as it rang out noon. The cogs of the arcane machine churned endlessly, powered by another long-lost art, tolling every three hours from dawn until nightfall. It was the legacy of the original architect of Setharis, the refugee Escharric magus Siùsaidh, whose other, and to my mind greater, creation had been the sewer system that kept the air of the Old Town fresh and fragrant. Doubtless her practical sort would have had no truck with the backstabbing politics that plagued the Arcanum nowadays.

As the last ringing echo faded, from the centre of the square the godsingers lifted their voices tower-ward in praise. Crimson leaves swirled around them as their hymn swelled, illuminations from the temple windows intensifying. Competition was always fierce for a place in the choir, a chance for the finely-voiced faithful to please their gods.

The temple of Derrish opened its doors and priests began taking tithes. Rich merchants handed over bags of coin to receive the god's blessings, and more practically, to gain the temple's political clout and financial advice in return. Derrish was widely regarded as the incarnation of Setharis, a bit of a money-grubbing scoundrel that saw himself as better than everybody else. Mind you, he was a god, so arguably he kind of was.

A line of bleeders shuffled towards crimson-robed priests of the Thief of Life, watching drops of their blood patter down into golden bowls as an offering, then drinking a tiny cup of his holy red wine. What Nathair got out of these transactions, no mortal knew. He had always been the least popular of the gods, his priesthood's cultish practices seeming uncomfortably close to blood magic. Despite dark rumour, it seemed that his popularity had grown tenfold in my absence, probably because he didn't hold with long, boring sermons.

The grey-robed priests of the Lord of Bones remained silent as they went about their business: bestowing final blessings on the dying, and taking in the corpses of all Gifted to set them to the pyre. The fate of mundanes was different, of course: the priests took those bodies down into the Boneyards beneath the city, where they alone had no fear to tread amongst the darkness and the dead, to lay them to rest somewhere within that maze of catacombs. As a god he was deathly dull. Quite apt really.

On my travels I had discovered that in many foreign lands they believed people possessed a strange and nebulous thing called a soul, which I understood as a strange sort of spirit locked in a cage of meat. People had a deep-seated need to believe that they didn't wink out like a snuffed candle when their physical end came, but like most magi my opinion differed: we believed that over time our lives slowly drained back into the sea of magic it had spawned from. The fact magi tended not to die of old age lent a measure of credence to that idea, the Gift constantly refilling our hourglasses with sand.

Lady Night was a mystery. She had no discernible aspect or interest save perhaps an association with the hours of darkness. She was said to be an ever-watching guardian but also a thief, both hero and villain. People called on Sweet Lady Night when traversing dangerous paths by torchlight, and cursed the Night Bitch when misfortune's silver eye fell upon them. She had no established priesthood, but every so often somebody would feel a deep calling and be drawn to minister to her worshippers for a few years. Legend said that the Lord of Bones and she had been lovers long ago and some folk liked to imagine that they still were, an immortal love lasting thousands of years. I chose to believe it even though I could only dream of finding such love.

And then there was the Hooded God. Only a handful of worshippers set foot in his temple, and they looked as guilty as any red-handed murderer, slinking up, looking left and right before heading in and closing the door behind them. It seemed that this new god had not built up any sort of real following yet. I couldn't think of any living magus both old and powerful enough to be anywhere near calling themselves a god, so which mortal had occupied dead Artha's position so quickly?

I had been picking at the old, dread secret in my head since I returned home, all the reminders helping to pry off the protective scabs. So near the site of Artha's temple, I couldn't help but use it to pick at the scab in my mind a little more.

Oh Artha, what have I done! His blood speckled my face, metal tang burning my lips as I plunged my hands into his splayed flesh, searching... A tidal wave of horror overwhelmed me. Everything went red and I toppled.

I regained awareness lying in a quivering heap of terror, with a raging headache and a pool of vomit by my mouth. The lines of worshippers had all shuffled forward and people were peering over at me with disgust, wondering if I'd been overcome by religious fervour. I shivered – I had cut him open, gutted like a fish. My heart pounded and sweat beaded my brow. Artha had died by my hand.

"Get up! Burn you for a fool, boy," Old Gerthan said. "Now is not the time to be drawing attention." I stood and pulled my hood lower, trying to walk normally away from the scene. I buried my horror in a corner of my mind, as I had to.

At the edge of the square Old Gerthan stopped and handed me a scroll. "This will get you in and out of the evidence room. Good luck."

"Thank you," I said. "I won't forget this."

He smoothed his beard, looking thoughtful. "What happened to your friend was terrible. I hope you find the answers you seek."

"I will."

"Oh, and Walker – you are dead to me."

I got the point: he knew nothing and I was on my own. Old Gerthan disappeared into the crowd. I looked up at the gleaming golden spires and gothic arches of the Templarum Magestus. Fear shuddered up my spine. I was a chicken about to stick my head into the maw of a sleepy fox and hope it didn't bite down.

CHAPTER 11

I took a deep breath – *this is for Lynas* – and then entered the great hall at the heart of the Arcanum. Whispers of mellifluous music greeted me as I traversed the marble floor of the nave, with its ornate spiralling columns and vaulted roof. Large globes of frosted crystal filled the hall with pale light and fearsomely fanged dragons swam through wood and gold panels while stylized magi fought back hideous daemons and dispensed words of wisdom through tapestry and mural. One scene depicted the war god Artha. My hands itched, felt stained red. I had been exiled and forced into forgetting, but if I was involved with the gods then it was no wonder I'd been terrified of breaking my bargain.

Heatless silver fire limned the ranks of obsidian-and-gold statues of past archmagi and great heroes. I wasn't impressed by the display of wealth, but instead admired the years of effort and artistry that had gone into the artwork – all this gaudy frippery could feed the entire city for years. The statues led to the centre of the hall, and the conclave dais where seven golden thrones awaited the Archmagus and the six other councillors of the Inner Circle. It was a conflicted feeling that one of those now belonged to Cillian. Five empty alcoves were set high on the walls, empty and awaiting a god's arrival if they chose to manifest.

I pulled my hood back and smoothed out my mop of hair as best I could before making my way down a side corridor towards the evidence rooms, smaller gem-lights studding the walls. Most of the people I passed were part of the army of overworked clerks and scribes involved in the minutiae of running a city and an empire. The Templarum Magestus and the Collegiate had been built in a time when there had been many more Gifted, but after the devastating losses suffered centuries ago it seemed like we were old folk rattling around the house long after all the children had gone. An entire wing of personal quarters had been closed off for the last two hundred years. There had been a time when those corridors buzzed with laughter and spirited debate, or so Archmagus Byzant once confided in me.

Such topics had drained the elder magus. The poor man blamed himself for the many mistakes made during the Daemonwar, and had never quite got over the loss of so many friends and colleagues during that daemonic invasion. He deeply regretted the resulting political deadlock that left the Arcanum sitting impotent and idle while the empire crumbled around them. Fortunately I had been able to alleviate some of those worries, when and where I could lend a subtle hand, in my own unique way.

Beyond a warded archway to my left, through studies and libraries and grim guards, lay the personal chambers of the Archmagus. What had happened to my old friend? He had taken a brat from Docklands under his wing, despite my loathsome Gift, only to disappear as I fled the city. Whatever happened that night I had nothing to do with it – I would have taken a knife in the gut for that man.

Next to his chambers were the offices of the Administratum, and below the feet of those merciless bureaucrats lay level upon level of locked vaults containing every ancient artefact ever dug from the desert ruins of the Empire of Escharr by the greedy hands of Arcanum magi. Deadly weapons and devastating magical devices slumbered beneath our feet in the most protected place in the world – so secure I'd never even seen the warded doors to those vaults.

I walked in the opposite direction. A pair of guards checked the scroll provided by Old Gerthan and let me pass into the Courts of Justice without any fuss. Further in lay the Arcanum dungeons, where rogue or corrupted magi were chained and guarded by sanctors until they were put down for good. I'd been on the run for ten years, and if I were caught here then I too would spend my last days languishing in those dank pits.

This area was mostly frequented by wardens and scribes so with any luck I wouldn't encounter any magi. I confidently entered a large room lined with bookcases and shelves. Eight scroll-laden desks lined one side, occupied by young scribes – those still with sharp eyes – transcribing scrolls. Their quills scratched across parchment, sounding like rats in the walls. One large and imposing writing table guarded the entrance, on the other side of which sat a stern-faced older woman with grey hair pinned back into a tight bob. She set down her quill and scrutinized me, mouth twitching with disapproval. "May I help you?"

I handed over my scroll. "I need access to the evidence rooms and the listed box."

She unfurled it and scanned the text. "Everything seems to be in order." She snapped her fingers. "Edmund, show Master Reklaw to evidence room three."

A lanky lad with a beaked nose jerked upright, chair scraping along the stone. "Right this way, Master."

He led me through the back and down a corridor to a nondescript door. "May I be of any further assistance?"

Another door opened further down the corridor. A tall woman appeared, wearing azure silken robes, her pale olive skin revealing some mix of Esbanian blood. An elegant gold circlet held back long dark curly hair. My stomach lurched: my old flame Cillian. And then it dropped away into a black pit of dread as a withered old hag of a woman followed her out: Shadea Saverna. With Byzant gone she was now the oldest magus in existence, an elder adept of most forms of magic and a member of the Inner Circle. She was the Arcanum's foremost expert on blood sorcery and her interrogations were a gory legend. If I was scared of Cillian spotting me, then Shadea made me want to piss myself. If either caught sight of me I was as doomed as a lame horse in a tannery. Spirit-bound blade or not, I wouldn't stand a chance. The more powerful the magus, the stronger the Gift, and the more their minds and bodies naturally resisted foreign magics. Shadea would be able to resist any mental attack long enough to burn me to ash with the flick of a finger.

I spun to put my back to them. "So how does all this work? I was given some numbers…" It was a poor ruse, but all I could think of.

The boy began explaining the evidence indexing system whilst I sweated and tried to ignore them walking straight towards me. I didn't listen to a word he said; instead waiting for any gasp of surprise from behind me.

"Indeed, Ahram remains locked in a vicious civil war after the assassination of three prominent philosopher-priests of the reunification sept," Shadea said, continuing a conversation as they made their way in my direction. "In truth only the impartial librarians of the Great Archive of Sumart hold Ahram together at all. As our main business partners in Taranai this will result in trade remaining disrupted for at least another year, and without those exotic goods coming through our ports the Esbanian merchant princes ply their trade elsewhere and war over more lucrative shipping routes."

Cillian sighed. "The smaller kingdoms and barbarian tribes across the Sea of Storms also vie with each other. Death walks every land these past few years. Speaking of which, what of the slain warden set to guard that warehouse in the Crescent?"

"If we are to believe the surviving wardens' story," Shadea said, "then something sent them to sleep while they were supposed to be guarding the Granton building."

Oh shite. If they were coming over to review the same evidence I was...

"Whoever this woman they encountered was, we will find her," Shadea continued. "I am curious – why go to the effort of killing one and disabling two others, then take nothing? One of my own wards was also discovered and broken, and that I did not expect." She huffed. "This may perhaps be related to the Skinner killings in some manner we are not yet aware of."

My heart pounded. They. Were. Right. Behind. Me.

"Have you found any trace of an alchemic substance in their bodies?" Cillian said.

"None," Shadea replied. "The corpse has also yielded no obvious cause of death. I shall obtain the living wardens and research the matter further; however the simplest explanation is most often correct. They shall rue wasting my time if I find they were drunk and taking alchemics on duty. Such incidents have become worryingly frequent of late." Those poor bastards I had left asleep at the warehouse had no idea what they were in for. Still, better them than me.

"In which case it would seem prudent to remind them of their duty," Cillian said. "Evangeline of House Avernus has excelled herself of late. The wardens may respond better to her presence than to ours."

Shadea cackled. "A good choice. I do hope she does not break too many this time."

They passed by while the boy continued through his list of instructions. I strained to listen as their voices gradually moved out of earshot.

"Master Reklaw?" I blinked, the boy had finished and was frowning up at me. "May I help you with anything else?"

"Ah, right. No, thank you. I'll be fine on my own." I opened the door and slipped inside, closed it firmly behind me and let loose a huge sigh of relief.

A broad-shouldered young woman with short dark hair sat at one end of a large bench in the centre of the room. She glanced up as I entered, and I noted gorgeous green eyes in an otherwise plain face. She wore an unadorned tunic and trousers rather than the lavish dress of noblewomen or the warded robes of a magus. She didn't have the plump flesh of a scribe chained to a desk either. A warden then. I nodded to her and she resumed digging through a box of numbered items, tallying the contents with her list on a scrap of parchment.

I browsed the shelves, trying to locate the box that Old Gerthan had indicated. It was on a high shelf, and as I stretched up to lift it down, my fingers slipped. I overcompensated and flailed to catch it, only for it to tip forward. A deluge of paper and scrolls rained down on me.

The woman failed to stifle her laugh. I flashed a sheepish smile and she came over to help me pick up the mess.

"Is this your first time?" she said. My confusion must have shown. "Being amongst so many magi, I mean. You appear a little flustered."

"Oh, yes," I lied, then took a deep, calming breath and wiped sweat from my brow. I needed to appear normal, happy even, when all I wanted to do was tear this place apart. "Two of the Inner Circle just walked right past me there."

She smiled and I felt a twinge of attraction; she wasn't a beauty by any measure, but there was that indefinable something in the honest mirth shining in her emerald eyes. Or perhaps I was just a dirty old fool who had gone far too long without the warm caress of a woman.

"They do tend to have that effect," she said. "Feels like when my mother caught me out drinking with rogues owning far more charm than sense." She chuckled, "More than once, I must confess."

"More charm than sense? Why that describes me perfectly," I quipped.

She raised an eyebrow, brazenly looking me up and down, gaze lingering over my scars. "You will not find me doubting you for a rogue, what with well-worn boots and scars that were surely no accident. That coat looks expensive, the sort of thing that a rich man might wear for travel, one that can surely afford newer boots. An intriguing discrepancy."

A thrill of danger washed through me. "Is that so?" I said, trying to appear nonchalant. "I only returned to Setharis recently. As it happens, I have indeed been travelling and didn't see much point in wearing better."

"What line of business are you in?"

"I suppose you could consider me a sort of investigator."

Her fingers drummed on the desk. "I see." She seemed amused, as if I were a puzzle needing to be solved.

I extended a hand, "Reklaw."

She took it, "Eva," then looked at the long list on her parchment and sighed. "Well, I really should return to my work. Good luck with your investigation."

"Thank you." I lifted my box to the opposite end of the table and took a deep breath, then began rifling through Lynas' papers. Every so often we both glanced up, and both pretended we didn't when our eyes met.

Any faint thoughts of a dalliance with the woman died as I began reading. It was impossible not to dwell on Lynas' murder when his hand stared out at me from every scrap of parchment. My mood grew darker as I worked my way through piles of letters and notes, invoices and inventories, not sure what I was even looking for. There didn't seem to be anything unusual, not until I found the stock take of alcohol imports. Only one week old and thirty jars of Skallgrim wine were present on paper, but missing from his warehouse, not marked as paid either. It was the perfect amount to fit on those empty shelves I'd noticed. I tapped my nail on the entry. I knew only a little of the Skallgrim, given how few of their traders ever made it across the Sea of Storms even during the calmer summer months. Their scrimshaw was a rare and desirable commodity to the High Houses of Old Town, but as far as I knew they didn't produce wine, being more partial to mead and ale. The ink was smudged, as if a grubby finger had swept over the entry several times.

Lynas was… had been a stickler for details. His profit and expenses would be tallied somewhere. It was, but, unlike his detailed entries for other goods, the buyer for the wine was listed as blank. Anonymous buyers and stolen wine meant that somebody had something to hide.

Charra was correct; Lynas had dabbled in a little borderline smuggling. If I could track down the missing wine then I suspected that I would find something different contained in those jars. But what would be so valuable that they would kill him for? Gems? Alchemics? And then I found a hasty note scrawled for one of his now-dead staff, containing a name I recognized only too well: "Off to see Bardok the Hock. Again!" That sour old bastard Bardok worked as a middleman for various unsavoury people, and I'd sold him more than a few items myself in the past. I would need to pay him a visit.

I spent hours going through the last of Lynas' papers, back growing increasingly stiff and sore, arse numbing on the hard bench. I sat up and yawned, stretching my arms out. The woman opposite had fallen asleep at the desk some time ago. She snored softly, head resting on her folded arms. A little spot of drool glistened at the corner of her mouth.

I smiled and walked over. "Excuse me." No response but a soft moan. I put my hand on her shoulder. "You'd better wake up before somebod–"

She jerked upright, grabbed my wrist and wrenched my whole arm round until the joints threatened to snap. I fell to my knees, gasping in pain as she twisted further.

She blinked away her confusion and let go. "Shit, sorry." She helped me to my feet. "I didn't break anything this time, did I?"

This time? "No harm done," I gasped, my whole arm throbbing like she had been a whisker away from breaking it. "My fault for startling you." She was strong. Really bloody strong.

She turned away and wiped the drool from her lips, face flushing red in embarrassment. "I really cannot apologize enough. The effects of a week of night patrols, I'm afraid."

"I always found bookwork tedious myself," I said, rubbing my elbow. "Ach, buy me a drink sometime and we'll call it even."

"Done," she said.

I wasn't sure who was more surprised at her answer. We stared at each other for a moment and then burst out laughing. It felt good to enjoy a brief moment of levity.

"One drink for an almost-broken arm does sound fair recompense," she said.

I stiffened as a thought struck me. Was Eva short for Evangeline? Surely she wasn't the magus that Cillian and Shadea had been talking about. I cleared my throat. "Er, you wouldn't happen to be a magus, would you?"

She frowned. "Don't let that put you off. I don't discriminate against mundanes."

I felt like diving head-first out of the nearest window but instead waved my hand at Lynas' papers and invented an excuse. "I'm kept busy for the moment, but how about we go for a drink some other time?" The strain of maintaining this pleasant façade was mounting.

She smiled and clapped me on the back, none-too-gently. "I will be at the Gilded Swan in two days' time if you are free. Assuming you have not been run out of the city by then."

We made small talk and exchanged a few bad jokes while tidying away our papers, her fishing for minnows of my real history, me ducking and diving. It seemed that I had piqued her interest, which was nice in one way and abysmal in others. For a magus she was blessedly unassuming, almost a real and normal person, and as I learned more about her, that joke about her mother catching her out drinking with disreputable men seem increasingly plausible. But she was Arcanum, and not to be trusted. The sooner I was back in the lower city, the safer I would be.

Eva insisted on accompanying me as I made my way back through the great hall and out into the street. She was heading in the same direction and there was no plausible reason to refuse her company. If I seemed any more suspicious then she might have me arrested. As a magus she had the authority to detain anybody for questioning, save another magus or high ranked members of the nobility or priesthood, and if she somehow uncovered who I really was, well, I was a notorious degenerate, dangerous, and also supposedly dead. I would be clapped in irons quicker than I could blink.

It was a huge relief to get out of the Templarum Magestus. The risk of wandering sniffers and magi recognizing me dwindled with every step I took towards Docklands. We pulled hoods up against the drizzle and made idle chat as

we passed through the thinning crowds outside the gods'
temples. Outside the temple of the Thief of Life, and in the
middle of discussing my utter distaste of sea travel, a man
called out to her. The hairs on the back of my neck stood on
end. A shiver rippled up my spine and bile seared the back
of my throat.

"Evangeline!" he called again. I glanced up to see high
cheekbones, bright blue eyes, immaculate ash-blond hair,
and absolute bastardry. Harailt, heir to High House Grasske,
had aged badly and was now painfully thin and gaunt. He
wasn't wearing the sort of showy finery I remembered from
the past; instead his plain robes blended in with the poorest
magi. I quickly looked away, face hidden by scars and hood,
and slipped amongst the worshipers wandering through
the columned portico of my patron god Nathair's temple,
hiding, watching, hating.

He made my skin crawl. Seeing his face again flung
me back to when I was entombed alive, and even now I
couldn't control my fear of dark enclosed spaces. When
they discovered what he had done to us, if he hadn't been
the heir to a High House, then the Arcanum would likely
have thrown him out. But he was, with all the wealth
and influence that brought. Every day after his crimes
had been exposed he had sought out ways to persecute
and vilify me, as if it would somehow excuse his own
villainy. It wasn't even entirely personal: he would have
treated any scabby little runt from Docklands the same
for dirtying up his hallowed halls of privilege and power.
He was the worst product of the Old Town, the type that
considered his blood pure and righteous, and ours tainted
with base-born blood little better than animal.

I kept my hands clenched to stop myself from grabbing
Dissever and ramming it through his fucking face, the
barbs biting deep. He had briefly appeared in Lynas'

death visions – but much as I wished otherwise, that didn't mean he had been involved; it was much more likely Lynas had been trying to tell me it involved the Boneyards.

"I am glad to have caught you," he said to Eva, his voice slick with the cultured tones of the High Houses. They all sounded the same, these honey-tongued, spoilt bastards. "The famed Ahramish illusionist Lucata of Sumart is performing a play at the amphitheatre tonight. I was wondering if you would care to join us?"

She groaned. "Always when I am working. I have night patrol with the wardens tonight."

"A shame," he said, sighing. "I find shadow-play fascinating. Another time perhaps. Fare you well tonight." With that he gave a slight bow and left.

"So," Eva said, once Harailt was lost in the crowd. "You know Magus Harailt?"

"Was it that obvious?" I had slid from mysterious into suspicious.

"You don't seem the bashful type."

She had me there. "I knew the heir to High House Grasske when we were young. It's a long story." I couldn't keep the venom from my tongue.

"Ah," she said. "I have heard about his old scandals. By all accounts he was a flaming prick back then."

I gritted my teeth. "Was? In my experience people like him don't change."

She made to reply, stopped, pondered it for a moment, and then chose her words carefully. "How much do you know about the disappearances ten years ago?"

Careful! A mundane shouldn't show that he knew too much. "A god died. And Archmagus Byzant disappeared."

She nodded, "Harailt and Archmagus Byzant were particularly close. It hit him hard when the Archmagus went missing so shortly after Artha died, and, well, there were a few accidents afterwards." Meaning Harailt had probably maimed or killed people and Grasske covered up the worst of his excesses. "His house disinherited him and the Arcanum shipped him off to work in our embassies based in city states bordering Esban and the southern Skallgrim tribes. When he returned to he had become an entirely different and better person. He is not that odious youth you knew so long ago, that I can personally vouch for."

Her taste was piss-poor. It still rankled that Byzant, a good and decent man, had shown that cock-maggot Harailt any favour after what he had done to Lynas and I. Maybe my old friend thought he could rehabilitate the swine.

"The bastard can burn, for all I care," I said. "Some things cannot be forgiven."

She shrugged, body language displaying her distaste. Not surprising – I was bitter and twisted, sour as any lemon at the suck.

We walked in silence for a while. "I'm sorry," I said eventually. "It's not a pleasant topic for me."

"We all have our wounds, and some go deeper than others. I rarely get to see a man's scars before I know him well." She looked at the ragged scars marring my cheek and neck. "How did you acquire those? I suspect that's an interesting tale."

"Bad jokes and worse timing," I said. It was close enough to the truth.

"Ha, I am surprised you are in one piece in that case. I would bet good coin that most of your jokes are terrible."

My mind was churning with anger, questions, and the acute fear that I would be caught if I stayed any longer in the Old Town. I was not in any kind of mood for flirting and small talk, and as for love or sex – pah, no time for that! She was far too sharp to risk revealing anything more.

"I might tell you that tale someday," I said, giving her a small bow, as befitting a noble of the Old Town taking his leave. I did have proper manners when I cared to use them.

"I will hold you to that," she said. "Hope to see you soon, Master Reklaw."

With that we went our separate ways. I kept my head down and hurried through the gate to the lower city, paranoia ebbing with every step I put between the Arcanum and myself.

I was finished earlier than I'd thought and not due to meet Charra until tomorrow. What to do now? The gaps in my current knowledge of Setharis were glaring. I needed to immerse myself in the underbelly of the city, to feel its ebb and flow before I could identify more links to Lynas' murder. I knew just the place, and it wouldn't hurt to earn coin while I did it; information would cost me dearly, and the people there would know who else Bardok the Hock was working with. It was time to toss the dice.

CHAPTER 12

Gold and silver are the greatest lubricants known to man. Greasing palms makes everything easier, everywhere, and black-marketeers and snitches were never less than ruinously expensive, which made my meagre stash about as useful as teats on a fish. It didn't take me long to find a gambling den in the Warrens; all you had to do was follow the sweet scent of alchemic smoke and the sour odour of drunken fools shuffling along with golden dreams in their eyes and poverty in their future. Sooner or later they all ended up in the sleaze-pit called the Scabs, the scummiest part of the entire city, an impressive claim considering the competition. The muddle of crooked lanes housed the very worst gambling dens, where underground slavers and pimps bet flesh as often as coin. It was also where the best information brokers plied their trade.

An old man doddered into me from behind and I felt a hand slip into my pocket. I backhanded him into the mud and gave it no more thought. Cutpurses were the least of my concerns – I was far more worried about the moneylenders. When I fled Setharis I'd owed a bucket of gold to various unsavoury characters and their sort never forgot or forgave, but to look on the bright side, hopefully they were all dead by now.

I ended up dicing in a copper-bit dive occupying the

mouldy basement of a raucous tavern. It was heaving with painted, pox-ridden doxies and hairy-knuckled toughs with overhanging foreheads taking bread money from the desperate and the drunk. It wasn't the sort of place to hear interesting snippets of gossip, not the sort of place I needed to be, so I stayed just long enough to grow my handful of copper into silver and got out before they dragged me into a back alley and kicked my head in. I didn't even use my Gift, just a load of bullshit and skill gained from a misspent youth and a downright wasted adulthood. I didn't even enjoy the games: amateurs like them exhibited too many tells and their attempts to cheat me were frankly embarrassing.

I went up-market, as much as you can in the Warrens anyway – at least the building wasn't in imminent danger of collapse, even if it did seem held up mostly by soot and mould. It was the kind of place a man might hear rumours dripping from loosened lips of gang bosses and their lieutenants, boasts of murders and dodgy deals. In short, it was exactly where I might uncover information on the Skinner and Lynas' murder. I walked through the door, past the cold eyes of gang enforcers on guard duty, the sort of men that wouldn't balk at breaking bones and cutting up bodies before heading home to tell their daughter a gentle bedtime story.

One big brute covered in scars was overly twitchy. The scar tissue was surgically straight and smooth, his skin a little flushed, the muscles too defined and bulky; all classic signs of fleshcrafter modifications to heighten reactions and muscle growth. It was highly illegal, but some magi with the talent for healing would happily pervert their calling in the cause of extra gold, or to obtain fresh research materials. Usually his sort were built for cavern-fights, their owners pitting prize fighters against each other in underground rings. His body would burn itself up and he would die early, but until then he would be like a daemon in a scrap, and earn extra coin for it too. He had probably accrued a hefty debt to the wrong people, but I supposed it was better than a knife between the ribs or selling your organs for a fleshcrafter to implant into the diseased and unscrupulous rich.

The brute's gimlet eyes lingered on my back as I descended to the card tables. A smile slipped onto my face. Oh, how I had missed the bluff and tumble of high-stakes gambling, the expectant thrill of my gold wagered on a single toss of the dice or flip of the last card, the sudden hush as one by one my opponents revealed their hands. Fleecing drunken farmers in the hinterlands lacked this dangerous lustre. If only I had the time to enjoy such frivolities.

I scoped out the smoky room, dimly lit by twinkling rush-lights on the tables and oil lanterns on the walls, taking in the padded booths at the back where purple-lipped khufali addicts reclined immersed in sweet smoke and vibrant dreams. Scantily clad men and women served drinks, occasionally slipping upstairs when they took a customer's fancy and their coin. I didn't dare use my magic here: with this much coin changing hands they would have a sniffer mingling. Still, that didn't mean I couldn't open up my Gift in a more passive way, soaking in the atmosphere and any stray thoughts; here those thoughts were dark and perverse, reeking of fear, aggression and despair. It was maddening to have my Gift open but not draw in magic, akin to wafting slabs of sizzling bacon under the nose of a starving man and telling him not to chow down.

After earning some gold at dice I slipped into a booth and engaged an information broker for details on the Skinner murders, and for events that occurred around that date. He knew only two things more than I already uncovered: the first was that the murdered magus had been a white-robe. The revered members of the Halcyon Order were the only magi that normal folk had anything good to say about. Healing was a rare talent that I dearly wished I possessed, and I would have traded my cursed Gift for that in the blink of an eye. I'd seen far too many people die while I looked on helplessly. They were the closest thing to sacrosanct that Setharis had. The other was that somebody had torched an old temple in the Warrens that same night. In my mind I was plotting distances from there to Bootmaker's Wynd, but the slums of Setharis stretched a good half-day's walk and I was going to need Charra's map. It might prove coincidental but I filed it away for investigation. On mentioning Bardok the Hock he proved a more bountiful source. That greedy old git was working with the Harbourmaster in charge of Pauper's Docks, who was on the payroll of the alchemic syndicates. Which linked to imports, and to Lynas.

Once I was done with the information broker I picked a central table suitable for mental eavesdropping, tossed some coin in and eased myself down onto the bench opposite a heavily built older man wearing a flat cap – a dockhand judging by his rope-burned hands – with a clay pipe clamped between rotten brown teeth. He glanced at me and then went back to studying his cards and puffing on a pipe with the tarry reek of cheapest tabac. The dealer flipped two painted cards my way and then placed another three face-up on the table. I peeked at my hand, kept my face still at the glorious sight of two High House cards. So the dealer was going for the usual hustle of letting me win small, then upping the ante until I was overconfident and bet all my coin on a single round of cards. Then some accomplice would wipe me out with an amazing hand, with the help of some dodgy dealing of course. Naturally I had no qualms about cheating outrageously myself when the time came. I tapped my highest cards thoughtfully, letting the tiniest trickle – barely a sip – of magic seep into them with each tap, building my trickery up layer by layer, each use far too subtle to be noticed by any sniffer they could possibly afford.

Usually I wouldn't resort to using my Gift for something so minor; it felt like cheating when I could win through skill and deception, but I didn't have the time to fritter away. It was easy to bluff when you could read people's expressions and body language as well as I could, no magic needed; all it took was a little attention to detail. Most people seemed to meander through life blindfolded when it came to the emotions of others. I couldn't quite fathom that sort of ignorance, but then I was hardly normal.

I let the chatter of customers wash over me, immersing myself in the mood of the room, keeping ear and mind out for any interesting titbits to fill in gaps in my knowledge. The Skinner was a topic on many lips and stray thoughts, but I learned little but unsubstantiated rumour and conspiracy theories. A tension filled the air, so thick I could almost taste it. It was the sort of atmosphere that built up slowly, thickening until it eventually exploded in somebody's face. It wasn't just the Skinner; this was something that ran much deeper. Too many bad things in such a short time, too many people gone missing, and nobody knew who, which let suspicion bloat into a loathsome beast.

I won the first three rounds before the dockhand threw his cap in and admitted defeat. It was a shrewd man who knew when to quit. Three others took his place around the table, lured by the chance of winning a share of my growing stack of coin. They just made my winnings rack up all the quicker. The gambling den's owners sent free drinks over, but that was fine with me, it'd take more than a little booze to throw me off my stride thanks to years of rigorous training in that respect. My winnings grew. You don't win that much without drawing attention, and I could feel people's eyes on me now, including one woman I suspected to be a sniffer from the distracted look as she walked past me, nose crinkling even though she wasn't looking for a physical scent. I flipped a smoke between my lips and lit it from a rush-light. I'd have to be careful to time my cheating just right.

Focused on the game, studying the cards being dealt, I sensed a woman slip down beside me and noted a smooth dark thigh and the subtle, exotic scent she wore. I knew the type, the sort of pretty leech that attached themselves to winners and drained them dry. Her mind gave away nothing, no strong feelings or stray thoughts. In a place like this it was possible there wasn't an alchemic-free thought in her sluggish mind, but it was surprising all the same.

"Sorry, love, I'm not in the mood," I said, watching the dealer's fingers deftly slip a card to an accomplice from the bottom of the deck. He was a very good cheat, but I had been taught by the minds of masters. I glanced at my cards. It was a damn good hand but his accomplice would have better. I frowned at the dealer. "Fold." He gave me a sick smile and started sweating.

The woman at my side gave a throaty chuckle, then leant in close to whisper in my ear. "You couldn't afford me, *Uncle* Reklaw."

I almost choked on my smoke, turned my head slightly to see Layla's raised eyebrow, the hint of a smile tugging at the corner of her mouth. She was wearing a tight fitted dress that showed a lot of leg and a hint of cleavage, positively modest for these parts, but far from how I'd seen her last.

"So, what brings you here?" I said. "Didn't take you for the carousing type." The dealer flicked out another round of cards, no cheating this time. I had good odds of an excellent hand. I tossed gold into the pot.

"Do I look like an old maid to you? I'm here to meet a man."

I tapped my nose. "Point taken. I'm to keep this as our little secret, yes? I doubt your mother would approve of this place."

"You had better. Don't worry, at the first sign of trouble I'm out of here." Then her voice hardened. "So this is why you returned? Gambling and drinking?"

"Hardly." I leant in close. "That tub of lard at the side there, dicing with his friends – he's cheating on his wife. Mind you, she's spreading her legs for the lanky fellow sitting next to him, so she's no better." Layla looked surprised, but I still felt nothing from her. She was as controlled as any magus. I nodded to an older man in velvet coat and tunic smoking an ornate pipe, his pupils dilated and his mouth slightly slack around the stem. "Him, he's a syndicate gang boss working with the Harbourmaster. Some of his best men disappeared a while back after they tried to break into the mageblood trade and he's never quite recovered. He blames Charra in public but actually fears that it was the Skinner. No proof though. People disappear in the Warrens all the time, especially these days." Him I was paying particular attention to. When he left I was going to follow and force him to answer all my questions.

"How can you possibly know all of that?" she said.

The dealer flicked out more cards. One of my opponents folded, but the other two slid piles of coin in. One seemed unsure, but the other exuded a quiet confidence that he was very good at hiding behind a twitch of fake worry. Not skilled enough though. I chucked more coin in anyway, calling their bets.

"I'm very good at listening," I said to Layla. "Most people hear but few listen."

The unsure man opposite laid his hand out. Two middling pairs. I made a show of scowling at my cards to waste just enough time and draw enough attention to me – the trick wouldn't work otherwise. Then I spread my hand out on the table. "A high court," I said. People murmured in the background, every eye in the room lingering on the large heap of coin at stake. All eyes turned to the fake worrier.

The man smiled broadly and finally spread his cards out. "All High Houses," he gloated. "I win!" He reached for the pot.

I cleared my throat. "What are you talking about, pal?" I tapped one of his cards, setting off the temporary glamour I'd placed in it earlier. "That's a two, not a high house. Just what are you trying to pull here?" Through some quirk of fate his high card seemed to have changed into a two for the observers. Almost without exception, people saw what they expected to see, and I had just given them a little nudge: part deception, part subtle magic.

He gawped at his card, picked it up and stared at the dealer, a question on his lips. Oh-ho, the crowd caught that look and a murmur of disquiet stirred as they looked between the two. The dealer turned to the sniffer, who stared at me trying to sense if I was using the Gift. The sniffer shrugged and shook her head. Beads of sweat appeared on the dealer's forehead and a sickly smile grew. "Another round?"

"Nah," I said, "don't want my luck to turn." I scooped up the heap of gold and silver, then turned to grin at Layla, but she'd already slipped away to find her lover. I packed away my winnings, pouch bulging at the seams.

A woman screamed. A tray of drinks crashed to the floor. One of the serving girls stood staring down at the twitching corpse of – ah, shite! – the gang boss slumped over his table, pipe still smoking. Blood oozed from a small wound between the base of the skull and the spine. It had been precise and quick, with minimal blood – this wasn't a mere stabbing, it was an assassination. And what's more, they'd used my game as the perfect distraction.

Layla was nowhere to be seen. Paranoia reared its head. Oh gods, was she safe? Then I spied her over by the far wall, unharmed and with a half-empty goblet of wine in her hand. She shot me a worried look, set it down and then slipped out of the door while everybody else was busy gawping. I sighed with relief; it was just another ganglands killing, they were not here for her or me.

The crowd edged forward to examine the body, prodding it out of morbid curiosity. Me, I tied the cord of my money pouch around my neck and tucked it beneath my tunic and used the distraction to slip out of the door before it got ugly. I was carrying a lot of coin and people might soon notice that unfortunate two now looked awfully like a High House card. I breathed a sigh of relief as I stepped out into the shadows, fumbling in my pockets for a smoke as the door closed behind me. Whoever had offed that gang boss had been good, and I'd had my back to them the entire time. Even with magic-wrought heightened senses there had been no–

My senses screamed a split-second warning before a hand clamped around my throat and pulled me backwards into a side alley. He stank of stale sweat and tarred leaf. Thick, calloused fingers squeezed. My head went tight and hot, pulse pounding. I flailed, ramming my elbow back into a man's hard stomach. He grunted but the grip didn't loosen, squeezed even harder. My Gift opened on instinct, magic lashing out into his skin. I savaged his mind like a wild beast. He choked, fingers going slack.

I slumped against the wall, wheezing for breath. The dockhand I'd beaten at cards earlier stared back at me dumbly, drool running down his chin. He dropped down in the muck, gurgling, fascinated with watching his fingers move. His memory was shredded. Seemed he had realized that he couldn't beat me and instead decided to wait outside to get his hands on coin in a different way. Too clever for his own good. Still, I'd been a blind idiot to walk outside as unaware as any innocent lamb heading to the slaughter. Even if I had been rattled by the assassination, there was no excuse. Too much was at stake to be that sloppy. I massaged my throat. It had been so very easy to break him. First the guards and now this... I seemed to have actual might at my beck and call nowadays, and it was thrilling.

I imagined the Worm of Magic's serpent smile growing wider as it waited for me to let go of all restraint. I'm not sure I wouldn't prefer it to be a real entity as opposed to something that only personified my own desires magnified through the lens of magic. Nothing is ever quite as terrifying as your own mind.

"Sorry, pal," I croaked. Reducing him to that infantile state had been a step too far. Instinctive reaction or not, I was powerful enough that I could have and should have left him puking up and cradling a broken nose, or, oh I don't know, given him a nasty memory of lusting after and sucking off a dog or something. That sort of thing could scar a man for life. I shook my head. It was a shame, but I consoled myself with the fact that he'd likely learn to walk and talk again, and he might even remember his own name someday. That was more than most people got in the Warrens. Usually it was a knife across the throat and a swim in the river. He was lucky really.

As I limped away into busier streets, three men burst through the door behind me, tumbling over the gurgling dockhand. I wasn't in the mood for teaching them a lesson now, and after using magic, I didn't care to linger. I slunk off into the darkness as they scrambled to their feet, cursing and kicking, looking around in vain for the man they were supposed to have beaten and robbed.

As dusk drew in I bought a packet of smokes and

spiced meat on skewers from a cart on Fisherman's Way. My teeth sunk into the hot meat, spicy juices dribbling down my chin as I wolfed it down while listening to a group of musicians drinking and playing on a street corner. Docklands might be squalid in comparison to the Old Town, but it was far more alive: a real and vibrant community in many places.

Whoever the Skinner was, he had nothing to do with the usual underworld strife. That lot seemed more on edge than anybody. When I met up with Charra tomorrow I hoped everything would slot into place.

As I passed the dark mouth of an alley something bright and fluttering in the breeze caught my eye. Hidden in the shadows amidst a pile of refuse was the green of a torn coat: fine Clanholds wool distinctively tailored by Arlsbergh of Ironport.

It was my coat.

I peered into the gloom with knowing dread. A man's corpse lay in the alleyway... well, not a corpse precisely, more like what was left of one. Chunks of raw offal had been strewn across the cobbles and tattered flags of flesh and skin hung from shards of stone and wood gouged from the walls by massive claws. I squatted down and picked up a silver earring of twisted wire still attached to most of an ear. Arse. It was the boy thief's earring.

I recognized the bite marks on a hunk of thigh, made by fangs the length of my hand. Shadow cats! Of all places, I should have been safe from daemons in Setharis. Lynas had seen shard beasts, and now these were here hunting for me. Somebody or something had to be protecting them from the city's corrosive effects.

My plans were just grand in theory, not so great when I was confronted by my own bloody handiwork. Still, the lad had been no innocent and had dug his own grave, and not undeserved either. Such a waste of a life. I took one last look at the remains and then ran for the inn.

I kept Dissever naked in my hand and found my eyes flicking to every darkened doorway, every corner and pool of darkness, watching out for anything lurking in the shadows. How had those damned shadow cats located me so soon? It could take a week, usually two or three before they narrowed down my location, and this time I had travelled over the accursed sea, which should have made it more difficult. A thought struck me: with their master here, perhaps some of the damn things had never left Setharis at all, had sat waiting and watching all these years just in case I should ever return. If one knew I was here then the rest of the pack surely did. I would have to keep moving from now on. There went any chance of a good night's sleep.

I blocked off the door to my room and carefully set an array of the nastiest wards that I could remember – things that would blast your mind and burn flesh from your bones. Only then, weary with the effort, did I shrug off my clothes, climb onto the pallet and pull the blanket tight around me.

My fractured dreams were stalked by a butchered boy in a tattered green coat running from shadows, and the night echoed with Lynas' screams.

CHAPTER 13

Somebody crashed into my door. I jerked upright, blanket
flying, and reached for my wicked knife. It was just a
drunkard staggering down the stairs, hacking up his lungs
as he went. I slumped back into a doze, immune to guests
clomping on the stairs, the creaking of floorboards and the
clatter of pots and pans in the kitchen below. For a single
sublime moment I just lay there, numbly cocooned in my
own safe little world.

My blissful numbness gave way to a growing itch. I sat
up and scratched at my hair and body, peering down at the
straw, at an almost imperceptible hint of movement. My
skin crawled. Bile rose up my throat. Swallowing, I looked
down at my itching crotch and with two fingers quested at
the root of the hairs, pulling off a tiny hard speck smaller
than a grain of sand. It squirmed between thumb and
forefinger. Lice.

Fucking Docklands inns and their mangy pig-faced
owners!

One of the first things that the Collegiate tutors beat into
initiates was cleanliness, both magical and mundane. Most
Gifted had one method or another, and luckily my meagre
skills at aeromancy proved sufficient to avoid the worst of
the beatings. Sod the risk; I wove a scouring blade of wind
to strip away all the dirt, grime, dead skin, lice and bits of

straw, and left a pile of gunge in the bed. My skin felt fresh, if a little raw, and the vile itching had ceased.

I beat the worst of the dust and dirt from my clothes and slipped them back on, then stomped downstairs to curse the sour-faced owner, telling her to burn her lice-infested bedding. She hissed like a startled alley cat and I was forced to duck a bowl flung at my head. I spat more curses right back at her as I stormed out into unexpectedly garish sunlight, quickly leaving behind the scabby inn and the hag shrieking obscenities at my back. If she was lucky I wouldn't be back to burn the place down myself.

The city din washing over me was cleansing in its own way. Setharis was a place of mists, sea fog and rain, and the hubbub of daily life was usually somewhat muffled; it was a rare treat to enjoy such fine weather. The city had sprouted sails: linen hung out to dry on ropes between buildings fluttered and flapped in the crisp morning breeze.

Despite the glorious sunshine, there was still an undercurrent to the babble of voices, an edge of intangible tension flowing through the city streets. Setharis was worried sick. It was more than the usual disaffection amongst the peasantry or the influx of refugees from coastal villages around Ironport, nor was it solely due to the Skinner murders and the missing people. The lower classes might even have cheered had the murders been up in the Old Town instead of right on their own doorsteps.

With the shadow cats already in the city, I wasn't about to linger where I'd used even a little magic, in daylight or not. I walked briskly towards Carrbridge, passing through the morning market at Pauper's Gate where men and women were gathering to sign on to ships and work gangs. If they were very lucky, a labourer might get hired by the Arcanum, or find a place on one of the various guilds' projects. For the few who excelled it might offer prospects of retention and steady pay. Of course such contracts were rare as diamonds.

A muddle of languages and accents filled the streets as travellers and foreign sellswords sought their fortunes, steady work, or to disappear. Setharis could easily offer that last. It was sometimes called the Dreaming City in the oldest of texts, depending on which translation you used, but City of Fever Dreams was to my mind the most accurate interpretation – for many newcomers it soon became a nightmare.

In the ten years I'd been gone the number of businesses and trading houses boarded up and abandoned had tripled, as had the number of beggars. Was trade really that bad these days? The poor clustered on every street corner, ragged figures squabbling over turf and doing their best to look worse off than any other: pinching their babes to make them wail piteously, grinning at me with soot-blackened teeth, cultivating fake limps or showing off bandaged stumps of missing limbs that were merely bent double and tied up. I knew most of these old tricks, had used many of them myself as a street rat. There was some real artistry on show here today and I wished them the best of luck.

There were only two tried and tested ways to climb socially into the upper city. One was by being fortunate enough to be born Gifted, and there was no shortage of sexual offers to male magi since the Gift tended to run in bloodlines. The parents of a Gifted child would quickly find themselves plucked from poverty and ushered into the relative luxury of the Crescent once their child became a full magus.

The other way was the old fashioned way: to get stinking rich and buy your way up. Of course, as Lynas' family had discovered, it was easy for the unGifted to fall back into the filth of the slums if they were not cunning enough to survive the politicking of the Old Town's magical bloodlines with their old money and old alliances. With extended family wielding political power in the Arcanum it was easy for the High Houses to remain in power and suckle from the flaccid teats of the city's dwindling riches. Thoughts of politics always made my stomach heave.

The month of Leaffall was at an end and it was only three days before the festival of Sumarfuin was held to mark the onset of winter. The market area had been cleaned up and given a veneer of respectability. Country folk from the surrounding villages had been pouring into Setharis for the festival and to bring their cattle in for slaughter before the snows and ice arrived. The incomers held hands, laughing and kissing as they browsed the wares on offer, or danced to the bards playing tunes on their pipes. Grim-faced locals avoided any festivities and resented their carefree joy. I smiled at children wearing hideous horned masks as they wandered through the crowds carrying baskets of white heather sprigs, rabbits' feet, boars' tusks, black cats' tails, and anything else that could conceivably be sold as lucky; others carried white quartz charm stone pebbles or strips of bright cloth that tradition claimed were offerings to appease the ancestors.

Sumarfuin must have held real meaning once, but these days it was just a bit of much-needed fun, a communal habit harking back to the tribal ancestors of both the Clanholds and the Setharii. It was older than the first words ever written by mankind during the era of tyrants, back when my wicked lot of bastards ruled. Some meanings and memories were probably better off forgotten.

The Arcanum and the nobility tended to frown on these old folk myths but some things even the rulers of the city couldn't control. They certainly couldn't stop young magi and nobles donning elaborate masks of their own and coming down to join in the revelry. It was the only time of the year when the social classes mixed freely.

A woman wearing some sort of foreign hedge witch costume, all bright beads and bones, thrust a necklace of carved wooden charms at my face. In a thick accent she declared it a talisman from some distant homeland with far too many vowels and apostrophes. She didn't fool me; her voice was undiluted Docklands however hard she tried to disguise it. Seeing my lack of interest she thrust a basket of dragon bones and teeth under my nose. "Gathered from the beaches of the Dragon Coast, they was," she said. "Grant you luck, so they will." The stone bones looked genuine enough, still with traces of the costal rock they'd been dug from.

I waved her off and she moved down the line of newcomers peddling her artefacts. In the taverns and inns I'd passed through while travelling I occasionally heard tales of dragon sightings, but in ten years of travel I'd never met a single person that had personally seen a living one – well, nobody that was both sane and honest.

I bought some onion bread and chewed with relish as I made my way up Fisherman's Wynd. The further from the market, the more sullen the city became. People kept their eyes fixed on the ground as if afraid to attract attention. A horse and cart tore down the street, causing a heavily-laden woman in the middle of crossing to leap back at the last moment to avoid being crushed. She fell to the ground. The cart didn't slow, and nobody bothered to help her up.

Amidst the crowd somebody stumbled and bumped into my shoulder. I turned, something inside screaming wrongness. A richly dressed man stared up at me, bewildered, his pupils wide and dark, the whites shot through with red. I noted the tiny red cuts in his forearms where he'd been making blood offerings at the Thief of Life's temple. He stank of stale sweat and sour puke, and his skin bubbled with pustules of corruption: low-level magical corruption at that. "All gone," he muttered. "Gone. Ran out."

A habitual mageblood addict too long without a fix. Panicked, I shoved the alchemic-addled idiot aside and hurried away. The man meandered his way down the hill, pawing at people and shouting obscenities, occasionally trying to bite chunks out of them. In that state it wouldn't be long before the sniffers caught wind. Then it would be a quick knife across the throat and another corpse tossed onto the pyres. I kept my head down and quickened my step.

The wardens stationed on the Carr's Bridge were carefully checking each cart as we stood in line to pay the toll and trickle over the hump of the bridge. No doubt my recent activities had caused the heightened security. Good, maybe if the authorities had been more vigilant they'd have caught the Skinner by now.

I filed in behind a gaggle of worshippers as they headed down onto East Temple Street. On entering the square a wall of incense hit me like a rock to the face. I'd never seen the point of the stuff; half the time it stank worse than the odours they were trying to mask.

By the time the bells in the Old Town tolled, the place was thronging with worshippers muttering prayers. I couldn't help but think that our religions were an oddity flying in the face of Setharii inclinations towards practical cynicism. It was as if people refused to believe their gods had once been mortal men and women. Granted, the gods had been born Gifted, but they had still soiled their swaddling and spewed milk all over their parents at the most inopportune of times. Given time and centuries of hard work – and knowing that secret in my head – perhaps even the likes of me could find a way to become a god. Hah, wouldn't that fuck them up!

I stuck a smoke between my lips and lit it from the sacred censor outside the Thief of Life's temple. A priest frowned at me, but somehow I didn't think my patron god would mind.

Finally I caught sight of Charra entering the square, dressed in soft brown leathers cut for travel, a short sword sheathed at her hip and a small satchel slung over one shoulder. I gave her a wave and made my way over.

My tabac smoke wafted over and her nose wrinkled in disgust. "Do you have to use that muck?"

I shrugged. "No." I took a long drag, then turned my head away and blew a long slow plume of smoke.

She scowled. "I hope your search was fruitful."

"It was. I also discovered that the titans glow now. When did that happen?"

She shrugged. "Started about a year ago and has been getting steadily brighter. It's a great mystery."

I chuckled. "I can imagine the Arcanum's consternation. Not knowing must be driving them mad. It certainly gave me pause when I was heading to Lynas' warehouse."

"I can imagine. Well, let's go somewhere quiet and get down to business."

At the entrance to East Temple Street we met a squad of wardens coming from the opposite direction. "Oh, come on," I muttered, heart sinking as I recognized Eva in the vanguard. I forced myself to smile.

Those glorious green eyes flicked from Charra to me. "Well, well, if it isn't Master Reklaw." She inclined her head to Charra. "Business is well, I trust?"

Charra smiled thinly. "And entirely legal as always, Magus Evangeline."

"Oh, I am positive that we wouldn't find a single thing out of order," she replied. "If I may offer a word to the wise: I would keep my eye on this one. Your lover, is he?"

"Ha!" I blurted. "As if."

Charra stared daggers at me. Eva's eyebrow quirked.

"I have better taste than that," Charra said. "He's all yours, if you want him?"

"Perhaps another time," Eva said. "I am on duty at the moment. Good day to you both."

After we turned the corner, Charra stopped and wagged her finger at me. "I thought you were supposed to be laying low? Be wary of that one, she would snap you like a twig."

I rubbed my arm. "I'm already aware of that. Have no fears of me dipping my wick there."

She led me to a near-deserted tavern called the Fuddled Ferret. We sat at a bench and ordered ale, being entertained in the loosest sense of the word by a hungover bard in a colourful patchwork coat plucking the strings on his lute in vague accompaniment to the lacklustre tale he was telling to two snot-nosed pups staring up at him, rapt with wonder.

After the drinks arrived she busied herself sorting her map and papers while I listened to the bard's tale. A poor rendition but it still evoked golden memories. I knew this story well: *The Journey of Camlain Calhuin* had been one of my mother's bedtime stories. Young as I'd been, the sense of wonder my mother's tales evoked in me was still vivid. It had been one of the last before the voices in her head finally drove her to fevered madness and death. This dreary-tongued bard was mangling it. Perhaps it was a cultural thing between the Clanholds and the Setharii, but this version had none of the details that made my mother's so real to me: it lacked her gritty humour as she told of the time Camlain learned which mushrooms were safe to eat, and which gave him explosive squats, or how he'd tried and failed and tried again to learn hunting and fishing on his epic journey north. It had been as instructive as it had been fascinating to hear Camlain Calhuin grow from boy into doomed hero. This bard's hero was seemingly born with the innate ability to be the greatest at everything without putting in the sweat to learn, and I suspected that none of this bard's heroes ever took a shite, ate a dodgy meal, got ill, or had wounds that took months to heal. Pah, a pox on that! Still, it was a happy reminder of my youth.

"Are you ready?" Charra said.

We barely touched our drinks as I related what I'd discovered in Lynas' warehouse and the Templarum Magestus, and what I'd learned from the information broker and gang boss in the Scabs.

"Why chase him through the Warrens and kill him there if they could just steal what they wanted from his warehouse?" I said. "If the Skinner had wanted to murder him beforehand then he would have. No, Lynas had been snooping into something, I'm sure of it." I massaged my temples, trying to recall the fractured details of the vision. "Something big. He bought us time, paying with his life."

Charra cleared her throat and studied the map in front of us. It was fairly crude and the further away an area was from main thoroughfares like Fisherman's Way the less detail it depicted. The Warrens was mostly just blank space with a few older points of note marked. It would be nigh-impossible to keep a map of the Warrens current: by the time you finished such a time-consuming task you would find entire areas had already changed due to fire, collapse and construction.

"While you were up in the Old Town I compiled all the information I have on what occurred on the fourteenth of Leaffall," she said. "This…" she swallowed, "this is where Lynas died." She had marked Bootmaker's Wynd with an X, smudged where a charcoal stick had broken from pressing down too hard.

I clenched my jaw as resurgent terror drifted to the surface of my mind. I felt the ghost of the scalpel's bite and our hot blood pattering down across our face. "The air smelled of blood and smoke as he pounded on doors asking for help."

Her finger pressed down on a circle, not far from the first mark. "This old abandoned temple is within running distance of Bootmaker's Wynd. It burnt down that same night, which explains the smell of smoke." Two marks were next to it. "Multiple fatal stabbings here and here, a small-time alchemic-dealer named Keran and his gang, the Iron Wolves. Could be coincidence. Could be that Keran and his men saw something they shouldn't. Normally I'd say good riddance to the filth."

I gulped ale like water. "Did anybody live in that temple?"

"A few years back the area was ravaged by a flesh-rotting plague and it's been abandoned ever since. Rumour claims it's cursed. It was a rat-infested shithole by all accounts, occupied by a dozen or so alchemic addicts. None survived the fire so far as I know."

"Whose temple was it?"

"I suppose that it must have been inherited by the Hooded God after Artha died..." She let the comment drift off unsaid, studying me.

I examined the map, trying to trace Lynas' likely route. "I still don't know what happened that night." Not yet. All I knew was a deal had been cut amidst fire and blood. She had no need to know that I left to keep Lynas, Layla and her safe. I wasn't about to lay guilt on Charra that wasn't her fault.

I cleared my throat. "Assuming he started from the temple, the quickest way for Lynas to get to a public place and any hope of help was through the streets near Bootmaker's Wynd." *If only you had made it, my friend.*

"Where do we go from here?" she said. "We know Lynas was working with Bardok the Hock, who is apparently newly flush with coin, and we know Bardok works with the Harbourmaster at Pauper's Docks. The Harbourmaster is in the pocket of the alchemic syndicates and not exactly inclined to be friendly to me, but if all these murders are linked then the Skinner is a bigger threat to all of them than I am."

"True. Can you can get me in and out of the docks under the sniffers' noses?"

"Of course."

"Well then, it's settled. First we investigate that razed temple to see if there is anything left to uncover, pay that slimy git Bardok a visit on the way back and then, if needs be, we find out what the Harbourmaster has to say. We'll leave him to last, no point putting ourselves in danger if we don't have to."

She nodded agreement and fingered the hilt of the short sword at her hip. "Drink up. We have work to do. If Lynas bought us time then I won't waste it. Whatever it takes."

It was so good to work with people who didn't mind getting their hands dirty.

The reek of burning still lingered around the site of Artha's old temple. The blackened stonework had once been part of a proud and martial edifice, albeit latterly left to decay and swiftly hemmed in by cobbled-together wooden structures propped up against its walls. Ironically, that very sodden decrepitude had been what had saved most of the surrounding buildings from the worst of the blaze. We circled the site, kicking over the occasional cracked stone or burnt cinder. I squatted down and touched fragments of an arrow slit and a spiked iron rail twisted by heat, but if Lynas had indeed been here on the night he died I felt nothing, not a whisper of magic or hint of his emotions. Fire was the great devourer, and hungry tongues of flame had destroyed anything that might have been imprinted on the surroundings.

"Not much left," Charra said, stating the bloody obvious.

"There must be something here. Some clue they've overlooked." I picked up a sodden doll made from straw and flicked off grey ash. It had been bound into a human shape with clothes of coloured rags, two twists of yarn carefully woven and teased into the hairstyle a proper Old Town lady might wear.

The stone cobbles underfoot began shaking as another earth tremor shook the city. The building to my right creaked like an old man, gave a splintering crack and listed a hand-span towards me. A rain of rotted wood pattered down nearby. The place was an ill-omened death-trap; no wonder it was deserted. Soon it would collapse in on itself – hopefully long after we were out of here – and then it would be reborn once people got up the nerve to pilfer the stone from the ruined temple to build a new tenement.

As the buildings settled I sensed a tiny tremor of movement from a roof behind me. I opened my Gift, trying to sense any stray thoughts or emotions. I relaxed as a corvun screeched and took flight from behind one of the crooked chimney stacks that leaned like bad drunks over the alleyways.

While I was busy examining the buildings, Charra climbed over a pile of rubble and scanned the ground for clues.

"Walker, look at this."

Something cracked underfoot and she disappeared shrieking into a hole.

"Charra!" I scrambled over the rubble.

She was sitting on her arse in a muddy hollow half-filled with debris, wincing and holding her chest. Her face and hair were grey with ash. She coughed, spitting mud and blood.

I opened my mouth to comment.

"Don't you dare say a word," she said.

"As you wish, my lady." I lowered my hand to help her out. Stale fetid air wafted up out of a dark opening in one side of the pit, sending a shiver up my spine. "Merciless Night

Bitch," I cursed. "There is an entrance to the Boneyards here. This old temple to Artha must have been built to guard the exit."

She looked up at me in alarm, recalling our old stories of the things that lurked in those dark catacombs. Once upon a time she had liked to sit with us and listen to gruesome tales of the twisted, broken things gone howling mad down below her streets, but that was when our tales had merely been scary stories of a strange place she would never see.

The stink of the Boneyards summoned the foul taste of bile to burn the back of my throat. Dizziness and terror overcame me. I stumbled, foot falling over the edge, blood flooding my mouth from a bitten lip. Charra's eyes widened, her arms opening to catch me as I fell, racked by old nightmares of being trapped in the darkness...

CHAPTER 14

My breath misted the air of the dusty, disused cellar. I was starting to shiver so I pulled the threadbare cloak tighter around my bony, gangly body, feeling like a shabby street rat amidst the finery of the high-born boys that surrounded us. There wasn't any chance of escaping; they were older and bigger than me, already with hair on their chins, and more importantly they were blocking the only way back. I had no idea how Harailt had got the keys to this room and disabled the wards – the lower levels of the Collegiate were forbidden to initiates and usually heavily guarded, but the corridors had been strangely empty today as they marched us down here. I supposed that Harailt *was* Archmagus Byzant's favoured student...

"No," the fat boy beside me pleaded. "I... I don't want to go."

The chorus of older boys kept up the chant: *"Boneyards, Boneyards, Boneyards, Boneyards, Boneyards."*

"Are you quite sure of that?" Harailt said. "We have all taken this challenge. Do you not want to be one of us?" I could see the dangerous twitch start at the corner of his mouth. The fat boy was in far more trouble than he realized. "Are you really going to let poor little Edrin here go into the tunnels all on his own?" His half-dozen idiot cronies kept up the heckling chant.

The fat boy looked back at me, swallowed, and lowered his eyes. He edged away from the steps leading down past the huge steel gate that yawned open into unknown depths below the Old Town. The darkness loomed behind me like a living, breathing thing, and I clutched the lantern they had given me even tighter.

The group of seniors pushed forward, herding the fat boy towards me, and towards the entrance to the catacombs. *"Boneyards, Boneyards, Boneyards, Boneyards."*

Harailt glowered at me and jerked his head towards the darkness.

I took the hint, and began to descend the steps, taking my own good time about it as some sort of lame protest. Heir to a High House or not, if Harailt had been alone I might have smacked him one and burst his nose, but I wasn't about to try to fight seven initiates whose Gifts had already begun to mature. Instead I satisfied myself by imagining my fists beating his face to a pulp and his silver-threaded tunic stained with his own blood. Lately it seemed like he found an opportunity to harass me every other day. If things got much worse I'd have to revert to my old Docklands ways and stick a knife in his back when he wasn't looking. I didn't want to have to do that. I'd tried so hard to fit in and I was every bit as good as they were! It wasn't my fault I'd been born in a Docklands tenement and them in lofty palaces.

I reached the gate and looked back, happened to catch the fat boy's eyes. I flicked a look at Harailt and back again, gave him a curt shake of my head. The boy finally seemed to realize that he didn't have a choice. He took a great shuddering breath, held up his lantern like a shield, and followed me through the gate.

Harailt gave a sarcastic cheer. "Finally! Go on then, find a relic from the Boneyards to prove your bravery."

We slowly edged forward into the darkness, batting cobwebs away from our faces. The light from the lanterns went nowhere near far enough down the tunnel. The air was dank and stale, leaving a foul taste in my mouth.

"Don't worry," I said, trying to show a confidence I didn't feel. "We won't be in here long. We'll just grab something and run straight back out." I almost dropped the lantern as the gate clanged shut behind us with an eruption of laughter and jeering.

"What are you doing?" I shouted. "Let us out!" We ran back but it was much too late. The gate was locked and they were running away, laughing and patting themselves on the back.

Harailt was the last to leave the room. He turned, silhouetted in the doorway. "Perhaps if you beg I will come back to free you both." His lips twitched with derision. "Beg."

To my surprise the fat boy didn't immediately fall to his knees offering to lick Harailt's boots. He was made of sterner stuff than I'd thought. I hocked up a blob of phlegm and spat it in Harailt's direction.

His face reddened at the insult. "Find your own way out then, you grubby little drudges. You poor excuses for magi do not belong in these hallowed halls. Better get moving before your oil runs out." Then he was gone. The heavy door thumped closed behind him, cutting off the sound of their mirth.

"I hope your cocks rot and fall off," I shouted after him, booting the gate and succeeding only in causing pain to shoot up my leg. The fat boy grabbed the spars and tried to wrench them apart, but the gate was completely and utterly immovable.

"Hello?" he shouted. "Hello! Is anybody there?" He kept up the shouting for a few minutes until it finally got on my nerves.

I prodded him in the side. He turned, and it was only then that I realized he was on the verge of tears. "I think we're on our own, pal," I said. "Those gangrenous scrotes ain't coming back for us." His tears started to well up. Great. Why did I have to be stuck here with the likes of him? "Well, I'm going to prove that those bawbags aren't better than me. I'm finding my own way out and I'm going to bring back something awesome to rub in their stupid faces." I backed away from the gate. "You coming?"

He stared at me for a few seconds, sniffling, then looked back out into the darkened cellar. He scrubbed his face with a sleeve. When he looked back the tears had dried up. I was surprised at his fortitude. He stuck his hand out. "Um, hello. I am Lynas Granton. Sorry about..." He waved a hand indicating the whole of himself. "I... I guess we do have to go down there."

We clasped wrists. "Edrin Walker," I said. "Call me Walker. I hate Edrin. Bloody parents, eh."

He frowned. "I haven't heard of a House Walker before."

"Ain't no house at all," I said, preparing to judge him by his response. "My father is a dock worker. Walker comes down from my mother's side. It's a clan-name." It was how I chose to honour her, that and I preferred it to dreary old "Edrin of Hobbs Lane".

Lynas looked embarrassed, but showed no sign of the derision I'd learned to expect from high-born magi and initiates. "Oh. Sorry." He took a few deep calming breaths and seemed to relax a bit. "So they pick on you as well?" he ventured.

I shrugged. "No more than anybody else who isn't from a High House. What about you, pal, are you...?"

He shook his head. "I'm not one of them. I'm the heir to House Granton, but we are just a Low House. Grandfather distinguished himself during the last big war in the colonies and bought his way up into the Old Town. My family have..." He seemed to search for the correct words, but gave up. "We've lost almost all our money, to be honest." He looked at his feet, face reddening. "It's my father. He gambles."

He didn't need to elaborate. That particular curse hit high and low alike. He may have been low nobility but he didn't seem the same as those arrogant, self-entitled pricks who thought that locking us down here was a bit of a lark and a jolly old jape. Their families probably had enough money and power to let them get away with anything they liked – especially when it concerned little first-year initiates like us without any connections, and whose Gifts hadn't matured yet, and might never.

I uncorked the oil reservoir of my lantern and peered in. "Stinking book-lickers have left me hardly any."

Lynas frowned. "Book-lickers?" He checked his own and cursed.

I sneered. "You think those boil-brained buffoons have any idea what to do with a book?"

The tunnel ahead sloped away into the yawning darkness like we were sliding down the gullet of some huge beast. We shivered and clutched our lanterns tight. "I'd better turn this down low," Lynas said. "We need to ration the oil."

I blinked. He was right. To my chagrin I hadn't thought of that; instead I'd been wanting both lanterns up full for as much light as we could get. I turned mine down as well, the darkness creeping closer as the light dwindled.

At first the tunnel was square and formed from blocks of cut stone, but as we trudged on into the depths it changed, becoming a cruder passage hacked though the black basalt rock below Setharis. Yellowed skulls grinned at us from niches cut into the walls. They might have sat there for unfathomable eons for all we knew.

We paused to scrape an arrow into the wall with a shard of stone, joining a collection of other symbols that valiant adventurers like us had left in past years, decades, or even centuries. We took the right-hand passage and walked for a good half an hour, carefully marking each new turn and split until we came to a circular chamber with five stone archways leading off into the depths. Human bones carpeted every wall and each block of stone in the arches was inlaid with grinning skulls. Lynas shuffled closer to me.

"They're just bones," I said, but it didn't seem to comfort him much. Their hollow stares were a little unsettling, but I wasn't about let him know that. We made idle chatter as we walked, more to hear the comforting sound of our voices than anything else.

While Lynas had his back turned studying a tunnel, I grabbed a skull and held it up at his head. He glanced back, "Which way do you–" He shrieked and I dissolved into laughter.

"Not funny!" he grumbled.

"Oh come on, it was a little bit funny," I said. "It's just bones, they can't hurt you. Don't be so serious." He glared at me, but his lips quirked into the first smile I'd seen from him.

"Let's go through here," he said, waving me to go first. The tunnel walls were slick with damp and stalactites grew from the bones of the ceiling and doorways. The only sounds were our ragged breathing and the steady *drip-drip* of water.

We felt compelled to keep our voices down. Everybody knew that monsters made their lairs deep in the catacombs, their burrows dug into piled bones of the dead.

"Why am I the one in front anyway?" I said. "I'm no leader."

Lynas just shrugged and scanned the room, peering into each doorway in turn.

I carefully slid my eating knife from my belt. I'd concealed it at dinner after seeing Harailt watching me, then lean in close to his lackeys and laugh. Dull-edged as it was, I felt safer with the knife in my hand.

Lynas noticed, gave a scared little chuckle. "That's why you go first."

Despite my fear, I returned a grin. "Smartarse." That caused him to smile again.

Some of the doorways led nowhere, fresh rubble and piles of shattered bone filling the tunnels beyond. Above one blocked passage I noticed a small opening in the ceiling. I edged closer, listening for any sign of further collapse. A faint breeze caressed my skin.

"Lynas," I whispered. "Over here."

He crunched over, gaze following my pointing finger. "Is it a way out?" His voice trembled with hope.

I bit back the caustic reply I was about to make. No wonder I didn't have any friends. "Hope so," I said instead. I put away the knife and tried to scramble up to check it out, but the scree was too loose to get good purchase and I refused to let go of my lantern. "Give me a hand."

Lynas interlocked his fingers to create a foothold, hoisting me up. The extra height allowed me to clamber up over the lip of the hole. I lifted up my lantern, turning the oil flow up to illuminate the room.

"What's up there?" Lynas said.

The cracked walls were slick and black, made of some queer sort of stone, and the ceiling was high and tapered to a point. "I don't know," I said. "An old bedroom maybe. There's a rotted old heap of slime in a wooden frame that looks like it used to be a bed, and what might be the remains of a wardrobe, table and chairs. There's a breeze coming from beneath a big door up here so it could be a way out. No bones, so maybe Old Boney's priests haven't been here in before." Which meant it might have something worth stealing – no, recovering, I corrected myself. It wouldn't be stealing this time.

I placed my light to one side and stretched a hand down. Lynas passed his lantern up and then scrambled up to join me. By the Night Bitch, he was heavy! With one last heave that almost dislocated my shoulder he was up and through the hole.

He sat panting, craning his neck around the room. His eyes were bright, curiosity overcoming his fear for the moment. The floor was strewn with rat skeletons and desiccated droppings and the ceiling mostly obscured by curtains of cobweb. In the centre of the room was a shattered stone block, the eerie carvings covering every surface defaced or hacked off. What I could see of them made my vision swim. We decided to give that a wide berth.

Every initiate had heard thrilling stories of adventures in the Boneyards, of people coming back laden with jewels and sacks of gold. Somebody a few years back had even claimed to have found a spirit-bound sword amidst a pile of skulls. But then there were the other stories – the ones we whispered to each other at night, huddled under blankets in our dorms – the stories of people that just disappeared, their bodies consumed by ancient traps or ravenous monsters, and of the agonized wails heard at night that were said to be the cries of warped magi gone insane, their minds and bodies consumed by the Worm of Magic. The tutors themselves told us those dark and cautionary tales as a warning not to succumb to the lust for power and the lures of our Gift. But for the moment we were both far too excited to care: Gold! Jewels! Magic stuff! I'd never go to sleep hungry again, and I could even get a new cloak, a warm one for those cold winter nights. My dreams were small and simple things.

We crept around the room hunting for treasure, wincing at every crunch of stone and bone underfoot. I caught a whiff of something dead and rotting in the room. "Ugh. Do you smell that?" I said, fully expecting to find a maggot-ridden corpse. "Something reeks like a dead..." I caught Lynas' guilty expression, and laughed.

"Whoops," he said. "Sorry about that. I do not think dinner agreed with me." He began poking through the ruins of the wardrobe, muttering about cabbage. I chuckled and picked up a length of petrified wood, whacking what I assumed had once been a bed. Beneath a crust of hardened slime, layers of rotten cloth and mould had fossilized into a hard shell surrounding something underneath. With my stick extended at arm's length, I carefully started chipping away at it. My avaricious little heart hoped to find a skeleton still wearing jewellery. Not much else would have survived for long down here. I wasn't squeamish when it came to money or corpses; Docklanders couldn't afford to be.

Lynas sighed and grumbled as he sifted through his pile of debris. Me, I was filled with morbid curiosity as the shape of a person gradually emerged from its cracked coverings. I whacked it again and the whole shell shattered. I squeaked in surprise as three mummified rats plopped to the floor right next to my foot.

Lynas yelped in fright at my sudden noise. I leapt back, spun, stick whipping up. We looked at each other sheepishly. He padded up beside me, glancing back at the pile of junk he'd been investigating and then shrugging despondently.

I couldn't take my eyes off the bed. There were no jewels or gold rings, but what we did have was a bloody huge skeleton. The bones were all wrong, surely too large to be human. Desiccated skin clung to it, and a mane of straggly white hair was still attached to a large skull with a strange hole right in the middle of a thick sloping forehead. It wore intricately crafted bronze armour that looked like it was designed more for show than out of any sense of practicality. Arcane wards the likes of which I'd never seen had been inlaid into the cuirass in untarnished silver that glimmered in the lantern light. A black hilt jutted from the chest piece, piercing wards and armour both to stab through the heart. I swallowed and exchanged a glance with Lynas.

He moistened his lips. "Finders keepers."

"Hold up the light," I said.

He held his lantern over the bed. We stood in silence for a few moments, staring at the skeleton.

"Who do you think they were?" I said, then after a moment's silence added: "What do you think they were?"

Lynas shook his head. "Look at the armour. That exquisite workmanship was wrought by a master smith." He pointed to the one side where the metal was melted and stained dark. Looking closer the armour had numerous gouges and scrapes as if it had seen battle. I tapped the bronze with my stick, then again, harder. The end of the stick snapped clean off. The armour was still solid, and might even be worth something.

"Do you think that there is still magic in it?" I croaked.

Lynas shivered, shrugged, and eyed the wooden door that was our only exit. I wanted to leave, badly. Standing in front of a weird skeleton in this horrid place was creeping me out; it wasn't anything as ordinary as being back in the Warrens and coming across somebody that'd been stabbed. Lynas looked sick and terrified. What brave adventurers we were. But I refused to leave without a prize to prove Harailt hadn't made us cry like babies and piss ourselves down here in the dark. Even if it was almost true. I placed my stick on the ground by my feet and wiped sweaty palms on my cloak.

My hand hovered over the black hilt jutting from the skeleton's chest. Then I thought better of it, picked up the stick and handed it to Lynas. "Just in case," I said, mimicking him using it as a club. You could never be too sure where magic was concerned.

My hand was back over the hilt. I extended my index finger and forced it down, bit by bit until it was almost touching the hilt, then that last little push. I snatched my hand back, heart hammering. Was my skin tingling? Was I imagining it? Was it magic? Was I being paranoid? Yes – my finger was fine. I took a deep calming breath.

"Don't scare me like that, Walker," Lynas complained, his knuckles white around the stick.

"Sorry," I whispered. Steeling myself, I wrapped my hand around the hilt and pulled. It slid out easily in a shower of bone dust and curled bronze shavings.

We stared at the large barbed black iron knife in my hand. It was a hideous and crude weapon, but the sort of crudeness you could only get from a careful and studied artistry in brutality. I hefted it in my hand. It felt perfectly balanced despite the strange design. This was more like my idea of a magic weapon, not a poncy prettified sword all shiny silver and gold. To my mind, weapons were made for killing.

"Is it magical?" Lynas said. "It looks stupid."

Each to their own, I thought. "I have no idea. My Gift hasn't begun to mature yet. Yours?"

"Not yet, though I have high hopes it will happen soon."

I examined the blade, carefully touching one of the barbs and finding it still sharp. I upended it to examine the plain hilt for sign of any maker's marks. Nothing. I blinked, realising that blood was gushing from my finger and down the blade, dripping onto the skeleton below. When had that happened? Suddenly my finger started to throb. I hadn't even felt it cut my flesh.

"Ow, this thing is sharp as–"

Fuck? a searing voice said in Old Escharric. I winced in

pain, the word burning into my mind. I only knew what it meant because curse words were the first ones I'd researched after entering the Collegiate.

I brought up the knife and spun around, scanning the room. "Who said that?"

Lynas looked confused. "Said what?"

I glanced at the bloody knife and then to the skeleton. I froze in horror. The skeleton's empty eye sockets and the hole in the forehead now pulsed with septic green light.

There needs be a pact, the voice said. *Be quick.*

"W-w-what?" I stammered. "I don't know what you are talking about. Who are you?" The knife throbbed in my hand.

Runes on the skeleton's armour flared bright. The hardened shell of slime dissolved into ropes of ooze that squirmed over the bed, snatching up and absorbing the dead rats as it went, transforming them into ribbons of pulsing flesh that twisted up the bones and across the crude skull. The huge skeleton lurched upright, at least seven foot high, eye sockets and the hole in the forehead blazing with eldritch fire. It reached for me while I stood like a statue.

Lynas saved my life. He shrieked and swung his stick. It crunched into the skull and caved it in.

The thing collapsed back onto the bed, into a mass of writhing flesh that flowed in and around it. Dust swirled up from the floor and into the corpse. Pink and grey organs formed, slurped through spaces between bone and bronze to pulse obscenely in its abdomen. A mutely screaming inhuman face of glistening muscle began to form on the skull. Jellied eyes oozed into sockets, one forming right in the middle of its forehead.

"Run!" Lynas shrieked, shoving me towards the door, his stick raised defensively.

Something dug into my mind, barbs of alien thought ripping their way inside me. I staggered and fell to one knee.

When the barbs retreated I knew what I had to do. A quick glance at the undead thing reforming convinced me that it was the only option.

A name coalesced in my mind. "Dissever," I intoned, slicing the knife across my forearm. "My blood, your blood. My flesh, your flesh. My enemies, your enemies." A frisson of energy ran through me, linking us. This pact, it went both ways. It urged me to attack.

The knife punched straight through enchanted bronze into the undead thing's insides. The creature reeled back, shrieking. I stabbed and cut, reeking fluids spurting across my face. A mad energy filled me. I was out of control, wild and screaming with rage that stormed into me from the knife.

"Run!" I snarled at Lynas, struggling to resist the urge to tear his throat out with my teeth and gulp down hot spurting blood. Instead I hacked away at the fleshy thing growing from dead bones. An unbearable pressure began building behind my eyes.

Lynas ran. I heard the door crash open and glimpsed his light receding down the tunnel, chased by my manic laughter. The black knife cut though the thing with ease, and the armour may as well have been soft cheese. My vision ran red as bloodlust howled deep in my heart. The pressure in my head exploded. Something inside me broke.

My Gift awoke.

Wind shrieked around me, tearing at stone and rubble. Unearthly strength flooded through me. A thousand fragmented thoughts from the city above roared into my mind. Too much. All too... much...

When my senses returned I was drenched in blood and covered in bits of bone and gobbets of flesh. The thing's head – a ruined mass of cracked bone and rotting flesh – gaped at me like a freshwater pike, impaled on a spike of wood rammed into the floor, its over-large jaw still gnashing. Light guttered behind its three malformed eyes. Whatever the thing had been, even it couldn't handle what I'd done to it. I both laughed and cried as we stared at each other, my body trembling with the afterbirth of magic.

Parts of the ceiling had collapsed, burying both the doorway and the small hole through which we had originally entered under blocks of stone I hadn't a hope of moving. I was trapped, but held onto a shred of hope that somehow Lynas had got out and was running to summon help. I sobbed at the thought: who would come back for a nobody like me? Lynas barely knew me. If the streets of Setharis had taught me anything, it was that you could only rely on yourself. And even if Lynas did get out, nobody would get up off their arses to dig all the way down here. My lantern was almost out of oil.

After the last flicker of light died away I spent days – I didn't know how many – in that near-darkness, the dim septic green from the thing's eyes my only source of light. I went a little mad, I think, shrieking for help and clawing at the walls until my fingers were raw and bloody. My throat slowly dried to sandy parchment, lips cracking and hunger churning in my stomach. Eventually I took to licking damp from the walls, and then, eventually, gnawing putrescent flesh from the undead thing's bones while it watched. In my delirium a macabre amusement filled me at the foul act, supposing that it was one way to ensure the thing did not rise again. Consciousness came and went. I talked to the head, even asked it questions about its past, though it never answered. The knife, however, whispered incessantly inside my head, promises of war and slaughter yet to come.

I'd given up hope, had no energy left to fight, and had curled up to sleep, maybe for the last time. I slept for what felt like an age, barely stirring as hallucinated sounds of digging drew closer. That's where the magi found me as they dragged out the last boulder – curled up on the floor in front of the still-living head, my black knife cradled in my hands. I blinked as torchlight seared my eyes.

Archmagus Byzant was first to squeeze through the gap, his craggy face and neat white beard streaked with dust, emerald ring glowing like a verdant sun. He took one look at the head on a spike and held up a hand to still those behind him. He approached carefully, his eyes never leaving me, ignoring the blinking head completely.

"Are you well, boy?" he said softly, comfortingly. "Are you able to talk?"

Kill, Dissever demanded. *Blood. Strong blood.*

My body throbbed with the illusion of strength. I almost did it. I almost snarled and tried to leap forward to kill and eat the Archmagus. What stopped me was the sight of the two initiates behind Byzant tasked with holding lanterns. The look on Harailt's face, the shock and disbelief as he stared at me, the naked fear in him, stirred something inside of me, a wordless and horrible rage – I needed to split his face with an axe and hack him into quivering pieces. But it was something more powerful than anger at Harailt that stopped me flinging myself at them; it was the honest worry – for me! – on Lynas' face that shook me to my core and threw off the bloodlust. He was a wild mess of scrapes, cuts, and bruises. He must have suffered terribly on his flight out of the Boneyards, and his hands still shook with fear. He had crawled blind through the tunnels for days to reach help and then insisted on coming back down to retrace his steps to find me. I didn't think I could have done the same.

My eyes hurt, vision blurred with tears. *I owe you my life, Lynas Granton. One day I'll do the same for you or die trying.*

"I'm fine, Archmagus," I croaked. "I just had to deal with this… this…"

"Revenant," he said. "It is the Worm-taken corpse of some sort of magus, mindless and animated only by magic." His eyes narrowed as he noticed Dissever. "Hand me that blade, boy."

I swallowed. My hand shook but didn't obey me. "I… I don't think I can, master."

He looked at me, looked into me, nodded, lifted his hands and snapped his fingers. "A blanket, you fools, fetch water and a blanket. You are very lucky that he lives, Harailt, you boil-brained whelp."

Byzant studied my weapon, his frown deepening. Dissever did not like that one bit. It hunkered down in my mind and went quiet. I felt my hand loosen around the hilt.

The Archmagus pried it from my hand. "A spirit-bound blade," he said. "A most impressive find. The making of such objects is a lost art. Only the gods can forge such items now."

He did something to me. I felt it happen, but didn't know what. I sagged, eyelids drooping. "Mine," I mumbled.

"Yes, boy. I understand now how you survived. This knife is undeniably yours."

The last thing I saw was Lynas grinning at me, his joy and relief piecing my heart. As sleep crushed down on me, I couldn't help but wonder: had I actually, somehow, acquired a friend?

CHAPTER 15

Soft warm skin brushing across my forehead. Soothing. Stroking my hair. I opened my eyes to Charra's dust-streaked face. Dank, stale air from the catacombs filled my nostrils. Boneyards. Walls. I was surrounded by walls crushing down on me! I panicked, then shuddered with relief at the sight of the clouds overhead. I was just in a pit, not buried alive. Just a stupid hole in the ground. I sagged, panting, Charra patting my back awkwardly.

Oh Lynas. I couldn't save you after all.

"I'm so sorry," Charra said. "The old nightmare?"

"Nothing I can do about it," I said gruffly. "It happened and it will never leave me. That's all there is to say." Old memories of Dissever drenched in blood stirred. "I'm falling to pieces here, chased by daemons, and if the Arcanum discover me I'm in no shape to resist."

She scowled. "Well you'll damn well have to keep it together. You're not the sort of man to whine and go easily. Oh no, you'd spit in death's eye socket. I'd do the same myself." Her expression grew serious and she looked away from me. "We'll figure this out. We have to."

I smiled for her. The only people who had a chance of being able to help me with my daemon problem were the Arcanum, and they'd rest easier in their beds with me dead. They might even toast sweetroot on a stick over my pyre.

The only reason I wasn't already collared and leashed was that I'd taken great pains to fake my death.

She cleared her throat. "Walker, ah, there is a tunnel. I think somebody has been using it fairly recently."

I stiffened, palms slicking with sweat at the sight of the rubble-choked tunnel. Footprints were visible in the muddy floor leading down into the darkness. A line of scrapes accompanied the prints, as if something heavy had been dragged through.

"Somebody has been moving goods through the catacombs," Charra said. "Smugglers perhaps."

I swallowed and looked at her pleadingly, mentally begging her not to say those next words.

"We need to go in," she said with regret.

"Only if Bardok the Hock and the Harbourmaster can't give us answers," I said hoarsely. One way or another I'd make them talk. Anything was better than going back down there. But if I had to, I would. I owed Lynas everything.

We hauled ourselves out of the pit, dusted ourselves off and headed for Bardok's shop.

The Warrens are the rocky shore that a tide of diseased and decrepit humanity washed up on when they were shipwrecked by life. Anybody that made any real sort of money would be out of there quicker than a whore could lift her dress for a high lord, if they didn't squander it all on gambling, drink or alchemics first of course. As strange as it seemed to me, some folk took to the squalor like rats to refuse, revelling in lawlessness and decay. Bardok the Hock was typical of that sort.

He still kept shop in the cellar of one of the older and sturdier tenements that had somehow survived fire and neglect, a full four storeys of solid stonework located northwest of the ruined temple and almost half way to the wealthier streets of Westford. The slimy worm had holed up in there seemingly forever, a touch of the Gift granting him rude health well into his old age. After my father's death I had sold him more than a few items of dubious origin to fund my way through the Collegiate years.

Under a cracked sign painted with the golden globes of the hockers' guild, I pounded on the heavy door. Nobody answered but we knew he was in there; he always was. Charra kept watch while I struggled to pick the shiny new lock. After a few minutes of my fumbling she nudged me. "Want me to do it?"

I scowled and pulled out Dissever. "I'm good." The knife carved through the wood and steel as easily as flesh. Not exactly subtle, but I was past caring.

We descended the steps into Bardok's dimly-lit, cluttered shop and discovered that it was as much a mess as it ever had been. Black and green mould carpeted one wall and the room smelled of dust and rotten wood. We wove past heaped baskets of hocked chisels, hammers, tongs, spades, tools from every sort of trade, past shelves of pottery and cheap jewellery. I paused at a mound of coats to finger a carefully repaired slit in the wool where a knife had gone in. The brown stain was barely visible in the seams. Pots and pans hung from hooks on the walls and chests of brass fittings, fire pokers and old locks clustered next to the door to his back room.

Charra volunteered to take the first bash at trying to get the old goat to talk. She went in alone armed with the blunt force approach of bribes backed up by threats and intimidation. After a few minutes of eavesdropping it became apparent that there was bad blood there, Bardok having declined her protections recently. Maybe his new benefactors had given him the brass balls he'd never had back when I had dealings with him. Charra began dropping curses every third word and her threats were getting inventive. I amused myself by tampering with the magical wards that somebody had set up for Bardok. Sloppy but potent work, as if somebody both powerful and skilled had set them up in a hurry. They were designed to be activated remotely in the same manner as the city gates and Bardok would have a similar activation crystal on him. As I broke the wards I smiled at the thought of his face if he tried to use it on us. The stored magic now leaking out to fill the shop also served to mask any trace of my own Gift.

"Is that your last word?" she said loudly after they had both been silent for a few seconds.

"Away and fuck a dog, you braying donkey," he snarled, making little sense, but being admirably offensive all the same. "Get out of my property, you saggy old whore."

I thought I'd better get in there before Charra killed him, so I shoved open the door and sauntered into a room lit by a miserly single oil lamp on his desk. His room was stuffed to the gills with scrolls, books, sheaves of parchment and artefacts from around the world. On the walls hung a variety of exotic weaponry: a beaked Skallgrim war axe etched with angular runes, an ornate Esbanian gladius, an Ahramish khopesh, and an acid-etched Clanholds broadsword, as well as others unknown to me. Small stone dragon skulls and assorted bones were propped up on a table at the back by a clay tablet carved with the flowing text of distant Ahram. One small statuette of a jackal-headed human was of Escharric origin, hideously expensive and almost certainly smuggled in illegally from a dig site. The old goat would wear clothes until they fell apart but didn't mind splurging coin on his precious collector's items, and undoubtedly cared more about them than people.

Charra had risen from her seat, short sword naked in her hand, and was leaning over a wide desk cluttered with odds and ends, scraps of parchment and old crumbs of food. She settled for scowling at Bardok, who had pressed himself back into an oversized red leather chair. He looked old and cadaverous, entirely bald now, the lines of his face set into a permanent scowl.

I slipped on my nastiest grin. "Well, well, if it's not Bardok the Hock. So good to see you again."

It took him a moment to recognize my face and the voice. Then his watery eyes goggled and the blood drained from his face. "Oh shit," he whimpered. "I thought you were rat food."

Charra remained standing as I eased myself into the creaking chair in front of his desk. "That's what I wanted folk to think."

I wasn't exactly a big fish in a little pond, more like a fat minnow covered in huge and venomous spines that you would do well not to aggravate. In my own element I was as dangerous as any magus in Setharis. "So…" I said, stuffing a smoke between my lips and lighting it from his lamp. I took a draw, then blew the smoke right in his face. "Go fuck a dog, you say? Braying donkey, was it? And we mustn't forget saggy old whore. Quite the muckspout today." I looked at his cherished collector's items on the walls. "It would be a shame if I had to start breaking things." Sweat burst across his face and he looked ready to throw up.

Amidst the hodgepodge of objects on his desk a brass cone the height of my thumb caught my eye. For a second utter horror overwhelmed me. I suppressed the shudder before he could notice. The fool had an alchemic bomb sitting right there on his desk!

There couldn't be half a dozen people in the world that had ever seen one: as a Collegiate initiate I'd been earning coin running errands for an artificer magus named Tannar who was conducting unsanctioned experiments with alchemics. His workshop had been a thing to behold, full of strange smells and bubbling liquids in glass alembics, and it was not every magus who could claim to have ventured into an artificer's innermost workshop. The trouble with the Arcanum, Tannar told me, was that they had spent the last thousand years trying to rediscover the glories of ancient Escharr instead of actually using their brains to invent something new. That sort of opinion was anathema to the Arcanum, so of course that endeared him to me.

He had come up with the idea of blowing holes in mountains to get at seams of ore, and had made a dozen or so alchemic bombs to be tested during an initial mining expedition. Unfortunately that expedition never departed, but his inventions must have been a success in a way since his workshop had turned into a smoking crater overnight. And here Bardok was using one of the bloody things as a paperweight!

He quivered, about to buckle, then suddenly flipped to anger. He glared at me with a surge of aggression I hadn't thought he'd had in him. He slammed a fist down on the desk, making the bomb jump. I almost soiled myself, but couldn't let it show or I would compromise my position of power. "Get out of my shop," he said. He spat on the floor, not seeming to care that it was his own. "You still owe me money, you cur. Think you can step all over me? You don't know who you're dealing with now." He sneered as his hand reached for the underside of his desk, pressed his thumb against the activation crystal embedded there. He pressed it again, eyes darting down, then up to look at me in shock. His expression was everything I had hoped it would be.

"Something wrong?" I said, slouching back with a mocking smile plastered across my face, trying not to look at the bomb sitting three feet away from me.

He swallowed, stood, pointed towards the door. "If you are not here to buy something then get out," he said. "I have friends in high places. You have no idea–"

"Sit," I said.

And he did, slumping back into his chair and deflating into the weaselly coward I'd known and hated. "What do you want?" he said, rubbing his forehead with one hand as if we'd given him a headache.

"Lynas Granton," Charra said.

I watched his expression change. Not guilt exactly, but he was definitely hiding something. "Who?" he said, fooling nobody. His reactions were too rapid, his emotions changing too quickly, like he had taken an alchemic.

"Bardok, Bardok, Bardok," I said, wagging a finger at him. I leaned forward and patted his hand. "Don't make me hurt you." He knew I was alive now, so there was no point in my holding back, and nobody who mattered would lift a finger to help scum like him anyway. I eased open my Gift and reached for his mind, only to find myself plunging into a churning maelstrom of alchemically heightened emotion and magic. I flinched back in confusion and pain. Mageblood. I was certain of it.

Somehow he felt it and laughed at my suddenly queasy expression. "You think you are so dangerous with your petty magic tricks. You have no idea what real power is."

Fine. I was in no mood to play. I tried again, forcing my way in past the pain. "Slap yourself." His hand snapped up, cracking hard across his face. "Harder." *Smack*. The next slap bloomed as a red hand-print across his face. He would tell me everything he knew, anything that meant I didn't have to enter the Boneyards. I smirked, not showing the strain I felt invading his alchemic-addled mind. "And aga–"

"By the Night Bitch, stop it!" he cried.

"Lynas Granton," Charra repeated.

"Fine!" Bardok said, rubbing his cheek. "Look, I don't need the trouble. It's got nothing to do with me. He was importing some goods for a client, that's all, I swear."

"Which client?" Charra asked.

He shrugged. "You think I ask for names in my line of business?"

"So what did he wear then?" she snarled. "Height? Accent?"

"Didn't see his face, hid it under the hood of his robes," he said. I exchanged glances with Charra. "Medium height, slim build, bad fake accent."

"Fake accent?" Charra asked.

Bardok nodded. "Trying to sound like a Docklander, but he wasn't. Was one o' those rich slicks from the Old Town."

I mulled that over for a few moments. "What was Lynas importing for you?"

"Expensive wines," he said. I glared, so he swallowed and continued. "Leastways it came in big jars. Just a normal shipping contract, but it were right queer the way it was collected. I swear I don't know more. The Harbourmaster – he's the one who'd know where the things came from."

"Is he also where you got the mageblood you're on?" I asked.

He licked his lips, nodded. "I… yes. He's the only one that has any supply in the whole city. He has contacts abroad."

I frowned. "So what happened when these jars arrived?"

"Lynas came to notify me he had them in stock."

Charra's eyes lit up. "And then you contacted your client to pick it up?" she said. "Where?"

Bardok shook his head. "You got it wrong. He always contacted me after Lynas had been and gone. Guess he wanted a middleman for some reason."

"How did he know they'd arrived?" I asked.

"Fuck knows," Bardok said, scowling. "Ask all the godsdamned beggars. Somebody had eyes and ears on me. Now get out of my shop unless you are buying something.

That's all I know." He was telling the truth for once, so I gladly pulled out of his cesspit of a mind.

"One last thing, Bardok," I said. "When was the last time you saw this client?"

He scowled, hands twitching. "Not since the fat bastard got himself skinned."

I went for him, but wasn't nearly quick enough. Charra's fist rammed into his face, flipping him and the chair over to crash to the floor. His feet rattled off the desk, sending his lamp and collection of objects spilling to the floor. Heart in my throat, I leapt forward to grab the alchemic bomb as the brass cone wobbled, then fell. I caught it with my fingertips and held the damn thing at arm's length, sweating. Charra was oblivious to my terror, her boot pressing down on Bardok's throat. He choked and scrabbled at her leg as his oil lamp teetered on the floor next to a pile of browning papers.

"If there's something you haven't mentioned, now is the time to tell us," she said.

He choked a negative. She sighed and removed her foot from his neck.

I had everything I needed from Bardok, so now it was time to kill him. He had facilitated Lynas' death, even if his hands were clean of the actual deed. I couldn't afford to leave him free to spread tales of my death being greatly exaggerated, and he wasn't worth the risk of using more magic on. Once I would have felt Lynas in the back of my mind urging mercy. I listened for it, but now there was nothing. I reached for Dissever, intent on slitting his throat. His eyes flew wide as he saw death bloom in my eyes.

Charra's hand latched onto my wrist and refused to let go. "He's not worth it, Walker. Leave him be. For now." She stared me down until I reluctantly let go of the knife. As we made to leave I held the bomb ever-so-carefully in one hand and tossed a few silvers onto Bardok's desk. "See, we did come here to buy something after all. Let's hope we don't need to come back for a refund." I glanced at Charra. "You should be thanking her."

He shuddered, nodded.

"We were never here," Charra said, lifting two unlit oil lanterns off hooks on the wall, both sloshing with full reservoirs of oil. She didn't offer him any coin.

He swallowed, grimaced, and clutched his bruised throat. "I beg of you, please fix my wards. They'll kill me without them. Somebody is out to get me."

I ignored him, and it felt good to slam the door behind us and leave that mouldy dungeon behind. I really didn't do well in dark enclosed spaces below ground. It was surprising that Bardok was still alive. With Lynas dead surely his client had no more use for the greedy old weasel? Perhaps he'd thought Bardok didn't know enough to implicate him, or maybe he hadn't got around to ending him yet. I carefully slipped the alchemic bomb into my pocket. It was wildly dangerous, but something like that might prove useful.

"You've grown too cold, Walker," Charra said. "You would have killed him if I hadn't stopped you."

I shrugged. "And?"

"It doesn't suit you. I know the Forging does something to you all, changes a magus' mind in subtle ways to make you loyal, to resist…"

"Losing control," I supplied. "It makes us less prone to emotional instability, amongst other things." *Or it breaks you, like it broke Lynas.*

She nodded. "Nobody will ever believe anything a rat like Bardok the Hock says, and in any case, I've never known you to kill in cold blood like that."

Oh, but I have, Charra. I killed for Byzant on several occasions. And you have no idea what I did to survive before meeting you and Lynas.

She looked up at the gods' towers looming over the Old Town. "Lives are meaningless to alchemic dealers and most of those Arcanum bastards up there. I know you spent ten years on the run, and I do know what it's like being forced to look out only for yourself in order to survive, but be careful you don't end up as heartless as they are. You are better than that."

"I can try to be," I said. It was all I had to offer. Had I really changed that much during the years we had been apart? I had killed six men in the last ten years, mostly for good reasons, and I didn't feel a shred of guilt at the thought of killing Bardok either. Perhaps I was becoming more like those stony-hearted elder magi than I had ever suspected. It was an unsettling thought.

Charra coughed. Then she leant against a wall, hand over her mouth as a full-on coughing fit erupted. When it subsided she cleared her throat. "How he can live in that mouldy slime-pit I don't know. The damp and dust would drive me mad." She cleared her throat again and spat in front of his doorway. I eyed the glob of red-speckled spit and my stomach lurched. It was the same as ten years ago, when she had been ill. I said nothing for the moment, praying I was being paranoid.

We'd both lived in worse places, but I took her point. He had more than enough money to do better than live in that midden, but some people knew where they truly belonged.

She straightened her clothing and started walking toward Pauper's Docks. It was time to roast the Harbourmaster over hot coals.

CHAPTER 16

The woollen dress and cowl Charra insisted I wear prickled my skin, a nauseating reminder of the sensation of crawling lice. She could get me through the gates easily enough but as she was usually accompanied by women I had to masquerade as one to avoid drawing notice. My disguise was passable if I hunched down to hide my height, pulled the cowl up, and hid my scarred face behind veils of hair. I grumbled about it but Charra knew best; if I was going to be noticed then it would be at the gates rather than amongst the unwashed masses of Docklands. If that meant I had to feel like a fool then so be it – I was emphatically not blessed with the bone structure for this sort of thing. Charra found the sight of me shoehorned into a dress amusing. Insufferable woman. For her part, she just threw on an old cloak to hide the short sword hanging at her hip, and looked smug.

We passed though Pauper's Gate and down to the docks. Fortunately she knew the gate guards well enough – and paid enough – to get us in and out without fuss or bothering the sniffer. If the Arcanum ever discovered that little arrangement all involved would be burnt alive.

Once we were out of sight of the wardens Charra lost her composure and started sniggering. "I can't believe you fell for that."

It took me a moment. I looked at my dress. "Oh, you little bitch," I said, careful to keep my voice down. "Don't you dare tell me I didn't need to wear this."

She swallowed and took a deep breath to calm herself, hand clutching her chest. "There was a very good reason for it actually."

I mock-growled. "Your own amusement doesn't count."

"Walker, there is too much darkness in the world just now. We have to enjoy what lighter moments we can. All too soon they will be dead and gone."

I rolled my eyes and lowered my head to hide behind all that hair again. For a moment it felt like old times, and she had got me good again. I was stuck wearing it for a good half hour until I found a quiet corner to strip it off. She was right enough; there wasn't much laughter and joy going around these days. I doubted I'd live long now I was home in violation of my old bargains, so who was I to deny her a few last, good memories of me? Besides, you'd drown in darkness if you couldn't laugh. Life is a farce and death an arse. Charra got that, just one more reason why I loved her dearly.

Pauper's Docks lay outside of Charra's sphere of influence, deeper inside the alchemic syndicates' territories than she usually cared to venture. She didn't exactly see eye to eye with them, and funnily enough any alchemic dealers that happened to stray onto her streets had their legs broken, if they were lucky. It made finding somebody willing to talk to us somewhat problematic, but my coin loosened their tongues. It seemed that the Harbourmaster had gone to ground after the recent assassination, and the local rumour mill didn't have much information on his whereabouts. People were more interested in gossiping about overdue whaling ships and fishing boats lost at sea.

It took a few hours and a small fortune in bribes before we were able to track down the name and description of somebody who had the answers we sought, an Esbanain ex-pirate named Aconia involved in the illicit distilling of dockhouse rums. We found her in one of the dozens of small drinking dens that littered the stretch facing the docks, each shack cobbled together from the same mix of driftwood and scavenged debris.

Charra pulled back the tarred canvas sheet that served as a door and we slipped into a room that reeked of tabac smoke and sweet rum. A ragged young juggler was frantically flinging balls up into the air and flailing to catch them. They bounced off his upturned face to the laugher of the dozen or so people crammed onto barrels and crates. We had been told that Aconia was middle-aged with a harsh look, long black hair tied back out of the way and scarred skin like tanned leather, weathered by decades of salt and sun. The woman matching her description also had a distinctive heavy machete tucked into her belt, and judging from the notches it had seen a lot of use. She was leaning back against the wall, long black boots up on the only table as she chuckled at the juggler's antics. She spotted our scrutiny and sized us up with a glance. I pointedly rubbed my chest, tunic cloth bulging around the hidden money pouch. That got her attention.

She flashed a bawdy grin and inclined her head towards the men occupying the rest of the room, eyes never leaving us. "Be leavin' us now, you dogs. Aconia has business." One tucked the squawking juggler under an arm and carried him out while we took their seats.

Aconia ran her gaze down my scars, noted the hilt of Dissever at my hip, and then looked to Charra, dismissing me as some sort of hired muscle. "So what can Aconia of the Fortuna Esban do for you?" she said.

"We're looking for the Harbourmaster," Charra said. "You know where he is."

Aconia's eyes tightened, jaw muscles flexing. It wasn't a comfortable topic for her. "Ah, my lovelies," Aconia said, licking cracked lips. "Answers depend on how much you can pay. In a hurry, yes?" She set to haggling with Charra like a pair of corvun squabbling over the corpse of a seagull. Aconia's initial reaction bothered me; she didn't strike me as the worrying type. I could have taken her mind and forced her to reveal all she knew, but I refused to become the monster the Arcanum always feared I was. Nor did I want to alarm Charra with a vivid demonstration of what I could do if all it took was a few coins to gain the same information.

Eventually they came to an agreement and I handed Charra my coin pouch. When she passed it back it felt distressingly light.

We followed her along a winding alley past streets deserted due to a collection of tanneries reeking of a heady mix of salt, ammonia and dung. As we approached a row of derelict mossy-stoned workhouses I sensed her tension growing and eased open my Gift, tasting the ether for stray thoughts and emotion. Aconia lit up like a Sumarfuin bonfire, radiating anger. It was not, I thought, directed at us. We stopped before a thick iron-bound door with a grilled peephole slat that would take a battering ram to open. Somebody had glued broken glass to the windowsills to deter climbers.

"This is the place," Aconia said. Her muscles tensed, heart beating quicker, breathing faster, fists clenching.

I was about to say something but Charra beat me to it. "So what do they have on you? Perhaps we can help each other."

Aconia's hand caressed the hilt of her knife, but didn't draw it. I didn't want to see her dead but I'd not bat an eyelid putting her down if she forced my hand.

I stiffened and scanned the rooftops. For a second there

I thought I'd sensed a presence, a hint of movement and a whisper of thought...

Aconia shrugged and lifted her hand free. "My business is my own."

I locked gazes with her. "Fair enough. If things get heated in there, will you stab us in the back?"

"If I stand to gain from it," she said with total honesty.

At least we all knew where we stood. I cracked my knuckles and held out a hand. "No hard feelings. I appreciate that you've been straight with us."

Aconia pursed her lips, stared at my hand for a moment, then her calloused palm slapped against my own. A jolt of my magic stabbed through into her mind. She stared at me with horrified eyes as I cracked open her mind and set my compulsions in place.

I sighed and leaned in close. "I like you, Aconia, and if I'd time left when all of this is done and dusted then I would happily toss a few ales back with you. Sadly, that's never going to happen." I didn't give a rat's arse about meddling in the minds of scum, or in self-defence, but she'd been honest with me and my actions left a sour taste. It was a violation to enter her mind and subvert her will. I hated myself for doing it, but didn't see any safe alternative.

"Stop flirting, Walker," Charra said.

There would be no flirting with her after this, unless I chose to wipe her mind clean afterwards. "Aconia has decided to help us out in there if things go wrong," I said.

For a moment Charra looked confused, then her eyes narrowed. "What did you do to her?"

"Hey, I can be charming when I want to be."

She stared in silence for a few seconds. "We'll have words about this later."

I cursed under my breath. Charra was no fool and I fully understood how uneasy I'd made her: she was only just realising how unprotected she actually was around me, and being vulnerable was something that Charra couldn't abide; she had shaped her entire life around that fear. I didn't think she had ever truly thought of me as a real magus before now, not like those rich pricks up in the Old Town. To her I was a friend first and a magus second, and I'd always been very, very careful not to let her see the worst of what I could. Now she suspected I was more than I claimed.

"If we have to," I said, sighing. "After you, Aconia. Give us a real nice introduction." Her mind screamed at me, but her face smiled.

We followed Aconia to the door and she rapped three times, paused, then four more.

"Who's there?" a gruff voice said from the other side.

"Aconia of the Fortuna Esban. Open up, you dogs."

A slat in the door slid open and a pair of suspicious eyes peered out. "What do you want?"

"Have some people needing to talk to your boss, Clay."

"That so? Well, he doesn't need to talk to them."

"Call your master, dog," Aconia growled. "Have I ever steered you onto rocks? I am trying to pay off my debts, and if you get in my way I will gut you like swine."

The slat clacked shut. Almost a minute passed before they unbarred the door. It swung open and Aconia sauntered straight through, seeming entirely unconcerned. Which was a damn good act considering half a dozen burly men were aiming crossbows at us.

For a supposedly derelict building the insides were in good repair, if a little bare, with only seven chairs and a table complete with dice and piles of coin. At the back of the room a set of stairs led up to the second floor.

A portly balding man with dropping grey moustache and bushy eyebrows stood watching us from behind his wall of muscle. They all wore hard-wearing brown leathers for ease of disguising blood stains. "This better be good, Aconia," he said. One of his men slammed the door shut behind Charra and dropped the bar back into place.

"It always is, Clay," Aconia replied. "These two need a word with Raston."

"The Harbourmaster ain't seeing nobody," Clay said. He drew a knife from his belt and fixed a glare on me.

Charra stepped forward, slowly, her hands kept in clear sight. "He'll want to see us. Tell him that Charra will owe him a favour in exchange for some information."

Clay laughed. "You could be a bloody magus for all I care. I got my orders. You'll bleed out the same as any other ugly bastard. The alchemic syndicates will thank me for it."

Charra's lips tightened. "Raston is neck-deep in shit. Do you really want to be the one to dunk his head under and tell him to get swallowing? You let him know that Charra wants to talk to him. Right fucking now. Otherwise he'll have more than my boot on his head pushing him under."

Aconia started, staring at Charra. My hastily implanted commands were already starting to break up and she was regaining a measure of control over her body. She was strong-willed alright. But my commands would last until we were done here.

Clay's eyes flicked to his henchmen and their crossbows. "And what's to stop me just killing you and that chewed-face mongrel next to you?" I winked at him in reply. He found that off-putting.

Charra sneered. "You think we didn't plan for that? We'd be fucking stupid to come in here without any backup waiting outside." She shook her head. "Every one of you will die in excruciating agony if you so much as lay a finger on us." Her bluffing was superb, totally calm and very reasonable. I couldn't have done better myself. "All we need is a few answers from Raston, nothing more. And a favour from me is worth more to him than your lives."

Clay ground his teeth and put away his knife. "Fine." He scowled at his men. "They move, you shoot." He stomped up the creaking stairs.

I relaxed, glad that blood didn't need to be shed. For a second there it seemed a civilized meeting with the Harbourmaster would be too much to ask for. Sadly we still needed to suffer the tedious back and forth of bargaining and threats in order to get the actual truth out of him.

Clay screamed. His cry cut off to a gurgle.

Four of Clay's men dropped their bulky crossbows, drew knives, and charged upstairs, leaving behind a pair of nervous guards with itchy trigger-fingers.

The men upstairs roared in challenge, briefly. A few seconds later they flopped back down the stairs in a crimson mist of arterial spray, each dying of a single lethal cut to the throat.

"Run!" I said to Clay's remaining men. They dropped their crossbows and fled into the street.

Power flooded into my body, strengthening muscles and quickening reactions beyond human limits. My senses were pin-sharp, mind reaching ahead, Dissever finding its way into my hand. Weakening spurts of blood spattered my boots as I took the steps three at a time up to the landing and launched myself into the Harbourmaster's room faster than anybody could possibly react.

The room was cluttered with ledgers and shelves groaned with sheaves of parchment. In the corner lay a pile of smuggled Escharric artefacts, a fortune in pottery and statuettes, coins and inscribed tablets. The room was as empty of life as the Escharric desert itself. Clay lay crumpled at the feet of an older man, dead on his chair, a single puncture wound gaping between skull and spine. The assassin had killed them both. If Clay hadn't had the bad luck to go upstairs at that exact moment then he'd still be alive and the assassin would have slipped away without anybody noticing. I cursed, scanning the room. A breeze set loose window boards creaking, boards with nails torn free of the sill. I peered out and up. Specks of dust drifted down from the roof.

I stepped out and swung myself up. Steel flicked out at my face before I found my footing. Dissever came up, shearing through the twisted steel hilt of a grey-clad assassin's knife. Taking advantage of the momentary surprise, I grabbed a hold of their suddenly weaponless hand with my left and rammed my knee into their belly. It was a woman, eyes widening in shock behind a black leather mask as she crashed down in a clatter of tiles.

"Didn't expect that, did you?" I snarled, leaping on her. "Who sent you?" I crushed her against the roof with brutal strength.

Her own knee snapped up into my belly like a kick from a horse – far too strong for a normal woman. I gasped in pain as her blow launched me backwards off the roof. The ground rushed to meet me but an outflung hand caught the window sill and I jerked to a stop, arm nearly wrenched from the socket, broken glass gouging skin. If I hadn't had magic reinforcing my body I'd be a broken mess on the street below.

I hauled myself back up. The assassin was already two rooftops away, steps flowing with unnatural grace and speed. I had badly underestimated her. She was a mageborn with magic-enhanced physical abilities.

I leapt over the gap to the next rooftop. It was daylight and sniffers weren't likely to loiter this far from the city walls. To the pyre with subtlety – she'd just offed our best lead. In the same manner I'd killed the warehouse guard, I gathered my power and struck at her mind, hoping her stunted Gift would allow her to survive it.

She stumbled, fell, but was back on her feet in seconds; seconds too late: I had already closed the distance. I leapt onto her rooftop, fist lashing out. She spun, leaned to one side, and casually deflected my blow with one hand while the other smashed into my stomach. Air exploded from my lungs and I doubled over. Her elbow cracked into my skull as I fell. She stamped on my hand while I was down, heel grinding, forcing me to let go of Dissever. I grabbed for her leg and she pulled back, cloth tearing. My fingers brushed dark skin. I had her!

Magic roared into her, throwing her body into spasm. We rolled across the roof struggling mentally, coming to a rest with me on top. Her will was stone, but I hacked my way in, exposing layer after layer of rocky strata. Her fingers clawed at my eyes. I blocked, tried to push her arm down and pin it to the roof. Her arm didn't move. Instead she shoved me aside and started to beat me like a fishwife beating a dirty rug. She was stronger than me, faster, better, and she hadn't spent the last ten years lost in ale cups. The heel of her hand thudded up into my jaw. I saw stars and made a feeble attempt to bring my hands up to ward off the inevitable deathblow. To my surprise, instead she made a run for it.

That was a mistake. I'd been in her head already, and that made it easy to get back in. She should have pressed her advantage in hand to hand. I gathered my will and speared deep into her. Her legs stopped working and she fell. I approached as she groggily tried to rise, and failed.

"It's over," I said.

"Think so?" she rasped. A length of fine chain flicked out from her wrist, weighted hooks embedding themselves in my coat. She gave a mighty pull and I lurched towards her. She seized my leg in one hand, the other going for my crotch.

Panicked, I forced my will through the last of her mental defences.

I heard a creak of gutstring and wood off to one side of the roof. Charra had climbed up a ladder and was aiming a crossbow at the assassin. Her finger squeezed. I sensed the assassin's instinctive urge to spin around and use me as a shield – immediately discarded – then her utter horror. In that moment I knew her thoughts. I knew her. Terror iced my spine.

"No!" I screamed, blocking the shot, far too late to stop it.

String thunked against crossbar. The bolt flashed past my leg, taking a chunk of cloth with it. I sagged in relief. Charra had been able to force the shot wide at the last moment.

"Have you gone horseshit mad?" Charra said, dropping the crossbow and clambering onto the roof with a knife in her hand.

I swallowed, then carefully removed the immobilized assassin's mask.

Layla.

CHAPTER 17

Charra's jaw dropped, as did her knife. Her stomach heaved as if she was about to be sick.

I stepped back to give them space, rubbing my many new bruises. "Want me to release her?"

Charra's glare could have melted steel, torched entire villages and boiled oceans. I slunk out of the girl's mind with utmost care, like she was on fire and I was driest tinder. Layla shuddered once, and then rose to her feet, face composed.

"Explain yourself, daughter," Charra said through clenched teeth.

Layla edged away from her mother. "I disposed of an alchemic-peddling piece of filth. What of it?"

She had a fair point. As damned inconvenient as the timing was.

Charra glanced at the leather mask in my hand, hissed, plucking at Layla's clothes. "These are not your own. You murder people for coin now? Is this how I raised you?"

"I..."

"I gave you everything I never had: hot food, a soft bed, love, security, education. A chance for a good life. And this is how you repay me? You know what I went through w–" She cut off, glaring furiously in my direction. The view of the distant Old Town suddenly demanded my attention.

"Mother, you cannot–"

Charra lifted her hand, palm up. "Shut your mouth, you stupid little girl. Pretty words won't cover up what you are."

Layla's face froze. "And you haven't killed people, mother? How can you claim this is any different?"

The crack of hand on skin made me glance back. Layla's cheek bloomed an ugly red. "Don't you dare," Charra said, angrier than I had ever seen her. "I killed because I had to. You think I had any choice?" She caught me looking and cut off what she was about to say next. My eyes fixed on the gods' towers wreathed in cloud.

"And as for the alchemic dealers," Charra continued, "they all know my rules. The first time, you get warned not to deal alchemics on my streets, then you get your legs broken. If it happens again, you die. You rape, murder or enslave? Then the Smilers cut you up. Simple rules. Good rules. I don't go off murdering people in their own homes. Nor do I take coin for ending a life." Her hands shook with fury. "People's lives are not commodities to be bought and sold!"

Oh gods, I thought. No wonder this was hitting Charra hard: she had been property.

"And another thing, daughter," Charra said. "That man was our last solid lead on your father's murder."

"What? No. That's not... I was told–"

"How are we supposed to ask a corpse what he had your father importing?"

"Layla," I said. Charra shot me a venomous look but I steeled myself and ploughed ahead. "Did you have anything to do with getting rid of an alchemic-dealer called Keran? Or a gang called the Iron Wolves that claimed a part of the Warrens?" She'd also been behind that neatly done assassination in the gambling den, but I thought it better not to mention in front of Charra that she'd been in the Scabs. One scandal at a time.

Her mouth clamped shut, but I could read the answer in her body language well enough. Perhaps not personally, but she was involved somehow. The temptation to pull the information from her mind was powerful.

"Who commissioned you?" I asked.

As expected, she said nothing. She physically couldn't. The group she apparently belonged to had a magus or some sort of artefact to enforce the silence of their members. I would be able to break through that sort of geas though, given time.

Layla sighed. "I can say that somebody claiming to be an altruist is behind all of this," she said. "Somebody rich, powerful, and anonymous. They wished to see Setharis cleansed of undesirables and provided a list of criminals for removal."

"But why the Harbourmaster?" I asked. "Why now?"

Layla glared at me, fingering a knife. She might feel besieged by her mother, but she didn't really know me or owe me anything. Whatever Charra's opinion, Layla saw me as a threat. My fault for getting so angry at Charra for sharing my secrets with her. "It took me some time to locate his latest bolthole. He helps the syndicate lords bring in alchemics and slaves from the continent. He profits from pain and flesh."

"As it turns out, so do you, Layla," Charra added. "You profit from pain and dead flesh. Just what do you think assassins are? Some merry band of avengers righting wrongs?" She spat at Layla's feet.

"I think no such thing!" Layla snapped. "I am under no illusions as to what we are. I'm no hero. I pick and choose my own contracts, mother. It's not the same. I am cutting out the rot."

"Or so you think," I said. "They've been damnably clever."

Layla glared at me. "What do you mean?"

"Don't you find it a huge coincidence that you just happen to be killing the very people who might be able to give us answers about your father's murder? I'd wager good coin that somebody is getting twisted pleasure out of making his daughter dance to their twisted tune. And even better, they have you thinking it's all your own doing."

Layla lifted a hand to her mouth, looked like she might vomit. "No, I... I didn't mean to. I didn't know."

Charra's face softened. "And that's why you don't kill for somebody else, Layla. Always make it your own choice, if you must. And then you live with the consequences."

Layla's hands clenched, nails digging into her palms and drawing blood. Her eyes went cold, suppressing wild fury. Clearly you didn't get to be an assassin of her prowess without iron discipline and self-control. I'd felt her mind, and she had barrels of the stuff to spare.

Charra reached for her daughter. "You will come home with me right this second."

Layla shuddered, then spun and leapt across to the next rooftop, fleeing as fast as she could. Charra started after her but I seized her arm.

"Let her go," I said. "She needs to figure this out on her own." Charra tried to pull away, but I held on tight until her daughter was long gone.

She didn't cry, didn't show any emotion whatsoever. She felt numb, and didn't look at me as she descended the ladder.

"Charra..." I didn't have the faintest idea of what I could say, had no clue how to help.

"Leave it be, Walker. She's big and ugly enough to make her own mistakes. She doesn't hang onto her mam's skirts anymore." She paused in her descent. "Was she telling the truth or was that all an act? I don't know her as well as I thought."

"Layla wasn't lying," I said. "She's not the heartless thing you fear she's become. Not yet anyway."

"How can you possibly know that?" she growled.

"I know."

She said nothing as we made our way down to street level. Charra was in a daze, not noticing the people gathering on the street to stare into the building, or the suddenly hushed chatter from people spotting my bloodstained boots. I was acutely aware that the wrong people might recognize Charra and draw conclusions. This deep in syndicate territory I didn't have a hope of protecting her if they mobbed us. I brushed a veil of hair across the unscarred side of my face to give me some disguise but resisted the urge to hunch down again – that would get me marked as having something to hide. Instead I stood tall and tried to look at ease. Just another scruffian out on the streets.

Her friendly wardens and sniffer spotted Charra and waved us through without fuss. She didn't even acknowledge them. We passed through the hubbub of the market, tension rising with every step, and we were halfway up Fisherman's Way when she stopped dead. A sick feeling rose up my gullet – she was going to discuss what I'd done to Layla, about what I did to people's minds.

I finally found my voice, tried to divert the subject. "I don't know what to say," I said. "At least she can take care of herself. She was more than capable of killing me up there. She went easy on me." I stopped in the street, a horrible suspicion occurred and somehow I was certain it was true, another flake of that locked-away secret ripped loose. "Charra, Layla is mageborn. After what happened to her father during the Forging, you never sent her for testing, did you?"

She shook her head. "After what they did to Lynas? I would never allow those butchers to lay a finger on my daughter.

Lynas took care of it just before you left. He arranged forged papers proving she had already been through the testing."

No, he hadn't. Neither Lynas nor Charra had that sort of influence. Their safety was my payoff from the deal I'd made and I'd made him believe it. They had no need to feel any guilt over my exile; that truth I kept for myself.

The Arcanum could not risk magic running wild, or disloyal magi and mageborn working against Setharii interests. There were so many checks and protections in place to prevent such things that even the Archmagus and the High Houses were helpless to interfere. Only a god had the sort of clout necessary to fake that. Thinking about it made my head hurt, literally.

"Walker," Charra said, sounding utterly drained. "Layla is still a stupid child in many ways, still naive. Promise me you will look out for her when – if…"

"Hey, hey – none of that," I said. "We both will. I promise to look out for her if I survive that long."

She gave me a wan smile. "We can hope." She closed her eyes and loosed a deep sigh. When they opened again it was the old, harder Charra. Her dark eyes nailed me to the wall. I swallowed and prepared to weather the storm.

"Have you ever done that to me? Been in my mind?" she said. "Changed things?"

There it was, the beginnings of fear and paranoia. "Of course not," I said. "I'd never do that to you."

"All these years you led me to believe that you were just a swindler with a few clever magic tricks, maybe a little more. You pretended all that raw talent as a magus was wasted on you. You, just a copper-bit trickster? After what I've seen today? Hah! Do you take me for a fool?"

I hung my head, waiting for the righteous anger.

"You're a bloody fool, Walker. I've always known that you were so much more than you ever said, and I always suspected you were hiding your real power. Why keep it from me?"

After so long hiding it all away from her I found it difficult to voice. "I didn't want to scare you."

"Did it never occur to you that if I didn't trust you with my life then we wouldn't be friends at all?" she said. "You of all people should know that I don't trust easily. Just because you can do something doesn't mean you will."

My head lifted. She looked exhausted, worn paper-thin. She patted me on the arm. "You always seemed to live without a care, drinking too much, getting into stupid scrapes and dangerous schemes. It was hard for anybody to see you as anything other than an unreliable, weak-willed, piece of shit on a mission of self-destruction. But that was all just for show, wasn't it? A grand con. But then you always were good at fooling people."

She was mostly right. But there was a large and twisted part of me with a scurrilous tongue that constantly urged me to dive headfirst into danger, to endanger my life for no good reason.

"You think I didn't do some digging after you ran away?" she said. "Lynas' lips might as well have been nailed shut." She looked at me funny, as if pondering for a second if maybe he couldn't have said anything; but no, Lynas was just Lynas, he'd have taken a secret to the grave if asked to.

A moment of pain as part of me reminded myself that he did take them to his grave.

"I knew that other magi distrusted you, thought you were scum barely worth noticing," Charra continued. "But in truth you are a really nasty piece of work, aren't you, Walker? Given what you did to Aconia and Layla I'd wager you are far more powerful than anybody ever suspected." She locked gazes with me. "No tricks, Walker. Cards on the table now – tell me everything."

Unable to meet her gaze, I studied my hands, wondering if I really knew that myself. "Have you ever heard the old stories of the tyrants who ruled the tribes of man long before the empire of Escharr arose?" I said.

"The enslaver-kings?" she replied, using the old Ahramish name.

I met her gaze, nodded, pointed a finger at myself. "In Kaladon they just called us tyrants."

It took her a moment. "You?" She snorted. "As if."

I didn't say anything more, didn't need to as my sincerity filtered through.

She swallowed. "That's what you did to Aconia, and what you were doing to Layla?"

"Exactly. That's why the grand deception. That's why I've always downplayed what I can do. I told them I could only use my power through touch, but that was also a lie I told for good reasons. The magi don't hate me, Charra, they fear me. Not because of what I am, but for what I might become."

She squeezed my hand. "Don't be a fool. You will never be like that. However much of an annoying prick you are."

I offered a half-hearted smile. "Uh, thanks. I guess."

"If you were that way inclined then you wouldn't have spent half your life penniless and puking in a gutter – you'd be off in some marble palace somewhere living like a lord and drinking yourself blind on fine wine. You wouldn't be slumming it with a godsdamned lady of sheets to find out who killed an old friend."

"Charra–"

She waved a dismissive hand. "I own the words, Walker. They can't hurt me. Other people won't forget what I was, so neither should I. And I meant every word."

"Thank you," I said, looking up at the grey sky as a soft drizzle started falling. *Don't let her see you tearing up like a wee babe*. It was such a relief to hear her say that. I had always been adamant that I would never become crazed with power like everybody expected me to, but the lure of magic was so subtle that sometimes I woke in a cold sweat wondering if I'd changed and just didn't know it, or if some creeping doom was gradually overtaking me. Would I even notice? It was never far from my mind. My first physical changes had been so gradual that it had taken me a year to realize I had developed senses keen beyond normal human ability.

I grinned at her. "Hah, I guess as long as you're around there is nothing to fear. You wouldn't be slow in telling me I'm in the wrong."

She looked away. "True, I wouldn't." She seemed to crumple into herself. The whole thing with Layla must have finally sunk in. She cleared her throat and looked me in the eye with a gaze as cold as winter and with just about as much life. "Just so we are clear," she said. "If you ever do that to my daughter again, I will kill you." And she meant it.

I swallowed. "Noted."

She looked me in the eye. "Thank you for finally telling me what you really are. I know it couldn't have been pleasant."

"Since we are exchanging secrets," I said, "how about you tell me what you really are? You're no lady of sheets and you never have been. You've always been too self-assured and much too handy with a knife. We've been dancing around secrets all our lives. Let's be done with it. What does it matter now?"

She smiled coldly, gazing up at the sky. "We both wear masks, it seems. I was six, I think, when my parents died from the Grey Pox."

I winced, remembering that disease running rampant through the Warrens and the grey seeping lesions that had consumed my aunts and uncles, my cousins and my friends. It was not a swift death.

"A group of alchemic dealers took me in off the streets. There were too many starving orphans after the pox struck for anybody to care about one or two going missing. They trained me to kill. A child assassin can reach places, can cater to certain tastes that adults can't. I lost count of the lives I took to hide their activities." When she looked back at me some of that old, wild Charra reappeared in her eyes, a hint of desperation as I now recognized.

"They kept me like a pet. I was sick of watching people living their lives, laughing and playing with friends and family. And then ending them. You have no idea what that does to a child." She tapped her chest, "I was empty in here. All I had were my kills and serving their so-called grand purpose."

I swallowed. "I'm so sorry."

She shrugged. "I'm just glad I got out. One night our leader Anders staggered in from the tavern with a girl on his arm. He was so drunk he couldn't get it up. The girl laughed, laughed in our glorious leader's face!" She glanced at me, meeting my eyes for a moment before her gaze jerked skyward again. "You need to understand that I'd never dreamed anybody would dare such a thing. Anders snapped her neck and dumped the body in an alley. It wasn't for any grand purpose, it was just murder. It hit me then, young as I was – it was all just murder. That's all it had ever been. I think I went a little mad."

She cleared her throat. "They would never let their property leave, so I waited for them to fall asleep, then cut my way out and made a run for it. I met Lynas and you a few days later and I had thought about covering my tracks afterwards, but I'm very glad I didn't."

"Me too," I said softly. We'd had no idea we were so close to getting our throats slit. She didn't need sympathy and she didn't want forgiveness, she just wanted me to finally know what she had gone through. No wonder she had dedicated her life to ridding the streets of alchemic dealers and to helping the lords and ladies of sheets escape the gutters.

She sighed. "I figured that claiming to be a lady of sheets sounded much more wholesome than admitting I cut throats for alchemic dealers. It's certainly a more honest profession."

She paused, a hand covering her mouth as she coughed and cleared her throat. I suspected she was struggling not to throw up. "It would seem that the apple does not fall far from the tree," she said through gritted teeth. "She betrayed everything I went through, but I blame myself for hiring the best fighting masters gold can buy. I've been a blind fool not to think that one or two might have been scouting for such a rare talent." Her eyes met mine again, now filled with rage. "They seduced my daughter right in my own home!"

She shuddered, and drew her cloak tight. "Well that was depressing. Best we head back to that ruined temple. We're wasting time, and that's the one thing I don't have to spare." She wasn't in the mood for small talk after that, and I knew she would never speak of her past again.

CHAPTER 18

"I'm so sorry," she said, standing before the entrance to the Boneyards. "It's our only lead." She retrieved a small flask of whisky from a concealed pocket in her cloak and handed it over. I took a big gulp.

She was right, but it was all I could do not to piss myself. *You need to do it, for Lynas.* It took me a few minutes to compose myself and shrug off the terror. "I survived it once and I can do it again." I tried to put bravado in place of abject terror. "You bringing along some of those big brawny guards of yours?"

She shook her head. "No, they'd just get in the way in narrow tunnels. I couldn't ask them to risk their lives like this, not down there. I'm expendable, and I know exactly what I'm getting myself into."

She was hiding something, but I had already pushed her more than enough in the last few hours. When we arrived at the temple I stashed the alchemic bomb into a hole in the wall. If it exploded amidst these plague-haunted ruins then at least nobody would die. I was certainly not taking it underground with us. What if I slipped and fell? The thought brought me out in goosebumps.

From the rooftops an entire flock of corvun watched us in eerie silence, their black eyes unblinking as we descended into the pit. A tad unnerving, but nothing compared to the dark, narrow entrance to the Boneyards that threatened to swallow me whole. I couldn't look at it without breaking out in a cold sweat, and was about to take another fortifying swig of whisky, lips already touching the neck of the flask, when Charra grabbed my arm.

"You need to stay sharp," she hissed, prising the flask from my death-grip and stuffing the cork back in. She stowed it away out of reach. "We will have earned a drink afterwards."

I stared into the yawning darkness. The walls squeezed in around me, suffocating. I shuffled backwards, mouth ash dry, and then forced myself to stop. I couldn't run: this had to be what Lynas was trying to tell me in his last moments by sending me a vision of the Boneyards. He had been telling me to look below the ground for answers.

"Walker," she said, her hand firm on my back. "Edrin, I need you, but I will go in there alone if I must."

I shook my head. "Stop. You know that's cracked." I took a deep cleansing breath. "It's far too dangerous down there. The sort of danger that needs magic, or an army."

She knew that fine well, and said nothing as she adjusted the short sword buckled at her waist. We both knew there was no way I would allow her to go in alone. It was just taking me a while to gird my loins for battle – whatever that actually involved. It was just a phrase to me but I had a vague notion that it was something to do with lifting the hem of your robe up and tying it around your groin to stop your cock from flapping about near all that sharp steel. I wished I could do something similar to strap down my imagination. It was strange to think that in the days of ancient Escharr robes had been common garb; by law only magi and priests were allowed to wear robes within Setharii lands, and–

"Walker!"

I blinked, dragged out of my escapist musings. "Right. Yes. Sod it. Let's go." I lifted my lantern and stomped into the tunnel without a backwards glance. If I were to look back at the diminishing circle of light my courage would crumble. Instead I focused on the light ahead and on putting one foot in front of the other. Most of all, I focused on Charra, Lynas, Layla, and on just why I found myself back in these foul catacombs I'd vowed never to set foot in again.

A soft moaning breeze cooled my sweat-slick forehead – the Boneyards' dank breath. The tunnel of ancient stone blocks swallowed me. The light from the entrance dwindled and I slowed, panting, the handle of the lantern slippery in my grip. I couldn't do this. I had to turn back, to–

"Did I ever tell you why I got together with Lynas instead of you?" Charra said. She never had, and her voice was incredibly welcome right then.

"No." I couldn't say anything more, voice catching in my throat, but she continued anyway, to give me something to focus on. It took everything I had to keep moving forward.

"Oh, he was cute enough, and both kind and funny, but he also made me feel safe," she said. "He wasn't like you and me."

"Innocent?" I croaked.

"No, not that. How could he be after spending so much time around us? It was more like some part of him just didn't get the point of lying and backstabbing. You know?"

"I do," I said. It was the very thing I hated the most about the Arcanum. Her voice was soothing, and intimate despite all the years apart.

Her boots squelched in the mud with each step. "I found it so refreshing. His world was so much better than ours. So bright and shiny. Hopeful where we always expect the worst from people."

With everything she had been through, somebody else might have called her damaged, and deduced that was why she'd wanted somebody safe. The simple truth was that she recognized Lynas had been made of something finer and better than we were. And with her history that had been like finding buried gold, even if they hadn't lasted.

"All those years," I said. "And you couldn't just tell me that? I must have asked you a dozen times." We both knew that I'd never been in love with her, or ever wanted her that way beyond a few fleeting boyish desires – it would have felt unnatural and ruined our friendship. No, we were family and I was just being nosey, whereas she liked to keep her cards close to her chest, which was not the best combination of attributes.

"I'm just as awkward as you then, I guess," she replied. "Well, that and you are a big, ugly, gloomy bastard."

I laughed. In this claustrophobic pit I actually laughed! The panic retreated to a scream inside me. "I've missed you," I admitted, trudging forward. "And just for the record: you've always been too skinny for my tastes, and you have a foul mouth. It's not attractive at all." The tunnel twisted round to the right and led into the remains of an ancient slime-covered cellar strewn with rotted refuse.

It was all too similar to the room I'd been trapped in once before, but this room had two yawning exits. The bone-walled tunnel to my right led down, cut steps descending into the depths of the basalt hill. I froze, hands shaking, lantern light dancing across the walls. Charra pushed past me and bent low to study the ground. Most of the footprints leading down to the right had filled with water, with long lines gouged on either side from whatever they'd been dragging.

Charra followed a set of footprints as they split off from the others, heading left to the entrance of another tunnel, this one smooth and organic, not formed by the hands of men but by some strange natural process. Empty niches lined the wall where skulls had once been placed to rest, but it looked to me like they had all been purposely cracked open and scattered across the floor. That trail ended at the entrance where mud had been ploughed by fresher prints. These prints were from no human, had taloned toes splayed out.

Air stirred my hair. My enhanced senses screamed as a pressure wave of warmer air pushed out of that lefthand tunnel, the reek of corrupt magic billowing with it. I grabbed Charra's arm and yanked her back.

Something white and glistening surged from the darkness, fangs snapping shut on the air right where Charra had been standing. It had been human once, mottled hide covered in weeping sores, its empty breasts flapping loose. The face was broken and stretched into a fanged maw crusted with pus and filth, the hands and feet warped into the claws of a beast. But the eyes were wholly and unmistakably human, screaming silently. The thing mewled, sniffed the air, head lolling round to face me. I dropped the lantern and drew Dissever, bloodlust singing through me. The thing's jaw split wide, revealing a squirming pink tongue and jagged yellowed teeth. It leapt for me.

Dissever sheared through one pale limb. Hot blood spurted across my face. My left hand clamped around its throat, barely keeping snapping teeth from tearing off my nose. My battle blood rose, heart hammering, barely feeling the claws raking down my shoulder, cutting through coat and flesh.

We rolled across the floor. I stabbed, missed, stabbed again, this time hitting flesh. Its mind was a churning mass of animal instinct, barely human. I forced my way in through the maelstrom, seeking some sort of mental purchase. It rolled on top of me and an elbow crashed into my forehead, snapping my head back to expose my throat. Claws cut down.

A steel blade crunched through the thing's skull, the point quivering right in front of my eyes. Charra wrenched her short sword out and flicked off blood and brains. The thing twitched once and collapsed, pinning my legs beneath it. I rammed Dissever into its side, and just for good measure stabbed it twice more.

"Thanks," I gasped, wriggling out from beneath it. In death it looked pitiful, just skin and bone instead of a horrific danger. But with magic, appearances could be wildly deceptive. My shoulder started throbbing.

"No," Charra said. "Thank you. Was that a daemon?"

I shook my head. "Just some poor wretch with more Gift than sense, corrupted by something it couldn't control. That's why the Arcanum forces all Gifted through the Forging: it breaks you or it makes you. This sort of corrupted creature cannot be allowed." I neglected to mention it could also be the end result of habitual mageblood use – I didn't like to think that in some small way I'd been a part of that trade.

Charra shivered, her eyes avoiding me as she picked up her lantern.

I nudged the corpse, jerked back as its muscles twitched. I leaned in closer and lifted its chin with the flat of my blade. A red-raw wound circled its throat. I looked up at Charra and she furrowed her brow.

"Collared," she whispered, fingers absently rubbing her own neck. "And for quite some time, I'd say."

I held Dissever ready in my right hand and the lantern clutched in the left as I advanced down the tunnel it had emerged from. Dissever's bloodlust kept my fear at bay.

The tunnel opened into a smooth bubble of rock with a bricked-up exit at the far side. Two sets of shackles dangled from iron spikes hammered into the walls, the collar and wristbands hanging empty. Charra gasped, eyes wide. "Two!" She swung round, her sword up and ready.

"Don't worry," I said, pointing over to one side, to what I'd taken to be a pile of sticks at first. "Looks like she got hungry." Looking closer, it was a heap of gnawed bones that had been cracked open to get at the marrow.

She lowered her sword. "Guard dogs?"

"Looks like. Poor twisted bastards."

I peeled back bloodsoaked wool from my shoulder to check the damage, grimacing in pain. Angry red furrows bled freely.

"Stay still," Charra said. She held up the lantern and peered at the wounds. "Can't see too well down here but your skin looks inflamed."

I cursed. That blasted thing's claws had probably got filth into the wounds. Normally I wouldn't have been too worried, since even for a magus I was a fast healer, but that thing had been corrupted by magic, and those sorts of changes came with danger of magical poisons and plagues. Joy. Still, better me than Charra. UnGifted people were so brittle.

She told me to stop squirming. Her whisky flask was open and in her hand. I winced, knowing what was coming. She poured the alcohol over the wounds. Searing pain left me shaking, my jaw clenched so as not to cry out.

Charra groaned.

My own pain forgotten, I looked her over. "Are you hurt?"

"No, it's not that," she said. "It's criminal to waste good whisky on your sorry hide."

I huffed. Good old black humour; after all these years she still knew me well. If by some miracle we survived all of this then I'd need to come up with a spectacular revenge for the dress and the whisky comment.

We backtracked and turned right, feet crunching through bone shards as we followed the trail. My battle blood was still up, and Dissever was far from satisfied with feasting on something already half-dead. My claustrophobic panic retreated into a grim and blessedly numbing acceptance, allowing me to open my Gift. The tunnels oozed magic, a miasma seeping from the very rock hanging like a fog in front of my Gifted eyes. It made any sort of magical detection impossible.

We doggedly followed their winding trail through passageways so choked with fresh rubble that we were forced to scuttle along like rats, cheeks brushing against the remains of the dead. Picking our way round a ledge above a gaping chasm, I accidently dislodged a rock and we listened for it hitting the bottom. No sound ever came. I kept Dissever in my hand, relying on its anger to distract me from dwelling on the tons of stone crushing down above my head. It kept me sane.

Legend said the tunnels and caverns were wont to lead to different places at different times, and whatever the cause, maps of the Boneyards had never proven reliable beyond a few years of their penning. I was paranoid we would lose their trail, our only clue to Lynas' murderer. And then we did, the tunnel ahead blocked by a very recent rock fall. We frantically searched for signs, finally finding a single boot print in the dust pointing into a crevice and up a crude staircase into an area of more solid human construction. Scents of honeysuckle and sage enticed us into a high-vaulted chamber of white marble blocks and tumbled pillars of faded beauty. The whole chamber slanted to one side, floor crazed with cracks, as if over centuries an entire building had sunk down through the stone. A broken statue of a woman lay on its side, half buried in rubble and shattered pottery. Her arms and face had been destroyed long ago, but there was still a lingering echo of once-powerful benign magic.

It felt so peaceful and open, a soothing balm to my besieged mind. There were no skeletal remains as a reminder of my own approaching demise. It seemed that even the priests of the Lord of Bones found no cause to bring the dead here. The pain in my shoulder subsided to mere gentle warmth. I took a deep breath of fresh air and forced Dissever back into its sheath – which it resisted – and then became aware of my utter exhaustion. Charra settled on the floor, stretching out cramped and sore muscles. She yawned, infecting me with one of my own. Gods, I was so tired. We needed to rest.

My eyes were gritty and I found it difficult to focus. I sat down, resting my back against a warm pillar. My eyelids started to droop. A sudden spike of interest forced them back open to squint at broken pottery piled at the foot of the statue. Below the potsherds a dark stain had spread out across the cracked marble. A plug of forest-green wax still clinging to the broken neck of a wine jar stirred a vague recollection of having seen that exact colour somewhere before. Drained and aching, it was difficult to think, but I struggled to stay awake – this was important.

I groaned and heaved myself up, dragging my sorry arse over to squat down beside the statue. The pottery was still covered with a sticky residue of what looked like red wine. I dipped my fingers in and lifted it to my nose. It smelled oddly metallic. I dabbed it on my tongue. Tasted of iron – and magic! A fiery surge of alchemic euphoria blew away the cobwebs of exhaustion, like nothing I had ever experienced before. I felt like a god! By the Night Bitch, no: I'd just supped mageblood. The life-force of other magi surged through my body.

My mental fog was blown away by alchemic-fuelled storm winds. "Son of a sow," I growled, snatching up the disc of wax. It was the exact shade I'd found in Lynas' warehouse. I dashed it to the ground and crushed it beneath my feet. Then I stamped on the pottery, exulting in destroying the remains. This was why they killed Lynas – he had been unwittingly importing mageblood, and when he found out what they were doing, the virtuous fool must have tried to stop them. It sounded like something he would do. I staggered to and fro, panting, hands clenching spasmodically as alchemic and strange magics both took hold, wanting to rip and tear something apart. The air took on an acrid, sour scent.

I shook with fury. I'd kill them. Destroy them. Cut them to pieces and swim through rivers of blood. I'd tear into their minds; turn them into my wailing playthings. I would – *No!* This wasn't me; I refused to let myself become everything that I despised. This was the alchemic's influence.

Wrongness assailed me. The air stank like a midden, not the sweetly floral scent I had smelt at first. Neither was the chamber pure white marble, but was instead stained and mottled with a spongy carpet of pale mossy growth. Two mounds of reeking compost lay wrapped in some sort of fibrous cocoon and– Ah. A pair of hob-nailed boots poked out of the bottom of one mound, the tough leather half eaten away. The mageblood smugglers had encountered that recent rock fall and had been forced to carry the jars through this chamber, but some had fallen foul of whatever ancient power lingered in this place.

Charra was curled up on her side and slumbering peacefully. Tendrils of white root had squirmed up from the cracks in the floor and wrapped around her. Where they touched flesh, her dark skin was red and puffy.

"Charra!" She didn't stir at my shout. I charged over to tear at the sticky roots with my bare hands, heedless of the stinging pain. With a sound like straining rope more tendrils writhed up to clutch at my boots. I opened my Gift, reached for power. Unspeakable agony exploded in my head.

I came to a split second later, mid-collapse. Checking my fall, I crashed down to one knee, head ringing from magical backlash. I'd never felt anything like it. It was akin to a thousand people screaming in my mind all at once. Impotent alchemic-driven rage lashed my ego.

I snatched up my lantern and broke it apart, pouring a circle of oil around Charra. I stepped in close and flung the burning wick down. The room flared bright as flames roared up to encircle us. Roots charred with almost animal squeals and withdrew back into the cracks in the floor. What was left I tore from her and flung into the flames. Red-raw fury throbbed inside me but there was nothing more to kill. My stinging hands burned with the itch to rip and tear and – *Charra!* – I shook my head, clearing some of the alchemic haze. I'd fought Dissever's bloodthirsty influence for so long that it helped me shunt the alchemic's effects aside and squash it down to a dull throb of madness in the back of my head.

I slung her over my shoulder, and carefully lowered myself to pick up our one remaining lantern. Seconds trickled by as the surrounding flames waned. I had to time it perfectly because there would be no other chance. An overwhelming malevolent presence emanated from the statue as it creaked into life, stone muscles flexing as a broken and forgotten idol woke to find more clumsy intruders in its temple.

Before I leapt the flames I spat foul insults at the statue, in a medley of languages. The ground rumbled and more cracks spread through marble. A crazed laugh burst from my mouth: it seemed to understand me. Charra snoozed on, a blissful expression on her red-streaked face. I suppressed an irrational surge of anger towards her and cursed the alchemic taint in my body.

As the flames flickered low, pale roots began reaching towards us again. I held onto Charra for dear life and leapt. Fire licked the seat of my trousers, and then I was past, boots pounding across the marble, crushing clutching roots with every step. I could barely see the crumbled archway out of the chamber, lantern light swinging crazily, praying it wouldn't fall or dash against rock and plunge me into suffocating darkness. The presence surged up behind us moments after we passed the archway. The doorway shook from the impact.

I glanced back to see the statue stopped in its tracks, seemingly unable to cross the threshold, hacked-away face turned to regard me. It stood immobile in the doorway, still as stone should. Roots trailed from its feet, burrowing into the cracks and into the cocooned people it was digesting. I wasn't about to wait for it to change its mind and took off as fast as I could manage.

CHAPTER 19

I ran, heedless of direction so long as it was away. Charra grew heavier and heavier until she felt like a lead weight in my arms. My breathing became ragged gulps and my muscles burned and shook. The false strength I'd been imbued with by that dab of alchemic was fading fast, leaving behind a greasy, queasy feeling akin to a whole-body hangover. It was potent stuff. I forced myself on, to create as much distance between us and that thing as possible.

Lathered in sweat, wounds in my shoulder stinging, I slipped and slid down a set of steps and then staggered across a subterranean stream running through a half-collapsed corridor. My head cracked off a low-hanging stalactite and everything went fuzzy for a second. We fell and I bruised my knees trying to keep Charra and the lantern from crashing to the ground.

I placed her down on a dry area and slumped to the floor, chest heaving. We had to be far enough away from that thing now. We had to be, because I didn't have much left to give. The back of my throat burned with a little bile that had forced its way up from the effort. I retrieved the whisky flask from the pocket in her cloak. It seemed to take forever for my jellied muscles to prise the cork free. I took a swig to wash the foul taste of bile and alchemic from my mouth, swilling it around and spitting it out, then a swallow to soothe my burning throat.

Charra slept on, peaceful as a babe. I was on my own, buried somewhere in the dark depths of the Boneyards with only a single lantern, an unconscious friend and unknown thousands of the dead all around me. It hadn't been so bad when we'd had a trail to follow. The darkness closed in around me and my pitiful little light. I started panting, panic rising from within like poisoned water drawn up a well.

"Shite, shite, shite, shite," I muttered, teeth clamped together, eyes screwed shut. My knuckles whitened around the handle of the lantern. Visions of my fate stormed through my mind as I tried to control my fears; if I didn't they would consume me. I had to keep Charra safe and see this bloody debacle through to the end. I'd accepted that I was going to die, but not like this, not in this dread place, gone howling mad and blindly clawing at the walls. I folded my legs beneath me in a meditation position and tried to concentrate, to clear my mind as I had been taught so long ago.

Deep breaths – stuck in an ever narrowing tunnel, unable to turn...

Calm yourself – lantern running out of oil, plunging into darkness...

Peace. Quiet. Relax – crawling things nipping at my flesh, squirming all over me in the dark...

One with natur– buried alive under tons of earth and stone. Corpse dust on my face, in my mouth, choking...

Peac– the revenant's hungry eyes as it rises from its deathbed...

My eyes snapped open as the vision of that old undead thing materialized before me, echoed in every leering skull and scattered bone, a palpable presence hanging in the darkness that resurrected a child's terror. *No – I destroyed you!*

I was going about this all wrong.

Dissever was in my hands as I stood and opened my Gift. Anger and power flooded into me, blasting through the pain barrier caused by alchemic poison. I was a magus. I was no longer that powerless cringing child shivering in terror from crawling bugs and long-dead monsters. I didn't need mind-rotting drugs to feel powerful.

"I am the fucking monster here!" I roared at the vision of the revenant, my voice reverberating back in hollow echo.

I closed my eyes and plunged into absolute darkness. Except, that didn't matter. The air currents washed over skin and super-sensitive hairs, and the earth vibrated with almost imperceptible movement and pressures. In a mess of panic and fear I'd suppressed and forgotten my magic-given gifts. I couldn't see far in my little island of lantern light, but then I didn't need to actually see.

I sensed no malign magic or movement in the tunnels nearby, no revenant creeping towards me in the darkness. An ever-so-slight air current cooled my skin. I took several deep breaths of moist, warm, stale air, and then turned around. The air was slightly cooler in that direction, and a mite fresher. It seemed a possible way out.

I opened my eyes again and stamped down the last remnants of my panic with bloody-minded will. It was still there waiting to break free, but Charra's breathing was ragged and her skin covered in a swollen lattice of angry red streaks. I cursed myself for an idiot and ran to her side, scooping handfuls of cold water from the stream to scrub her exposed flesh to get rid of any lingering poisons. She didn't stir.

"Charra," I said, shaking her. "Charra, wake up. Please wake up." No response. I peeled back one eyelid. She didn't even twitch. Her pupil was huge and dark, not natural.

I gritted my teeth, wishing again that I had the Gift to heal. But, no, all I had was a manipulative curse. All I could do was to get her to somebody that could help, whatever that cost me.

I winced as I hefted her back on my shoulder. Lantern in hand, I followed the hint of fresher air, staggering through a winding maze of dank tunnels and excavated caverns, forced to fortify myself with magic and take frequent breaks to stave off complete exhaustion. I stood at a crossroads, peering into the darkness down each path. Something slammed into rock somewhere down the tunnel to my left, causing stalactites to crack and fall. I shuttered my lantern so only a glimmer of light showed my way, and edged towards the source. Every few years the Arcanum sent coteries of magi into the depths to clear out warped creatures, and if this was an Arcanum party they would have a healer with them.

I made my way down towards the vibrations. Warm, humid air washed over me in rhythmic cycles. As I got closer the air carried a rancid meaty smell akin to a bad Docklands butcher sited next to a tannery.

I carefully set Charra down and propped her up against the wall. "I'll be back soon," I whispered.

It took an almighty force of will to prise my hand from the handle of the lantern, and shuffle forward in the darkness, ever wary of stepping on bones. Gradually my eyes picked up a dim light ahead, and with it, muffled voices.

"Pour it in the pool, not over my feet, you cretin," a man said. "That spill is worth more than your entire village!" At that distance it was difficult to make him out clearly, but his voice was slick with the cultured tones of the Old Town.

I slunk forward, back to the wall, until the tunnel opened out into a torch-lit cavern. The whole space was awash with a hiss of stray magic, masking lesser magical traces. Four rough men in tattered homespun, their skin mottled with rashes and sores and unnatural growths, were pouring the contents of large jars into a pool of black water a hundred paces wide. A dozen empties had been discarded behind them and, sat closer to me, only a single remaining jar remained sealed with green wax. Their robed leader's face was hidden in the shadows of his hood and a pair of fresh corpses lay at his feet. My gut instinctively clenched – he was Gifted, and surely had to be an elder magus from the insanely potent aura of magic that cut through the haze of stray magic. Or something more – a god perhaps.

The men finished and scurried back from the pool. The hooded man pulled back his sleeves and plunged his arms up to the elbow in the water. The aura of power drained away and the air reeked of blood sorcery. At a word his cringing minions tossed in the two corpses. The surface of the water churned to pink froth as something snatched them under.

The ground shuddered. Stalactites fell from above to splash into the black pool. The hooded man turned in my direction and I slipped further behind the safety of the wall, holding my breath as he scanned the cavern. I resumed breathing as he chuckled and said, "How they struggle, trapped so deep below the city. Trusting fools."

I scowled as the sweet scent of blood and alchemical spice reached my nostrils. I recognized the green wax around the necks of those jars and was certain they were pouring mageblood into the pool, more than I had ever believed existed.

It was impossible to obtain that much from a few down-on-their-luck donors. Somewhere, somebody was farming Gifted like cattle, draining their blood and smuggling it into Setharis. But why? What could they possibly gain by pouring it into the water? With that much you could have sold it to amass entire armies of mercenaries.

"Fetch the last of it," the man ordered.

One of his minions scrambled closer to my hiding place and picked up the final jar. It seemed the perfect time to get into his head. Hidden by the magical haze, I eased my Gift open and carefully snuck into the depths of his mind. He was half-deaf and his knee ached from an old breakage. I learned he was a simple, weak-willed country man come to Setharis to find his fortune, and been consumed by the dark underbelly of the city. Sadly his memory was damaged by years of alcohol and alchemic abuse and he knew little of worth, but he was deathly afraid of whatever the magus kept beneath the water. Oh well, he would just have to ask this hooded man a few leading questions. It was a simple task to gently take his reins and guide his lips.

He lumbered towards his master and considered the jar in his hands. I could smell the heady reek of mageblood through his nostrils. "Master, how long until we are ready with... whatever we are doing?"

The hooded man paused, surprised at being questioned. "The date is set and we cannot afford further delay. Three days left until the city is full of lazy peasants fat from food and wine. I had hoped my creature would be fully mature and already able to scale the walls of the Old Town by then – curse that fat fool's interference! Now pour that last jar in unless you want to join it in the pool. In three days you will have all the women, wine and gold I promised you."

Fat fool? I almost said it out loud, catching myself just in time. He was planning something terrible for Sumarfuin. This wasn't some pissy little blood sorcery ritual to bolster a weakling's power; this was on a grand scale, like something straight out of the histories of the fall of Escharr. If the sorcerer could enact a ritual this huge and complex he was dangerous beyond anything I'd ever dealt with. Suddenly the invasion of Ironport seemed a mere portent of far worse to come. My anger grew, causing the minion's knuckles to go white around the jar. I took a deep breath and calmed myself, bidding my puppet to begin pouring slowly. I had to find out everything I could.

My puppet frowned. "That fat fool was a bad man?"

The hooded man sighed and muttered something unintelligible. "Yes, yes, he was the bad man who burned my stockpile and caused so much delay. Now please stop asking stupid questions and pour."

It crystallized in my mind. The green wax and pottery fragments on Lynas' warehouse floor, imports from the Skallgrim lands. The robed man with inhuman strength and daemons at his beck and call. The butchering of mageborn. It all fit together: Lynas had picked up a new delivery from the Harbourmaster and accidently broken a seal on one of the jars, then realized he'd been importing mageblood. When he investigated and found out what it was to be used for, he torched that old temple trying to destroy their whole damn mageblood supply. He had delayed the birth of this monster before running to warn people. They murdered Lynas to cover up the truth, then paid Layla's assassins to slaughter everybody else that might know anything, like the Harbourmaster and the Iron Wolves, and Bardok the Hock huddled alone in his warded shop.

Lynas, you stupid bastard. Why couldn't you have just run away instead of trying to be a hero? Because Lynas wasn't selfish like me. He didn't leave me in the Boneyards to die alone in the dark, and he bloody well wouldn't have turned his back on everybody else. He'd been through the Forging, and that carved loyalty to Setharis into every mageborn's heart, but he'd have done the same by choice even if it cost him his life.

I watched through my puppet's eyes as a bloody hand lifted from the water to caress his master's arm. No, that wasn't water, it was thicker. It couldn't possibly all be mageblood – so, blood of the unGifted perhaps? That meant hundreds or even thousands of bodies. It seemed likely this was where the missing people of Setharis had ended up.

He pulled his glistening hands from the pool and dozens of arms burst from the depths, grasping towards the sorcerer, their human skin replaced with thick grey leathery hide. Faces surfaced – men, women, children, and animal – with mewling cries of hunger. Ropes of flesh and muscle writhed across the surface like the tentacles of some great sea monster. He stroked them, murmuring sweet words. "Hush. You will feed soon."

Hunger and pain blasted through my mental defences. Blind animal rage. All-too human horror. A maelstrom of madness. Overwhelmed, my eyes were drawn to a single face among that vast melded bulk, only now rising from the depths of the pool. Free from the heavy cloak of blood magic, the Gift-bond pulsed into a weak and twisted semblance of life.

Lynas. My brother in all but birth, his face now a mottled grey mockery of life. I scrubbed at my face and looked again, found it all too real. His eyes stared at me, devoid of anything that had once been my friend, then his mouth opened and began screeching.

The sorcerer stiffened and spun to face me. "Edrin Walker! Still alive and breathing we see."

I stepped out. "You know me then, sorcerer?" I did my best to ignore the animalistic urges pulsing in the back of my head.

He chuckled, voice almost lost amongst the gibbering mewling cries of the thing in the lake. "Oh yes, we know you. And you know parts of me very well indeed."

Parts of him?

He looked left and a glittering shard beast crawled down the wall, he looked right and two burning green eyes stared from the shadows. "The Arcanum were fools to believe your false death. My shadow cats should have torn you to shreds years ago, but when they didn't return with your head I knew you must still live."

Flames licked up his hands and robed sleeves, burning him not at all. "Such a happy day when I finally get to dispose of filth like you. All these years I have wanted to see you burn and now my god has granted my wish." He waved a hand towards Lynas, "Say hello to your fat fuck of a friend. Will your screams be as pathetic as his when we skin you alive and feed you to my pet? When I am done with you perhaps I will pay his lovely daughter a visit." He noted my shock, "Oh yes, we know of her. I have learned many things these last few years."

Power filled me to bursting. God or magus, this fucker needed to die. Dissever leapt into my hand, lusting for blood.

He laughed, voice subtly different. "Such a unique pleasure seeing you again. It's been far too long, my little Edrin. Bring him to me."

Three of his minions pulled out knives and shambled towards me, my puppet remaining where he was, still pouring. The magus opened himself up and pulled in more power than I could dream of handling. He levelled burning hands at me.

The magus was the bigger threat. His Gift would instinctively resist my intrusion, so I put the full might of my rage behind the blow. His mind was a fortress of control surrounded by a spiked moat of alchemic haze. Fuelled by rage and hatred, I blasted through his first lines of defence. Inhuman thoughts tainted his mind, fragmented shards both unknown and unnatural. There was something unspeakably alien inside. As flames roared up around him I pressed in deeper, touching something of immense power. It flinched, inexplicably fearful of me. Then a third power scattered my attack with a surge of more-than-human will

– it felt like a god – and its relentless force tore me out of the magus' head. We both screamed.

He fell to his knees, dazed, grip on his power lost. Fire exploded from him in an uncontrolled sphere. One of his men was blasted through the air to crunch into the cavern wall. The thing in the pool surged up in a glistening mass, enveloping and consuming my puppet and not shying from the flames but lapping them up. I stared in shock as its heaving bulk devoured the otherworldly fire.

Two of his servants had almost reached me when the shockwave of hot air reached us. They stumbled, disorientated. I clamped a hand to one's arm. With the skin contact I was able to smash through his drugged mind with a mental war hammer, then crudely twist his perceptions. It was all so easy and I felt like a god playing with a new toy.

He drooled idiotically, then turned and stabbed his friend in the belly. In his mind his friend wore my face, and me his beloved master's. He sawed open the man's belly, intestines spilling out like links of sausage.

The magus blood sorcerer climbed to his feet. Flame began spiralling round his hands, faster and faster, building to a firestorm. He cocked his head to one side, listening. "Really? Must you find out what this secret locked away inside his head is? I know, I know, you don't like anything kept from you."

I went cold. Who was he talking to? *What* was he talking to?

The flames intensified. "Surely it is safer to burn him to a crisp? Oh very well, if you only need his head intact, your wish is my command, my god."

I went cold. A god. He said there was a god inside him.

The thing in the pool was agitated, bulk crashing against rock. Earth and pebbles trickled from the ceiling. From the darkness above, a handful of glittering shard beasts scuttled down stalactites towards me.

There was still a small chance I could kill this murdering bastard. I could open myself up beyond my limits and rip my way into his mind. If I did that I'd likely die, or end up a twisted insane wretch even if I succeeded. If I fought and failed then this blood sorcerer would be free to carry out his foul plans. For Lynas' sake I almost risked it, but with Charra sick he would have beat me black and blue for even contemplating it. Charra's life was not something we would ever gamble with. If only I'd kept that damn alchemic bomb, then I could have blown the bastard to little pieces – yes, and no doubt bury Charra and yourself in the resulting cave-in.

From around the feet of the magus, pebbles and rocks were sucked up into his vortices of flame, glowing bright red.

I tore myself away from dreams of vengeance and ran for my life back down the tunnel.

WhumpWhumpWhumpWhump – flaming bolts of rock blasted from the vortices to explode against the cavern wall. Razored fragments of old bone and stone scythed out. The tunnel shook from multiple impacts. My left leg collapsed beneath me. I tried to keep moving, using the wall to keep myself upright. Explosions deafened me as I lurched blindly down the passage. The ceiling cracked and groaned, and finally came crashing down behind me. A dust cloud enveloped me. Choking and coughing I dragged myself forward. Visions of being buried alive kept me moving. Fragments of rock bounced off my back in eerie silence, my ears stunned and useless.

Eventually the air cleared and my ears started working again, the only noise that of my battered body scraping across the ground. A dim light in the darkness made my heart soar. I'd never been so eager to see light. No, that

wasn't true – visions of being a child locked in that room
with the revenant flicked through my mind. Sweat burst
from every pore.

Have to get to Charra, I told myself. Get help. My leg
throbbed, the pain ramping up to searing agony that
eclipsed that of my shoulder. I focused on the pain and used
it to blot out my terror, crawling into the light to discover
I'd left a bloody smear along the floor behind me. Jagged
shards of hot rock had torn through boot and trousers to
bury in flesh. My clothes still smouldered and I realized that
my wounds being cauterized was the only thing saving me
from bleeding out. Charra's breathing was ragged, the red
streaks angry and weeping. I had to get her out of here. If
the poison didn't kill her then that magus would when he
came looking for the remains of the intruder.

The Worm of Magic was awake inside me and yelling
promises to help if only I would let myself go. It was only a
small terror compared to Charra dying in front of my eyes.
My body was a wreck. What other option did I have? With
a useless leg and a torn-up shoulder I couldn't possibly
carry her.

So I swallowed my terror and did what every part of my
Collegiate indoctrination and common sense had trained
me to deny. For the first time in my life I gave in to the
Worm, flung wide the doors of my Gift and welcomed in
unrestrained magic.

Power roared into me. I was a demigod filled with all the
power of life and death. All tiredness and pain washed away
and my wounds itched with quickened healing. Strength
returned tenfold. The darkness retreated to a crystal-sharp
half-light.

My sanity cracked. The physical world wavered around
me, glimpses of other worlds and strange dimensions
drifting past my eyes. I slid towards Charra, tripped out

on the majesty of creation, trails of thought billowing out behind me. Below my feet lay a yawning abyss of darkness, a place I knew I could never escape. A cloud of creatures darted in and out of my thoughts like a shoal of silverfish. It was so tempting to drift off on a wave of magic, my mind gone elsewhere, leaving my body behind as a mindless animal host for the Worm of Magic, or perhaps an empty suit of meat for something else to take up residence. A dark mass blotted out my vision. The feeding things fled from a vast predator. I shuddered and flinched back to the physical, focusing solely on Charra.

I picked her up, light as air, and cradled her carefully, afraid I might crush her brittle human bones. Tendrils of dark magic were spreading towards her heart. Convinced of my own god-like power, I almost reached into her body to rip them out, but managed to stop at the last moment. My confidence was a delusion; I didn't have the knowledge or skill to heal, and probably never would. The tides of magic roared through me, trying to twist my mind and body, but through force of will and the mental conditioning required for my talent, I resisted the worst of magic's seductions. For now.

I broke into a sprint, feeling my way through air currents towards the freshest air, through cavern and corridor and tomb, until I came to a place that shook me to my core. My delusion of godlike power cracked and dropped away beneath me. I staggered through a doorway cut through a rock fall and into the room where I had been trapped as a child. The old stone block with strange carvings had been removed, but otherwise the room remained untouched.

I couldn't control myself – my hand snapped out and blades of air lashed out to shred the room, gouging stone. I howled with the effort, power straining mind and body. Vulgar magic was arduous for me, something like this normally impossible. The walls started to crack and crumble. Pain roared through me. I drew deeper on the magic and flung out all my fear. I had to destroy this room. These nightmares haunted me and destroying them was the most important thing in my world.

Charra groaned, her breathing too rapid. It cut right through my self-absorbed fear – my only living friend was far more important. She was the only light in the dark of my heart that kept me human.

I tried to stop, and found that I couldn't halt the magic. I had opened myself too wide and drawn too deep. Panic tried to rise and failed, swamped by the pleasures of pain, power and promise. It hurt, and it was ecstasy. My Gift shuddered, threatening to tear itself apart due to the torrent roaring through it. I'd be little more than a gaping hole through which magic flowed into the world – an abomination, warped and twisted at the bestial whims of the Worm. I found myself at peace, not caring. Maybe it would even be a good thing? Pleasure pulsed at the thought.

Agony exploded in my leg, cutting through pleasure and disrupting the aeromancy to drive me to my knees. A few flickers of air swirled in the dust. The surge of magic slowed. Dissever had somehow managed to slice through its sheath and into my leg. Before I knew what I was doing my hand found the hilt. Bloodlust and rage swarmed through me, fighting back the pleasure and dreamy confidence, and stamping down my terror of the dark.

I*diot,* Dissever thought at me. *Brainless bald ape. Do not. I will not be lost again. Care for the female, you fool.*

Charra!

Fucking weak idiot, letting myself get sucked in. I clutched her to my chest and glanced at the half-destroyed room of my nightmares. Then I turned my back on it and ran for the way out. I sped through the tunnels I'd been carried from as a child, wishing that I was once again safe in Byzant's arms. The magic stormed through me and my mind kept drifting off in scattered directions. Dissever's counteracting influence rapidly waned.

An archway lay ahead, closed by a gate of massive warded steel bars blocking my exit from Boneyards. Barely pausing, I hefted Dissever and sliced through. Warded steel sparked, then parted and thudded to the ground. I stepped through the hole and an array of hidden wards activated. I spun to shield Charra with my body. An alarm shrieked and a web of force squeezed me like a giant fist. Despite being filled with a torrent of power, I was held fast, barely able to breathe. Magic built up inside me, screaming to be unleashed. These paltry wards couldn't hold me. Nothing could hold Walker. I shuddered, trying to fight the madness down.

A trio of magi tore in, magic crackling around them ready to destroy whatever twisted monstrosity had emerged from the depths.

Dissever writhed from my grip. Jagged metal teeth pierced my wounded leg and then the enchanted weapon sagged, black iron turning into a viscous liquid that flowed into the cut, hiding inside the wound. The pain felt distant, like it belonged to somebody else.

"Help her!" I pleaded. "She's been poisoned." The floodwaters of magic rose inside me, an unstoppable tide breaking through every shred of my restraint.

The magi gasped, seeing Charra's arm dangling limp. All three lifted their hands and unstoppable power slammed into me.

Survive, Dissever commanded. *I am not done with you yet.*
Everything went dark.

CHAPTER 20

I drifted in and out of consciousness, living more in dream than reality. Every so often I woke in agony, followed by a vague sensation of soup being spooned down my throat before something sweet and sticky was squirted into my mouth, flinging me back into the dream...

"Stop fidgeting, boy."

When the Archmagus tells me to stay still, I dare not even blink – even if he does have my eyelid peeled back and is blinding me with a candle held in front of my eye. He goes through the same checks and tests again and again, every day. It is tedious. At least the beeswax candles favoured by the Archmagus fill his chambers with the delicate scent of honey rather than the reeking incense used elsewhere in the Collegiate.

"Move your eyes from side to side again," he orders.

I look back and forth across his personal quarters while sinister animal heads mounted on the walls stare back at me with glassy eyes. His rooms are packed with an assortment of intriguing mechanisms and bubbling vials and tubes that beg to be poked and prodded. His possessions are obsessively orderly and despite the amount packed into the room everything has its set place; I suspect that his servants live in mortal fear of moving something when cleaning. It is cold in the Archmagus' rooms and all I want to do is huddle next to the hearth and savour the warmth and the light – especially the light. It has been weeks since I was carried from the Boneyards, but I still can't be alone at night without a candle by my bedside, and even then I only manage to sleep thanks to exhaustion. The nightmares are relentless.

My eyelid slaps back against my eye. I reach up and rub the tears away, multi-coloured wisps dancing across my vision. Byzant strokes his beard, deep in thought. I stay put, keep my eyes down and hope that he is finally done with me. I say nothing, fearful I won't speak properly to the Archmagus and get punished, even thought he has only ever been considerate towards me.

"Has the fever abated?" he says, concerned, his hand cold against my forehead.

"Yes, Archmagus. Over a week ago."

"Eating well?"

My face twists. "Mistress Sellars makes sure that I eat nothing but stin… uh… healthy foods."

"Mmm, good, good," he replies, distracted. Eventually he lifts up my chin with a liver-spotted hand. "Try once more. What am I thinking of?"

I swallow and stare into his eyes, take a deep breath and concentrate on opening my Gift, reaching out to him. For a moment everything seems to go fuzzy and I feel lightheaded, but that's all. I try again, and all I get is a headache.

After a while the Archmagus sighs and shakes his head. I couldn't manipulate fire, water, earth or air, and now this, whatever it is. I've disappointed him yet again. I'm useless. He strokes his beard, great emerald ring glinting in the firelight. "That is enough for today, young Edrin." A twinkle appears in his eyes and a smile creases his lips. "Go and get yourself something decent to eat. Perhaps something that does not stink." My face flushes red. "If Mistress Sellars objects then tell her to pass her protestations on to me. What do you desire?"

I grin. Finally I'll get some decent grub in my belly. "I can't wait to tuck into some smoked haddock." I frown and scratch my head. "Sorry, I don't know why I said that. I hate fish. I meant to say that I fancy a big slice of cheese and some roast pork."

The smile on the Archmagus' face is worse than death-grins on corpses, and I've seen a fair few. His eyes are lumps of ice. He says nothing, just shivers, turns and waves me away. I am halfway out when he unexpectedly speaks. "I will help you to manage this special Gift that you have been granted. You will come at the same time every week without fail."

"Yes, Archmagus," I squeak, walking from his quarters as quickly as I can without running. Outside the great iron-bound doors I sag against the wall, shaking. Have I said something wrong? I don't even know what all of this is about. Surely private tuition with the Archmagus is a rare privilege reserved for children from the High Houses? It is almost like he suspects me of something bad. I find myself shaking and don't know why. I mull it over as I walk to the kitchens.

My belly rumbles and my mouth waters as the scent of a pig roasting on the spit wafts down the hall. I dump all those confused thoughts into the back of my mind.

The dream began fading, piece by piece, until it dwindled away to nothingness. I felt myself clothed in heavier, aching flesh.

I cracked open sleep-crusted eyes, feeling like they were filled with broken glass. A blurry blue shape sat on a chair by the foot of the bed, tinkering with some sort of glinting metal object. I was dozy and weak, barely able to focus. There were no windows in the room, but a gem-light embedded in the wall gave off more than enough light for me to recognize the fine stonework and the distinctively ornate vaulted ceiling. I was in the Collegiate? I tried to push myself up to peer at the figure by my bed, but found myself chained to the steel frame, manacle bands digging into wrists and ankles. I was naked and covered only by a thin blanket, but didn't feel unhappy having been stripped and chained, even though I should. I didn't feel much of anything but numbness and a raging thirst.

"Byzant?" I said, my tongue thick and swollen. "S'that you?"

The figure stood. "Hardly," she said, voice firm but with an edge of something more – a mix of resentment and relief. "Archmagus Byzant went missing ten years ago. Would you happen to know anything about that?"

Her voice seemed naggingly familiar but I couldn't quite put a name to it. I blinked away the gunk and peered through one eye, unable to focus with two. She wore robes of finest blue Ahramish silk, and curly brown hair spilled around her shoulders. A name floated up from somewhere. "Cillian? That you?" As my vision cleared I noted the odd device in her hands, comprised of metal circles holding coloured glass discs. It looked harmless, but in this den of vipers it was wise to distrust everything. "What do you have there?"

"It is I, Edrin." Cillian sighed and shook her head. She flicked out a disc of red glass and held it up to the oil lamp, splashing red light across the wall. "No need to be afraid, it is merely a tool for new initiates, a visual representation of the Gift." She flicked out a blue disc to turn the light magenta, returned them and then held up a lone disc of yellow to filter the light. "I intend to use it to demonstrate that the source of light, representing magic, is the same for all, but that each Gift filters it differently." She held the disc closer to the lamp – to the source of magic – and the glass disc bubbled and melted. Sugar-glass rather than true glass. "I also feel it to be an elegant illustration of the inherent dangers." She studied my face. "Tell me, Magus Edrin Walker, why did you flee Setharis shortly after the god Artha died and Archmagus Byzant disappeared? Why did you go rogue?"

She said nothing more. The silence stretched and deepened while she waited for an answer. On a small table beside the bed a jug of water called to me, my throat dry and rasping, but chained to the bed it was just a different kind of torture for me. I frowned, head clearing slightly. "You can't blame me for every ill."

She stared at me, face unreadable. "You claim it to be mere coincidence? If it was not you, then why flee? Who else would we suspect under such circumstances?"

"Byzant would have squashed me like a bug." Which he would have. Effortlessly. Byzant had been older and scarier than any magus in existence, that old crone Shadea excepted. "My leaving had nothing to do with that, and in any case I left before he disappeared."

"We only have your word for that, and I am certain it is merely blind coincidence that you leave the very same day a god dies and then you return shortly after the rest of our gods go missing," Cillian said, voice oozing sarcasm. "You really must forgive my entirely unwarranted scepticism. We have had you tested and the loyalty of the Forging is still in place; without that I would not believe a single word you say." It wasn't like she had any cause to trust me, not after the way I'd treated her in the past, but it still rankled. She looked over the scars running down my face and neck. "What happened to you?"

"Bad booze and worse women," I whispered. "What's it to you?"

She scowled. Cillian was colder and harder than she had been, but people could change a lot in ten years. You didn't become a member of the Inner Circle by wearing pretty flowers in your hair and filling out your robes nicely; you got there by power, skill, manipulation and ruthlessness. Time passed, people and places changed. That was the way of things. I pulled at my chains and realized that my arms barely worked, the muscles slow and unresponsive, my body almost completely numb. There was no feeling at all in my left leg where I'd been wounded. I suffered a moment of panic until my toes gave an obliging wiggle. They'd taken the shards of stone out but it was still wrapped in a bloodied bandage.

She shifted, crossing her legs. "I shouldn't bother. Those chains are unbreakable. In any case, you are lucky to be alive after allowing your magic to overwhelm you. You always were weak and contrary, but I had not thought you to be a complete idiot. You were a survivor, more inclined to scurry off like a rat than stand and fight for something worthy."

A niggling worry that I was too groggy to understand everything made me ask: "How long have I slept?"

"Two nights."

A dark and urgent thought reared its ugly head. My tongue juddered over cracked lips and I struggled forming the right words. "Boneyards – Charra."

"Charra? Ah, so that was your dirty little friend," Cillian said, a sour expression on her face. "She is alive. For now."

"If you are threatening her then I'd think very carefully," I said, with only a hint of a tremble making its way into my voice. Something was wrong with me, my body flipping between hot and cold, some sort of alchemic wearing off.

A look of haughty scorn on her face. "Or you will do what? You cannot even get out of bed."

Dissever purred from somewhere inside my body, letting me know it could slice through my leg, chains and Cillian herself all with equal ease, but physical or magical threats wouldn't do any good. I had to hit her where it would really hurt, threaten something she'd dreamed of for so long. "Or you'll lose your council seat."

Her brow furrowed in surprise. "What do you mean?"

"How many favours do you think Charra is owed by

people of power and influence? How many precautions do you think she's taken?" I said with a forced smile, futilely straining against my chains. "Those crusty old traditionalists can't be pleased a young upstart like you sits on the Inner Circle. How many more votes against you do you think it would it take? Do you even have a clue who you are dealing with, Cillian?"

To her credit, she didn't let her mouth run away with her. She scrutinized my face. I didn't have to bluff, which was good since if I'd had to lie I didn't think I'd be the least bit convincing in my current state. I knew fine well that Charra could call in favours – she'd called in Old Gerthan to look at the murder scene after all – and you didn't get as rich and influential as Charra was without greasing a large number of palms and bartering favours with both the gangs and the nobility.

Finally Cillian nodded. "It would seem that I have underestimated her, in that case," she said. Her cold and controlled facade cracked, lips twisting into a snarl. It was good to see that some of her old fiery nature remained. "In any case, you arrogant buffoon, I was not making a threat. I simply meant that the healers have purged the poison from her body, but they cannot halt her disease progressing further."

I went still. "What do you mean?"

Her anger shattered: lips parted, eyes softening as realisation dawned. "You don't know, do you?"

"Know what?" The numbing effects of the alchemic they'd given me was fading fast, draining from my body like I was a leaky bucket, leaving me shaking and bonecrushingly tired. I waited for the pain that would be arriving shortly. You couldn't do what I'd done, physically and magically, and not reap the consequences, but at the moment all I felt was my stomach dropping away into a bottomless pit. "I have to see her. Please. What's wrong with Charra?"

"It is not my place to discuss your friend's health," she said, silk whispering as she paced the room. "Edrin, do you have any idea of just how much trouble you are in? After ten years supposedly dead you suddenly burst out of a warded entrance to the catacombs with your magic out of control and a dying woman in your arms. There are many questions needing answers, not least your actions on that night ten years ago. You know as well as I do that magi whisper *tyrant* when they speak of you. However unwarranted." That last bit she didn't seem entirely convinced of.

I creaked open my badly abused Gift. A trickle of power seeped through. It felt not dissimilar to plunging my head into a barrel of shattered glass and I couldn't hold it open. Cillian was fortunately not endowed with senses acute enough to detect that sort of attempt. What she was, however, was potentially the most dangerous magus I'd ever met, Byzant and Shadea included. Cillian didn't go in for fire and lightning or flashy tricks, nor inhuman feats of speed or strength; her affinity was for water magic. Fire, earth and air, and even the rarer talents such as mine, took a little time to channel the power and weave a magical attack. Hydromancers boasted the swiftest of all Gifts, but even amongst those Cillian was special. She could use her Gift as fast as thought, could stop my blood pumping or burst my veins before I could blink. I had to first break through people's will to affect them, while she suffered no such restrictions.

"Fine," I said. "I'll answer whatever questions you have. Just get me out of these damn chains and take me to her." My head started throbbing and I was burning up, pain finally arriving to kick down my door and fling in an oil lantern. She'd timed her visit perfectly. I didn't think it a coincidence.

Cillian held up a finger. "Not so fast. Answers first, your friend second. No negotiation and no room for you to wriggle out. That is the way this will happen unless you want to spend your life in chains."

She held all the cards and she knew it. Well, all but one. "Let's cut the crap," I said. "Take me to see Charra, and I'll tell you what I was doing in the Boneyards, or whatever else you want to know."

She sighed. "For once in your life do not make things worse for yourself. You will see her only when I am satisfied with your answers."

I ran my tongue over dry, cracked lips. "Cillian, fuc... uh, the gods know you have no reason to trust me, but you can't afford to dick about on this one. You need to know this, and you need to deal with it right now. Let me see her."

She shook her head, moved to leave.

"Then on your head be it, Cillian. Go right ahead and open that door if you really don't want to know about the monster that grows beneath your very feet, the monstrous creation of blood sorcery that will be unleashed tomorrow."

Her hand paused on the latch. "Oh, very well," she said. "But if it is not worth my time then you stay chained. As will your friend." She turned back to me, eyes cold and calculating like the politician she now was.

It was hard to concentrate through the pain: Gift and muscles torn, bones aching, bruises throbbing, leg and shoulder wounds burning.

"Can I have a drink please?" I was frustrated by my own weakness.

She picked up the jug on the table, poured me a cup and carefully tipped it to my lips. Up in the Old Town the water was always pure and crystal clear. A chill balm soothed my lips and raw, parched throat.

"Thank you," I said. So how to spin this... "How much

blood magic has been going on lately?" Her lips tightened. "Let me guess: my friend Lynas Granton's murder wasn't investigated properly because there was a damn sight more going on than the Arcanum will ever publicly admit to?"

Her silence was answer enough. I cleared my throat and continued. "I followed the Skinner's trail down into the catacombs."

She looked at me incredulously. "And just how exactly did you find his trail?"

The pain was distracting and my head was thumping, making it difficult to manipulate truths and think up believable lies. I almost blurted out the actual truth, but the last thing I wanted to do was sully Lynas' name by telling her that had been importing mageblood. Instead I said, "Because I actually give a shite about Docklanders."

"As foul-mouthed as ever, I see." She chewed on her lower lip. "I find it difficult to believe that you would go back down there after what happened to you in the past." At least she believed me.

"For Lynas, Charra and Layla, I would." The sooner this was over with the better.

"Who is Layla?"

Damn – I had to avoid any mention of their daughter. If they investigated and noticed the Forging rite papers for Layla had been falsified then they might start linking it all up to whatever deal I'd made ten years ago to haul everybody out of the fire. I was in no condition to attempt to match wits with Cillian. She was dangerously intelligent and had no doubt acquired a goodly dose of cunning if she'd risen this far this quickly.

"Charra's daughter, not anybody you would know." Fortunately she seemed to accept my answer. I proceeded to detail our encounter with the living idol and then my discovery of a magus blood sorcerer, the one that I suspected had a god inside him, and something else truly alien. She went ashen-faced as I described what he was growing in that pool of mageblood, the thing that ate magic.

She thumped down into the chair at the foot of my bed, her eyes burning into me. "Go over that again. Every single detail." When I was done she looked ill, her face pale and sweaty. She had some idea of what that creature was. If a member of the Inner Circle was this scared, with all the arcane might at her disposal, then I found that downright terrifying.

"What was that thing in the pool?" I asked.

"None of your concern. You will not mention it to anybody."

I was exhausted and in too much pain to put up a fight. "Please take me to Charra. Then you can go and poke about in your beloved book stacks."

When we were more than friends she had spent most of her spare time with her nose buried in dusty books, Escharric scrolls and stone tablets, pouring over obscure histories and ancient texts written in dead languages of long-vanished civilisations I couldn't even name. I resented it at the time, wanting her to spend more time out carousing with me than curled up with her beloved books. And who had done well for themselves in the end? Not me. Never me.

Absently, Cillian nodded. She chewed on her bottom lip, something she had always done when worried, and a habit I suspected she had tried hard to eradicate. Without a word she turned and wandered from the room, deep in thought.

"Come back here," I croaked.

She didn't.

CHAPTER 21

An age passed before three men entered the room: two muscular guards in chain and leather and a tired-looking young man in dust-streaked travelling clothes with a pack still slung over his shoulder. I didn't recognize him, but from the sour expression he knew exactly who and what I was.

A strange dislocation washed over me. My Gift felt fuzzy and distant. A thrill of instinctive fear ran through my abused body – he was a sanctor, a magus-killer. I wasn't in any condition to try to use magic, but they considered me dangerous enough to deny any chance of that.

"A damned tyrant," the man groaned, hand clutching his head. "You are in my charge now that you are awake."

The two guards carefully donned thick leather gloves before unchaining my ankles. It seemed the Arcanum still thought I could only use my power through skin contact. With the tyrants before me all dying so young they had little else to go on but what I had previously told them. The fools. Did they not know I was a liar?

"I've been accused of bringing on headaches before," I said, "but never so quickly. Has to be a record even for me." The sanctor looked at me like he'd happily stab me in the face. Luckily I was on familiar ground there. I tried to engage him in conversation but he found the bare walls far more interesting.

The guards hauled me to my feet. My legs were locked into a solid mass of cramping muscle. I gritted my teeth and ignored it. Pain belonged to somebody else. The numb stiffness in my left thigh made it difficult to walk; it felt like somebody had rammed an iron rod through the muscle. Blood seeped out to stain the bandages as they dressed me in plain grey tunic and trousers, no modesty spared.

They half-carried me down a deserted wood-panelled hallway with guards posted at every door, the sanctor never more than three paces behind me. I wondered if he kept his distance out of habit, or if he too feared my touch. Ah, if only – the things I could do with an enslaved sanctor! It would be so simple to control the Inner Circle then; to shut down their Gifts and beat them unconscious, to dominate them while they slumbered. In a month I would control the core of the Arcanum. In six, the city. Everybody who mattered anyway: peasants swarmed like vermin in the lower city, far too many to take them all. Then I would have the power to change everything. The only problem would be... My thoughts crashed to a stop. Peasants as vermin? This wasn't me. I looked deep into myself, scrutinized my own mind. The Worm of Magic stared right back out at me, larger and more cunning than ever.

If I wasn't who and what I was then I didn't think I'd ever have noticed the taint to my thoughts. There was no way to know how much the magic had altered me in body or mind. I shuddered, horrified, fighting the urge to vomit. When a magus gave in to the Worm it didn't create something that wasn't already there, it was far more insidious than that: it took what already existed and twisted it, stretched it out in obscene directions. Those thoughts were horribly, and entirely, the darkest whispers of my own mind.

I stumbled and would have fallen if the guards hadn't kept a firm grip on my arms. I always hated those crusty elder magi, so cold and inward-looking, but now I finally understood. Magi could live a long, long time, and generations of mundanes came and went whilst we remained almost unchanged. It was too painful to watch them wither and die. It was natural to come to believe a mage's life was of far more importance than brief mortal flames, inevitable to assume that with greater experience you knew better. It was logical to want control, for the greater good.

A chill of paranoia shivered up my spine. Hair and senses tingled in response, possibly my old magic-induced changes reacting to the new alterations in my mind. I had no way to know what else was happening inside me, burrowing like invisible worms through my body, devouring the old and excreting new flesh. Before I could horrify myself further, the guards stopped outside a door and dragged me into a small room with a table and chair, and Charra lying on the bed.

She looked little better than I felt. Scabbed red lines crisscrossed her face, neck and hands, and her skin held a peculiar grey tinge. A wide smile of relief appeared and she sat up.

The guards dumped me into the chair and one stepped outside, the sanctor and the second man loitering inside the doorway to keep watch over me. It was too early to tell if I was entirely sane after what I'd done to myself. I had held on long enough to prevent the worst consequences, but if I wasn't sane I would think that.

"How are you feeling?" I said, putting aside personal worries for later paranoia.

She coughed, wet and phlegmy, and glanced at the guards. "Mostly just confused. They haven't told me anything."

I scowled. It was typical of the Arcanum to treat mundanes like children. I had to keep telling myself that I was different, that to me normal people were not just dupes to manipulate and discard. But they already were: I'd barely set foot back in Setharis before I chewed up and spat out that young thief who'd taken my coat. Because I'd found it convenient. Not to mention that warden whose mind I had burned out, or the infantilized dockhand who had tried to take my winnings. Charra had called me cold, but I figured that as long as I still felt a little bad about it then I wasn't entirely lost. I was walking a hair-thin path.

Charra stared at me with big bewildered eyes as I told her about the statue, and the roots wrapping around her while she slept. She shuddered, but stayed quiet until I finished. I decided not to tell her about what they'd done to Lynas' body. She had enough to deal with right now without being forced to suffer that horror.

Instead I began telling her about the blood sorcerer and the creature in the pool, omitting certain details like the true extent of my powers due to eavesdroppers. Cillian would have taken that badly, and in my position I couldn't afford to aggravate her more. I was part-way through the tale when the sanctor cleared his throat. Loudly. Pointedly. I ignored him. He apparently didn't hold with Docklanders knowing details of Arcanum business.

I continued: "...so this blood sorcerer was a magus–"

The sanctor cleared his throat again.

Again I ignored him. "–and I could tell from his voice that he was from the Old Town."

A hand gripped my wounded shoulder. I winced as the fingers squeezed. Not the guards, they were too stupid to know what I shouldn't be discussing. The sanctor then. His bare finger rested against my neck. Oops.

"You will cease discussing this subject," he growled. "Or your time is up and you will be back in chains."

I looked at his hand on my shoulder. Then slowly lifted my head to meet his gaze. My lips twisted into a mocking smile as I reached for my Gift, letting none of the excruciating pain that caused me show. He snatched his hand away, backpedalling and staring at his hand as if it had been poisoned. It seemed to me that he was frantically searching his thoughts for any trace of tampering. Good, let his paranoia grow. Sometimes the superstitious fear of tyrants came in useful. I could still feel magic lurking beyond my Gift, but an invisible vice clamped it closed and kept me from using it. At the moment it was oddly comforting to know I couldn't, however much I needed that surge of supreme confidence right now.

I licked my lips. My head was pounding and my energy drained, but I couldn't avoid voicing my fears any longer. "Cillian, she… said something; a disease." My voice cracked. "She said they can't heal you."

Charra frowned. "No idea what she is on about. I'm fine, so no need to worry."

"Liar."

She flinched and looked away, eyes tracing the lines of mortar in the wall. "You like your answers straight, so here it is: I'm dying. My own flesh has betrayed me. It's killing itself and the white-robes tell me the disease has spread through my whole body." She lifted a hand to her mouth and coughed some more, then stared at the blood flecking her fingers. Her gaze drifted to meet my horrified stare. Her voice reduced to a whisper, "Sorry I didn't tell you. I had a similar scare once before, but I got better. Not this time."

My world dropped away. The deal had been broken, and those bastards I'd bargained with ten years ago never had fully healed Charra, they had just stopped the disease in its tracks.

"I'm so, so sorry, Charra. There must be something we can do. I'll force the Arcanum to help."

She shook her head. "There's no more to be done, my old friend. Magic can't fix everything."

Healers used their magic to quicken a body's ability to mend what was broken and fight off infection, but if her own flesh was killing itself then any attempt at magical healing would just hasten her end. But I couldn't accept that.

"You're wrong," I growled, hands shaking. I was no healer, but there had to be something. "There must be another way. We'll go to the Halcyons, try something else. They–"

"They tried, and they failed," she said. "I've accepted it. In this life you can do everything right and the worst can still happen. Sometimes it craps on you at the roll of a dice; mine just happened to come up all ones."

I slumped, mind thrashing through options: gods, great spirits, daemons, ancient Escharric texts of forbidden knowledge, even blood sorcery; I had to find a way to fix this. I'd lost Lynas – I couldn't lose Charra too. If only I was stronger. If I had more power I could... No, that way led back to the Worm's false seductions. I dismissed the possibility of obtaining and translating ancient texts that might be of any use as unrealistic. Pacts with great spirits or daemons of the outer realms? Risky. Illegal. And more importantly, I didn't have the faintest idea where to begin, which put it in the same bucket as blood sorcery. Which left me gods, of whom four were missing and one a traitor to Setharis. If I tore off hunting them then I would be leaving her at the mercy of the Arcanum and that thing growing beneath the city.

I swallowed and took a deep breath. "How long do you have?"

"Months?" She shrugged, oddly calm. "Weeks?"

No time at all. My unseeing eyes stared at the floor. What was the point of going on if she was just going to die on me anyway, whatever I did, however hard I fought?

Charra's hand cracked across my cheek. The guards started, seemed confused between the sanctor's sudden horror and Charra's slap. They didn't know what was happening but didn't try to stop her.

"Don't you dare wallow in self-pity," Charra growled.

"Charra, I–"

"Not while…" She bit her lip, eyes boring into me. "I've accepted I'm dying, and so must you – you promised me you'd look after her." I had, but then I'd only known Layla as a child and that was an age ago. I seemed to be having trouble caring, about anything; I didn't know if it was the magic changing me, the residue of the alchemic they'd given me earlier, or if it was just me being a cold bastard worn far too thin by the world. There was only an ember of life and love deep inside me and I held onto it grimly, hoping it would reignite. It was too terrifying to consider what I might become if I lost that.

The door creaked open and Cillian entered with an aura about her like a grizzled veteran contemplating a coming battle. She glanced at the sanctor who was still fretting over our momentary touch, and her lips tightened.

"Your time is up, Edrin," she said. "We will take care of your friend until she has recovered enough to leave." It was a polite way of saying she was hostage to my good behaviour. Cillian had learned the game of politics well.

Charra grabbed my sleeve. "Promise me."

How could I refuse? "You have my word."

A small sigh of relief escaped her lips. "Do whatever you have to." She was telling me she was expendable and that her daughter needed me more, whatever the cost.

A strange emotion surfaced, one that took me a while to recognize: shame. It had been a long time since shame and I had last been acquainted. I'd had my fair share of regrets over the years, but not shame.

I knew fine well that the Arcanum had ways and means to discover Layla was Lynas' mageborn daughter, and they might even find out that we had hidden that fact against the law of Setharis, whatever any falsified papers said. The Arcanum would destroy everything belonging to Charra as an example, and they would hunt Layla down and send her to the pyre. She was much too old to go through the Forging so they would put her down like a rabid dog. And there wouldn't be a damn thing I could do about it.

A magus could fight another magus, our loyalty belonging to Setharis and the Arcanum as whole, but the mageborn law was magically ingrained, so if they found out the truth about Layla then even I wouldn't be able to lift a hand to stop them.

I hugged Charra tight, like it was our last. Tears blurred my sight. "Goodbye, my friend." It had been all too brief and I doubted she would be allowed to see me again. I fixed her face in my mind, so I could remember it until my end.

She coughed, struggling not to cry. "There's been absolutely no pleasure in knowing you, Walker."

"Vile woman," I said, smiling so I didn't cry.

Cillian narrowed her eyes at us, not understanding the ripples beneath the surface of our conversation.

I stood on cramping and burning legs and waved off the guards. I welcomed the pain as I hobbled from the room.

As they escorted me down a hall back to my cell I caught sight of the very last thing I needed to see, my old tormentor, Harailt. I was so deep in despair that I couldn't even bring myself to dredge up all the old grudges. I said nothing as the guards ushered me past him.

"Wait," Harailt said. The guards halted. Cillian tapped her foot impatiently, but otherwise remained silent.

I turned my head to face him.

"Edrin Walker," he said, with less hatred in his voice than

I might have imagined, and showing no surprise at the sight of me.

"I'm not in the mood," I said, lacking the strength to headbutt him. "Leave me be."

"I owe you an apology, magus," he replied.

I glared.

"For my past actions," he continued. "I was less than gentlemanly. I hope you can forgive me." He extended a hand.

I slapped it aside. A bright bead of blood welled up in my finger from a cut.

"Sorry," Harailt said, holding his hand up to show the scuffed signet ring on his finger. The gold and onyx emblem of House Grasske was cracked and bent. "I found I could not part with it, even after... well, in any case I was foolish and petty in the past. I think you were the first to show me that. I am ashamed that I was not a better man. There are many things I would change if only I had the opportunity."

"I..."

"All I can plead is an arrogant and ignorant childhood," he said. "Events have transpired to educate me and put me on a new path."

People could change a lot in ten years, but I couldn't forget the terror he caused and I wasn't the sort who forgave: by nature I was the sort of man who would let a grudge fester and then wait in a darkened alley to break your kneecaps with a hammer. Or I was before meeting Lynas, but without him I was slipping back. I refused to believe in this new Harailt. I sagged into my guards' grip, not knowing what to say. In the end I just nodded, too dazed to reply. For years I'd nursed a variety of elaborate and brutal revenges, but now I was sick and tired of it all. What was the point? Cillian finally had enough of the delay and started walking again, the guards dragging me in her wake.

"What happened to him?" Had Eva been correct as to his changed nature? I refused to believe it.

"For a time he looked likely to succeed Lady Ilea," Cillian said. "Instead he was cast out of his House. He is no longer the heir to House Grasske. His cousin sits in his stead. It has been commonly viewed as a wise decision."

I couldn't help but agree. The thought of Harailt with all the power and influence of a High House at his fingertips was madness.

Harailt ran after us, "Ah, I forgot to say; it has been... such a unique pleasure seeing you again. It's been far too long, my little Edrin." He chuckled, leaning in until we were almost touching. "I hope we meet again, very soon."

That intonation. Those slick tones of the Old Town – the very words of the blood sorcerer!

Out of the sight of the others he mouthed "I skinned your friend" and smirked in malicious amusement.

I snarled and tried to tear his fucking throat out with my bare teeth, only to be wrenched back by my guards. "He's a monster! Harailt is a fucking blood sorcerer in league with the Skallgrim! I'll gut you, you–" They slammed me up against a wall, knocking the wind out of me.

Harailt staggered back and fell on his arse, a look of shock on his face as his eyes flicked from me to Cillian. "The man has gone mad. I was just trying to be nice."

Liarliarliarliar!

I lost it. Biting and clawing, thrashing to get free. *Kill! Come Dissev–*

Something slammed into my skull and I sagged, everything gone blurry. A noxious rag was placed against my mouth, its alchemic stench making everything hazy and distant.

I woke wrapped in chains as they dumped me into the bed. They may as well not have bothered – my body was a wreck after letting the magic roar through me like a wildfire. And I hadn't even saved Charra in the end, just delayed her death. Exhaustion, despair and gnawing fury crushed me down.

The sanctor settled into the chair at the bottom of the bed to keep watch.

"Get some rest," Cillian said. "You will need it. I hope for your sake everything you told me was true." She chewed on her lip. "I hope for our sake that you were wrong."

I screwed up gritty eyes, tried to focus. *I'll kill you Harailt! If it's the last thing I ever do.* But darkness descended, fatigue dragging me down into a safe and welcome nothingness.

CHAPTER 22

I yelp and try to flinch away, but for a young girl Charra's grip is strong as iron.

"Don't be such a baby," she chides. With a cloth already stained red she dabs away crusted blood from my mashed lips and swollen nose.

Lynas sits on a stool to the side of the bed, a wry and knowing smile on his face. His knuckles are skinned and raw, but otherwise he's come through the fight without a scratch. How I always come away worse off I have no idea.

"Is it broken?" I say, peering down at my nose.

She flicks it with a finger. I shriek and scoot back, clutching my face. "That'll teach you," she says, faking a scowl. "Did I say I needed saving?"

"No, but–"

"But nothing. I've been on the streets all my life." She glances around the tiny room that consists of nothing more than a straw pallet, single stool and a wobbly table with folded rags stuffed under one leg. "Well, until now." It barely has enough room to fit all three of us but her eyes still shine with pride. It is her room, bought and paid for with her own coin.

I gingerly pat my nose, wincing at each spike of pain.

"You know I can handle sleazy old men like that," she says. Her mirth at my bruised face and sheepish expression makes me smile. My burst lips object. That feral child has changed remarkably over the last two years. Somehow without me even

254

realising it Charra has become the practical backbone of our trio. "We both know I fight dirty. Make you a deal: if I ever want your help, then I'll ask for it. Good enough?"

I nod. "Sorry."

"What were you thinking? Just charging in like that?" She smiled, knocking a fist against my shoulder. "Idiot. His sort of slime treat women like dirt all the time." She shakes her head. "You wouldn't last a week as a woman."

I grin. "As if you will ever see me in a dress! As for what I was thinking…" I shrug. "You know me, always leaping before I look." In truth I'm bloody well worried something is very wrong with me, and even Archmagus Byzant's constant ministrations haven't convinced me otherwise. Ever since the Forging I've grown increasingly cracked in the head – I always need to have that last little needling dig, to stick in a barbed comment at exactly the wrong moment. I'm scared I'll get myself killed. I've been in more fights in the last few months than in the whole two years previous. If I keep going like this I'll wind up with a knife in my back lying cold and stiff in a gutter somewhere.

Lynas smiles and shakes his head at my foolishness, but he isn't the same as he used to be either. He's come out of his Forging a shadow of his former self, and it isn't only the discovery that he isn't Gifted enough to become a magus. He is merely going through the motions of living, a puppet dancing on strings of habit. Something deep inside has been shattered.

For once I am the lucky one. For unknown reasons Archmagus Byzant has taken a personal interest in me, listens to all my fears and tells me not to worry, that the world will all be set right again, given time. However, things are getting much worse. Charra can't possibly understand what we went through, but Lynas and I both know we've been changed. Nobody ever remembers their Forging, but each and every Gifted wretch is carried out of that ritual chamber the same way: skin slick with sweat, throat raw from screaming, head bursting with pain and sobbing uncontrollably. I came out a magus, others come out like Lynas: broken. Some don't come out at all.

Lynas rises and looses a huge yawn. "Better get going. I have to get back to my accounts." He waves goodbye and leaves.

Charra frowns. "He seems obsessed with numbers lately. He's never shown an interest in accounts and coin before, but in the last month he's had his nose buried in ledgers and his fingers are constantly stained with ink."

"He told me he's thinking of starting his own business," I say. "He has a whole bunch of ideas. Keeps wittering on about taxes and tariffs and asking me what I think – as if I'd know anything about all that."

"I hope he's well," she says, looking thoughtful.

I carefully explore my cuts and bruises with fingers that feel like knives. "Take care of him, will you? I think he could use somebody looking out for him right now."

Her dark eyes study me. "Of course I will. What did those bastard magi do to him up there?" It doesn't seem to have sunk in that I am one of those bastard magi now.

I shudder. "Nothing good. But that's all over with now. I'm sure that he just needs time to recover. Something to focus on." We could hope…

She stares at the door, doesn't say anything and doesn't have to. She is as worried about Lynas as I am. I can't be sure if he is throwing himself into business as some sort of way forward after his hopes and dreams were crushed, or if it was a strange effect of his Forging. Either way, I hope it helps him heal.

It is a huge mental effort to haul my sorry, beaten body up off the pallet. "I'd better head back to my room or they'll have me washing the privy floors again." I struggle to ignore the self-destructive impulse urging me to stay longer. "Goodbye, Charra."

She smiles sadly, her face growing more lined, hair greying. "There's been absolutely no pleasure in knowing you, Walker."

• • •

A sudden panic shattered the dream memory. My eyes shot open, the world a dull smear of grey, heart slamming, body aching. I jerked upright, muscles screaming in protest. Chains rattled around my ankles and wrists. Crusty blood bunged up my nose and for a moment I was back in my dream with burst lip and swollen nose. But no, that was long gone, being home was just dredging up old memories. Dried blood covered the straw where I'd laid my head.

The sanctor rose from the seat at the bottom of my bed and rapped on the door to let them know I was awake.

I didn't have much time left and I had to do something right for once: Harailt had to die, and I should have done it long ago. I ground my teeth and thought of Layla. I had to see her safe before there could be any reckoning, but it was impossible to ensure her safety while I was locked away like this. I'd have to be sneaky, have to unbalance the bastards, kick them in the balls and leg it while they were busy puking. I would probably have to do something monumentally stupid, but that shouldn't be too hard; I'd pretty much refined that to a high art.

The guards came for me again and shovelled a thick and salty broth down my throat. Afterwards I felt strangely improved for having had a few hours' sleep and some food, which was far from right. My body ought to be completely crippled, muscles seized up and solid as cured ham, much like my left thigh still was thanks to Dissever's presence there. How had the damn knife even fitted without ripping me to shreds? It had gone fluid, hadn't it? My memory was somewhat vague. I should not be healing as fast as an elder magus, not at my age. It was not something that could be caused by briefly giving in to the Worm. The realisation washed my grogginess away with a thrill of distilled fear.

I couldn't bury my head in the sand anymore. A hundred little things over the years piled up into one inescapable conclusion – that something fundamental had changed inside me during the last ten years. The Worm of Magic was burrowing deeper into my flesh, changing me, and it had quickened on the day a god died.

My power was swelling, my Gift grown stronger. I found it much easier to reach into people's minds than I could ever remember. Breaking into those stolid and unimaginative guards outside Lynas' warehouse should have proven troublesome and yet I'd cracked them open as easily as tossing eggs at a rock. I healed quicker than I should and as the years ground on I was growing increasingly resistant to alcohol and alchemics. Every magus lived with the fear of change – we had all seen the warped flesh and bizarre mutations, the seeping wounds and howling madness, that resulted from somebody using more power than their Gift could handle. Even if they somehow pulled back from going over the edge it always changed a magus. I was terrified of losing control.

My introspection was interrupted by the door opening. I looked up expecting to see Cillian. Instead my blood chilled at the sight of the wrinkled countenance of Shadea. Whatever horror I felt at my body changing paled in comparison.

"Leave us," she said.

The guards and sanctor scurried out and secured the door behind them. She eschewed use of the chair, instead stood scrutinizing me with the same passion she might show a corpse splayed open on a table. I was in deep shite. I shivered as her grey eyes judged me and found me contemptible. If the hag wanted to she would take me apart as easily as a snot-nosed pup pulling the legs off spiders, and probably with more curiosity. I had no doubt I would tell her everything she wanted to know. People said they'd take a secret to the grave but they had no concept of what real torture was. Everybody broke sooner or later, and what little

I knew of Shadea's practices was more than enough to give me nightmares.

"To what do I owe a visit from you?" I said, finding my voice.

"Guard your tongue, boy," she said. "You will show me the respect I have earned." It was not a demand but a statement of fact. Coming from Shadea, I dared not disagree. Even if I hadn't been chained I would never dream of attacking her.

She tutted. "I had some faint hope for you once, despite your background. You showed an aptitude for unconventional thinking and a dynamism that the cliques of traditionalists lacked. I wonder if it is the nature of your unfortunate Gift, your base personality, or your lowly upbringing that has led to the situation we must now deal with. What might we have made of you if only the sniffers had discovered you a few years earlier?"

I clamped my jaw shut to stifle the retort. Instead I shrugged, chains creaking.

She caught and held my gaze. "However, I am aware that in the past the Arcanum frequently assigned you to Archmagus Byzant's service, and I suspect some of the tasks he set you."

I swallowed, suddenly nervous. Over the years I had done many unpleasant but necessary tasks for Byzant throughout Docklands, the sort of things that were best never recorded in Arcanum records. How much did she know?

"Not that there was ever any proof, of course," she continued. "But I have known Archmagus Byzant far longer than you have been alive, Magus Edrin Walker. I know him, and I know you, and for that I am willing to delay judgment on your activities pending a thorough investigation of both your recent claims."

"Did you capture that bastard Harailt?" I growled. "He must reek of blood sorcery."

"The man passed my own personal testing," she replied. "He is not corrupted. No magus can do what you claim and show no evidence."

I blinked, gawping at her. "What? That's not possible. He is a blood sorcerer and he commanded daemons. Test him again!"

"You are a liar or you are mistaken, Magus Walker. Which is it?"

"Neither," I said, struggling to escape my chains. "Whatever lurks inside has managed to fool you. I told you, I felt a traitor god helping him! He needs to die, and die now." I considered trying to use my power to convince her, then quickly discarded such a foolish thought. Even if she didn't detect me opening my damaged Gift – a vanishingly unlikely chance an adept like her would fail to notice – she was an elder, and I didn't fancy my chances of surviving after intruding into her mind.

She shook her head sadly. "Ludicrous. The gods of Setharis are all missing and Magus Harailt Grasske has neither the power nor the skill necessary to fool an elder magus such as myself; however, he has been confined to the Templarum Magestus pending further investigation. We agree that something did happen to you in the Boneyards. Councillor Cillian has been successful in persuading the Inner Circle to investigate those warnings. You will be coming with us."

My stomach clenched and I almost threw up. The Boneyards terrified me beyond all reason. I had to stay calm, act reasonable, then seize my chance to escape and ram Dissever through Harailt's black heart. He had tried for ten years to kill me and now it was my chance to return the favour.

Somebody knocked on the door. "Enter," Shadea said.

Old Gerthan hobbled in, cane clacking across stone. He nodded to Shadea and approached me, looking me over with his droopy eyes. His back to Shadea, he gave me a crafty wink. It was nice to know that I wasn't universally hated.

"No skin contact during the healing," Shadea ordered. "He is unstable and we will take no chances without a sanctor present."

"I will not be able to effect a full healing in that case," Old Gerthan replied. "You understand this?"

Shadea nodded. "Heal him enough to walk but not run. I do not want him capable of fleeing. He has a nasty habit of that." Her eyes never left me. It seemed she would only allow a single small and calculated risk and not a grain more.

Old Gerthan carefully unwrapped the bandages around my wounds, grumbling over the inflamed and swollen mess of my left thigh. I gasped and bit my lip. I didn't have to pretend to be in pain, I just had to exaggerate it for maximum gain. Perhaps I could tease out a little extra healing.

"Very well," he said, stretching a near-skeletal hand out over my legs. "I will do what I can." He was looking into my eyes when he said that last bit, but Shadea took it as meant for her.

A warm tingle crept from my toes up my legs, washing away pain and replacing it with tiredness as my flesh exhausted itself in quickened healing. He was facing away from Shadea, and she couldn't see the confusion in his eyes at the discovery my body was not as wrecked as by all rights it should be. I winced as torn muscle knit back together with sparks of ragged pain. And then the tingle reached the wound gouged into my leg. Dissever writhed inside the wound and I shrieked, no longer faking anything.

"What is this injury?" Old Gerthan said, his hand held over my leg. "It refuses to heal."

I opened my mouth to tell them, but a deeper pain wrenched within my thigh. I screamed as something squirmed inside every muscle of my leg. *Idiot*, Dissever's voice rasped into my mind. *I will not be caged by ignorant children.*

I clamped my jaw shut to muffle the screams. Dissever was more talkative than I remembered. *No. More awake,* it said. It sent a feeling like a tongue lolling over jagged metal teeth. *Walker blood has matured well. But your war god's blood was far stronger. Nourished. Woke.* A chill cut through the agony. The secret in my head rattled its chains and mocking mirth was Dissever's only answer.

Somehow Dissever was hiding inside my body. That should not be possible – it shouldn't even fit. The exact words of our spirit pact rose unbidden to make me shudder: *My blood, your blood. My flesh, your flesh...* Now those words sounded horribly literal, it had merged with my flesh, become a part of me...if it wasn't already. This was no normal spirit-bound object, it was something far more sinister. As it stirred inside me blood welled up from the wound to soak through trousers and bedding.

Old Gerthan grumbled as he tried again to heal Dissever's cut. "I cannot heal him without contact. That wound is passing strange. I have never seen the like."

Shadea's eyes burned with curiosity. "Very well. Heal the rest of him as you think best and bandage that leg up for now." She would not forget – she never did – and would take great pleasure in exploring one more mystery when this current task was done.

The healing magic bypassed Dissever's hiding place and the absolute agony subsided to mere abundant pain. I lay limp and moaning while he painstakingly healed the rest of me. Shadea lost interest and stared at the wall, deep in thought, eyes flicking to and fro as if reading texts from memory.

He leant over me as his hands passed over my neck and whispered in my ear. "Be at ease. I shall do my best to see

Charra out of here should the opportunity present itself. I can give you a chance, nothing more."

"What did you say?" Shadea asked.

"Just an old man mumbling to himself," he replied.

The pain was too much for me to reply, but shrivelled up old prune or not, I could have kissed him full on the lips. By the time he finished the old magus was leaning heavily on his cane. I was physically exhausted, but it felt like I had been healed more than Shadea had wanted. My Gift would take a while to restore itself, nothing anybody could do about that. I coughed, wincing with exaggerated pain. "Thank you," I said. He looked shattered and I couldn't help but feel he had fed his own energy into the healing process to reduce the toll on my body.

He grunted, pointedly ignored me and turned to face Shadea, an expression as if he'd just stepped in a mound of horse dung on his face. I wasn't the praying type, but if there had been a great spirit or a god out there somewhere who wasn't a complete arse-rag, then I'd have sent my thanks.

"It is done," he said, then left without another word.

As he exited the room Cillian marched in wearing cerulean robes so heavily woven through with metallic wards that soft clinks sounded with every step. The sanctor came in behind her and I could see the shadows of others lurking in the hallway. They were here to force me back down into the Boneyards and they would collar and leash me like a feral dog if they had to.

As the guards removed my chains and began dressing me in clean clothes and new boots, I decided it was time to play the con man again, to take every edge I could get. I groaned and exaggerated the damage to my body, tried to walk, failed and slumped back down on the pallet, face twisting in pain.

"Stop faking, boy," Shadea said. "You are well enough to walk."

Cillian glared at me, then looked to the sanctor. "Martain, stay close to him. He is as slippery as an eel and we still have many questions that need answering." Her eyes warned me to behave. Even if I did what they wanted then I had a hunch that somebody would see to it that I didn't survive captivity for long. It would be arranged to look like suicide – just another cursed tyrant putting himself out of his misery. It was a crying shame I'd have to find a way to disappoint all these fine magi.

My hands were pulled out in front of me and Cillian fastened cuffs around my wrists. "Oh my," I said. "In public too. How lewd. You might have asked me first, Cillian, but I'm fine with you being in charge." She didn't show any emotion on her face, but did pull away to fuss with her hair. I didn't imagine many people had enough of a death wish to speak like that to a member of the Inner Circle. Shadea looked more murderous than usual.

Martain punched me between the shoulder blades. "Do not speak to her that way, you viperous mongrel." I noted he wore gloves now.

I stumbled forward, then turned to smirk at him. He seemed overly protective of Cillian, and from the way he glared at me he probably knew we had once been involved. Angry people didn't act with forethought, and that I could use. "Viperous mongrel? Is that really the best you can come up with? Why don't you just piss on her to mark your territory?"

His face went red. He started forward, but before he could do more than growl Cillian snapped her fingers. "Restrain yourself, Martain, don't dance to his tune – he always was good at angering people."

Two guards stormed through the doorway, wrapped gauntleted hands around my arms and dragged me out into the corridor where two other magi waited, young men with an edgy, angry air to them that stank of pyromancer. You didn't as a general rule get old pyromancers. They tended to, hah, burn themselves out quickly.

"Does anybody require anything before we begin?" Cillian said.

I almost asked for a strong drink and a last meal just to be annoying, because I'm the sort of git that likes to rile up serious people for my amusement.

"How about a gag?" Martain said. She seemed to be seriously considering it.

Just because they needed me right now didn't mean they would shy away from inflicting pain. I had to stay calm, keep my mouth shut, and try to squirm my way out of this midden I'd fallen into.

While I withered under Shadea's scathing glare somebody in clinking chainmail and creaking leather marched up the corridor to my right.

I turned. Eva started, pretty green eyes widening in shock. She was armoured for tunnel fighting, wearing metal gauntlets with spiked knuckles and a heavy knife sheathed at her hip. Longer weapons would just get in the way down in the Boneyards. I swallowed. Of all people, why did it have to be her? If Shadea or Cillian found out we had spent time together in the evidence rooms it would not be pretty, and she didn't deserve that.

"Well, hello there, pretty lady," I said, forcing a sleazy grin onto my face. "Are you my bodyguard? You had better stay very close. What's your name, my lovely?" She stared in confusion. I turned to wink at Shadea. "You lot really spoil me."

Shadea was not impressed. "Careful boy, if one more base comment escapes your lips I will sew them shut. If you irritate Evangeline she has my leave to break your fingers. You do not need those to walk." Her liver-spotted hand slapped into my crotch, held firm. I kept very, very still. "Or perhaps I will take these instead. Anger me further and at the end of this I will have a rarity on my dissection table." She licked her cracked lips in anticipation.

Eva regained her compose, catching on to my ploy. She was not a good liar, but fortunately all eyes were on Shadea and myself. "So you are Edrin Walker?" she said, scowling with real anger simmering behind her eyes. "I thought you'd be bigger from the way they described you. You look like a lying rogue."

"Well," I said. "Don't say you weren't warned."

If she had thought about coming clean she had just missed her chance. Our mutual secret was safe for now. Eva had guts as well as a bit of a mouth on her. I liked that. Shame about the timing. The unsavoury part of me filed all of this away as possible leverage to use later – after all, she had far more to lose than I did.

"Enough delaying, Edrin," Cillian said. "It is time to begin our descent." The guards dragged me forward and there was nothing I could do to resist.

CHAPTER 23

Cillian marched us through corridors and down staircases, winding deep into the very bowels of the Collegiate. Martain and the two guards flanking me were a constant thorn, but I was more worried by Shadea's soft footfalls behind me. Her gaze stabbed my back, burning for a chance to cut me open and dig about in a tyrant's still-living innards.

My panic rose with every step taken towards the entrance to the Boneyards, until it filled my throat and started choking me. I dug my heels in and tried to pull back but the guards' big hands clamped onto my arms propelled me onwards. The steel door to the old cellar came into sight and the three magi guarding the gate unlocked it and stood to attention. *Oh gods, no.*

Somebody had already set out gem-light lanterns, rope, and supplies. I gritted my teeth to avoid begging for my freedom; I refused to give them that satisfaction. Instead I spent the time they took readying supplies trying to control my emotions, to calm down and think. I almost had it all in hand too, a carefully crafted look of indifference on my face – until they dragged me into the inky darkness waiting just beyond that old portal of fevered nightmares. Air wafted up from the depths to caress my face with stale fingers and fill my lungs with musty terror. The clang of the gate locking behind us echoed in my ears once again, followed by the ghost of Harailt's mocking laugh. I couldn't do it, not again.

I bucked and jerked, snarling and biting like a feral beast. Suddenly Shadea was there, two gloved fingers clamping down on the fleshy part of my hand between thumb and forefinger, jabbing into nerve and muscle. Unbelievable agony devoured me. She didn't use magic, just two fingers. The guards let me fall to my knees.

"Look at me, Edrin Walker," Shadea said, squeezing harder. She wore a look of profound disgust. "You are already under suspicion of murder, tyranny, and magical corruption. I would recommend you exercise utmost restraint."

She gave one last agonizing squeeze and then let go. I slumped there in the arms of the guards, not even able to clutch my hand to my chest. She cupped my face with her bare hand, as if daring me to attempt to take her mind. "I have dealt with your accursed kind of magus before," she said. "Though none have lived so long. This is me being exceptionally lenient. Do not test me further."

I shook my head. I really, really didn't want to test her. Only a fool would fail to fear Shadea.

"Good," she said. "Now behave like a magus. You have proven a disgrace to Setharis thus far. You will comply with each order promptly and efficiently."

Her tone stuck in my craw and made me vomit up a bile of words. "Me? A disgrace? You all think you are so damn virtuous, so *righteous*," I said. "This city is rotting, drowning in a pit of poverty and despair. Ever since I was a young pup I've seen people starving and selling their flesh for a few copper bits down in Docklands, but you lot don't give a damn, haven't ever lifted a finger to help them."

I stared Shadea in the eye. We both knew that I was all bark and no bite, for the moment. "And you, looking down your nose at me; I might be scum by your cold calculations but at least I still live out there in the real world, not closeted up in my chambers for years on end. You've been buried in your scrolls too long and forgotten what it's like for normal people. The rest of you are well on your way. Me, I still care about people, and in my own haphazard way I still try to help. I'll be damned if I apologize for that."

Eva had the good grace to look embarrassed at my rant, but then she was still young and vital. There was a hard truth in what I'd said. Every magus eventually felt the dislocation and knew they drifted away from the world of normal people as time passed. Less so for those that came from the High Houses, of course – they already lived in a privileged world of money and power that had little to do with the lives of normal people. The two pyromancers and Martain looked furious that I'd shot my mouth off in the presence of Shadea and Cillian.

"You can never help yourself, Edrin, not even once," Cillian said. "Always with the brash words, always about you and what you think. You have no idea of the issues we must contend with." She shook her head, a sour twist to her mouth, and then turned her back on me. "You must think me a fool if you expect me to believe your drinking and gambling ever helped anybody."

I chuckled low and hard. How little she knew, how low her opinion of me. Not that I expected anything else, after all had I not expertly crafted my own wastrel image so that they wouldn't think me a threat? Still, it stung. So maybe I hadn't improved everybody's lot in life, but I had damn well stopped things from getting a whole lot worse. My mentor Byzant had known that, and Shadea suspected.

The withered crone showed no reaction, my words like raindrops off oilcloth. "There will always be peasants toiling in the mud," she said, "and there will always be impoverished wretches working day and night. What of it? Cheap and abundant labour is necessary for the efficient running of an empire." One long-gone, I thought. "The smallfolk breed like rats and live near as long," she continued. "They are just a herd of cattle to me, a resource. Do you expect me to care for them as if they were my own children?"

I lowered my eyes. "No. Sadly, I don't." I was horrified at the thought of how she might treat her own children.

Shadea pursed her lips. "A tyrant's insight is most interesting. Let us hope that you are found guilty and we can engage in a more thorough discussion."

I shuddered at the thought of the horrors she had in mind. "I'm no tyrant."

"Magi with an affinity for fire magic are pyromancers," Shadea said. "The usage and degree of power at their disposal is irrelevant. You are a tyrant."

"I prefer peoplemancer," I muttered.

"I'm sure you do," she replied.

I wasn't about to accept that from her. I opened my mouth to start arguing when Cillian finally had enough and snapped her fingers. My escort dragged me forward. I shook and scrabbled to open my Gift but the sanctor was close behind me, just far enough so the other magi remained unaffected.

"Control yourself, Edrin," Cillian said. "If what you told me is the whole truth then you have nothing to worry about."

"Well, not about this," Martain said from behind. "There are other crimes to answer for." I could well imagine the slimy git's smug expression.

"Give me a damn moment," I snapped. "None of you know what I went through down here." But I knew I had to go. Today was Sumarfuin and we had to stop this blood sorcerer.

"No time," Cillian said. "Evangeline – lead the way."

I struggled, but it was useless. Eva advanced with her

heavy knife in one hand and a lantern in the other, clear, bright, unwavering gem-light flooding the tunnel ahead. Her face looked daemonic in the lantern-light, a painting of shadow and malice. She was familiar with blades and was not the bookish type. She had to be a knight with full mastery of body-enhancing magics. No wonder she had almost broken my arm. If she had been serious she could have torn it off and beat me to death with it.

"If he will not walk then tie and carry him like a sack of grain," Cillian said.

I was about to lose any chance of escape and couldn't do a damn thing about it – a black scum of paralyzing terror oozed through my mind. The light shed by the lanterns seemed to fade away to pinpricks and everything went hazy. Then a spark of blood-red light appeared in my guttering mind. Fury exploded. Searing pain from my leg accompanied that familiar, inhuman surge of rage – Dissever.

My head snapped round to grin at my guards. They flinched. It took all my willpower to stop myself ripping their throats out with my teeth and letting their salty blood fill my mouth. I barely managed to choke down the bloodlust. "I'll cope," I snarled, walking on my own again. "Let's get this over with."

Shadea's eyes narrowed, scrutinizing my abrupt change. Not knowing what it was had to be killing her. As soon as I was no longer needed I was going to be in trouble there. It didn't bother me; it wasn't like I was going to live long enough for that.

They followed my directions, descending to where I'd been trapped as a boy and had nearly gone insane. Shadea froze as we entered the room, staring at the black stone ceiling tapering up into darkness. Something like astonishment, then anger flickered across her face and I thought I caught her mouthing Byzant's name. She hurried us onwards.

After a while she bid us hold at a rockfall. "I sense the corruption of blood sorcery beyond." She waved a hand and the rock rippled and receded like water, revealing a large and familiar cavern whose walls bore recent scars inflicted by superheated rock and flame.

The pyromancers sent fizzing globes of fire soaring across the chamber to reveal a huge empty pit in the centre. Instead of the lake of blood and the fleshy abomination there were now only shallow dregs of black water and a stained lip of crusty brown. The entire far wall had collapsed into a mess of shattered bone and rubble, a hole knocked through to remove the thing in the lake and then resealed. Even with the sanctor shutting down my Gift I could feel a miasma of foul magic tingling against my skin. The magi all looked decidedly queasy. Maybe having a sanctor around to shut down my Gift did have some benefits.

"Is this the location?" Cillian asked.

I nodded.

Shadea bent down and ran two fingers across the lip of the pit. She rubbed the wetness into her fingers for a few seconds, lifted them to her nose and took a sniff, then licked them. Her face twisted like she'd bitten into a lemon. She spat into a kerchief. "Residue of blood sorcery," she said as the cloth incinerated in her hand. She looked at me with perhaps a little less distaste as she wiped her fingers. "The strongest I have ever encountered, with traces of the Gifts of many individuals, which partially verifies his story of mageblood." She turned to me. "Show me where you entered the cavern."

I raised an eyebrow, glanced at the guards holding me in place.

"Oh, very well," Cillian said. "Let him loose, but stay close. Do not let him touch your skin." Even with the sanctor shadowing me they were taking no risks.

The iron grip of the guards vanished. I cricked my neck and stretched manacled arms, pointed over at a small rubble choked alcove. "I entered from there."

Shadea looked thoughtful. "You fought this blood sorcerer, you say? A pyromancer magus?" She studied the heat-scarred walls and traced the origin of the conflagration, fixing on the circle of melted stone down by the edge of the lake where the hooded magus had been standing. "Tell me then, how exactly did you fight him from all the way over there?"

It was difficult to keep the sudden stress from my face. I had two choices: to reveal the true extent of my swollen powers, or to lie. I chose a half-truth, the very best of lies, just enough of the truth to make it believable.

"Harailt wasn't alone," I said. "He had four men with him. Disciples or apprentices all with bodily corruption. I grabbed one of them and send him into a killing frenzy." I talked them through a revised version of the events up until the shard beasts attacked and the tunnel collapsed as I fled.

One of the pyromancers looked at Cillian curiously. "Shard beasts?"

"Daemons summoned from a strange realm of living crystal," she replied. "Scant knowledge of them exists, mostly references from Archmagus Byzant's personal library." She raised an eyebrow at me. "A curious connection, since Edrin was once a favoured pupil of Archmagus Byzant."

I snorted. "Yes, and what of it? Aside from yourself, Edell, Ailidh, and a half dozen others also had personal tuition from Byzant. That insinuation isn't worth the spit I'd waste on it. Guess who else Byzant taught? Harailt."

A shiver rippled through me as the air currents changed and swirled across my hair and skin. Something was moving overhead, something big. I peered up into the gloom where only the tips of stalactites were visible. A glint in the dark caught my eye, then another. Dull splodges of colour began pulsing into life all across the ceiling. Not something big – lots of things.

"Shard beasts!" I shouted, preparing to grab a lantern and hobble to freedom while the magi were distracted.

Dozens of crystalline spiders clittered and clattered down the stalactites, glittering like grotesque jewels. If I hadn't seen the thing in the lake I wouldn't have believed it was possible for one man to tear so many daemons from the Far Realms. This was unheard of outside of peasants' wild tales told in dingy taverns by firelight. How were they even alive? Daemons died in Setharis, everybody knew that. *Much like the shadow cats then.*

"Form a circle," Shadea barked. Martain dragged me back and the magi formed a defensive ring a safe distance outside of the sanctor's disabling effects. Palpable auras of power rippled up around them and the air vibrated. The guards drew short swords and planted themselves on either side of me. They swore like sailors – displaying some shred of personality at last – but didn't show the fear normal people would have when confronted by such creatures. The sanctor remained behind me, no doubt intending to use me as a meat shield.

I tried to slip my hands from the manacles. "Let me free, damn you."

The sharp point of Martain's blade pressed into my back. "That will not be necessary."

As the shard beasts advanced into our light they began moving faster. Bulbous obsidian eyes glistened as they fixed on us. They dropped, flipping in mid-air, knife-legs stabbing down at our heads.

Martain shoved me to the ground. The guards dropped with me. A deafening concussion thumped me on the back, searing my skin. I lifted my head, the only sound a ringing in my ears. Most of the shard beasts had been flung across the cavern by a pyromancer's explosion but were already righting themselves and scurrying back. A good dozen of the things had darted through the flames and were now waging silent battle amidst the smoke, rearing and slashing razor limbs at Eva.

The knight slammed her fist through the bulbous abdomen of one beast, shattering it in a spray of glittering dust and glowing fluids. She tossed it aside and caught another mid-leap, knife-legs splayed to envelop her. Jagged crystal tore through leather and chain, but left only shallow scratches on skin gone hard as steel. Her mouth twisted into a savage grin as she crushed the creature between her hands. Two dead in two seconds. She drew her knife and set to work like a demigod of battle, destroying everything before her. This was the girl I had lied to and flirted with? Shite.

My hearing returned as Shadea and Cillian loosed volleys of crackling incandescent energy into the things, leaving twitching and jerking husks of blackened crystal.

The pyromancers spat roaring jets of flame across the cavern. Shard beasts glowed red hot and squealed, a teeth-on-edge sound like tearing metal. Cillian lifted her hand, sucking moisture from air and rock and drawing up the dregs of the lake to form a wall of water. With a wave the wall hammered into the super-heated daemons. They shattered like dropped glass and clouds of steam billowed upwards. Only a few of the daemons were left, and those were cracked and leaking stinking luminous liquids.

One last, enormous, spider dropped from the ceiling to land directly in front of Cillian. It reared, limbs slicing at her face. She ducked, quickly backed away and created a globe of black water around the daemon, hiding it from sight. Razored limbs burst from the sphere, thrashing as it lurched this way and that, blindly hunting its tormentor. Then it crashed to the floor and stopped moving.

"Impressive," Shadea said. A compliment from her was rarer than diamond.

"Byzant's records state that shard beasts breathe light instead of air," Cillian said. "It is likely they were left as a trap and roused from hibernation by our lanterns." The globe fell apart, splashed down and flooded back into the pit. Shadea loosed a lash of energy that cleaved the larger creature in two. The cavern trembled, followed by the unseen crack and tumble of a few rocks falling near the far wall.

Shadea carefully prodded the corpse with a toe. "We must discover what manner of power enabled these creatures to survive in Setharis, and who is behind it." She looked to me, troubled.

Eva crunched through shattered crystal, heedless of the shards shredding her boots. She dispatched anything still twitching. "I thought you said this would be dangerous?" she said, re-sheathing her knife. From a shallow scrape a few droplets of her blood pattered to the floor.

The cavern floor collapsed.

I plunged into icy water. The lanterns sank to the bottom, dimming blobs of light leaving me almost blind as the weight of my manacles dragged me under. Something huge barged into me, sent me tumbling with a slash of pain across my side. Bubbles erupted from my mouth as I screamed. The water tasted of salt and iron. I winced as my Gift suddenly wrenched open. I was out of Martain's range. Awareness exploded. The magi above me radiated panic as they struggled to pull themselves from the water. A mass of ravenous insanity surged up towards them.

Dissever shifted inside the meat of my thigh. The strange numbness blew apart, agony racking me as black tendrils of living iron speared through the bandages. Dissever birthed from my flesh and crawled up my body, leaving pinpricks of pain, its edge slicing though the manacles. The hilt squirmed into the palm of my hand.

A current dragged me to one side of the pit where a hole in the wall sucked at my clothes – the exit to an underground stream that somebody had hastily blocked off to keep the creature contained.

Flashes of light exploded overhead, silhouetting something large and misshapen in the water above me. It was far too puny to be the gigantic thing that I had originally seen.

My lungs burned for air. I kicked upwards, feeling my way along the wall until I broke the surface. I took great heaving breaths and clutched onto the wall, coughing as smoke tickled the back of my throat. One of my guards floated next to me, half his torso bitten off, pink and red organs drifting free. Above, a jet of flame engulfed a fleshy abomination. The formless thing of churning flesh sprouted arms and legs and gnashing jaws as it dragged itself from the water towards a terrified pyromancer. The magus shook with the torrent of power flowing through him, his flames intensifying. The mass of churning flesh rolled over him. His magic cut off with a wet crunch. Patches of rock glowed and burned but the creature's rippling flesh was undamaged by the magical flames. It swelled as it absorbed him. The man's horrified face sank into its body, the light of intelligence in his eyes guttering, decaying into feral hunger. He howled at me, jaws snapping.

I shrieked as my Gift clamped shut and something grabbed me by the collar, yanking me up onto the rock floor. I flailed behind me, Dissever slashing. Something grabbed my wrist and held it. "You are going nowhere," Martain said, spinning me round to face him.

"Is that so?" I replied, smashing my forehead into his face. His eyes bulged, mouth gaping, as he lurched back, blood pouring from his nose. He'd spent too long dealing with magi who relied on magic as the answer to everything. I hobbled away until my Gift reopened.

Eva was down and bleeding, a gaping wound in her shoulder. I missed a step, torn between fleeing or helping. Her skin had been all but impervious to the shard beasts' legs, how the f… Of course – this thing fed on magic just like its larger sibling. It had eaten straight through her magically hardened skin.

A swarm of green lights buzzed though the gloom to detonate in the thing's flesh. A dozen conjoined mouths gibbered and cried out in pain, limbs jerking and thrashing. The skin was scorched but showed no other effects. Eyes appeared on its back and bulged out towards its tormentor. Shadea pulled the other pyromancer unconscious from the dark waters, a raised welt on his forehead, and then calmly loosed a lance of incandescent light that could burn a man to ash. All it did was blast a small crater into the thing's hide. She tutted as her second attack also failed.

A dozen malformed limbs sprouted and it lurched towards her. Shadea grimaced, and then unleashed a dozen different attacks with bewildering speed, globes of fire, bolts of lightning, darts of purplish crystal that solidified mid-air. The thing shrugged them all off.

She paused, confounded for a moment but showing no hint of fear. Shadea was an elder magus, an adept of magics beyond her natural affinity and a magus who had faced down insane murderers, blood sorcerers, corrupted wild beasts, grotesque daemons and heathen god-spirits, and had defeated them all. If she couldn't take this thing down then nobody could.

"The creature is resistant to direct attacks from magical sources," she said. "Switch to secondary effect attacks."

Cillian rose from the dark pool, feet planted firmly atop

a pillar of water. A second pillar snaked up into the air beside her, tilting until it faced the creature, then swung forward. The giant fist of water hit it like a battering ram. The controlling magic broke apart as soon as it touched the creature but the weight of water slammed it into the wall in an explosion of dust and debris. The cavern shook, stone rumbling ominously as dust and fragments rained down. The light was growing dim as the pyromancer's flames died and slagged rock cooled. I gritted my teeth against the pain and forced a trickle of power into my eyes. The darkness retreated. It was all I could manage after the abuse my Gift had taken, but even that damage was easing with uncanny swiftness.

Moans and wails bubbled from the thing's shattered mouths and torn throats as limbs flopped aimlessly. Cillian started to smile, but it was stillborn. Broken bones cracked back into place somewhere inside its bulk. Torn flesh and spilt blood slurped into the body, reforming. All-too human faces burst from its skin, screaming in panicked animal pain.

I turned to make my escape, found Shadea between me and the exit. Eva staggered towards her, one arm hanging limply but the heavy knife clutched in the other. Her wound was already knitting together and scabbing over. There was no escape that way. Whoever won here, I lost. Or I could take the chance and break through into that underground waterway and hope it carried me out rather than drowning me in the dark or smashing my head open on a rock. It seemed a preferable way to die, and it had to empty out somewhere. If I wanted to gut Harailt I had to risk it.

The creature shambled forward, tentacles darting out at everybody simultaneously. One wrapped round my waist before I could react, small gripping spikes stabbing into my skin. I screamed. Not from torn skin, but from the sudden suction on my Gift. The creature was ravenous for both meat and magic. It hauled me towards gnashing human teeth in inhuman mouths.

I hacked my knife into the tentacle, heedless of the possibility of Dissever's magic being devoured – but instead of devouring the enchantment, raw power exploded into me. Dissever drank deep and I felt the creature's life-force pulsing with the Gifts of more than one mageborn. I was drunk on power and riding high on a wave of rage, cutting deeper.

The thing shrieked and broke off its attempts to snare us. Cooling flesh unravelled from around my waist and plopped to the ground. The thing had severed its own tentacle rather than let Dissever feast further. I held up the black iron blade and licked the side, savouring the bloody warmth. Even in my power-drunken state disgust rose up inside, but I couldn't stop myself. My body felt healthy again, pulsing with a potent vitality.

"Edrin!" Cillian shouted from her platform of water, voice booming unnaturally loud. I blinked and looked up, realized that she'd tried to get my attention more than once. "What did you do?" she said.

I didn't have time to answer. The creature launched itself at her, moving impossibly quickly for something of its bulk. She didn't have time to scream before it enveloped her. The platform of water burst apart and they plummeted towards the water. Her terror hit me hard. Before I knew what I was doing I flung myself onto its back. Dissever rammed into the twisted flesh as all three of us plunged deep.

My skin burned as the creature tried to devour my magic and absorb my flesh. I shoved Dissever deeper, sawing. The beast flinched as I stabbed through pulsing muscle and hit something hard – I glimpsed a glow through the wound, something vital. A heart of magical crystal. I hacked at it, once, twice. It cracked and gave way. Light flashed and heat bloomed as the arcane core of the creature exploded. It convulsed, smashing into the rock wall, body breaking apart as the inner light guttered and died.

Cillian's motionless form floated free of the mess. The wall crackled and crumbled, water pouring through a hole into the watercourse beyond. I didn't believe in worship, but right then I started praying to everything I'd ever heard of. Dissever wrenched itself from my grip and flowed back into my wound rather than risk being lost in the watery depths. I grabbed hold of Cillian and held on tight as the torrent sucked us through.

CHAPTER 24

The current tossed us around like rag dolls. Dazed, I scrabbled for purchase on slick rock, nails cracking. I clutched Cillian tight to my chest, blindly trying to keep our heads up and snatch breath from pockets of air. Icy water flooded my mouth and up my nose, choking me. The water fell away, as did my stomach, and we were washed down a long chute. All air exploded from my lungs as I bounced off a wall and tumbled end over end, one of my boots tearing free.

I flailed in vain, tried to slow down, couldn't tell which way was up. My lungs screamed. Panic filled me, the need to breathe overwhelming. Our heads burst out into air and I sucked in another desperate lungful before a surge sucked us under, submerging again and again until a roaring filled my ears. We went over a waterfall and plunged deep into a pool; the impact tore Cillian from my grasp and the river pulled me backwards. I flopped this way and that, unseen tunnel walls pummeling me like a hundred hidden fists. With one last surge those walls were abruptly no longer there. The current dissipated.

Saltwater stung my eyes and a wavering light filtered down from what had to be up. Cillian's motionless form was blurry shadow above me. Foul-tasting gunk clogged the back of my throat, like I'd bitten into something rotten. I tore off my remaining boot and took hold of Cillian's arm in one hand, pulling great handfuls of water with the other as I made for the light, the wound in my leg burning with each kick. The surface neared with agonising slowness. Panic set in as the need to breathe overwhelmed me. My vision started to darken. With one last desperate stroke my face burst free and I took ragged heaving breaths. I'd never take air for granted again! Cillian didn't move, unconscious or dead.

Coughing and spluttering, I wiped blurry, stinging eyes and treaded water, struggling to keep us both afloat amidst a froth of sewage and refuse. I gagged and spat at the foulness in my mouth. The underground river had washed us out to sea near Pauper's Docks.

I started a painstakingly slow and pathetic paddle towards shore, towing Cillian behind me. Clumps of splintered wood and debris floated nearby, evidence of a ship going down. A dozen Setharii navy cogs were limping into the docks, their sails torn, hulls charred and studded with arrows. One of them was listing badly, a gaping wound in the starboard side bearing what looked like teeth marks. The road winding up to Pauper's Gate thronged with wounded coming off the ships, and people running back and forth carrying tools and weapons.

I wallowed my way through the waves, already tired from the exertion of flailing around like a diseased hog. By the time I dragged us both onto the shingle beach I was panting and aching all over. I rolled Cillian onto her back. She was covered in angry welts and patches of raw skin where the creature had touched her. Four long bloodless gashes marred either side of her neck, as if something had tried to tear her throat out. She wasn't breathing so I opened her sodden robes and fumbled for a pulse in her neck with frozen hands. Nothing. I had no idea what to do. I pressed on her stomach and water gushed from her mouth and from the gashes in her neck.

"Breathe," I snarled, pumping her stomach. I tried to get it all out, but she still didn't take a breath.

"Come on, Cillian. You are better than this. You were meant to do great things, not drown in the dark. Burn it, breathe."

She didn't.

I collapsed to the stones, trying to marshal enough will and strength to haul myself up and stagger towards the docks. My stomach growled, informing me that I was literally starving after all the quickened healing I'd had.

There wasn't much of me left that wasn't battered, bruised or bleeding. Some homecoming. If I wasn't a magus I would have died five times over. How often did we shrug off injuries that would cripple or kill a normal person, without so much as a thought? It wasn't surprising many thought themselves so far above mundanes as to be a different breed.

Eventually I managed to stagger to my feet and peeled off my torn clothes to wring most of the water out. I tried not to look at Cillian. I had no reason to feel guilty, but I'd known her well once and couldn't help but feel responsible in some way. My body was a tapestry of black, green and blue bruises. Some were already blooming out into yellows and purples. I probed my head with my fingers and fortunately it didn't seem like I'd broken anything after battering it off rocks, but then my medical skills extended as far as wrapping bandages and hoping for the best. Lynas always said I was thick-skulled. A hand raked through my hair dislodged squidgy debris it was better not thinking about.

The weeping hole in my leg burned from the saltwater. "Get the fuck out," I said to Dissever, imagining the pain belonged to somebody else.

Tendrils of liquid black writhed from the wound. I clamped my jaw shut to muffle screams as Dissever birthed itself in a welter of blood. It clanged to the stones, jagged blade embedded a hairsbreadth away from severing my big toe.

"What are you, you vile thing?"

It replied only with alien mirth.

I scowled and tore off strips of tunic to bandage my leg, grimacing as I took a few experimental steps. Dissever was carefully hooked under my belt and it was obvious I carried an unnatural weapon, but the time for subtlety was long past.

I wiped the worst of the blood and filth from Cillian's face. We had not been friends at the end, closer to enemies in truth, but I could never hate her. In some other world I might have saved her, been a hero. But that wasn't me. I sat her up facing the sea, dabbed away some more filth from around her eyes and nose. She would have liked to go with a view of the sea. "Goodbye, Cillian. And... I'm sorry."

She opened her eyes.

I jerked my hand back, fell arse-first onto the beach.

She doubled over, coughing up water and clutching her head. "Where am I?"

My mouth opened and closed like an idiot fish.

She probed her matted hair with her fingertips, wincing as she found a lump the size of an egg. She looked at me blearily. "Edrin? What... Where are we?" She suddenly realized that her shoes were missing and her robes torn open and absolutely indecent. She hastily rearranged them and shot me a suspicious look.

I swallowed. "The beach near Pauper's Docks. We, uh, got washed out into the sea." I couldn't quite believe this was happening. "You weren't breathing. I thought..."

She tried to rise, groaned and sagged back. "I am a powerful hydromancer, you fool. You think I can drown? That a councillor of the Inner Circle is so weak amidst her own element? All of us with sufficient power have our adaptations."

I wasn't the fool she thought I was. Not entirely. "That creature ate magic. I felt the stolen Gifts of magi inside it and didn't know if there was anything of you left."

Her eyes flew wide with sudden remembrance. She shuddered, leant to one side and quietly vomited. I waited patiently for her to finish heaving up her breakfast of eggs and bread. "Dear gods, what happened?" she said, wrapping her arms around herself. "How am I alive? I felt it devouring my magic, eating me."

"I cut the fucker's heart out," I said, sounding cockier than I felt.

"How? It ate magic and our blades would have been useless."

"Your blades maybe." That was all the answer I fancied giving a magus of the Inner Circle, even if she did happen to owe me her life. With Cillian the Arcanum would always come first. Nobody needed to know Dissever was more dangerous than any spirit-bound blade I'd ever heard of. Even I didn't know the full extent of its powers. It was more aware than a crude hunk of metal infused with a spirit should ever be. And now it was mobile. Terrifying.

She studied Dissever's barbed blade and tensed, but said nothing, for once letting me have my secrets. "That abomination was a thing of blood sorcery created to kill magi. It ate magic. You had to know that. And you still leapt onto its back to save me. Why?"

I groaned like an old man as I levered myself to my feet, stones sharp against my soles. "I'm a fool," I said, shrugging. "Surely that's not a revelation to you?"

She stared at me for a long moment, face inscrutable. "Thank you."

"I'm just glad we both made it out of there," I said, trying not to think about it.

"There were rumours," she said, "about your involvement

in various atrocities ten years ago. I did not like to think the worst of you, Edrin, but you must understand how the Forging changed you. Something dark entered your head and twisted your personality. It set you on a self-destructive path I feared would see you dead. Or worse."

I shrugged, too tired to know how to react. "Did you believe the rumours?"

"I was uncertain, but I did know that you would never harm Archmagus Byzant."

"And now?"

"I believe you had nothing to do with any of it."

Words held great power. They hit me right in the heart. Cillian believed me, even after everything I had done to her in the past.

"Thanks," I said gruffly. Of course, I had been involved in killing a god, but she hadn't mentioned that part. Perhaps it was too unbelievable.

She sighed in relief. "At least that thing died before the sorcerer could unleash it. Thwarting this evil plot will go a long way in proving your innocence with the Courts of Justice."

She caught my sick expression. Her brow furrowed. "What is it?"

I licked my lips, a sudden foul taste flooding my mouth. "The thing I told you I saw in the lake? Well that creature we killed wasn't it."

"What do you mean?"

"That thing in the lake was vast. The one we just killed was a pup in comparison. Lynas' body and Gift weren't a part of that one. His Gift still lives. I can feel it somewhere underground, though the bond is faint and disrupted."

"You can't possibly know that for certain. The only way you could is if–" Her eyes widened and her throat spasmed, threatening to throw up again. So now she knew that I had

Gift-bonded Lynas all those years ago. Instead of chastising me she struggled to her feet, brushing off the hand I offered. "We must warn the Arcanum."

"You go do that. I have Harailt to kill."

My body seized up as foreign magic flooded my veins and threatened to burst every blood vessel in my body.

"You will come with me," she stated.

I gurgled a negative. She gave my insides a squeeze and then let go.

I staggered, nearly fell. "Nice way to treat somebody that just saved your life."

"Grow up. This is bigger than either of us. To save this city I would tie you to a horse and drag you over every cobble if necessary."

"So what is the bloody big secret here?" I said. "Why do you need me when you have the rest of the Arcanum at your beck and call?"

She suddenly wavered, eyes glazing over, stumbled and nearly fell. I instinctively steadied her, despite my distaste. She groaned and leant on my arm, still suffering from that knock to the head.

She blinked and refocused, looked up into my eyes for a confusion-filled moment before brushing me off and backing away. "I'm sorry," she said. "I'm not being vindictive. I suspect that we will need every magus we have."

"Why?"

She chewed on her lip. "If this creature is what I fear then we will need every resource of the city to withstand it. You are involved in all of this, and you did manage to kill that smaller one."

"Then dust off your old war engines and all those artefacts locked away in the vaults below the Templarum Magestus," I said. At the height of its empire Setharis had fielded a bewildering array of deadly weapons dug from the ruins of old Escharr, so why not just use those? "If it's really that bad then have them raise the bloody titans. You don't need me."

She hesitated for a moment before shaking her head. "The titan cores have been buried in the deepest of vaults behind layers of protection that even the archmagus cannot easily remove. It would take weeks to access them. In any case, the Arcanum will never again sanction their use. We are already worried about their strange luminescence."

"Old Boney's balls, it's like pulling teeth – just tell me what that bloody creature is! I have a right to know."

"If it is what I fear, then its nature is chronicled in fragments of ancient scrolls recovered only recently from an Escharric dig site, knowledge meant to be restricted to the Inner Circle." She hesitated. "Damn the rule, that time has flown. The creature's attributes perfectly match all those reported of the Doom of Escharr, the monstrous beast that devoured the heart of that ancient empire. It is the thing those few surviving magi named Magash Mora – the Devouring Flesh." She shuddered. "Oh dear gods, all those disappearances in the city, the skinned mageborn! How could we have suspected anything of this scale?"

A cold shiver rippled up my spine. Hair prickled all over my body. "How is that even possible?" I said, grabbing her tattered robes, knuckles white. "Was it not destroyed with the rest of Escharr?"

She shrugged me off. "We cannot know for sure if this is the same creature. It was reputed to have eaten all it could and then starved to death. Its insides eventually burned to ash under the desert sun."

I goggled. "The Arcanum have been digging up their ruins for centuries – how could you not know? Even with help from the Skallgrim, it would be impossible for Harailt to create a new one." My hands trembled. "Impossible."

He brought this monstrous thing here to my home, to my city. He'd murdered Lynas, tried to abduct Layla, and now he wanted to take even more from me? Something inside me teetered on the edge of losing control and tearing loose as a rabid howling beast. "Harailt is not powerful or clever enough to enact all of this alone. Only a god could fool Shadea like that. He is in league with greater powers. This new Hooded God, he–"

"Calm yourself," she interrupted. "I cannot imagine the gods are involved in the destruction of their own city. They have protected Setharis for a thousand years, and the Lord of Bones, Artha and Lady Night were gods here before there even was a Setharis."

"They have all protected Setharis for an age, all except one."

That gave her pause. "You were proven correct about one claim. I would be a fool to dismiss the other. When I return Harailt will be subjected to every test possible, however invasive. We will determine the truth beyond any possible doubt.

"That creature we encountered was not merely resistant to magic," she continued, "it fed on it, and if that was a mere spawn then even the gods may have cause to fear. I can only imagine the horror we now face. We must retreat and formulate a plan of action."

"Your plan is to hole up behind the walls of the Old Town until you think of something better." Her expression told me I was correct. "What about Docklands? What about every other poor sod living there? Just going to abandon them to that creature, are you?"

Her mouth opened and closed. She looked surprised, and didn't quite know what to say to me. I scowled and turned away. "I'm not sure what's worse, that you are abandoning them or that you forgot to consider them at all." She was a good person, but sadly still a product of her upbringing and environment.

"We are simply concentrating our power," she said. "It is the logical solution."

"Logic be damned, I…" My words drifted off as plumes of roiling smoke caught my eye. Ships berthed at Pauper's Docks were burning. So were maybe a dozen sites spread across the city, what looked to be the warehouses that held a goodly portion of the city's grain. A vicious melee erupted on the docks as a mob cornered a number of armed men – surely the arsonists – and began beating them to death.

"We are out of time," she said.

Cillian ran for the docks, heedless of sharp rocks and sucking mud under her bare feet. Despite taking a hefty hit to the head, she left me puffing and panting in her wake. Knowing her, she probably rose at first light and followed an exacting exercise regime. She had told me that "a healthy body means a healthy mind" at some point in the past. My dislike of her grew.

A chain of people were ferrying buckets of seawater up onto the burning ships with impressive efficiency. Even so, sooty flames grew higher, hissing tongues of red and orange crawling up their masts. Rigging and sails flared as they went up. On the other side of the city, a pall of black was rising from Westford Docks.

"Are they trying to burn every seaworthy ship here?" Cillian said. "This is deliberate. But why?"

I licked my lips. "To stop us escaping."

"Explain."

"The Skinner – Harailt – was hunting down mageborn, and then he moved on to full-blown magi to fuel his blood sorcery. It seems to me he's stepping it up, that he wants our people confined within the city walls. In an evacuation of the city, who or what would be on the first ships out?"

"The Arcanum and the High Houses of course," she replied. "Along with our most dangerous weapons... Son of a whore!"

"Exactly. Nothing is getting out now." It was strange hearing her swear at something other than me; always a rarity, and now that she was a high and mighty councillor I didn't imagine it ever happened in public.

A soot-smeared dockhand, yoke across his shoulders weighed down by two full buckets, slowed and glared at us as he passed. "You two scruffians just goin' to stand here and watch? There's goodly folk trapped. Get in line and lend a hand."

Cillian straightened and hoisted her chin. "No need." Her magic flared up around her and she stretched a hand out towards the nearest ship. It started to pitch and rock as the sea churned to brown froth beneath. Gasps rippled up the waterline of people as tentacles of seawater rose around one of the ships like a sea monster about to pull the vessel under. Instead water crashed down across the deck, snuffing out flames in clouds of steam. It was an awesome display of power, more so for me than the people on the docks – they had no idea of the obscene volume of magic Cillian was channelling.

The dockhand gaped, head snapping from the ship to Cillian and back again. A strangled choke emerged from his throat and his face reddened. "Beg pardon, magus," he forced out. "Didn't mean no offence."

"I took no offence, my good man," she replied, glancing at me from the corner of her eye. "Every life is precious, is it not? It is my duty to provide what assistance I can."

He bobbed his head and backed away from us as quickly as possible without actually fleeing. Everybody staring at us suddenly decided that gawping at the bedraggled magus was bad for their health and went back to hauling buckets of water down to the fires.

"Nice words," I said. "Did you mean them?"

She scowled, face taut with concentration as water writhed over a second ship that was already listing badly, flames consuming the starboard side.

"I am not a monster," she said, "whatever you may think. I will do what I must for Setharis and the Arcanum. However, I do accept that I am a product of privilege, and capable of oversight. I'm only human, you judgmental prick."

I grunted. "Well said. Anyway, see you later."

Her concentration almost faltered, but it took more than that to disrupt the focus of a magus of her prowess. Her eyes narrowed, lips thinning with both anger and the effort of directing so much complex magic. "You are coming with me, Edrin. If you try to leave you will regret it."

I nodded towards the ships. "People are trapped and you are their only hope. How many will die if you try to stop me? I won't make it easy for you." My smile crumbled. "Don't try to out-bastard me, Cillian. I'll win every time. I am going to find Harailt and I am going to kill him. There is no need for your tests."

My head ached from the strain both body and Gift had been under, and the secret locked away in my head was ever-present in my thoughts, the power that locked it away finally crumbling. I felt like a pus-filled boil ripe and ready to burst. The mere thought of reliving those memories caused me to break out in a cold sweat, but they were also the key to defeating the traitor god that was helping Harailt.

She shook her head slowly. "No, even you would not condemn innocent people to death. That would make you just as bad as all those uncaring, privileged bastards that you rant about with such vehemence."

I looked her right in the eye. I'd already killed one innocent man since returning. "Oh, I'm far worse." And I meant it. She'd no idea about all the dirty, devious, and just plain brutal things I'd done to survive over the years; the rich had no conception of that sort of life. I turned my back on her and headed for the city, every step exuding carefree confidence. In truth I was near pissing myself wondering if she'd stop the blood in my veins, or even burst a non-vital body part, maybe one I'd really not be keen to lose. But she didn't, instead she cursed and focused on saving lives. She thought I really was that much of a bastard.

I didn't examine myself too closely as to what I'd have done if she tried to stop me. I suspected neither of us would have liked the answer.

CHAPTER 25

A nearby warning bell tolled frantically. The wardens up on the walls hastily strung bows. Fearful faces stared out to sea. I followed their gaze. Hundreds of square sails studded the horizon, bearing the emblems of dozens of Skallgrim tribes. I licked my lips and swallowed, a thrill of fear rippling up my spine as I remembered those same wolf-ships unleashing red slaughter and daemons on Ironport. Of course Harailt was in league with those savages. He never had any empathy or mercy to begin with.

The sound of bells spread across the city as more wardens spotted the Skallgrim fleet. With the fires raging on the docks, most people were still tearing in and out of the gate to help, but some stopped to point and gawp in horror. The volume of traffic made the gate warden's work impossible and to the sniffer on duty Cillian's magic had to have been like staring into the sun, so it wasn't a surprise he didn't notice a filthy barefoot scumbag like me slipping through the gate.

Once Cillian was out of sight I felt able to breathe again, but I picked up my pace and resisted the urge to continually glance behind me. As soon as I entered the market I felt the crowd's panic, and I didn't need to be a magus to sense the riot birthing.

Blood stained the stones underfoot and food stalls had

already been picked bare and overturned. A wild-eyed old man with long straggly hair, dressed in nothing more than rags, deftly dodged the two armoured wardens pursuing him and clambered up onto one of the stalls so he could be seen by all. "The Skallgrim are coming," he screamed, pointing towards the sea. Then he spun to hiss up the hill at the gods' towers. "An end to the leeches that grow fat on our blood and toil. Rise up and put an end to the corruption of vile magic at our heart!"

The wardens caught him, one hauling him kicking and biting from his podium while the other hefted a club and bashed the old man's head. He flopped down unconscious, blood matting his hair. The wardens didn't check to see if he was alive or dead, and probably didn't care, instead hastily dragging him off with the angry crowd edging after them. Then the whispers started rippling through the crowd – High Houses – the Arcanum – gold – war – vile corruption – fat leeches – eat while we starve – our blood and toil…

More than swords and magic, words held real power. Regimes the world over had risen with a few whispered words in the right ears. And they'd also fallen to a few well-chosen words said to big crowds of scared people. People were like that in groups, a herd instinct sweeping them along in a flood of anger instead of fear, like cornered rats turning on a cat. I pushed in next to a gaunt woman wrapped in a ragged shawl, a refugee from Ironport by the cut of her cloth.

Setharis was ready to explode, and that old man had just flung in an oil lantern. I opened up my Gift – finding it oddly pain-free, if strained – and scanned the crowd, locating two other agitators without too much difficulty: they were the calm ones filled with a purpose verging on the fanatic. I skimmed the surface and tasted their thoughts, felt their disdain and disgust for the depraved cityfolk they found themselves surrounded by. They were not from Setharis, though they'd spent years here. They were Skallgrim infiltrators. Who had ever heard of subtlety from the Skallgrim? They preferred to fight each other over long-held feuds rather than looking to war with anybody else. Or they had done – times were apparently changing. The men were readying to fling more words into the crowd – more torches to help start the fire.

The tension was building to its peak. Somebody picked up a piece of horse dung and flung it at the retreating wardens. It splattered against one man's helmet and he turned, still holding his bloodied club. It had to be now. I placed my hand on the refugee's arm. She twitched as I entered her mind, then stilled.

"I'm from Ironport," she shouted. "And Skallgrim beasts skinned my daughter alive." For some reason I'd found that daughters usually had a more emotive effect. The crowd turned to stare. "Sacrificed for their sick, heathen blood sorcery," she continued. The crowd needed a reminder of the distinction between our magic and their sorcery. Even the crudest peasant knew dozens of dark tales about blood sorcery.

"No, the Skallgrim will save us," one of the agitators started up as the warning bells on the walls tolled louder, more urgent. "They bring all Kaladon a purity that was lost, and they offer Setharis, the Free Cities, and even the heathen Clanholds a life free from the yoke of magic."

Time to break out the emotional blackmail. Tears started rolling down the refugee's face. "Skinned her alive as I watched," she sobbed. "Just like the monster that's been killing people here." Eyes widened in the crowd as those words sunk in. Skinned alive by Skallgrim beasts. The Skinner.

"Lies!" the agitator shouted, drawing the eyes to him. "It is those leeches up in their palaces that caused this. They are the problem. The Skinner is one of them. They don't care if a few peasants die. We should march up there and take the wealth that should be ours."

I let go of the woman, leaving her sobbing her heart out and with no idea what she had just said.

"Sounds like he's in league with the Skinner and the Skallgrim to me," I shouted. "He's a traitor. The Skallgrim want to skin us alive and drain our blood. Everybody knows the Arcanum hunt and kill all blood sorcerers."

All it took was giving the man in front of me a shove with a shout of "Get him!" A few members of the crowd took a step forward, more followed, and then the whole crowd surged as one, grabbing at the Skallgrim infiltrator. All that fear and anger they'd been building exploded in his face. The mob took hold of the screaming man and started tearing him to pieces. Never before had I exerted such power over the hearts and minds of people on such a grand scale. Their emotions were in the palm of my hand. I could make them dance like a puppeteer's painted dolls and I found that I liked it.

A person could be clever, but crowds of people were stupid and easily manipulated. The problem was that once you built it up to a fever pitch, then somebody with just the right words could redirect it. Once a riot started they were difficult to control, but that wasn't my problem. I just didn't want dozens of innocent people incinerated by the defensive magics guarding the Old Town. I felt giddy with my own power, the Worm of Magic purring happily in the depths of my mind. I held a truly fearful power, and it was harder than ever to resist the delicious temptation to meddle, to dominate and direct, to *rule*. Letting my magic loose in the Boneyards had changed me, brought me closer to the mindset that the Worm – or worse, myself – desired. How could I cope without Lynas? He had always been my conscience, the hand on my moral rudder steering me back into safer waters. Even during my years of exile he had always been a presence in the back of my mind, mentally chastising me when I contemplated going too far.

Nauseated, I tore myself away from temptation and struggled against the tide of people, trying to avoid all the boots stepping on my bare feet as I followed the second agitator fleeing down a side street. He was the clever one, the one who had known when to shut his mouth and leave it well alone, which meant he was more dangerous than his fellows. He might know what Harailt's end game was. I followed him as he skirted the centre of the Warrens and headed towards Westford.

He stopped at an intersection and looked back. I slowed, made myself look exhausted, hanging my head and dragging bare feet through street filth. His gaze slid straight past me. Looking at the ragged state of me nobody would expect I was anything other than a deranged beggar, and Setharis had no shortage of those. He slunk down an alley and out of sight. I tailed him further west. He paused at a crossroads and I ducked into the shadows of a doorway as he carefully looked in all directions before heading right. I sidled up to the wall and carefully peered around the corner. He stood a mere pace away, dagger in hand. I lurched back as the point darted for my eye. A door thumped open behind me and I spun to see two heavy-set men emerge.

I backed away, holding up filthy hands. "I don't want no trouble. Just some food if you got any?"

The infiltrator sneered and the two men reached for me.

Back the way I'd come, somebody cleared her throat.

"Die," Cillian said.

All three men twitched, blood gushing from nose, ears and eyes as they crumpled to the mud. I winced, expecting to experience Cillian's wrath myself.

"Skallgrim infiltrators," I said, when her magic didn't burst me like a rotten tomato. "How did you find me?" I eyed my prospective lead's blood pooling in the mud and thought it wise not to rub her mistake in her face.

She gazed at the corpses, her face grim, and I wondered if she had ever before used her magic to kill – until now I'd only theorized her deadly potential. "I followed the trail of devastation," she said. "It took me a while to work my way through the angry mob. After that I followed the tracking ward I had placed on your clothing."

She'd done what? I started sweating, wondering if she'd placed some nasty surprise in me ready to explode on command.

She smiled thinly, glanced at the corpses by my feet. "It is war then."

"We have been at war quite some time," I said. "We've only just noticed."

She gave a terse nod. "You are not the fool you pretend to be, Magus Edrin Walker, and I am only just starting to realize that." Her eyes bored into me. "I am on to your game."

I swallowed, smiled sickly. "Ah, that."

She paced the cobbles. "The Arcanum had deemed it impossible for the Skallgrim to ever unite. Of the great powers, Setharis has been in economic decline for the last fifty years and our closest allies in Ahram and Esban consumed by infighting. We will receive no aid from them. It is an advantageous time for the Skallgrim to expand their territories."

If she was being straightforward with an untrustworthy cur like me then things had to be truly bad. Either that or the blow to her head had been worse than I'd thought.

"It stinks, Edrin," she said, "stinks of long and meticulous preparation for conquest, and patience is not something the Skallgrim have ever been noted for." She was reinforcing my own disquieting suspicions. "Over the years far too many of our ships have gone missing, and our agents in other lands have been turning up dead with depressing frequency. They must also be involved with the Magash Mora in some manner, but again the Skallgrim tribes lack the knowledge necessary to create such a creature. I feel an unknown power behind all these events." She chewed on her bottom lip, eyes widening, "Harailt was posted to our embassies bordering their lands ten years back. It cannot be coincidence this all happens here and now."

"You believe me then?" I asked.

"It would seem to match up. We have no time to debate this. Their infiltrators will be all over the city trying to incite the masses and there is no knowing how many of their warriors are already inside our walls.

"You did well," she said. "You played that angry mob as deftly as any minstrel ever plucked strings." Her eyes narrowed. "Now, tell me how you managed it without touching them all?"

I grunted. "You saved those sailors from a fiery death quicker than I'd expected."

"I sit on the Inner Circle for a reason. Don't change the subject."

We passed from the dark of the Warrens into a wider street, one lined with newer wood. It probably hadn't existed for long enough to acquire a name yet. People were dashing to and fro, some holding bloody noses or makeshift weapons, all avoiding eye contact.

I could have lied to her, come up with some pretty story wittering on about body language, expression and posture, but events were already too dangerous and spiralling out of control. "Oh, that?" I said. "I don't need to touch you to get into your head. I haven't since I was a mere initiate."

She lurched to a stop and a trace of fear seeped into her expression. "Just how strong are you?"

A woman ran down the street, toddler wailing in her arms. She hammered on a door, panting for breath. It creaked open, then swung wide. An older woman hugged her tight. "A mob is ransacking that fancy brothel," the first woman said. "Best keep your girls indoors."

Charra's Place. Layla.

I felt the air stir – too late to do anything about it other than drop to the dirt. An arrow thudded into the wall behind me. I scrambled to my feet, wrenched my strained Gift open and searched for the bowman. Sudden waves of agony made my attention snap to Cillian, who was staring at another arrow jutting from her chest.

Pink froth bubbled from Cillian's mouth and a dark stain spread across the front of her robes. She coughed, spattering my hand with blood, then slumped against the wall, a sickening sound of air wheezing from the wound. That sound, it… Blood gushed from my nose, head ringing like somebody had rammed a steel-shod boot into my face. Mental protections cracked and splintered, and bled out: *the sound of a god's agonized wheezing, my hands slick with hot blood so filled with magic that it sizzled against my skin. Artha's heart spasmed as I cut deeper and pushed a hand into it…*

Another arrow buried itself in the wall a hand span from my face. I didn't have time to think, panic stamping the surge of memory back into its pit. I scanned the rooftops as my mind expanded into nearby buildings. Snarls of thought and emotion marked dozens of people out of sight inside the walls. There – two bowmen inside fourth floor windows, their killing intent searing my senses. It was infectious. My urge to kill swelled.

One of the attackers stepped forward to the edge of the window and lined up another shot. I stabbed into his mind, scattered his thoughts and planted the urge to step forward for a better aim, onto a wooden sill that wasn't really there. I took grim satisfaction in the spike of confusion when his foot unexpectedly plunged down through air. It was much easier to fool somebody than go directly against their survival instincts. He fell screaming from the window, head hitting the cobbles with a sound like a burst melon.

His accomplice was no coward; after a quick glance at the mess on the cobbles he tried to take his own shot. His mind was calm and orderly, an experienced killer. He resisted mightily and was about to loose when his body exploded, painting the surrounding buildings red.

"Got... him," Cillian wheezed.

I held onto her arm in case she fell. Her breathing came in rapid gulps and her robes were drenched with blood. I reached to pull out the arrow. She hissed, her eyes not filled with panic but with a warning to back the fuck away.

"Wait..." she said between gulps, concentrating hard. The blood stopped spreading. Being a hydromancer had perks I'd never thought of before but it seemed she couldn't suck all that spilt blood back up after it had soaked into the muck under our feet. She groaned and clamped her hands around the base of the arrow. "Barbs... have to... break off... the shaft."

I gingerly took it in two hands, and made to snap it off to leave a short stump, then paused and felt bloody stupid as I took Dissever to it instead. The arrowhead barely moved, but she still shrieked as steel grated against bone. "What now?" I said.

She gritted her teeth and held out bloodied hands for me to help her walk. I didn't think it wise, but then I'd just been about to blindly rip an arrow out so what did I know. Somehow she stood on her own two feet. I didn't think I would be up and about with an arrow through my lung. She took a few faltering steps clutching onto my arm. "Get me… Templarum Magestus. No… time to spare. Magash Mora…"

"I'll get you there if I have to carve my way through," I said, bending so she could put an arm around my neck. She panted with pain as I took her weight. Magus or not, there was a limit to human self-control.

Feet pounded towards us down nearby alleys. Scuffles and cursing erupted as the narrow passages crammed with angry and frightened people. We slipped off the wider thoroughfare and into a narrow winding passage choked with filth. If they were Skallgrim then it wouldn't take them long to figure out where we had gone.

Cillian was lighter than I'd expected. Somehow she exuded an aura heavier than her frame could possibly allow. My body felt leaden and clumsy and I had to draw in a trickle of power and flush it through exhausted muscles. Magic was all well and good but I badly needed decent food and a few weeks of rest. It was a wonder either of us were still moving.

Through drifting smoke and crumbled tenement walls I glimpsed the gods' towers and we angled northwest, figuring it would be quicker heading for Westford Bridge rather than risk the centre of the Warrens. We hobbled through the small passages between listing buildings, bare feet squelching through mud and slime, Cillian hissing with each step. People were fighting and dying and a miasma of violence filled the whole area. Up ahead a cloud of anger and fear marked a full-blown riot, their emotions bleeding out into a communal torrent of rage.

Carrion spirits would be swarming over the city, drawn to the shedding of this much blood and magic like crows to a battlefield. The spirits would have a short existence in Setharis before the city devoured them, but they'd instinctively do their best to inflame the situation, to feed and breed and spread disease.

We burst from the gloom of the Warrens into a wider street, barging into some poor sap and knocking them to the cobbles. I turned to spit a quick apology but the words went unsaid as thick coils of smoke drifted past. Flames illuminated the black haze up ahead and terrified people were running for their lives towards us. I knew exactly where I was now. Charra's Place lay only a short distance up the street towards Westford Bridge.

"Walker," Cillian wheezed in warning.

I started, looked down at the person I'd bumped into. "Sorry, I–"

"Piece of dung!" The scars at either side of Rosha Boneface's mouth pulled white in a scowl. A dozen knives glinted in the gloom as more Smilers surrounded us.

I felt Cillian tense. "Easy now," I said. "Stay calm." These people had no idea how close they were to a very messy death.

Rosha scrambled to her feet. "Stay calm? I should cut your stinkin' cock off!"

"I wasn't speaking to you," I snapped, nodding to Cillian. "I was telling this magus here not to burst you like rotten fruit."

Despite Cillian's bloodied state she must have given a fearsome glare judging by Rosha's taken aback expression. "I have no time to dally… with the likes of them," she said, staring at their scarified smiles.

"A magus?" Rosha growled, voice wobbling with uncertainty as she took in the ruins of Cillian's expensive robes. The Smilers were used to intimidating people, but we weren't displaying the slightest smidgeon of worry. "What would scum like you be doin' with one of those daemon-touched bastards?"

"Councillor Cillian is right," I said, opening up my Gift and reaching for Rosha. "We don't have time for this crap."

Her eyes bulged as she felt me prod the inside of her mind. "So, are you going to get out of our way or are you coming to Charra's Place with us?" I asked, withdrawing but keeping my Gift ready.

A strangled choke erupted from Rosha's throat. "Councillor?" She coughed and cleared it, looking at us like we were daemons in human form. "That's the direction we was goin' anyways, you maggot." A shocked expression burst across her face, and she paled as it dawned on her what she'd just called the magus. Her bad habits would get her killed some day, but not by me.

"Uh, sorry, my, ah, maguses," she said. The rest of her gang looked like they'd collectively soiled themselves. Not surprising considering the dread stories that gleefully spread amongst the peasantry. Suddenly their knives seemed woefully inadequate. On the other hand, our reputation as magi was the only armour we had: all it would take was one idiot to stick a knife in my back and I'd be out of the game. I hoped they didn't have somebody insane enough to risk attacking us. Cillian would slaughter them.

"Get a move on," Cillian said, hobbling past two young Smilers, the puckered scars still red and angry on their cheeks. We limped uphill towards Charra's Place, closer to a bridge over the Seth and closer to help. After a moment's hesitation the Smilers followed us, their confidence returning with each step they took beside us. People coming downhill took one look at the angry wolf pack heading towards them and scattered, slinking off into darkened alleys or closing and barring their doors.

The smoke grew thicker, black coils writhing into the sky as flames licked up a nearby merchant house's walls and roared from windows on the upper floors. A mob surrounded Charra's Place, lusting for the riches inside, brandishing knives, sticks and broken bottles, flinging rocks and flaming debris at the shutters. The immaculate garden and delicate moonflowers had been churned into mud beneath their feet. A group of men had torn a heavy wooden beam from one of the burning tenements and was using it as a battering ram.

As we approached, a woman smashed a lantern across Charra's front door and the oil exploded in a black cloud. Another crashed into the upper wall, flaming oil bursting across a shuttered window. The wood was ablaze but it didn't deter the men with the battering ram as they continued pounding the door.

A wild-eyed woman in the torn and stained remnants of a dress turned to face us, her eyes catching sight of Cillian's robes. She snarled, revealing a mouth full of broken teeth. "Old Towners! Get them!"

"Oh, shite," I said, as the crazier half of the mob broke away and howled towards us. A few crossbow bolts zipped from slits in the brothel walls into the backs of the charging mob, dropping two to be trampled beneath their fellows without a second thought.

"Cillian," I said. "A little help here?" The front rank of the mob dropped mid-step as something inside them burst.

The Smilers didn't run. Maybe it was some sort of loyalty towards Charra and Layla, or perhaps this was part of their territory, but whatever reason they readied their knives and closed ranks around us.

The throbbing mass of rage surged towards me like an oncoming forest fire, and as much as I tried to keep it out, their emotion soaked into me.

I wrenched my Gift open as wide as I could manage. It was recovering astonishingly quick. Blissful power and pain roared through me in an uncontrolled wave to slam into the oncoming mob. One after another, I broke in and tore a part of their minds out. I felt laughter building up to eruption inside me as they fell face-first to the cobbles, drooling and blind. Only two survived to reach us, and the Smilers' knives made quick butchery of them.

I grinned. It had been so easy. Was this the pleasure of potency felt by elder magi? It was glorious. Sudden horror helped me wrestle that ecstatic torrent of power to the floor and stuff the laughter back down my throat where it met the rising panic and disgust at my grisly handiwork.

A terrifying and monstrous strength was biding its time inside me. I couldn't let the Worm of Magic take the reins again, no matter the cost. I glanced at the Smilers as they swallowed nervously and edged away from me. If I lost control I would take their minds, and they would be mine forever. I now knew exactly what it would feel like to be a tyrant. It was galling to admit the Arcanum were right to fear me.

Cillian stepped over a corpse and we advanced on the suddenly stilled and staring mob in front of Charra's Place, the human vermin in it for loot, rape, or the primal joy of destruction. The shitweasels that had just come to the horrid realisation they had attacked magi.

The Smilers trailed after us, didn't seem to have it in them to get too close. Rosha looked about ready to throw up and hung back out of our sight.

I stopped, my gaze sliding past the opportunistic bastards like a reaper calmly surveying a field of wheat. My brush with such a mass of vileness had affected me and it was a struggle to remain calm. If I hadn't been sickened by what I had just done I think I might have killed the rest too.

"Fuck off," I said. "Or I'll kill you all."

The mob burst apart like a flock of startled sparrows and the burning doors of Charra's Place swung open to disgorge a fully armed and armoured host, Layla at the head. The hulking forms of Grant and Nevin flanked her as she approached us, both of the big hairy clansmen gits bloodied and battered. Layla's clothes were bloodstained but it didn't look like hers. She ignored the twitching mindless bodies behind me. "Where is my mother?"

I swallowed. "She's safe. The Arcanum has her, but I'll get her back." It grew dark as a bank of thick smoke rolled over us, making it more akin to night than day.

Realisation suddenly crapped on me from a great height. *Idiot. You bloody fool!* In my worry over Cillian and Layla I had forgotten something vital, life and death even. I was covered in sweat and blood and I'd just used an enormous amount of my magic out in the open for any fool to sense – or any daemon. I shoved Cillian into Layla's arms. "Get her to the Arcanum alive and you'll get your mother back."

Cillian gasped for breath. "Edrin, what are–"

I didn't hear the rest, was too busy fleeing as fast as abused muscles could carry me. A sudden churning in my gut and a glimpse of luminous green eyes through the smoke warned me that my idiocy had paid off.

CHAPTER 26

Fuckfuckfuckfuckfuckfuckfuck...

I sprinted towards the Seth faster than I'd ever run in my life, feet barely seeming to touch the stone. They had caught my scent and I now had exactly one chance to live. I bolted towards the turgid roar of the river dead ahead.

A shadow cat the size of a horse padded from the smoke into the street right in front of me. It was Burn, scarred muzzle sniffing this way and that. My senses were befuddled by the smoke but it seemed she was affected just as badly. I slowed and circled right, trying to be quiet as I padded towards a side alley.

Matte black wisps of fur writhed across her body as her great head swung in my direction. Her shining eyes snapped to me and burned with hatred. It hissed, revealing obsidian incisors the length of my hand. Somewhere nearby yet more claws clicked on stone.

Cockrot.

Claws scrabbled behind me as I vaulted a low wall and leapt right. The shadow cat skidded past, sliding into an abandoned goods cart. The expected crash didn't come, instead a twisting racked my guts as she vanished into the shadows beneath the cartwheels – only to slide from a darkened doorway further ahead.

I lurched from the alley, trying to make it to the river

before the rest of the pack arrived. I was so close. Barefoot, I could feel the roar of water thrumming through the ground. A gust of wind thinned smoke to reveal the black bulk of cats stalking me on either side. It was pointless to try to fight.

Up ahead – the hazy forms of weather-worn statues lining the riverbank. I ran for my life. The tang of raw sewage and running water cut through the smoke. So near, but so damn far. Claws *click-click-clack*ed, gaining with every step I took. My wounded leg was about to give out. *Come on, not yet, not yet…*

A pitted statue coalesced from the smog. I panicked, dived blindly past it, hands up to cover my head. For a sickening moment I thought I'd misjudged, was about to smack face-first into the ground, but instead I plunged through smoke towards the river.

A great paw caught the back of my coat, jerking me to a stop. I dangled from Burn's claws like a fish on a hook, flailing to break free. The beast growled, slowly hauling me up to its fangs. I swung both feet up, planted them against the stone banking and shoved with all my strength.

I swung out towards the river and desperately tried to shrug off my coat. Something tore and I fell. Air gusted across the back of my neck as another paw swiped out, barely missing. The thing yowled and scrabbled for balance, failed.

I hit the Seth, a hard belly-slap that exploded the air from my lungs. Coughing and spluttering, I surfaced just in time to see a thrashing mass of shadow and claw plunging towards my head. I dived. The beast hit the water, shockwave and heavy weight on my back pushing me deeper until my feet scraped the mud. Water churned as the creature struggled to the surface. I clamped a hand over the wound in my leg and played dead, letting the flow carry me downstream. A swarm of pale and bony corpse-fish surrounded me, tasting my blood in the water, then as one they swarmed the struggling shadow cat. Horrors lived in the Seth, and things canny enough to survive centuries of eradication attempts by the Arcanum wouldn't have any hesitation in chowing down on my bones – if they didn't have something bigger and meatier to attract their attention.

I drifted up with desperate slowness. When my face finally broke the surface the shadow cat's screeches filled my heart with savage joy. After all these years I'd finally finished the damned fleabag off. Darkness steamed from Burn's exposed insides and the water around her writhed with fish more teeth than tail. My toes instinctively curled up and my balls attempted to retreat into my body. I loathed swimming, hated not knowing what was lurking beneath me – I couldn't help but imagine things with too many teeth eyeing up my toes like fat and juicy worms. I muffled a yelp as something big and spongy brushed past my dangling feet. The corpse-fish scattered. A second later something pulled the shadow cat under. Burn didn't resurface.

I forced myself to stay still and waited to be carried down to Sethgate Bridge where I could use the steps to climb back up to street level. Flapping tails and snapping teeth churned the water to froth upstream as scavengers fought over titbits of daemon flesh and magic. Once they'd finished devouring the cat I would be next. As soon as the steps below the bridge came into reach I flailed for the bank and heaved myself up onto solid stone, crawling until my toes were well out of reach.

I lay on my back panting and looking up at the smoke-filled sky, letting my heartbeat slow and the fear drain from my body. Patchy blue and sunbeams struggled through smoke and cloud. "Not dead yet," I said. My face felt strangely numb. I probed with a finger, finding something soft and squidgy attached to my cheek.

"Ew, ew, ew." I pried the fat black leech from my skin by sliding a fingernail under its suckers and then tossed it back into the river, wiping blood from my cheek.

I pried two more from my arms. And then something twitched inside my trousers. I shuddered, feeling sick as I undid my belt and whipped them down to my ankles. Horror stabbed me as something pale and cock-sized plopped out and rolled free across the ground. I cackled in relief – just a baby barrel eel.

I smiled at my crotch. "Still safe and sound, eh, old pal."

"What a disconcerting sight," Shadea said from the bridge above. "Just what are you doing, Edrin Walker?"

I groaned and looked up from my cock to see that old crone leaning out over the side of the bridge, eyebrows raised. Eva joined her, now dressed in full battle plate with a bastard sword strapped to her back. Both women were dusty, dishevelled and bruised but otherwise looked fine. I was glad that Eva had escaped the Boneyards alive but my feelings on Shadea's survival were conflicted.

Ah, fuck it. "I'm looking at my cock, Shadea. Must be a while since you've seen one."

Eva's eyes dipped to my bare crotch, brazenly ogling me. "Oh my." She choked back a laugh.

It didn't faze Shadea. "Not at all," Shadea said. "I dissected one last month. It was rather large in comparison to yours." She looked to Eva. "Be a dear and fetch the miscreant."

Eva vaulted the wall and dropped thirty-odd feet down to me, metal clad feet clanging. She bore the weight of all that metal like it was cloth. At least she had the good grace to look slightly embarrassed as I hastily yanked my trousers back up and tied my belt, not that she averted her eyes. She noted my torn and bleeding leg and then carefully swept me up into her steely embrace. I wrapped my arms around her gorget and held on tight as she climbed the steps back up to street level. Manliness be damned, it felt good. I couldn't remember the last time I'd felt so safe, and hadn't much fancied scaling those steps with a wonky leg either.

My illusion of safety evaporated at the sight of the horrid old hag waiting on us and two squads of armoured wardens busy erecting barricades across the bridge. Shadea's wards burned bright and baleful across the defences – nobody would get through those unscathed.

"What's going on?" I said as Eva set me down. She held onto my arm to help keep weight off my wounded leg.

"We are securing the bridges," Eva said. "Coteries of magi are currently moving forward to reinforce the wall guard."

Shadea's nose crinkled. "The stink of daemon spoor and blood magic clings to you."

"Oh, you know me," I said. "Always popular. A variety of interesting friends. Listen, Cillian's been hurt. She–"

"Has already passed into the Old Town," Shadea interrupted. "Your mageborn friend, Layla, is taking her to the healers. It is strange; I had thought that I knew the name of every living mageborn to undergo the Forging." I swallowed my sudden fear, but she brushed past it. "Councillor Cillian will survive. You have the Arcanum's thanks for that."

I needed to change the subject, else Shadea might pick at the discrepancy until it got Layla killed. "Did she tell you about the Magash Mora?"

She looked at me sharply. "Cillian has been divulging restricted information. She shall be censured later; however, given the circumstances I will say that it is merely an opinion, one that lacks sufficient evidence. I shall, however, account for every possibility. I admit to some surprise that you survived the underground river."

I smiled. "And spare the Arcanum the hassle of dealing with me? So sorry to disappoint. Where is Harailt?"

Shadea sighed and turned to survey the lower city. "He is currently being subjected to further investigation in the Courts of Justice below the Templarum Magestus. He passed every test I applied but it is a wise precaution given recent events."

"I've been proven right about everything so far," I said. "Just because you loathe me doesn't mean I'm wrong."

Columns of smoke billowed from many sites and the city gates were only now swinging shut after being choked by sailors, dock workers, and herdsmen driving in the last of their cattle ready for the Sumarfuin slaughter. The Skallgrim fleet would land shortly, unless the magi heading for the walls could burn their ships to ash before they even reached the beaches.

She pursed her lips, thinking. "Contrary to what you may think, Magus Walker, I have never harboured any particular dislike of you. In fact I feel nothing for you at all. Nor have I any solid evidence of you misusing your Gift, despite an extremely colourful variety of rumour to choose from." She glanced back, that impersonal gaze sending shivers up my spine. "If I had, then you would have been disposed of."

I bit back angry retorts. "As if I could believe that. None of you want a so-called tyrant walking about."

Shadea was silent for a long moment, thinking. Eva shifted, metal and leather creaking, uncomfortable at the reminder of what the man she'd just held in her arms could do.

"There are no written histories from before the era of tyrants," Shadea said. "However, I do believe that oral traditions contain a measure of truth distorted over time. The oldest tales all tell of an age where people cowered around their campfires, fearful of dire entities that stalked the night stealing children from their beds and spreading madness and disease. Humanity is not alone on this world."

I blinked, not entirely sure I was hearing her correctly. "Next you will be telling me you have samples of ghosts, ogres and darkenshae floating in jars in your creepy workshop, and that all the monsters of my childhood stories are real."

She snorted. "Is it really so strange when you have fought daemons born on alien worlds beyond the Shroud? Perhaps you forget the creature you uncovered in the catacombs as a boy."

Eva looked as flummoxed as I felt hearing this. I stared at Shadea, shuddering at the memory of huge bulky bones and a sloping skull with a third eye. "I thought that thing was an ancient magus changed by magic."

"It was the corpse of what we call an ogre," she said. "Ogarim, if you prefer the Clanhold oral histories which are less corrupted than ours. Other artefacts of those creatures' presence in Kaladon have been uncovered over the centuries, but it is not commonly disclosed to magi of your humble rank."

I licked my lips. "Then why now?"

"One last attempt to turn you from a dark path," she said. "Some creatures of myth were said to take on human form, and others to inhabit corpses of the wicked. If, as current theory suggests, magic slowly adapts its hosts and their bloodlines to survive surrounding dangers, then it is logical to assume that tyrants might once have served the purpose of identifying such disguised creatures. Sniffers too, perhaps: two differing human responses evolving to meet the same threat."

I must have looked incredulous, as she hastily continued, looking slightly irritated at getting carried away with her love of obscure research. "As fascinating as that conjecture may be, what I am suggesting is that you too may find a worthy purpose in the years to come. I deem it unwise to discard any tool unless it bites the hand that wields it."

I swallowed. Such a thing had never occurred to me before. A purpose? Me?

Shadea smiled, a terrifying sight. "By both tradition and familial ties, I was destined to marry a rotund oaf of a high lord and birth him a litter of squalling infants. I chose otherwise." Dear gods, Shadea wed? Children? I think all involved dodged an axe to the face there. "You too can follow a different path if you so choose."

Down below, three wolf-ships beached on Setharii soil ahead of the body of the fleet, the tribesmen glinting dots on the beach. Pyromancers on the city walls began incinerating them with bolts of fire.

"What madness drives them to dash themselves against our walls?" Eva said, shaking her head as she surveyed the slaughter.

Before I could reply with: *Bet it has something to do with a bloody huge monster underground*, Shadea's head whipped around to face the Warrens.

"Oh no," she said, and for the first time in my life I saw Shadea afraid.

The ground shook. Mortar pattered down from the surrounding buildings and pebbles rained from the cliff walls of the Old Town rock. My mind shook with it. Agony pierced right between my eyes. I screamed, barely feeling steel-clad arms keeping me upright.

"What's wrong with him?" Eva said, as I jerked and bucked in her grip.

I dimly sensed Shadea's fingers press first against my wrist and neck, then peel back my eyelid. The pain wasn't mine, was cutting in from elsewhere and bypassing every defence I threw up to block it out.

Eventually my desperate hands latched onto Dissever's hilt. Fury crashed into pain.

Shadea hissed and snatched her hand back. "Drop him!"

Eva let go and stepped away, drawing a green-flecked sword. I fell on my arse, but immediately rolled to my feet with knife in hand, lips twisted into a feral snarl. I barely noticed them, instead growling at the Warrens as an entire street of rotten tenements collapsed in a cloud of dust.

Shadea waved the wardens back, but I only had eyes for the source of the pain twisting behind my eyes.

In the distant heart of the Warrens wood and stone exploded upwards. A block of tenements bulged and burst apart as something huge and fleshy and glistening rose from the depths of the Boneyards in a cloud of debris and death. Mental screams emanated from the thing's insides as it absorbed the tenement's occupants. I could feel them all: a small town's worth of agony crashing into me, their minds not quite alive, but horrifically far from dead. Only a fraction of the thing had emerged but I could already sense a dozen mature Gifts of magi flaring bright with magic deep inside that screaming mass, surrounded by uncounted stunted mageborn trickling in power. I was instinctively drawn to one amongst the many, the source of my agony rising from the depths.

Lynas, my Gift-bonded brother.

I gripped Dissever in trembling hands. Hard to think. Pain. Fear. Confusion.

Shadea cursed. "Disable him. Be careful of that blade."

I brandished Dissever, growled at Eva and shifted my feet for a better stance. Magic flooded through my muscles, readying for the kill.

"Sorry," she said with a metallic shrug. She blurred and something slammed into my face. Everything went hazy as I toppled.

CHAPTER 27

When I regained my senses I was on my back with the tang of iron in my mouth and the right side of my face tight and swollen. There was a strange absence of mental pain. I tried to sit up but a steel-shod foot pressed down on my chest.

"Welcome back," Eva said. "Sorry about the face. I tried to be gentle, and I did pick the side with all the scars. Nobody will notice a few more."

I worked my jaw. At least it wasn't broken. Might be a few loose teeth though. "Remind me never to get on your bad side. Well, more than I already am." She lifted her boot and I sat up to see Martain loitering with a face like I'd shat on his pillow. Oh. No wonder I wasn't screaming in agony. Even without magic Eva was far stronger than me.

"Nasty weapon you have," Eva said. Dissever dangled by the pommel, carefully held between two fingers. "Such an ugly spirit-bound blade suits you. How did a rogue like you obtain such a rarity?" Smoke whipped past her head and with it came distant screams.

I rose to my feet, battered, bruised, and exhausted without my magic to sustain me. "Found it," I said, taking in the chaos around us. Armed and armoured wardens and magi rushed to and from the Old Town walls, weapons clanking, panic-filled voices cursing and barking orders. Ash from the fires raging in the lower city drifted down as grey snow.

319

Eva grunted. "Figures." Then she tossed Dissever to me. I suffered a moment of horror for my fingers before the hilt slapped into my palm. "Get ready to fight. We need every weapon we can get." She stretched a hand back over her shoulder to pull her sword from its fastenings. It glimmered strangely, odd green flecks flowing through the steel – another spirit-bound blade.

I licked my lips, glanced at Dissever. This was going to sound bizarre to her but I'd never had the opportunity to ask the owner of another spirit-bound object about it. "Does the spirit in your sword ever talk to you?"

She looked at me like I was cracked. "Did I hit you too hard? I thought your skull thicker than that."

I half-laughed, Dissever warm and pulsing in my hand. "I get that a lot. Never mind." Luckily they were linked to their wielder's life – if the Arcanum could have taken Dissever from me and given it to somebody more reliable then they would have. I had an instinctive feeling they wouldn't have lived to regret the attempt. Dissever's presence in my mind squirmed in response. Was it worrying that such a bloodthirsty spirit actually seemed to like me? Perhaps I amused it – a pet hound doing tricks: stab, slash, roll over...

DrooomDa. DrooomDa. DrooomDa. DrooomDa...

People crowded onto the walls of the Old Town to peer out to sea.

"What is that awful din?" Martain said.

"Skallgrim battle drums," I said, the sacking of Ironport vivid in my mind. *Sack*, such a sham of a word when slaughter and rape were far more accurate descriptions. A huge fleet of wolf-ships approached Setharis, their oars churning water to foam in time to the heavy beat, hundreds of ships cutting through the waves with red eyes glimmering balefully.

Cillian hobbled over, leaning heavily on a cane. She looked half a corpse, face grey and gaunt after magical healing. Two portly healers flapped around her squawking complaints but she ignored their protestations. She wasn't about to let a little brush with death keep her from important work.

"It is good to see you alive," she said.

"Likewise. You look like shite though."

"You are a silver-tongued fox, Edrin. Shall we see how well you fare after an arrow through your lung?" Her mouth twisted with a spike of remembered pain.

I held my hands up in defeat. "Where is Layla?"

"Being escorted to the Collegiate, and to her mother," she said. "And before you ask, no, neither are held hostage to your good behaviour."

"Where is that bastard, Harailt?"

She grimaced. "The traitor has escaped. Somehow he managed to murder five magi and a dozen wardens guarding him. It should not have been possible given his skills and the strength of his Gift. Some greater power is at work within him. You were correct."

I should have trusted my instincts and killed him the moment I'd laid eyes on him. Hindsight is a maddening plague on the mind.

Archmagus Krandus hurried down from the Templarum Magestus surrounded by a chattering swarm of attendants. He wasn't what people might expect in an Archmagus: he didn't look old and wise, instead he was physically in his early twenties with shoulder-length shimmering ash-blond hair held back by a warded golden circlet. Even in my biased eyes he was disgustingly handsome. In one hand he clutched a signal rod tipped with an inverted cone of gold that he barked commands into, carrying his voice to all such devices within a range of several leagues. "The gate guard and magi must hold off these Skallgrim savages," he said. "Remind the wardens that our walls have never been breached. We are readying to reinforce them."

Why was he bothering with the wardens and Skallgrim? Did he not know what was going on?

Cillian limped towards him. Children tore past ferrying armfuls of arrows to the archers on the walls and the wardens massing by the gate. Shadea was too busy directing the magi on the ramparts to pay us any attention, devising some plan to deal with the creature below. Wardens nearby laughed and joked as they readied to pass through the gate, boasting about how they were going to throw the filthy savages back into the sea.

"What are these fools doing?" I said.

"I have just awoken from healing," Cillian replied. "Archmagus Krandus must think we merely face a Skallgrim fleet and some kind of halrúna summoned daemon." She coughed and clutched her chest, face twisting in pain. "We must warn him of the Magash Mora before ignorance leads to a fatal mistake."

Martain and Eva held me back as Cillian closed the last few steps on her own. The Archmagus was being harassed by dozens of messengers all vying for his attention and one stern older woman was hauling others out of the way, desperate to personally hand him a note written by Shadea's hand rather than go through his aides. Ah, he had no idea what we faced. At Cillian's approach he ordered all to be quiet and gave her his full and undivided attention. The older messenger barged in and handed the Archmagus the paper. His face went ashen as he learned of the Doom of Escharr's rebirth.

The ground lurched as more of the Magash Mora exploded free of its stony womb. Boulders and fragments of buildings rained down over the city, smashing against the walls of the Old Town. The ancient defences groaned, cracks webbing out through the stonework. Blocks the size of horses shattered and fell outwards, crashing down into the Crescent below. Wardens screamed and scrambled away from the crumbling section of wall. Glimpsed through the gaps, limbs of writhing flesh as large as ships crushed whole streets as an abomination of flesh, blood and bone heaved the last of its mountainous bulk from the dark places below the city. Trailing tentacles snatched up corpses and screaming people and sucked them into its churning flesh.

Balls of liquid flame hissed from the magi manning the outer walls of the city, a flight of deadly fireflies. Incandescent forks of lightning stabbed out from a magus somewhere down in Docklands, thunder booming. The thing ate their magic the moment it touched flesh. Cries of shock and horror rippled through nearby magi.

Shadea signalled to Krandus. He glanced at her note again and ordered groups of pyromancers and aeromancers to the battlements. She snapped orders while several geomancers under her command prised blocks of stone from the ruined section of wall. The pyromancers concentrated their magic until the blocks glowed hot, red rivulets of flaming melt beginning to pool. Shadea lifted a hand, then dropped it. "Loose!" Aeromancers launched the fiery missiles out into the air.

It made sense. Molten rock was molten rock with or without magic. The missiles blasted into the creature, burning pitifully small holes in its hide and slowing it not at all.

Examining the great wall of the Old Town, it seemed that I was just noticing how shoddy it really was. Any defensive structures it might once have boasted had been left to crumble into picturesque neglect. They must have asked themselves, "What fools would ever dare to attack Setharis?" Such mundane defences as catapults and ballistae would be pointless to their minds when the Arcanum could use magic to obliterate any attackers. What arrogance. Instead they had wasted their coin on faerie lightshows and elaborate feasts.

"Harailt and the Skallgrim planned this well," I said as Cillian returned. "You were complacent." It earned me a medley of glares from every direction.

The ground shook again and despite the desperate attempts of a nearby geomancer, the damaged section of wall collapsed in a shriek of tortured stone. In the haze of smoke and flame beyond the gap a behemoth of twisted stolen flesh crawled through my city, crushing temples, workshops and family homes beneath its bulk. The magi attacks seemed pitiful against its monstrous mass. Somewhere dozens of voices shouted and screamed, too far away to make out what the clamour was about.

Archmagus Krandus ran over, dismissing me with but a glance before focusing on Cillian. "Our attacks are inadequate; whatever damage we inflict is replaced by new flesh as it devours all within reach." His face was grim. "I fear a full quarter of the populace lost in the creature's emergence. The Magash Mora grows ever larger." Screams and shouts again drifted on the wind.

I shuddered. With all the merchants and migrants flooding into the city for Sumarfuin, that had to be around two hundred and fifty thousand dead – worse than dead. The numbers were staggering. Unimaginable. My own plight as a hunted rogue was shown for the petty thing it was. I felt sick and powerless.

"We do have one thing that the capital of ancient Escharr did not," Cillian said. "We have the cliff walls of the Old Town. Newly recovered histories detailing the fall of their empire suggest the creature may starve itself to death. Something of that size must use up enormous amounts of both magic and physical energy. It likely needs to keep eating or die. If we can hold out long enough we may yet survive."

Krandus did not hesitate, "Agreed. If no other plan presents itself we will wait this out. The gates of the Old Town are to be kept closed. Make preparations to demolish every route up." He unfurled a small map-scroll of the city and began studying it with Cillian.

I looked around in shock, realising that all the people around us were well-dressed, all from the Old Town. The lack of sooty peasants scarred by fire, screaming mothers or barefoot children hit me like a hammer. Those clamouring voices and screams were people outside the gate pleading for safety.

"You callous bastards," I said. They would make the rock of the Old Town an inaccessible island. "You can't cut us off and leave all those people down there to die. If that thing doesn't kill them then the Skallgrim certainly will." Martain stayed close to me, hand hovering over his sword hilt.

Krandus narrowed his eyes. "As much chance for them to flee into the countryside as to stay. Likely more. We cannot take the risk of insurgents entering these walls as they did the lower city. Nor can we risk more magi being devoured. That would further strengthen the creature."

Rage grew inside me. I reached for my Gift, felt the sanctor's power clamping it shut, my mind scrabbling at a slick wall that offered no purchase.

"It is useless to fight," Martain gloated. "Your Gift is sealed." Oh, how he loved this, the smug little prick.

And then an insane idea reared its ugly head and burst into flames. I stared at Martain in utter astonishment. He didn't like that one little bit.

"Cillian," I said. "How many sanctors are in Setharis right now?"

"Three," she replied absently, glancing up from a map of the city. "Why?"

"What would happen if we stuffed them–" I pointed at Martain, then towards the gap in the wall and the Magash Mora beyond "–down that thing's throat? It draws power from stolen Gifts, so what if we get the sanctors close enough to shut them down? It might kill it."

A sudden silence rippled out from me as magi turned to stare first at me and then at Martain. His jaw dropped, face draining of colour. The signal rod slipped from Archmagus Krandus' fingers and clattered to the stone.

"Now wait just a minute," Martain said. "You cannot be serious."

"I know some of you can sense the Gifts open inside that thing, the torrent of magic pouring into its flesh through the magi and mageborn it has absorbed. Sanctors can block that source of power."

Martain's mouth opened and closed, not a sound emerging. His eyes bulged in horror.

"Cillian, is this viable?" Krandus said.

She shuddered. "Magus Edrin Walker would be the expert in this particular field. In the catacombs below the city he was able to destroy the smaller offshoot. If he says that their still-living Gifts are being used to draw in magic to grant that creature life…" Cillian glanced at me and I wondered if she was about to reveal the secret of my Gift-bond to Lynas, "…then I believe him. I felt it trying to absorb my own. It certainly explains how something so massive lives against the laws of nature instead of collapsing under its own bulk. Their massed Gifts working together may also suggest how it is able to warp reality in order to devour our magic."

Martain sensed which way the wind was blowing, his face going pale, fists clenching, but even he had to acknowledge the sense of it. "I cannot guarantee my power will work against that thing," he said with a shaking voice. "It may be immune." He was a smug git, but he was brave. That I could respect.

The Archmagus stood straighter. "I will not leave innocents to perish where it can be avoided." He clapped a hand on Martain's shoulder. "This is worth the attempt." With that he picked up his signal rod. "Find all sanctors and gather at the gatehouse. Be quick. Notify all commanders – we march to war!"

Martain's fate was sealed. "Sorry, pal." I meant it. Nobody should be asked to do something this insane. But I refused to let Lynas' body and mind be used to kill our people.

A series of explosions tore through the curtain wall in the west of the lower city, flames billowing skyward in clouds of greasy black smoke.

"Oil," somebody shouted. "The West Gate is burning and the Skallgrim have taken Pauper's Docks. More ships are heading for the West Docks and... oh, sweet Lady Night, flocks of winged daemons rise from their ships."

Krandus' signal rod chirped and he listened to it for a moment. His brow furrowed, jaw clenching. "The daemons scour the walls and an armed mob has rushed Pauper's Gates from the inside."

Even at this distance I could see people milling at both gates, fighting and fleeing, desperate to escape but trapped between the monster ravaging the city, fire, and a Skallgrim army pouring in through the docks. "They're trapped. Do something."

Krandus' nostrils flared. "There will be no escape now. With that many trapped the Magash Mora will gorge itself on the flesh of both human and beast until it can envelop the Old Town itself. To the gates! Gather your wardens and form coteries."

I shuddered and looked away as the creature wailed, a cacophony of voices like a thousand screeching newborns. It flopped and flowed and crawled and crashed over buildings and streets towards the trapped Docklanders. All the faces of the people I'd seen since coming home flickered through my mind's eye: the young girl's wide eyes as silver coins dropped into her bowl, the glowering clansmen brothers guarding Charra's door, Bardok the Hock and that annoying nobleman dubbed Lord Arse I'd had to endure on the voyage down the coast, and even the barber and his disturbing collection of pulled teeth. How many of them had already been devoured? The thought made me shudder. It was all too similar to the fear I faced every time I used my own magic: that the Worm of Magic would take me and I'd be trapped gibbering in a corner of my own mind, somehow still aware of my own monstrousness. There was no way to know if they were trapped in a similar living death, still horribly aware.

"I'm going down there too," I said, surprising even myself. I nervously examined Dissever's edge. I couldn't just sit back and let this happen. These were my people.

"You shall not," Shadea said, dropping from the walls and landing easily on legs that looked far too scrawny to allow her to leap about like that. "Did you forget that Magus Evangeline was forced to restrain you earlier?"

"I forgot nothing. You want the truth?" I caught Cillian's grim nod from the corner of my eye. "My friend Lynas was murdered by the Skinner. His mageborn flesh was used to help create that damned creature out there." I tapped the side of my head. "Lynas and me, we were Gift-bonded." More than one person gasped and whispers of *tyrant* rippled through nearby magi.

"There was no enslavement, we were closer than family, and damn what any of you have to say about it. That's why I'm back in this accursed back-stabbing rat hole of a city. Lynas sacrificed his life so that thing would not be fully mature before the Skallgrim arrived. Without him it would be a damn sight stronger and all of you would already be dead."

Shadea cocked her head. "Ah. So that is why the tyrant is so pained by the Magash Mora's emergence. On your Oath, can you bear this agony, Edrin Walker?"

Dissever's fury bled into me. I held up the foul weapon. "I'll ram my pain right down its fucking throat. I destroyed the crystal core of the smaller creature with this blade. If we can hack our way in then I'll bloody well do for this one too."

Krandus considered it for a long moment. "Very well. Magus Evangeline, assemble the siege-breakers and have somebody bring this magus his possessions. Be swift as the wind."

Eva nodded approvingly. "This suits me better than hiding behind walls while people die." She sprinted towards the Templarum Magestus.

Krandus spoke into his signal rod: "I, Krandus, Archmagus of the Arcanum, hereby order the seals broken on vaults three, four and five. Bring forth the articles of war."

Even through the beat of Skallgrim battle drums, tolling of bells and the screeching of the Magash Mora, the sudden silence of every magus resounded deeper and louder. The most powerful magical artefacts the Arcanum possessed had been sealed in ancient vaults below the Templarum Magestus at the end of the Daemonwar, all save the enormous titans which had been rendered inert. The Shroud where the Vanda city states once stood had been permanently damaged, and though the Arcanum had managed to block the open portals to the Far Realms long enough to allow the Shroud to scab over, the wound in the world there still festered. To this day all magi were forbidden from entering the Vanda desert.

They had sworn that never again would the full magical might of Setharis march to war.

Krandus looked like he would rather have slit his own throat than let those artefacts see the light of day again if he had any other choice. To my mind nobody should wield that sort of power. However, I also knew I would use that power myself if I needed to.

After an interminable wait Krandus' rod finally buzzed and a tinny voice replied, sounding scared. "The wardsmiths have unlocked the vaults." It was done.

A *crack* boomed across the Old Town.

It took everybody a few moments to locate the source. The spires atop the Templarum Magestus listed, snapped, and fell. The ancient building's steeple groaned, then caved in. With stately majesty the grand halls of the mighty Arcanum collapsed with a roar of tumbling blocks, shatter of stained glass and crackle of broken wards. Disbelief was written across every single face. This was inconceivable. A thousand years of Arcanum art and history destroyed, hundreds of lives snuffed out.

"No," somebody croaked. It was me. There would be no articles of war. Not for us. Once the Magash Mora scoured all life from the city then the Skallgrim would walk in and take everything the Arcanum had kept safe for centuries, all that dangerous knowledge and dread power just waiting to be dug up from unlocked vaults. The Skallgrim halrúna might be savages but even without Harailt's guidance, sooner or later they would learn to use those artefacts.

"How is this possible?" Cillian said, eyes fixed on the column of dust billowing into the air. She blinked and scrubbed at her eyes, as if not able to accept what she was seeing.

Krandus stared at his signal rod in horror, then flung it to the stone. "We are compromised," he hissed, grabbing a hold of a crimson-robed woman with wispy white hair and a harsh expression, councillor Merwyn if memory served. "Run. Spread the word that the rods are not to be used. Send seers to the site – I need to know what happened. No magus – no group of magi – should have the power necessary to break those wards. This could not have been done quickly, nor easily. This was years in the making. Somebody find that accursed Harailt Grasske and bring me his head!"

Merwyn scurried off, too shocked to notice that the Archmagus was treating a member of the Inner Circle like a messenger girl. Krandus studied the plume of dust rising without visible emotion but his mind had to be feverishly running through our options. When everybody else was rattled he was plotting and planning, and that was why he was Archmagus. Well, that, and he could have made a good attempt at devastating a goodly portion of this city all on his own.

"What is Harailt planning?" Cillian said. "Why do this?"

Krandus' fists shook with fury. "Targeting the magical centre of Setharis makes perfect sense if you want to crush your greatest obstacle to conquest with a single blow. I suspect that the wolf-ships are merely there to hunt down fleeing stragglers and sweep in once the Magash Mora has finished its feast." He exchanged glances with Shadea. "The Forging rite should have ensured the loyalty of all magi; however, we cannot know what strange powers are at work here."

"And what are our bloody gods doing?" I said. "Hiding away like scared children? This stinks. That thing needed serious power to create. Godly power most likely." The gods should be floating above the city, casting fire and lightning down upon our enemies, ripping the magic and life from their bones and opening the earth to drop their corpses into the Boneyards. All the beasts of Setharis should be rising up to tear down the invaders with tooth, claw and beak. Instead our gods did nothing.

"Ah yes, Cillian mentioned your previous ranting," Krandus said. "The Hooded God is not a suspect, whatever his old temple in the Warrens was used for." He gave a queer, sad smile as he said that.

"But–"

"Silence!" A vein throbbed in his temple.

I clammed up, simmering inside. He meant it, and now was not the time to push the Archmagus.

The clank of steel-shod boots and heavy armour drew our attention. A dozen dirt-caked figures marched up the street towards us, massive two-handed swords as tall as me held out before them. They were covered head to toe in an entire forge worth of steel plate, razor edges and wicked spikes. Their helms didn't have open eye slits, instead light glinted off some kind of clear crystal embedded in the metal, and artificer-wrought magical metal replaced leather straps, chain and vulnerable joints. They looked bulky and clumsy to my eye, awkward to fight in, and yet they covered the distance between us easily and fluidly, faster than humanly possible. Looking closer, Eva's green-flecked blade was strapped to the back of one of them. The immensely heavy armour suddenly made perfect sense – only knights could possibly fight in that.

A dark-haired boy and girl, twins by the looks of them, trailed a safe distance behind. They bore a passing resemblance to Martain, making them the other sanctors. They were far too young for the insanity we were about to put them through.

The knights formed a hulking line in front of the Archmagus, their boots stamping down like a thunderclap. "So few, Evangeline?" he said.

Eva's voice came out tinny and muffled. "The others were buried in the collapse, Archmagus."

Krandus grimaced, rubbed his temples, eyes falling. "It is not enough." Everything was failing and falling to ruin. He was desperate. It was the first time I'd ever seen him so weak, so human.

Somebody tossed me my old boots and grey coat. I buckled on the coat and tugged on the boots. It felt like donning armour against change: I felt like my old self.

"If only we could unleash the titans against the Magash Mora," Shadea said to the Archmagus. "I believe that is what they were originally created for, though completed too late to save Escharr. The puzzle of the titan's strange luminescence is no longer a mystery: it was a warning we were too ignorant to heed."

Krandus said nothing, didn't look at her.

Cillian sagged against me, her strength ebbing. "The point is moot. The activation keys are buried within the vaults."

Shadea said nothing, watched Krandus until he finally met her gaze.

He swallowed. "No. Never again. We swore an oath."

Cillian rallied, scrutinizing the Archmagus' face. She forced herself to stand on her own and let go of my arm. "Explain yourself. As a member of the Inner Circle I demand an answer."

"There is one," he said. "An activation key kept apart from the others. A… contingency. Is one monster not enough, Shadea?"

"Sometimes you need a monster to fight a monster," she replied.

Krandus raked a hand through his perfect hair and sighed. "So be it. Fetch it before I change my mind."

Shadea turned on her heel and disappeared into the streets of the Old Town. He straightened up and cast off his distress, and with it went that small measure of humanity he had displayed. He looked us over, eyes shrewd and calculating, and I knew we were nothing but pawns in a desperate game of life and death.

"Magus Walker," Krandus said. "You are in the hands of the sanctors until such time as you are needed. You will obey them without question." *Piss on that.* "Martain, a word before we march." The twin sanctors stood on either side of me as Krandus and Martain moved away for a private discussion.

When Martain returned he appeared troubled, refusing to meet my eyes. I didn't like the way Krandus had spoken to him in private. I was all too aware I was expendable. Others also owned spirit-bound blades…

The ground lurched as the Magash Mora loosed an ear-splitting howl and slammed its bulk down to pulverize a whole block of buildings. The creature squatted over the ruins, pulsing tendrils rooting about in the debris.

I had to look away as it slurped up maddened horses still hitched to a wagon. The massive gate between the Old Town and Docklands seemed impregnable: ancient oak bound with the hardest of mage-wrought steel and reinforced by centuries of potent magics. It was able to ignore besieging armies and battering rams, never mind screaming hordes of terrified Docklanders begging to be let in. All of our wards and protective magics would prove useless if that monster outside climbed the cliff and reached the gate. Mere wood, stone and steel was not going to be enough.

CHAPTER 28

Dozens of armoured wardens knelt before a gaggle of priests murmuring useless prayers to absent gods, while others were more interested in hurriedly scrawling notes to their loved ones before handing them over to a solemn-looking young lad with a sack. Eva formed her knights into a wedge of jagged steel in front of the gate and coteries formed into ranks behind them. Setharis had never done battle as lesser peoples did, with rank upon rank of spearmen, horse, and heavy infantry. Instead the core of our armies split into independent coteries existing solely to protect individual magi. With so few magi experienced in battle perhaps that had to change. A dozen wardens encircled the sanctors keeping me under guard. The girl sanctor took the front while Martain and the boy stood behind me.

The Archmagus and the other members of the Inner Circle, save the injured Cillian, moved towards the gate, giving the sanctors a wide berth. Shadea carried something bulky and metallic in her arms. I was disappointed to discover that a titan activation key was a plain metal box with little gold studs all along the sides. She was guarded by a wall of steel-clad wardens carrying tower-shields as tall as they were.

Krandus turned on his heel to face us. The wardens all shifted nervously, leather and metal creaking and clinking. They were terrified – and so were the magi, most of whom had never seen a street fight, never mind a battle. I didn't think it would take much to break them, and it didn't escape Krandus' notice either. His eyes found mine with an unspoken warning to behave.

"No time for a pretty speech," he said, voice ringing loud and clear over the background mayhem. "This is Setharis. We have always stood against blood sorcerers who cut out the beating hearts of children as sacrifice for their inhuman and daemonic masters. Kill them all."

The gate doors yawned wide and Setharis marched to war. A mob of sooty Docklanders spilled in pleading for safety. They pushed through the widening gap, then stopped and panicked, scrambling backwards as the steel wall of the siege-breakers advanced at a steady and unstoppable march. Beggars and dockhands, seamstresses, merchants and children shouted, screamed and begged even as they streamed back down the slope, pushing and shoving in a disorganized mess.

A few scattered cheers erupted from below as the bulk of our small army marched out after the siege-breakers and began descending the ramp to the lower city. It was as if they thought we might destroy the monster and the Skallgrim invaders at the wave of a hand. The might of Setharis was legend, and at its height none could stand against the ever-expanding empire: not kings, philosopher-priests, daemons or strange gods. Only the empire's overwhelming arrogance and lust for Escharric artefacts had proven a match for its power. All we had left to rely on now was stubborn pride and a tattered legend.

A female warden in old scale mail and pot helm who'd been keeping pace at my side stumbled over somebody's lost shoe and lurched sideways to jostle Martain. As the sanctor cursed them for a clumsy fool, through the eye slit I caught her aiming a wink at me. I frowned. Other than me, what kind of fool would wink at a time like this? A closer look offered dark eyes with scabbed lines across the skin. I cursed. What did Charra think she was doing being up and about, never mind armed and armoured? But damn she was a sight for desperate eyes! She mumbled an apology to Martain and slid back into position, blending in with the others and paying me no more regard.

I would never object to having a hidden knife up my sleeve, but I was more afraid of Charra's death than in confronting any number of ancient monsters.

As we advanced down towards the Crescent, people busy looting the fine houses looked up in terror, most fleeing with whatever they could carry. Some, crazed by fear or anger – or aligned with the Skallgrim – lashed out at us with nailed clubs, rocks, chair legs and rusty knives. A handful of arrows skittered down across the wardens' hastily raised shields. One lurched back screaming, with a shaft through his cheek.

That did it. The siege-breakers broke into a clanking run and the mob of innocent Docklanders that had been backing down the ramp splintered and fled, leaping off onto roofs, trees and gardens below. The siege-breakers didn't slow, smashed straight through their attackers in a welter of blood and shattered bone – and through anybody else unlucky enough to be caught in the middle. Any that survived that moving wall of death lifted their heads from the ground just in time to get their skulls crushed by the boots of wardens running in their wake. By the time we passed, the ground was slick with blood, and anything recognisably human reduced to mush.

The wounded warden got back to his feet. He bit down on the shaft of the barbed arrow pinning his cheeks and gingerly took hold of the feathered end. With a quick jerk, he snapped the end off. He slid the arrow from his cheeks, spat splinters and broken teeth, and then jogged off to rejoin his fellows.

The siege-breakers relieved the battered remnants of the bridge guard Shadea had left behind and cleared a sizable area of Sethgate, dripping blood and flesh while the rest of us caught up. Any peasants with a lick of sense had fled the area as fast as their feet could carry them.

In the lower city the ominous beat of the Skallgrim battle drums echoed weirdly through twisting streets and alleys. Drifting smoke stung my eyes and the air stank of charred flesh. I envied the black flights of corvun and flocks of lesser birds that wheeled overhead well out of danger's way. A corvun screeched and dropped like a stone towards us, with a last-second flap of wings settling on Krandus' robed arm. He whispered soothing words, not seeming to notice the vicious claws digging into his robed arm, and removed the message case tied to its foot. He unravelled and read a tiny scroll, then passed it on to three councillors of the Inner Circle that were nearby: Shadea, Merwyn, and a stern-faced man who was all bushy eyebrows and beard named Wyman. The others were busy marshalling troops elsewhere. I did my best to eavesdrop.

"The Skallgrim and their daemon hordes have overwhelmed the remaining gate guard. The bulk of their forces remain outside the city but an unknown number of units have entered and are herding the populace towards the Magash Mora. Prepare for battle." The magi began roaring orders to the coteries under their command.

Shadea and her guard broke away from the Inner Circle and came towards us, gathering three other magi and their coteries as she went.

"Your group are to come with me," she said to Martain. With the activation key held tight in her arms it looked like we were heading straight for one of the titans. A half-dozen siege-breakers led by Eva joined us. We had been given the easy job of sticking a metal box into a dormant titan. How could that possibly go wrong? Those other poor fools were going to hit the Skallgrim hard and try to draw the Magash Mora away from the fleeing populace. If the creature got much larger then even the cliff face of the Old Town would afford no protection.

"When the bulk of our forces engage the enemy we will make haste for the titan named Lust located at the far side of Westford Bridge," Shadea said. "We are short on time. When the signal is given do not fall behind, for we will not stop."

All I could do was wait and watch, trapped like a rat in a cage by ever-vigilant sanctors while the swarming streets of the Crescent slowly drained of activity as the Arcanum marched to war. Soon I too would be dodging axes and arrows amidst streets filled with daemons and death. I wanted to run and hide, but feared Lynas' pain coming through the Gift-bond would drive me insane before long – and where would I run to anyway?

The bulk of our army filtered through the choke of the bridge and began reforming orderly ranks on the other side. Small detachments of bowmen flung ropes with steel hooks onto the highest rooftops and ascended, pulling the ropes up after them as they took up positions overseeing the route of retreat.

The narrow lanes and streets of Docklands had to be a nightmare to try to implement any sort of coherent strategy, but fortunately that sort of thing was left to people far more competent than the likes of me. A handful of aeromancers were already drifting upwards amidst swirls of dust to act as the Arcanum's eyes. Those poor exposed bastards would probably be the first to die – even if they could whip up wind walls to keep out arrows, they still had the Skallgrim's winged daemons to contend with. *Good luck, lads.*

I paced, worrying at a hangnail, glancing at the Magash Mora every few minutes in fear that it might have changed direction and be heading towards us. Martain's sanctors stayed close, and he looked ill at ease, avoiding eye contact with me.

Charra leaned nonchalantly against a nearby wall, watching over me.

I envied her. I was a bag of nervous energy. It felt unnatural to loiter, doing nothing but wait for a signal while others fought and died. Bandits on the road or cutthroats in dark alleys I could cope with, but this was war. It was all new and it scared the shite out of me for two reasons: the obvious danger of an arrow or axe to the face, and the more insidious fear caused by its strangely impersonal nature – a communal us versus them instinct that tried to subsume individuality and merge me into the group. Even without my Gift I was infected by the army's emotions. With my Gift opened wide it might prove all too easy to get sucked deep into their flow, and only the gods might know what would happen then.

I sidled over to my foolish friend, trying to look bored and aimless as the sanctors shadowed at a modest distance. "How are you faring, warden? Did you manage to get down here without any trouble? How about your, ah, friend, is she well?"

I couldn't see much beneath the helm, only bloodshot eyes circled by darker shadows. She was exhausted.

She shrugged. "That wasn't any trouble, a few arrows is all." Then she lowered her voice to barely a whisper and answered what I was really asking: "I went for a nap, knotted the blankets and slipped out the window while Layla was reading a book outside my door. She's safer up there."

I groaned. "You don't look well, maybe you should rest here."

Martain narrowed his eyes as we spoke, but Charra tilted her helm just enough to spit by my feet and then stalk off.

The sanctor snorted. "We are going into battle and you are chasing women? Why am I not surprised? At least that warden has more sense than to have any truck with the likes of you."

"Maybe I should look elsewhere then," I said, blowing him a kiss. That shut the prick up. *Damn you, Charra, what do you think you are doing here?* Trying to save my sorry arse, no doubt.

It was then I noticed another warden had been watching us intently. They flipped a knife up into the air and caught it expertly, and I noted the twisted steel guard was a match to the assassin's blade Dissever had sheared through atop the Harbourmaster's roof. I groaned. These two women would be the death of me

Layla sketched me a brief bow.

I guess I couldn't blame her, I'd not have let my mother do this alone either. The best thing I could do was ignore them both. With any luck she would drag Charra out of harm's way at the first opportunity.

I approached Eva, my guards sticking to me like flies around horse dung. It seemed as good a chance as any to apologize for almost landing her in a cesspit of trouble. There might not be another opportunity.

"Stop," she demanded. "Come no closer."

I did as she asked. "I just wanted to say that I was sorry for the other day. Don't worry; I'll stay away from you now." She was like all the rest – afraid of the corrupt tyrant in their midst.

She sighed, a hiss of air escaping the helmet. "Don't be a dolt." Her helm jerked towards Martain. "Do you think I wish to wear siege-breaker armour without the strength granted by my Gift?"

I groaned. A dolt indeed. She was the sort to take people at face value rather than listening to hearsay; of course she had also believed that Harailt was a reformed character so her opinion was suspect. "How do you stay so calm?" I asked, nodding to the wardens and Shadea. "You are about to go into battle."

Metal plates scraped as she shrugged. "I spent a year with the legions guarding our colonies in the Thousand Kingdoms. War mostly involves a lot of waiting punctuated by periods of brutal violence. You get used to it. After a while you learn to focus on other things. Some wardens busy themselves checking and re-checking straps and buckles, or sharpening their blades. Others clutch charms and pray or share bawdy jokes and boasts about the coming battle."

"What's your method?"

Her helm turned to look up at the sky. "I like to watch the birds," she said, wistful. "They look so free. Sometimes I wonder if they feel pity for earth-bound creatures such as ourselves."

My thoughts leapt to the corvun with their wicked beaks and cruel black eyes. I didn't think they had any concept of pity or remorse. "I'll leave you be then," I said. "Take care out there." She didn't reply, already tracking a flight of swallows darting between buildings, entirely unconcerned with ancient evils, daemons and death.

My hands kept moving to Dissever's hilt, but each time they did the sanctors tensed and I returned to pacing and worrying at my hangnail until it was bloody. I tried not to look at Charra too much.

"Catch," Shadea said, tossing me a wineskin.

I frowned, uncorked it and sniffed suspiciously. It smelled like wine.

"Drink, boy," she said, "or I will take it back."

I took a swig. A silky texture and the taste of ripe berries bursting in my mouth. I wiped my lips on my sleeve. "It's good."

Her eyelids lowered. "That is Bourgasi red, the magus of wine, brewed by an order of silent monks for over five hundred years. It is imported from a delightfully quaint city-state bordering Esban, and each bottle costs twelve gold coins. And you call it 'good'?"

I took another swig. "Yes, good. I've had better. There's a small vineyard a few leagues south of Port Hellisen that produces the best wine I've ever tasted. On my oath as a magus and reputation as an itinerant drunk."

Her forehead creased. "I suspect the subtleties of quality wine are lost on you."

"Not at all. Drink is the one thing I'm truly educated in." I tossed the wineskin back to her. Despite her disdain I would bet good coin she had filed the information away for future investigation.

"Now that you have calmed down, stop that pacing. I find it irritating." She turned back to surveying the city.

I took a deep breath and forced myself to watch the bulk of the Magash Mora as it slowly gouged a trail of devastation through the Warrens. I ground my teeth, hands shaking. I wanted to tear it apart and lay Lynas' flesh on the pyre, but what could an ant like me possibly do to that monstrosity?

The wait to do something, anything, was excruciating.

CHAPTER 29

Finally a sphere of blue light flared bright above the warrens. "That is our signal," Shadea said.

We ran west. Shadea's guard ringed her with those massive shields held high while the armoured bulk of the siege-breakers ranged ahead. Our little group kept pace off to one side of the middle of the pack, two coteries on the opposite side keeping a safe distance between them and the sanctors, and the last formed a rearguard.

Cries of ravening hunger and gibbering insanity spewed from the Magash Mora's mouths, and the ground shook with each lumbering movement it took towards the masses of people trapped between it and the Skallgrim. My stomach churned as I caught glimpses of that mountain of deformed flesh and jutting bone through gaps in the buildings and drifting smoke. Flames scorched my hair as we clambered over debris and followed the road that curved in a crescent following the path of the Seth. We passed several pitched battles: wardens holed up in defensive positions fighting off looters and packs of Skallgrim infiltrators. Home owners and shop keepers had banded together to defend their families and property, and were laying into anybody poorly dressed that came too close.

A man screamed for help, his legs pinned beneath a fallen beam, flames slowly creeping up the wood. Shadea kept running. The distant *phwoosh* of burning missiles soaring through the air announced an escalation of the Arcanum's attack.

I was already out of breath and sweating like a pig. I glanced back, scowled at the sight of Martain and all the wardens making it look effortless while I puffed and panted and plodded onwards.

A thousand voices screamed from human and inhuman throats as super-heated rock and metal blasted holes in the Magash Mora's hide and began burning deeper into flesh. It was about as effective as throwing hot grit at an enraged bull for all the damage they did. But it did get the thing's attention. It didn't turn – the amorphous thing didn't seem to have a front or back – but the writhing mass of flesh and bone slowed its advance on Pauper's Gate and the masses of panicked people trying to flee the city, then it stopped and flowed in the opposite direction, gradually gathering speed towards the insects stinging it.

"Faster!" Shadea shouted. I didn't bother muffling my curses as I somehow dredged up enough energy to pick up the pace even with a wounded leg. All we had to do was get to the other side of Westford Bridge and then our job would be done. Charra stumbled, barely righting herself, labouring as much as I was, but I didn't have any way of sending her back to safety.

Across the river, Lust loomed through the smoke, a dark and deadly giant awaiting the return of her cruel heart. Alone amongst the titans it had been given a beautiful female countenance. Unsurprisingly, it had been named Lust by male magi. They were still men after all, still cursed to think with their cocks more often than was wise.

A knot of armoured Skallgrim blocked the far end of the bridge, their faces drenched in sweat from a forced run; they linked round shields to form a wall and hefted beaked war axes. A wild-eyed man with a face more scar than skin shrieked incoherent curses. I assumed it was the usual "I'm going to kick the shite out of you and fuck your mother" sort of boast. He began gnawing on the iron edge of his shield and frothing at the mouth, a vein pulsing angrily on his forehead as he worked himself up into berserk fury.

An old man and woman stood behind the shield wall, their cracked faces scarred with sigils and a motley collection of bone, hide and feather amulets around their necks marking them as Skallgrim shaman. The old woman opened her palm with a serpentine knife and began a droning chant in perfect Old Escharric. She sprinkled her blood in a circle. Not a good sign.

"Destroy those halrúna!" Shadea shouted, air shimmering in a sphere around her as she focused on protecting the activation key. The siege-breakers thundered towards the Skallgrim. A bolt of flame from one of our pyromancers roared towards the halrúna while the sanctors pulled us back to give the other magi room to manoeuvre on the bridge.

The male halrúna lifted a tattooed hand and a gust of wind deflected our firebolts to explode across the riverbank. It felt unnatural to be so close to magic and feel absolutely nothing; bloody sanctors! But the ghost of Lynas' pain still throbbed in my head, and it would be far worse if they weren't suppressing my Gift.

"How did they know we were coming here?" Martain said. Then his voice hardened. "More treachery."

The six siege-breakers smote the shield wall like an enormous hammer, wood and steel exploding from an impact that catapulted a dozen Skallgrim warriors backwards through the air. A few fell screaming into the murky river where their armour – and other things – dragged them under. The siege-breakers thundered straight through what was left of their line, hacking a path through mail and flesh towards the halrúna. Their enormous swords wreaked bloody ruin, limbs flying, heads smashed to pulp. Axes clanged off thick armour as berserkers picked themselves up and flung themselves back into the fray.

Halfway across the city the Arcanum pressed their attack, sky flashing incandescent with fire and lightning and more exotic energies. Flocks of chitinous daemons fell as burning rain. Closer to home, fire and wind writhed around the halrúna as our magi struggled for elemental supremacy. The old woman's murmurings intensified as she finished her circle of blood and began drawing unsettling runes inside. Bone charms around her neck blackened, somehow protecting her from the pyromantic flames raging all around.

A vicious melee erupted as the Skallgrim warriors used their superior numbers to try to drag the knights down so they could stab knives through joints in the siege breaker armour. They had no idea what they were dealing with and attached no significance as to why the wardens hadn't joined the fight yet. Four tackled Eva and succeeded in knocking her down onto one knee. She headbutted one on the way down, helm exploding through his face to leave a spurting stump, and elbowed another, caving in breastplate and chest. As they fell away she rose clutching a third by the throat. Her hand clenched and his neck burst like rotten fruit. She proceeded to beat the fourth to death with his friend's corpse, sounds of manic mirth bubbling out from her armour.

I'd never seen knights in a real battle before. It was terrifying and Eva was *laughing*. I was very glad she was on my side.

The enemy panicked and broke, leaving their halrúna to die. The male halrúna fell to his knees, drenched in his own blood, flames charring his skin as our magi overwhelmed his powers and protections. One of the siege-breakers charged the woman. She smiled and said, "My blood, your blood. My flesh, your flesh..."

A shiver rippled up my spine at her horribly familiar words.

A blade split her skull in two. Droplets of the dead shaman's blood hung in the air, then began spinning around her corpse with increasing speed. All the blood shed during the battle streamed over the ground towards the circle and was swept up into the ritual. A spike of gleeful alien hunger pulsed inside me, growing stronger with every second that passed – anticipation, as if a part of me knew what was coming. I gripped Dissever tight but the sanctors now had more to worry about than me.

Shadea hissed. "Too late – back away."

The whirlpool of blood drained down into the woman's corpse, far too much for any human body to possibly contain. Dark magic pierced the Shroud between worlds and opened a doorway. The shaman's belly bulged outwards and then ripped apart as something scaled with black iron emerged from a far-flung daemon realm.

The knight that had killed the old woman began backing away. A six-fingered hand tipped with metal claws burst from the old woman's flesh and speared through her killer's cuirass, exploding from the back in a shriek of steel. A second limb erupted from the corpse and buried claws in the ground. Sinews rippled and bulged as it pulled itself into our world. The reptilian daemon's massive form squeezed through a portal of flesh and blood much too small to possibly allow it, sloughing off corpse-meat as its serpentine tail slithered free of the portal.

It was easily ten feet tall and twenty long, with a serpent's head armoured in black iron crested with a jagged crown. Six golden slitted eyes opened and its jaw dropped in a mockery of a grin, revealing curved iron fangs the size of daggers. It tore the knight in two and tossed the halves into the river on either side of the bridge. Its eyes were not fixed in bone as ours were, instead freely sliding across flesh and metal plate alike to peer in every direction. Three eyes swivelled to look down at the male halrúna, now on all fours and weeping. A trio of forked tongues flicked out, tasting the air.

Shadea looked ill. Her wardens surrounded her in a nervous wall of steel. "It is a ravak queen," she said, eyeing the black crown. "During the Daemonwar their kind led entire armies of lesser daemons through the holes in the Shroud. I fought against one and almost died."

The creature's spiked tail lashed in agitation, and a dozen small serrated claws opened out on both sides all along the thing's torso like it was the bastard offspring of snake, scorpion and centipede. The creature's claws wrapped around the Skallgrim shaman's waist. Greasy vapour rose from its body as it lifted the old man to its maw, its flesh mottling with spots of grey as corrosion crept across the iron scales embedded in its flesh. Whatever power protected the shard beasts and the shadow cats from Setharis' virulent air did not extend to this daemon.

"You dare summon me to this place of atrocity?" it hissed in perfect Old Escharric.

"Mercy!" he begged. "We had no choice. The Scarrabus have our children."

Who or what are the Scarrabus? I'd never heard the name before. Perhaps this was who was behind the Skallgrim tribes' sudden organisation.

The man screamed – briefly – as the daemon bit his face off and wolfed down the rest, jaw extending grotesquely as it swallowed the squirming man whole: clothes, charms and all. The young sanctors gagged.

The ravak's tongues licked the air in the direction of the Magash Mora as it screeched. The distant booms and crackle of Arcanum attacks reminded us of our haste. Swarms of smaller daemons wheeled through the smoke-dark sky on iridescent wings, hazy forms darting down to pluck people from the ground and drop them screaming from a great height. Lightning flashed and a dozen blackened daemons fell. If the magi could hold out a little longer those smaller daemons would die off in droves.

We looked to Shadea. "Leave or be destroyed," she said, her power rising around her like a vast tidal wave ready to be unleashed. Everybody cringed back, instinct screaming *danger!*

The ravak didn't reply, didn't hiss, didn't do anything at all. What was this thing that it could ignore something like Shadea? It seemed to be listening to something. We waited nervously.

Its head snapped in our direction and it came for us, arcane energies crackling around the spikes of its crown. "The Scarrabus command your death. The lords of flesh cannot be disobeyed."

The wolf-ship raiders had lost two of their revered halrúna shaman trying to stop Shadea activating the titan – what power was this that could force them to sacrifice holy leaders more important than their tribal chiefs?

The daemon stretched out a hand and six feet of jagged black iron burst free from a sheath of flesh. I stared in shock at that vicious, barbed blade, then to Dissever. My knife was smaller but the resemblance was undeniable. An alien hunger tinged my thoughts, as if Dissever lusted to eat this ravak creature.

Shadea pressed the titan's activation key into Eva's arms. "It is primed and ready. Bring it to Lust and the war engine will carry out my command."

She moved to stand between the daemon and us. "This creature is beyond you. Run."

Some of her wardens stayed, loyal to the point of suicide. The rest of us fled as the elder magus and ravak queen unleashed their dread magics upon each other. The ground shook and air thundered.

The building to my left collapsed in on itself, angry flames roaring up beneath a cloud of black smoke shot through with sparks like dying stars. Smoke spun and writhed around us like a living thing, obscuring everything. We covered our faces in a futile attempt to keep the choking clouds from our eyes and mouths. Tears ran down my cheeks and my throat hurt worse than if I'd smoked a bucket-load of harshest tabac. The wardens were hazy shadows, but my sanctor gaolers stuck too close, giving me no chance to slip away even if I wanted to. Charra shadowed me, keeping me safe. Layla shadowed her, doing the same.

Somebody screamed. Hot blood spattered my face. Steel clanged all around. Our pyromancer staggered towards us, reddened eyes pleading as he pawed at the gaping wound in his neck in a vain attempt to stem the spurting blood. He went down and a pair of red-bearded Skallgrim burst from the smoke, vaulted his corpse and swung their axes at Martain's head. He sidestepped, his blade licking out across a face to leave jaw and neck a gaping ruin. He turned to exchange blows with the second. It was a mistake. That first ravaged warrior was deep in the red mist of rage and didn't even notice his mortal wound; he swung his axe at Martain's back. I instinctively rammed Dissever into the madman's side and cut it free. That seemed to do the trick; he dropped like a stone, almost in two halves. Martain glanced back, surprise writ all over his face, then had to focus on the warrior in front of him.

Charra fought beside me, nodding as she flicked blood off her sword, not a scratch on her. She had always been handy in a scrap. A horrendous childhood I wouldn't wish on anybody, but it had given her that. An axeman went for her, then fell with a knife through his eye. Charra scowled at the twisted hilt of the knife, and then at her daughter who had thrown it.

"Get your sorry behind over here!" Charra yelled.

Layla was in no real danger, dancing through the enemy towards us, leaving them pawing at slit throats and spurting blood. "I knew fine well where you had sneaked off to. I'm not leaving – you need me."

Charra grunted, knocking aside a wounded Skallgrim's axe and running him through. "Just stay close." It was far too late to argue and no chance of sending her to her room without any supper.

A massive, hairy beast of a man charged through the wall of smoke behind two of the siege-breakers. Tattoos and runic scars covered every visible area of skin, and the fine mail and helm marked him as a wolf-ship captain. He swung a two-handed beaked axe glowing with runes and malignant magic, once, twice. Both knights went down, heavy helms split.

He headed straight for Eva, mowing down every warden in his path with bewildering strength and inhuman speed. Gifted! She ducked, and his blow tore off her helm rather than her head.

The remaining siege-breakers charged him, driving him back, leaving Eva and ourselves to run for the titan. Steel shrieked, men screamed and magic burst all around us as we kept our heads down and ran for our lives.

Distant lightning flashed, setting my hair on end. Each flash of light silhouetted a mountain of writhing flesh against the sky. It had grown larger – no, closer. Perspective was skewed, the scale unbelievable. The Magash Mora was no longer heading for the Arcanum army. It was coming for us. We ran faster.

Soon the shadow of Lust coalesced from the smoke.

Eva skidded to a stop and held up the activation key. A rough coughing boomed somewhere high above and the air began vibrating with a high-pitched hum that set my teeth on edge. Then came a grinding squeal of metal and a *whomp-whomp-whomp* that steadily increased in speed until it became a deafening drone.

By Old Boney's barren balls I was not getting any closer to that machine! Our remaining wardens had no idea what was happening. Everybody cast fearful looks up into the smog and most began backing away. A prod of pointy steel in the small of my back stopped my retreat. I glanced back to see Martain shake his head.

"Are you mad?" I screamed over the drone. "Why do you want to be near that thing?"

"Shut up," he replied, the point of his blade pushing in to prick flesh. The other sanctors closed on me, swords at the ready, eyes on Dissever and ready to react. I didn't have a hope of fighting three of them – even if two were young they'd still been trained to kill rogue magi – so I stayed still. There was no point in escalating an already dire situation; I had to stay calm until a chance presented itself. Charra and Layla edged closer. I shot them a warning glare but they ignored it. Charra would help me or die trying.

The point jabbing my back eased slightly. "Why did you save me earlier?" Martain said.

"This is my home. We're on the same side," I said, puzzled. He didn't reply. "Aren't we?"

A breeze sprung up, whipping the smoke away to the east. An enormous armoured knee the size of a horse and cart crashed down by Eva's side, crushing cobbles to dust. A crust of dirt and bird crap broke loose to rain down on us. Lust's huge and inhumanly beautiful face descended through the thinning smoke. It held a terrible macabre beauty: that haughty metal smile was the last thing thousands of people had ever seen.

A sword the size of a grown tree lanced down through the street, followed by an enormous gauntlet that lowered to ground level. Eva placed the key onto the war engine's palm. Fingers clanked closed around it and lifted to its face. With a squeal of metal Lust's jaw dropped and swallowed it. Green flames flickered into life inside the titan's eyes.

A grinding thunk and screech of metal came from deep inside the great war-engine's armoured chest. It didn't sound right, but who knew if the damn thing would even work after all this time. The titan shuddered and ground to a halt. A dozen hollow metal snakes writhed from the titan's open mouth and began twitching towards us. With them came a tumble of old bones and a human skull.

Martain spoke, cold and hard, "As Krandus feared, the titan's source of power has been depleted. It requires another sacrifice."

Damn.

The flat of Martain's sword slammed into my wrist and Dissever slipped from numbed fingers. I cursed, ducking out of the way as a second blow whooshed past my head. A sick dread filled me. Blood sorcery hadn't been considered anathema until after the fall of ancient Escharr – the titans were powered by the sacrifice of a magus. It was grossly akin to the monster already ravaging Setharis and I refused to die like that.

"I don't know why I'm surprised," I said. This was what the Archmagus had been instructing him to do earlier during their little private chat. A glare and terse shake of my head stopped Layla from burying her blade in Martain's neck, for the moment. Whatever happened, I refused to let her or Charra die here. "The Arcanum have always wanted me dead." I spat on his boots and flexed my numb hand.

"You want me? Come take me. I'll tear your fucking throats out with my teeth."

Martain growled and menaced me with his sword. "Herd him towards the titan." Eva did nothing to help or hinder us, torn between obeying orders and committing an atrocity. The remaining wardens gathered around the young male sanctor, hands reaching for me.

And then everything took a turn for the worst. Across the street and out of the sanctor's range, Harailt stepped from the smoke. White-hot flame roared from his palms to engulf the young male sanctor and the wardens. They shrieked, turned into human candles. The sanctor's twin screamed and dropped to her knees.

Shock burst across on Eva's face. "Harailt? What are you–"

"I am so sorry, Evangeline," he said. "I had hoped you might join this new and glorious Arcanum I am building, but you would only refuse." I screamed a warning as Harailt's expression twisted, flickering between contempt, ecstasy and rage far too quickly to be natural. Something was very wrong inside him.

Betrayal was carved into her expression in the moment he flung his hands out towards her. Fire blasted her into the air, armour glowing cherry-red and starting to melt. Her flesh sizzled as she screamed through the twisting smoke into the ruins of a house. Nobody could survive that.

Harailt's expression dissolved into utter horror. "Evangeline, no… I did not mean–"

His expression hardened into an emotionless mask and he turned to face the five of us remaining: Charra, Layla and myself, Martain and the shaking girl sanctor. Martain grabbed her by the armpits and began dragging her away from me, to allow the use of my Gift.

I scanned the ground. Dissever was near my foot. If I could reach it then I could buy time for Charra and Layla to escape. I would die in agony, but there was a small chance I could take him with me. A fair exchange by any account.

A purple flash. A white line burned across my sight.

Harailt glanced at the gaping hole in his chest where his heart had been. "Ah." He didn't fall.

Shadea hobbled from the smog, one arm torn and limp and a missing foot replaced with a crutch made from a dead warden's sword. Her face was split, a red trench running through an empty eye socket. The other boiled over with virulent purple energy.

My jaw dropped as the hole in his chest writhed with reforming flesh. "Shadea," he spat. "You survived our little pet then. Perhaps nex–"

Light stabbed out from her eye, burning holes through his chest and neck.

"–t time we will find somethi–"

A sphere of blue fire coalesced around Harailt, so hot it drove us all back, the stone melting and sparking around him.

The flames burst apart. Harailt casually dusted off charred ends of clothing. "–ng more worthy of facing you."

"There is a god inside him," Shadea hissed. "Harailt is gone."

His face twitched into a sneer. "Not at all, elder. I am very much alive and in control. We three great powers, magus, god and Scarrabus, work hand-in-hand for our great cause." He waved to the looming bulk of the Magash Mora coming towards us. "You cannot kill us and you cannot stop the coming glory of the reborn Arcanum. Join us, elder, and we will rule this world entire, as we should, devoid of all restriction and petty politicking. Think of what you can learn from us." He glanced at me. "Him, we must kill."

She smiled, a horrific sight even when she was whole. "You are deluded." She flicked a finger towards him and

Harailt was yanked into the air, screaming as he disappeared into the distance. Somewhere across the city a building collapsed from the impact.

Martain looked to the titan awaiting its sacrifice, then to me, and finally to Shadea, a question on his lips.

"No," she snapped, spraying flecks of blood.

A carpet of flesh now flowed through the streets nearby, gnashing canine mouths and wailing human cries, grasping fingers and horse hooves all crawling towards us, the nightmarish main body of the creature looming dark and terrible behind it.

"Speed is now the essence of victory," she said, hobbling towards the titan. "As I think young Edrin here might say, I am no longer a dog in this fight. We fight where and however we must." She let the metal snakes swarm her, hollow heads burying in her withered flesh and lifting her off the ground towards Lust's mouth.

She gasped in pain. "Fight in my stead, tyrant. Share my wrath. Kill that traitor." Her eyes flashed with furious hope, "Destroy that traitor god."

I gave her a single nod as they drew her back into the depths of the titan. Harailt was exposed and the collusion of a god confirmed. It had to be this newly ascended Hooded God who had protected those shard beasts and shadow cats from Setharis' corrosive influence. Had the god's newfound power driven him mad?

Nathair, Thief of Life, where are you when I need you, eh? He stood for freedom and independence, everything that Harailt despised. I'd half expected him to rise from the earth and rip the life from our enemies. What use were gods if they didn't protect their people? Bloody gods, leaving me to clean up their messes again.

Again? My mind shuddered.

Beneath my trembling hands, Artha's skin is hot as a furnace.

The god's face twists in agony, "Cut deep and cut now."

An eerie song shivers through me and I press down, Dissever cracking bone and plunging into his heart...

I scrambled for the knife and clutched the foul weapon to my chest, letting its flood of hunger drown the memory. I killed a god – was this why the Hooded God wanted me dead? Because I was a threat to his insane ambitions? I had killed Artha and that meant there had to be a way to kill the Hooded God too.

Martain was dazed and despairing. He no longer cared to fight me and didn't think to try to shut down my Gift again. We collapsed beside the foot of the great war-engine, waiting in silent dread to see what manner of horror would be unleashed.

CHAPTER 30

It was all very anticlimactic. Minutes dragged by with no sign of life from the titan. We waited in tense silence for a while, then looked at each other and shrugged.

"What now?" Martain said. He put an arm round the young sanctor's shoulders, "I am so sorry Breda." Her shoulders shook with great heaving sobs.

I swallowed. "Guess it's up to us."

"Oh, dear gods," he said. "We are all doomed." It was a sentiment I wholeheartedly echoed. Then he cleared his throat, staring at his feet. "It did not sit well with me."

"What, trying to murder me?"

Charra shifted so she was behind his back, hand on the hilt of her sword. Layla tested the edge of a knife. He didn't seem to care.

"Yes." At least he wasn't hypocritical enough to try to couch it in prettier terms. "The Archmagus instructed me that a sacrifice might be necessary for the greater good. Whatever sort of degenerate you are, you did save us in the Boneyards. I apologize."

"Worthless," I said. "We both know you'd do it again in a heartbeat. Take your apology and shove it up your arse."

"I see there is no reasoning with you. I shall not persevere."

"Finally," I said, mocking a cheer, "some good news!" Something prickled my senses, a vibration on the air. "*Hsst* – do you hear that?"

"Is that coming from Lust?" he said, brow furrowed.

A muffled whine from the titan's insides grew into a thrumming shriek of barely-constrained power.

"Er, perhaps we should move?" Martain said, staring at the thing. By that point Charra, Layla and I were already in full retreat.

A heat haze shimmered around Lust. It rose with a hiss of steam and clank of metal, looming above the tenements. Massive as the war engine was, it was dwarfed by the mountain of flesh and bone flowing towards us. Undaunted, it tore its massive sword from the earth and took a single ponderous stride towards the Magash Mora, testing its balance, and then another, each step a small earthquake. It picked up speed and began ploughing straight towards its target, carts, bodies and buildings crushed beneath anvil tread.

Without the terror of battle to distract me, the waves of agony radiating from Lynas' mind were threatening to pull me into madness. All I wanted to do was claw my eyes out to get to the source of the pain and tear it from my skull. I'd thought I was prepared for it this time. I was wrong, but with the thrill of magic singing through my body it had become a perverse union of pleasure and pain that proved bearable. Just.

We followed the trail of devastation left by the titan. If killing that fleshy abomination wasn't the only way to ease the pain, the only way to let Lynas rest, then I might have laughed at myself. Me, acting like a sodding hero. Ha! Even if I made for a poor one, it was ludicrous. In the end it came down to a simple animal truth: fight or flight, and I'd had a gutful of flight – ten long years of it.

Martain drifted closer to me. I brandished Dissever and glared. He got the message. He looked cast adrift and confused, and rightly terrified. "What now?" he said, voice lifeless.

"We let Lust tear it a new arsehole, and if needs be we ram ourselves up there and cut out its heart." I hoped the titan would do all the work for us but I never relied on anything as ephemeral as hopes and dreams.

Whatever else I thought of him, Martain didn't whine and snivel or try to run. Perhaps it was loyalty induced by the Forging, but to my chagrin I suspected that it was just a man making a hard decision. The right decision. If the titan failed then nobody else would be mad enough to try to save this dark and dangerous cesspit of a city by diving in to headbutt death.

The other magi were doing their best to incinerate chunks of flesh and bone but it was nowhere near enough. With the creature's resistance to magic they couldn't hope to destroy such a vast bulk while the strongest artefacts the Arcanum possessed were buried deep below the ruins of the Templarum Magestus.

Lust crashed straight through an already-listing tenement and waded deeper into the warrens. Shoals of terrified people parted before it, fleeing their homes. Packs of armed looters and Skallgrim infiltrators were overwhelmed and trampled underneath the feet of the terrified mob. The shattered bodies of a dozen families who'd hid behind barred doors lay amongst the ruins, blood winding in little rivulets through the dirt. A dog with a broken leg whined and licked a dusty hand jutting from a pile of broken beams and stone. I lowered my head and ran on, avoiding tendrils of warped flesh that wormed through the debris. The dog yelped once and then fell silent. I shuddered and detoured to avoid another questing tendril.

Earth and sky burned as the Arcanum assault reached its climax. We passed through a ruined intersection choked with bodies. Breda ceased her sobbing.

Martain held her close. "Are you well?"

THE TRAITOR GOD

The girl's eyes were bleak. "I am well enough to do my duty," she said. "For my brother."

Martain's reply was blotted out by a droning horn blast from the titan, louder than a thousand trumpets.

The massive sword began cranking upwards as the ancient war engine closed on the Magash Mora. Outlying worms of flesh latched onto metal feet and began crawling upwards. The titan didn't shudder to a stop, drained of all magic; instead it looked down and the seething magic in its eyes bubbled over to blast the ground with liquid fire. Flesh that ate the Arcanum's magic charred and died, smoke and ash billowing into the air. I was shocked, was this ancient Escharric magic? Or was it artificer alchemy beyond anything Setharis had ever dreamed of? The titan resumed its advance, leaving flaming footprints in its wake.

"Breda, stay close," Martain said, holding her tight. "Can you do that for me?" The girl was terrified, but she fought it down, loosed a shuddering breath, and nodded. He patted her on the shoulder. "Let us watch the titan end this." His words lacked conviction.

The five of us chased after the metal giant, the sanctors in the lead. All around us the Magash Mora's appendages burrowed through debris and crept through windows. The closer I came to Lynas' flesh the greater the pain in my head became. It sizzled like a red-hot nail in my skull.

Charra limped beside me, barely keeping pace as I puffed and panted down a ruined alleyway. Layla had no such problems, eyes darting to every window and doorway checking for threats. She gaped in amazement at the armoured bulk of the titan ahead of us. "I had thought those old stories about the statues were just stupid legends."

Old? I guessed most adult Docklanders lived, what, into their thirtieth or fortieth year? That would make it about eight or nine generations since the titans had last walked.

An age to them, but not so long to the mind of a magus. The gulf between them and me widened.

"Would you care to explain why are we running towards that monster and not away?" Charra said.

"You don't get to come," I said. "There is nothing you can do to hurt it."

"We can kick your head in, old man," Layla replied. "You fight like a drunken oaf so don't dare try that with us. I could take you both at once so it should be me that goes. I have trained for years to fight and kill. What is the point if I run away from this, when my skills are needed most?"

"I'm not going to kick it in the head," I said. "You two will be in our way. Layla, if I needed somebody offed I would ask you in a heartbeat, but only magi can fight something like this." *And more importantly, I need to keep you both safe.*

Layla shook her head. "But, I–"

"I don't have time to debate," I shouted. "Cut your way out of the city if you can, or hide deep underground if you can't. There is an entrance to the catacombs below the Collegiate if those tunnels survived the collapse of the Templarum Magestus. Gather what food, drink and oil you can find and stay down there as long as you can." Charra started to protest but I cut her off and rattled out directions. "If you don't go now then I'll force you. You know I can do it."

We locked gazes. She was seething. "You swear to the gods that we would be of no use?" she said, looking up, and up, at the mountain of flesh. It was close, and the smoke was thin enough to make out individual faces amongst the revolting mass looming over the Warrens.

Charra should have known better: I didn't give a toss what the gods thought of me and I'd quite happily lie to their faces if I could get away with it. "May the Night Bitch rip my balls off with rusty tongs if I lie," I said. "Even if the titan falls, and we fail too, it might just delay that thing long enough for both of you to lead people to safety. You need to go. Please, I can't trust anybody else." Charra gave me a terse nod, grabbed her daughter and sprinted back the way we had come. She wasn't one to hesitate. A weight lifted from my heart. Whatever else happened, they would survive, and a little bit of Lynas with them.

The titan's horn blasted again, footsteps thundering as it picked up speed. The Magash Mora's babbling voices wailed as it surged to meet it with a vomit-inducing liquid slurp. The magical bombardment from the Arcanum slowed as magi strained their Gifts to the limit, pushing themselves close to succumbing to the Worm of Magic. An army of twisted magi without any restraint would be worse than anything the enemy could ever imagine, but Krandus would never allow that to happen. Any that succumbed would be immediately reduced to ash by the Inner Circle.

"Hurry!" Martain shouted. "It's about to begin." He pulled ahead and turned a corner to get a better view of the fight. I ignored my burning leg and the tightness in my chest and ran faster.

Docklanders streamed in the opposite direction through the narrow alleys: mothers and fathers clutching wailing infants, wide eyed priests muttering desperate prayers, gang-marked youths carrying the old and infirm, and even a handful of bloodied wardens helping to direct them and keep everyone calm. Each and every one of them looked at us like we were cracked for running towards the monsters. It was a fight for the likes of gods and elder adepts or legendary heroes, not for mere mortals and shitty little magi like us, but the gods were missing and we were fresh out of heroes. But then, perhaps every hero was just a desperate fool who did what needed to be done, and the songs and stories washed off all the blood and muck, the fear and the pain. Maybe someday a bard would write a song about me, one without all the swearing and drinking and pissing myself in terror.

Ash fell like grey snow, and with it the fleeting thought of corpse dust drawn into mouth and lungs. I felt cut off from reality, sunk in a fever dream of darkest insanity. The number of people on the streets dwindled.

The titan approached Bardok the Hock's shop, destroying everything in its path. The greedy old man was still there, red-faced and heaving at a bulging sack too stuffed with gold and goods to possibly fit through his doorway. He looked up in time to scream as Lust's foot fell, crushing body and business both to a flattened paste as it advanced on its foe.

A towering club of bone, claw and hoof, rose straight up from the Magash Mora, spiked tip lost in the smoke. The club listed, then it fell like a toppled oak, crushing buildings beneath the trunk before smashing into the chest of the titan. Lust shivered like an enormous gong, the shockwave of impact spraying living shrapnel, shredding everything nearby.

We ducked into doorways as fragments of bone and nail ricocheted down narrow alleys. My heart hammered as I stared at a splintered human femur embedded in the wall only a hand span away from having torn off my face. Breda hissed in pain, a line of red welling up across her cheek.

As Lust resumed its march, the sanctors charged ahead and I followed. Bardok was slippery and squishy underfoot and I didn't dare look down. The titan staggered, steam hissing from cracks spider webbed across its torso. Armoured feet stamped down as it righted itself, leaving craters. Flesh sucked and squelched as the Magash Mora drew back and reformed the club for another blow. An enormous metal gauntlet plunged into the remains of the club and took hold, metal and muscle straining in a contest of monstrous strength.

With glacial slowness Lust was dragged towards gnashing maws and spiked tentacles. The titan's sword cranked higher for another blow, shearing through the club's trunk. Separated from the main body, the fleshy weapon the size of a block of tenements exploded from the inside. It crashed to earth and slumped in on itself, spreading like a landed jellyfish.

The Magash Mora's throats howled in pain, stump flailing like a headless snake, hot blood raining clear across the city. Something that huge had to have thousands of human hearts pumping a staggering volume of blood under a pressure that only flesh strengthened by stolen Gifts and foul magic could possibly withstand.

Lynas' agony burned in my mind and everything went hazy. I slumped against a blood-slick wall and tried to regain control. We were so close, and the sanctors waited up ahead, unsure of what to do next.

Another volley of burning rocks fell from the sky like Elunnai's fiery tears. They exploded into the creature's gaping wound. Scattered cheers erupted in the distance as idiots clambered onto roofs and walls to watch the battle. Sheets of flame roared from the titan to immolate more.

The flailing club-stump ceased spewing blood, and bones slid through the skin to form another spiked maul. Huge red bulges appeared on the thing's body, swelling up like boils desperate to burst. It convulsed and thick ropes of muscle and bone hooks burst out to snare the titan. Its bulk surged forward, a thousand limbs grasping.

I wiped its blood from my face and stared at my red-smeared, fragile hands. Even Dissever seemed tiny and useless. I'd taken leave of my senses to think we could get anywhere near the core of that thing, never mind hope to cut it out! My heart pounded and my hands were slick with sweat and blood. I couldn't bear the thought of being absorbed into that thing – not like Lynas. I backed away.

"Walker!" Martain said. "What is wrong?"

What had I been thinking? I was no damn warrior. I turned tail when things got difficult – that was me, the pathetic coward.

I thought about running, but couldn't take a single step. My retreat was blocked by a ruined figure limping towards me.

CHAPTER 31

The figure wore half-melted siege-breaker armour, sword dangling from a limp arm and scraping along the ground, while the other hand was fused to the remains of the cuirass. Their hair was burnt to stubble and the left side of the face was a mottled mess of black and red, cheekbone exposed, teeth showing through burnt flesh, the eye socket a charred and empty pit. The other side was almost as bad, skin broken and weeping, what was left of the cheek twisted into agonized grimace, but one pretty green eye was intact – and I recognized both eye and the iron will behind it.

Fear forgotten, I gawped at Eva. "How are you still alive?" She emanated indescribable agony, pain enough to beggar what I was feeling though the bond from Lynas' Gift. Even for a knight those wounds surely had to be beyond healing, and yet she fought on. Shame overwhelmed me. We had left her for dead.

Her breathing was ragged and wet as she struggled to speak, her voice emerging as tortured groans. Instead she dragged her spirit-bound sword forward into guard position and glared at me. Her intention was clear: she intended to finish this. I shuddered, forcing myself to turn back to face the Magash Mora. If Eva could fight on in that state then so could I.

Martain recognized her sword and his face crumpled, trembling on the verge of losing control. He lifted his sword in salute.

Titanic metal met bone, tooth and claw in ponderous battle: it was not the cut and thrust of merely human fighting but awesome blows exchanged between two giants so massive that even the vast power granted by magic could not entirely overcome their incredible weight.

The mountain of flesh split open like a giant maw to engulf the titan, and once inside I imagined the sheer weight of its body alone might serve to crush the ancient war engine. Blood and charred meat rained down as the titan hacked an entire cliff-face from the beast and spat more liquid fire into the wound.

For a moment I thought it was all over – how could a creature of flesh ever beat solid metal? But then I noticed the severed parts of the monster were being reabsorbed by the flowing mass, and meanwhile metal chipped and dented, cracked and leaked steam where maces and spears of bone slammed again and again against its armoured form. Hooks and claws worried at the cracks, trying to pry them open. I had a horrible feeling that one titan was not going to be enough. Lust waded through the mass of churning flesh, sword cutting vast chasms into the Magash Mora's body, but it all flowed back, as futile as fighting the sea.

"What do we do now?" Breda said, looking at Martain, then Eva, and finally me. As if I had any more brilliant ideas.

Eva wheezed, struggling to speak. She gave up and instead pointed a trembling finger first at me, and then to her head. I shuddered, but did what she wanted: I opened my Gift wide. The miasma of blood sorcery in the air made me gag, feeling like plunging head-first into a plague-pit of rotting corpses. I struggled to tread water above the sea of fragmented screaming thought. Somehow I managed to rise above it to latch onto Eva.

A torrent of magic was roaring through her broken body, more than she could possibly handle for long. She was hanging on by a thread, but then she didn't expect to survive. With her mastery of body-magic she'd managed to dull her pain, the signals from her dying body throttled down to mere agony.

She let me right into her tortured mind. She trusted me, and that was not something I often encountered. I endured her pain and did my best to wall it away from her consciousness, but her will and Gift were strong and my hasty tampering wouldn't last. Her ruined face wasn't capable of conveying much emotion but I felt the cooling balm of relief wash over her, then a throb of gratitude.

Drops of burning liquid splashed nearby, setting tenements smouldering as another wave of flame engulfed the Magash Mora. It flinched back, retreating until the flames ebbed, only to surge forward once again, swinging a bone battering ram into the titan's side.

A whole section of the titan's torso caved in with a squeal of tearing metal. It staggered, leaking steam and spraying thick black fluid from the wounds as blow after blow slammed into it. Metal plates were wrenched apart as the Magash Mora wormed into its guts. Lightning flashed from inside and thick greasy smoke poured out. The war engine shuddered.

A spike of bone tore through that inhumanly beautiful face and lodged inside. The titan stumbled and nearly fell, limbs now afflicted with a palsied shake. Lust was dying.

I voiced Eva's fractured thoughts for her: "She says we must wait for an opening and then charge in and cut out its heart."

The titan righted itself and waded into the flesh for one

final strike, shearing though the mountain of flesh and the stone beneath. I felt a surge of animal fear as the huge blade cut near to what had to be the heart of the beast. Gifted minds pulsed with momentary agony before fading as a meatslide of severed flesh the size of a small town buried the shady gambling dens of the Scabs. I felt Lynas' Gift anew, a beacon shining amongst a cluster of Gifted minds, and I knew exactly where that part of him was.

"There!" I said, pointing to the gaping chasm of red and pink left by the titan's last attack. "The heart is in there."

We broke into a crazed sprint, vaulting up onto the debris of the meatslide, Eva slower behind us. The sanctors ran ahead, splashing though puddles of creamy fat, and wherever they went Gifts that had been absorbed into the mass shut down and died. The thing's body began to fall apart in the sanctors' wake; mouths and eyes ceased moving, limbs flopped like their strings had been cut. Nodes of brain-meat exploded, coating our legs with a wet pink splatter. Without magic surging through their Gifts to strengthen the flesh around them the sheer weight of its own body was crushing them to pulp.

I fed my muscles on magic, feeling a mad exhilaration burst out of that self-destructive part of me. Hysterical laugher bubbled from my mouth. The carpet of meat was spongy and slick with juices, the air hot from body heat and stinking of blood, sweat, and bile. Wind whistled in and out of severed tubes all through the thing's flesh.

The titan struggled to break free, but the Magash Mora was relentless. A shard of metal the size of a horse slammed down a few paces away, spattering us with blood and strings of jelly.

The vast wound in the beast's side began to close up as tentacles quested out to reabsorb and reattach the section we were running over. If that happened the thing would swallow us and strip the meat from our bones. A pink worm, thick and sweaty as a fat man, squirmed towards the sanctors and promptly had a seizure. I felt a Gift die. The worm crashed down. The Magash Mora responded to their threat by withdrawing the bulk of its Gifted minds deeper into the main body.

"Veer left," I shouted, tracking the source of my pain. We reached the end of the severed flesh-cliff and paused. The ground pulsed underfoot as it began to re-attach, to live again. I felt the suction on my Gift slowly return and cursed my old boots' worn soles. We had to hurry. The sanctors could shut down Gifted minds if they were close enough, but they could do bugger-all else.

Fire spewed from the holes in Lust's ruined face. Flesh sizzled and hissed but still wrenched at Lust's left arm. In a squeal of metal it tore free.

The titan's horn blasted one last time, then exploded. Lust's head spun off into the sky, trailing black smoke. The body screeched and fell. Lightning flashed and crackled from its wounds.

– Blinding light and a deafening boom –

– Searing heat –

– A wall of air slamming into me –

I was face down in something warm, wet, and throbbing that was suckling magic from me. I struggled to my feet. I'd been lucky to land on a part only barely attached to the main body. It took a few moments for the lurid spots of light to fade and deafness to wane. I blinked away blood and tears to behold a scene of utter devastation.

The ground where Lust had stood and fought was now a smoking crater. Twisted fragments of the war engine had gouged lines of destruction clear across the city. Huge chunks of the Magash Mora were missing and a cavernous hole gaped in its belly where thousands of dangling tubes spewed fluids and organs plopped and slid down steaming foothills of offal. It quivered and wailed in confusion, throbbing with agony so intense that my eyes watered. I gripped Dissever tight and leant heavily on its rage.

The ground pitched and yawed beneath me, but on seeing Martain and Breda staggering ahead I lumbered after them into the cavern. It was far too late to back out. If there was a chance to save Setharis then it had to be now.

For the first time in decades I prayed properly to my patron god, the only one who might give a damn, the outsider like myself: "Nathair, Thief of Life, I don't know if you can hear me but on the off-chance you can, some help would be much appreciated. Charra needs healed, and me... I need a fucking miracle." He didn't answer.

The walls thudded with heartbeats. The babble of uncountable thousands of thought fragments washed over me, lapping away at my sandcastle of reason. They were less than human, just mindless remnants put to abhorrent use, but every so often I felt a flash of knowing horror and despair.

Some part of the abomination sensed me and roused from agonized spasms, eyes and limbs sprouting from its insides. Pustules grew and burst, birthing clawed limbs that quested towards me. There was no possibility of the sanctors making it to the heart in time if they were spotted, so I had to draw all the attention.

Sweat poured down my face as I wrenched my strained Gift open as wide as possible, drawing in as much magic as I could without giving myself to the Worm. Even without touching the flesh some of my magic was being drawn off and devoured.

The Magash Mora was a simple creature, its mind easier to infiltrate than a still-living human. These pitiful remnants lacked the walls of will and self-consciousness that resisted mental intrusion. I sent out a pulse of anger to draw the attention of its many conjoined minds. "Over here, you stinking carcass!"

My ploy worked far too well. It only took a dozen steps before my feet were sucked beneath the surface. I waded through jellied meat, managing another few paces before something seized my feet from below. I screamed as it sucked on my Gift.

Sudden terror made me lash out, trying to dig myself free using Dissever, as I had with the lesser monster. As quickly as the flesh parted it flowed back, and only then did I think to fear that this far more potent monster might have damaged Dissever's enchantments, but the spirit-bound blade held firm.

A woman's supple hand with too many fingers dug jagged nails into my leg. I flailed wildly, leaving the arm a twitching stump. A nightmare of teeth and gnashing jaws rose from the living ground. I dodged, barely managing to save my face from being torn off. Tendrils wrapped around me as it gathered itself for another attack. I was dead. The thing launched itself at me, jaws gaping.

A flash of steel and its head flew to one side. Eva entered the fray like a storm of slaughter. She was shaking and bleeding everywhere. This was her last great surge of strength, only a temporary reprieve. The sanctors still had a way to go and she was already slowing.

In blind panic I lashed out with my mind. Every bit of power I possessed slammed into the mass of minds – and slid straight through the Gift-bond into what was left of Lynas. Mental shock exploded through the remains of my friend and cascaded though the entire creature. A fit took the Magash Mora, hundreds of limbs shaking and flopping uncontrollably, eyes rolling, mouths drooling. Its bite on my Gift disappeared.

My power twisted deeper into the mass-mind, tearing and cutting, sowing confusion. I could only compare what I found to invading a hive of bees. Deep in the centre of the thing was a searing source of alien magic – the queen of the hive-mind. But it rebuffed my probes.

There were too many people absorbed into the beast for me to contend with for long. Thousands of minds gathered scattered thoughts and desires and threw them against me in instinctive self-preservation. What they lacked in finesse they made up for in numbers. I grimaced, eyes screwed up tight, and drew even deeper on my magic. The Worm of Magic howled for release. I held on for a few more moments as the living cavern shook around me. *Run, Martain. Faster!*

I screamed inside and out as my already-strained Gift threatened to tear apart. And then blessed relief bloomed in my mind. I opened my eyes to see the sanctors had finally made it to the heart of the beast. Dozens of Gifted minds died as the weight of tons of magic-less meat crushed down on what was left of their human selves. Tentacles and hands slapped blindly at the source of death, but the sanctors skilfully dodged. Their power couldn't reach every Gifted mind but it was a dire blow.

The grip on my legs slackened and I hauled myself out, clamping down on the flow of magic before the strain tore my Gift apart. But I couldn't stop the leakage entirely. My Gift was damaged and magic seeped through the cracks, however hard I tried to stop it. Glutted on magic, I grabbed Eva and dragged her towards the inhuman heart of the beast. She could no longer stand but that didn't stop her sword arm.

My thoughts were too embattled to speak anything of sense so I let Dissever show Eva the way by slicing a doorway into the throbbing wall. Her sword proved far more effective, cleaving a full five and a half feet of meat and bone with each stroke. A hazy light shone through walls of palpitating tissue. It was grotesque butchery, hacking an orifice deeper into the centre of the monster.

A crystal the length of my forearm and thick as my thigh, banded with gold graved with elaborate eldritch runes, was embedded in a socket of bone and cartilage at the very centre of the Magash Mora. It throbbed with sickly yellow light that hurt my eyes and mind. The raw potency of magic seared my skin and Gift. Eva gurgled and forced herself up onto her feet. She hefted her spirit-bound blade and smote the crystal a tremendous blow. Her sword exploded into a thousand pieces. The spirit in the sword screamed in agony, flickering in and out of visibility as its magical life-force was devoured by the crystal. The spirit dissolved with a soft sigh.

Eva stared at the smoking hilt in her hand for a moment, then crashed to the floor. I didn't have time to help, instead busied myself hacking away at bone and cartilage until the crystal wobbled when I booted it. The heartbeat steadied around me. Flesh pulsed faster and squeezed in to smother us. The tunnel we'd cut was healing up. It was now or never, time to do something stupid – I stowed Dissever away, then grabbed hold of the crystal and pulled.

All my magic drained into it. We were one, and countless howling insane minds tried to consume me. Among the mass of once-human and once-animal thought were three coherent minds directing the beast from someplace else. One was a vast and potent force, something human, or had been once – a god, that Hooded Bastard surely. Fortunately it didn't hold the reins of the beast and could do little more than dribble its power into the other – a magus. Harailt. The third was something utterly alien and incomprehensible. I didn't have time or power enough to fight all three mind-to-mind.

I set my feet and pulled, arms and legs shaking with effort. "Come on, you bloody thing. Move!" I growled, heaving until every muscle shook with the effort. The crystal finally broke free in a welter of blood and the screams of thousands pounded my skull more franticly than ever, then... ceased. Lynas' presence quietened and faded, a soft mental exhalation of all purpose and direction. One by one the sources magic died. I grabbed Eva, and somehow we marshalled enough strength to get out of the collapsing tunnel. The huge crystal felt unnaturally light in my hand, and also strangely right.

The sanctors were already fleeing by the time we emerged from the cavern of flesh. Rivers of blood and fluids burst from the walls as the thing's weight crushed down. The ground decayed quickly, making our footing slippery and treacherous, but we made it back onto solid ground before whale-sized ribs snapped and the mountain of flesh collapsed in on itself.

The Magash Mora was dead.

Now you can rest in peace, my old friend.

It was a small but comforting mercy.

CHAPTER 32

I lay gasping for breath, drained of all strength, a gentle breeze cooling my sweat-slick skin. The crystal was hot in my hand, pulsing with life, its alien whispers stroking my mind as it fed on my magic. The traitor magus, his pet god, and that other thing flailed away in the back of my mind, crude but strong, their grip on the Magash Mora's core slipping with each second it spent in my hands.

The mountainous corpse of the Magash Mora twitched and jerked, jets of blood still spurting but weakening. To our relief it showed no signs of reviving.

Eva lay unmoving, and with my magic leeched away I couldn't be sure if she was still amongst the living or if her agony had ended with her mission. I was too exhausted to feel more than a numb sense of loss. Numbness was the mind's way of coping, and that scab would fall off soon enough. Her bravery didn't merit this kind of fate, but then neither had the countless thousands of other lives devoured today – I swallowed and avoided thinking about that.

Martain and Breda picked their way through rubble towards us, stained and sore and looking every bit as awful as I felt. They stopped a safe distance away, swords sheathed at their hips. "How is she?" Martain said.

Eva was encased in a warped shell of steel so I put my ear to her mouth listening for any sign of breath, but the breeze made that useless. I shrugged. "There's nothing we can do anyway," I said. "Even if she is still alive, I doubt there is a healer who would even try." Under the armour her skin was crispy as crackling and most of her exposed flesh was seared to the bone.

Breda sobbed, more from shock and relief than for Eva. "How could she walk like that, never mind fight?"

I shook my head. "She is possessed of a rare iron will. As if a shitty daemon and a traitorous pyromancer could ever stop Evangeline of House Avernus from carrying out her mission."

"She will be remembered," Martain said.

"You had better," I said, grimacing as I hauled myself to my feet. "You two will likely be the only ones to tell of what she did here."

"What do you mean?" Martain said, eyeing the crystal in my hands. "Is that what I think it is?"

"Yes, this is where it all began. They fed it mageblood to create the Magash Mora." I winced as I took a tentative step on my weakened leg, pain spiking. I set the crystal down – just for a moment – to let my magic wash away what tiredness it could. My stomach rumbled as wounds burned and itched from quickened healing. My hands shook with fear and shock and starvation.

"That sounds more like a job for a sanctor," Martain said.

"You would take it to the Arcanum," I said. "I mean to destroy it."

After a moment's hesitation, he nodded. "Perhaps that would be for the best."

Breda slammed into Martain, knocking him aside. Flame engulfed her as Martain landed awkwardly. She shrieked and fell, kicking and screaming and sizzling.

"Drat. Missed," Harailt said, appearing through a bank of smoke.

A dozen huge Skallgrim warriors in blackened mail and blood-soaked furs marched beside him, led by the Gifted wolf-ship captain. Harailt's eyes glossed over Eva's burnt figure, not even acknowledging his vile handiwork on somebody that had called him friend.

Martain surged to his feet and drew his sword. "Breda!" But she was already a smoking corpse. "You murdering scum. I'm going to cut your rancid head off!"

"Ah, ah, ah," Harailt said, waving a finger. "No, you won't."

I sought out his mind but it rebuffed my exhausted fumblings.

He chuckled. "I must admit that it was gratifying to skin your fat friend after his arson destroyed my stock of mageblood. The timing was perfectly terrible you know. The Magash Mora was supposed to have emerged in all her mature glory, fully capable of scaling the cliffs of the Old Town. The Skallgrim fleet sent by my allies was meant to arrive in time to help me rebuild and consolidate my control, not to waste manpower in pointless battle." He sighed, then smiled. "Ah well, these things happen. One must be adaptable."

"And what did you plan to do with the Magash Mora once you'd won?" I asked. "Did you think such ravenous hunger would just go away?" I itched to smash his face repeatedly into a wall until it was paste.

He shrugged. "I would unleash it upon my enemies, you stupid tyrant. One land at a time until all bowed to the new Arcanum and its new archmagus."

"And you call him a tyrant," Martain said. "You are offal, filth that deserves to be scraped off the boots of decent folk."

Harailt twitched, expression flickering through horror and fear, then anger before settling back on a mocking grin. He ignored Martain's jibe to focus on me. "It amused me to make your friend Charra's daughter dirty herself cleaning up my loose ends, but can you imagine my joy when I found out that you were still alive? That I get to dispose of you is a lovely gift indeed. There is no place for base-born vermin like you in the true Arcanum."

"What about your loyalty to Setharis?" I said. "What kind of monster would willingly bring this horror down on us? Look at what you did. Look, you sick fucker! The city is burning."

"I..." A shadow of confusion passed through his eyes. He shook his head and his gaze swiftly hardened. "Setharis is riddled with rot and its leaders are corrupt and impotent. I know you see this. To heal the Setharii empire I must cut off the head of this sickly serpent, and if a few lives need be sacrificed then so be it. I will rebuild anew, lacking the weakness and cowardice of past leadership. I will lead the new Arcanum to a golden age beyond even the wildest dreams of ancient Escharr."

"Oh, will you now?" I said, picking up the crystal core and backing away. "What about–"

The Skallgrim captain cut off my attempt to stall for more time, speaking in coarse Setharii. "Just kill them already."

Harailt waved acceptance and their men charged. "Kill the fools. Bring me his head and that crystal." He grinned, enjoying this deadly game.

I took one look at the advancing warriors and did what I do best – ran away. Harailt shrieked for them to give chase as I dodged his premature spurt of flame and legged it down the ruins of an alley. Axes thunked into the wall behind me. I hoped Martain had enough sense to run instead of making a futile last stand over the corpses of our companions. Honour was an admirable thing but I much preferred living; I'd been running from death for ten long years and I'd be damned if I allowed an odious little shite like Harailt the satisfaction of finally offing me. One way or another, I'd end him.

When I was young I'd made sport of losing people in the narrow lanes of the Warrens, getting away from bigger boys and brutal gangs with my hide intact. The trick was to get far enough ahead and make so many turns and twists that they had to pause at each intersection just to discover which way you'd gone, allowing me to gain a little more lead each time. But my natural strength was nearing its end and all that steel and leather the Skallgrim wore didn't slow them down. They were hard on my heels and gaining.

I scrambled over a pile of rubble and headed left, then took a sharp right down a narrow passage choked with refuse. If it was a tight fit for a skinny bastard like me then those hulking armoured lads would have trouble following. The sound of steel scraping along stone and guttural curses gifted me a fleeting pleasure.

I burst from the passage into a wider street, wheezing for breath, legs threatening to cramp. A few blank-faced Docklanders scraping through the ruins of their collapsed homes looked up and scarpered at the sight of me. A blood-stained madman holding a huge glowing crystal encrusted with weird runes wasn't somebody you wanted to be around. I shifted the murmuring crystal core to my other arm and scrambled down a side-street as shouts in the guttural Skallgrim tongue roared from behind.

Damn, they were gaining on me again. I vaguely recognized the area and realized I was heading towards the plague-ridden ruins of the old temple. I risked a glance back, dreading the sight of men pouring around the corner. They hadn't found my last turning just yet. When I looked forward again it was just in time to see the outstretched arm that yanked me through an open doorway. A rough hand clamped over my mouth and a cold blade pressed against my throat instead of through it. The door slammed shut and a bar thunked securely into place, plunging the room into a darkness lit only by sickly yellow crystal-light. I glimpsed perhaps a half-dozen faces before somebody flung a blanket over it.

I got the message: stay silent and stay still. Boots pounded down the street outside, stopping at the door. It shuddered as something hit it hard. Finding it barred, they hurried on. After a few minutes my captor removed the knife at my throat.

My eyes had adjusted enough to make out the scarred faces in the room and I looked up see which one of the Smilers had pulled me off the street. Tubbs' pockmarked face grinned down at me as she took her hand from my mouth. She lifted her fingers to cracked lips and licked them suggestively, then blew me a kiss. On most days I would have shuddered at the sight, but right then I could almost have kissed her. Almost. The Smilers were up to their gills in weaponry and jumped at every creak of wood in this old tenement. They were terrified. I moved slow and careful, not wanting to surprise anybody.

"No time to play with 'im, Tubbs," Rosha Bone-face whispered. "That cracked bastard has a whole army of foreign nutters after 'im." She gave the blanket covering the crystal core of the Magash Mora a fearful look and edged away. "Charra got the word out you were heading into that..." she shuddered "...that thing. Thought you might need your arse pulled from the fire and she was right enough. But we wasn't goin' to get closer to that monster, was we, girls?" They grumbled assent, even the big bearded Smiler at the back with a meat cleaver in his hand. "Wasn't until we seen it go down that we came lookin' for you. Good thing too."

Rosha cleared her throat. "What you doin' with that big hunk o' rock?" she said.

"Buggered if I know." What could I do with the damn thing? It whined and nuzzled at my mind. The last trace of Harailt's control had withered and died and the core now belonged to me. It wanted me to control it, to use it and abuse it in an orgy of devouring. I couldn't trust the Arcanum to destroy the thing; they would try to use it if they could, and study it if they couldn't. That power and knowledge was too seductive, and sooner or later, perhaps centuries down the line, somebody would use it again. With a god involved there was nobody I could trust. I had to get rid of it myself.

Eva's spirit-bound blade had shattered on the crystal core so I wasn't about to risk Dissever and I didn't have anywhere near the sort of personal power needed to destroy it. Which left what? With Skallgrim and looters still roaming the streets it was too dangerous to move about. Where could I go? And then inspiration struck: if I made it to Carrbridge then Lynas' warehouse already had wards set up. With a bit of luck perhaps I could use those defences while I holed up and tried to figure out what to do. That ruined temple was on the way, not far from here at all, and if the walls were still standing then I could retrieve the alchemic bomb. That might hold enough destructive power to destroy the crystal: after all, one of those bombs had turned their creator's entire workshop to dust, and it wasn't magic, so the crystal couldn't absorb it.

"I need you to distract those hairy brutes while I make a run for it," I said. "Then I can end this." The Smilers looked at me dubiously.

"Nah," Rosha said. "That there sounds like warden work."

I removed the blanket from my crystal and stained the room yellow. "Otherwise we're all dead. Or worse."

Rosha chewed on a bone piercing, mulling it over. "Fine. Whatever gets rid of you quickest."

We piled out the door and headed along a street running north-east. Two Skallgrim raiders turned a corner, came face to face with us. Before they could raise a shout the Smilers swarmed them, knives rising and falling. We left them choking on their own blood. The ruins of the old temple were mostly intact and I paused in our flight to stick my hand into the hole in the wall and retrieve the bomb. As a last resort I could always set it off and try to take Harailt with me.

"What are you doin' dawdlin'?" Tubbs said, coming up behind me and slapping my rear. "Get that sweet arse movin'."

We took off towards Carr's Bridge and a shout went up behind us – I'd been spotted. We led them a desperate chase though twisting smoke-choked alleys and rubble filled passages, bursting out onto Fisherman's Way. Relief surged as the bridge came into sight.

A wall of flame roared up all across the street. Some of the girls beside me shrieked and cringed back. Gutter-rats like them weren't used to magic; they scattered and ran for their lives. I turned to face Harailt, knowing there was no chance of outrunning a pyromancer in the open. The Skallgrim captain stood beside him, a sour set to his face. He probably couldn't abide Harailt either.

Tongues of flame licked up my clothes to scorch my face. He was enjoying toying with me. More and more raiders found their way back to their captain, standing around looking pissed off I'd led them such a merry chase.

"Put the crystal down," he said. I did as he asked, and as soon as my hands left it new strength flooded back through my Gift. Godly power emanated from Harailt and he wasn't trying to hide it any more.

I slipped a hand into my pocket and wrapped it around the alchemic bomb. He could kill me, but I wouldn't be going alone. I refused to let that slimy bag of arseholes win.

I gathered my power and lashed out. His mental defences weathered the storm. It *hurt*. His mind was drenched in alchemic, and I tasted mageblood in my mouth after even that briefest of touches.

He growled, "If only those idiot shadow cats had managed to track you down and tear you limb-from-limb as instructed."

"Why? What did I ever do to you?"

His eyes bulged. "You lowly runt! What did you do?" his throat spasmed and he had to start again. "What did you do? Everything went wrong for me the day they dug you out of that tunnel: you shamed my house and humiliated me in front of Archmagus Byzant. Why could you not just bow to your betters and cry at the entrance for a few days until we returned to free you after you'd learned your lesson? Oh no, Edrin Walker had to try and find his own way out."

He snarled. "As soon as I gained power from the Scarrabus I sought my revenge."

He was angry and unstable, ripe for letting something slip. "What is that, some sort of mind-rotting alchemic?" I jibed. "You pathetic addict."

His face flushed deep red. "You know nothing, ignorant peasant! My ancient allies ruled worlds beyond number long ago, and will again. They aid me in ridding the halls of my beloved Arcanum of filth like you."

I laughed at him. "And to think Eva claimed you had reformed, that you were a better person now." I spat on the ground. "Well, congratulations, you sure fooled her."

His snarl cracked. He frowned, confused. "Evangeline? No, I didn't mean to…" His eyes glazed over for a second, then he blinked and shook his head. The snarl returned.

The god's power suffused him, mingling in blood and bone. I felt its hunger for the crystal at my feet. Aha! So that was what it wanted. While Harailt had control of the

Magash Mora the god couldn't take it without disrupting years of careful work. A ritual that powerful and complex could not have been done quickly.

"You deluded bastard," I said to Harailt. "You have no idea, do you?"

That stung him. "What do you mean?"

"It's not yours anymore."

He didn't get it.

I helpfully clarified the situation: "Your god no longer needs you, you blind, bloody fool."

It took a second for realisation to sink in. His eyes widened. "No. We three have an alliance. The Scarrabus and I spent years preparing for the cleansing and rebirth of Setharis. You promised that we would rule together, and you–" His eyes bulged as blood welled up over his bottom lip. "Please, no, I promise to lead the Arcanum in your name – for your glory! Please, my god, don't you betray me too." His voice cut off in a gurgle as his belly swelled, split, and then tore wide open.

Flesh burst in a welter of blood and from his insides a god came forth. My guts churned and my Gift burned as if I stood too close to an inferno. I'd boasted that I would kill *this?* What hubris. It sloughed off Harailt's meat suit to reveal a male figure covered head to toe in glistening blood and slime, hairless and horrible. Harailt was left a boneless, bubbling, shivering mound of discarded flesh, and yet somehow still alive. It seemed that a god's blood and power coursing through your body for so long made you hard to kill, the Worm of Magic reluctant to let go of such a desirable host. Harailt's one remaining eye looked up at me in agony and horror.

I recognized this god and shuddered. It was something ancient, more potent by far than any poxy hooded upstart. This was my patron deity, Nathair, the Thief of Life. He was physically unimpressive: short of height and hairless, features obscured by gore, but his sheer presence struck me like a brick to the face. My legs trembled, threatening to give way and fall to my knees before him. The Skallgrim were similarly struck, swaying in silent shock. The god stank of mageblood and corrupt blood sorcery and I sensed the magic of countless Gifted churning inside him, a deluge of different flavours. Their Gifts and blood had granted power to the Magash Mora and Nathair seemed to have learned to copy that. My god was now a damned mageblood addict.

He bent down and tore a pale creature the size of my fist free of Harailt's exposed spine. It resembled a segmented beetle with too many legs and dozens of translucent threads instead of mandibles. It squirmed in his hand, frantic squeals hurting my head. "It would seem I am surrounded by tyrants this day. One of the mind–" he winked at me "–and this so-called 'lord of flesh' the ravak daemon spoke of. Pah."

The gory figure tutted at Harailt's remains. "Are you even aware how much this wretched parasite manipulated your feeble mind? I suppose not, it is their speciality. They certainly managed to enslave the Skallgrim tribal leaders with ease."

His hand clenched and the squirming beetle-thing crunched and burst into flame. Then the god turned to me. "Greetings, Edrin Walker. You are more resourceful than I had given you credit for, a veritable pain, in truth."

"What are you talking about?" I said, staring at him in horror. "What... what was that thing?"

Nathair cackled. "The creatures call themselves Scarrabus, an ancient and forgotten power waxing strong for the first time in millennia. The monsters hinted at in your oldest children's tales have awoken and they are returning to rule the fearful human masses they left to run free so very long ago. Did you really believe those Skallgrim savages could organize and wield such potent magics on their own? They were useful to me for a time. No longer."

I swallowed and stared him down. "And you, what is it you want?"

His mind probed my own, crude battering rams slamming into my defences, cracking them. I would not be able to keep him out for long. He pursed red lips, peeved I dared resist. "The Far Realms align in grand conjunction, allowing old powers to awaken and new powers to rise. Two hundred years ago a partial conjunction and the Arcanum's arrogance led to the Daemonwar. This is an age of change that enables me to break free of the chains that bind me to this damned city. This is the dawn of Nathair's dominion. Exciting times, no? Let us discuss the use of that lovely crystal after I have had a little snack."

He turned to the Skallgrim and his jaw cracked open to reveal serrated fangs and a forked tongue. The Skallgrim captain and his men – brave bastards all – attacked instead of fleeing. They chose poorly. Before their next breath he was on them. The Gifted captain was fast, the god faster – he plunged a hand through the captain's breastplate and tore the beating heart from his chest.

Nathair bit into the twitching organ with relish, slurping down Gifted blood while the wolf-ship raiders set about him with axes. He didn't even notice their blows, his flesh healing as soon as it was cut. The poor fools didn't have any idea that they were already dead.

A second Scarrabus parasite squirmed from the hole in the dead's captain's chest. Its pale and writhing head turned towards me.

I picked up the crystal and fled while the god was busy feasting. I had many failings, but not knowing when to run away wasn't one of them. My god was ratshit insane.

CHAPTER 33

The door to Lynas' warehouse dangled half off its hinges. A looter had taken an axe to it judging by the great gouges in the oak and the blackened corpse sprawled outside that was welded to a stick topped by a blob of deformed metal. It was no great loss to the world – only a fool would take an axe to something protected by big glowing Arcanum wards.

I stepped over the lump of stupid meat and bone and made my way over to the window, hauling my leaden body up and through, smearing a trail of blood across the wall. I dropped the murmuring crystal core of the Magash Mora, denting the floorboards, and slumped down into the regal comfort of the Esbanian merchant chair, desperately trying to think of any way to get out of this mess.

Harailt was dead – if he was lucky – but that didn't let Nathair off the hook. That traitor needed to burn, but how was I supposed to kill a sodding god? I'd done so once before, and as I scrabbled frantically at the locked doors in my mind a snatch of ethereal music whispered through my memory. I doubled over, vomiting and gasping as agony exploded in my skull. The seals were weakening but there was not enough time to pry them loose. I couldn't hope to face Nathair head-on, but even if I could come up with something desperate and sneaky enough to have a hope of thwarting him, he would rip that plan from my mind and body before I ever succeeded. *Fuck fuck shitting fuck.* There was no way to hide it from him.

Destroying the Magash Mora was more important than revenge for Lynas; whatever else happened, that thing could not be allowed to live again. My nails dug into the smooth curved armrest. An idea began to coalesce. I knew what had to be done, and what I'd need to sacrifice to do it. I could never tell him anything about a plan if I physically burned out that part of my brain afterwards. I swallowed my bile and did not hesitate.

What was I doing? My head hurt like I'd been stabbed with a spear. Why was I standing in the middle of the room facing the back wall where a majestic tapestry of gold and red hung? My left hand twitched and trembled and I seemed unable to stop it. The regal merchant chair had been dragged from its corner to the centre of that wall, and behind it the foreign king's woven image bestowed his blessings. It looked like a seat for an arrogant prick. Was I giving Nathair a damned throne to sit and gloat on while I grovelled at his feet and begged for mercy? No, that wasn't my style.

A small sack sat open on the floor in front of me, containing two glass jars. My index finger throbbed as I noticed blood beading my fingertip, a small wound already healing. In the centre of the room a circle of fresh wards surrounded the crystal core, inscribed in my own blood but not yet activated. Blood was a potent medium to channel magic but it made me uneasy; even using my own was too akin to sorcery for my tastes.

Wind gusted through the gaps in the front door. Shutters strained at their hinges as the building creaked and groaned, trembling at the god's unhurried approach. My enhanced senses told me I had only minutes left before his arrival.

I probed my memory, trying to find out what had just happened, and discovered a hideous gaping wound, a dead zone where part of my brain had been burned out. I gagged, shivering in horror at the self-mutilation. A thousand pathways of thought and their connected memories were broken and burnt along with that single tiny piece, the effect cascading through everything, changing what it meant to be me. I had mutilated and killed Edrin Walker and now a new me stood in his place. I clenched my trembling left hand, now sure it was a symptom of crude and hurried self-butchery.

Somehow I knew what I was supposed to do. Dazed, I placed both hands inside the circle and activated the matrix of wards and protections I'd woven through those the Arcanum had previously set up to protect the warehouse. The hiss of stray magic caused the hairs on my arms to stand on end. It was a work of brute force rather than finesse, but in my experience finesse was vastly overrated – a shovel to the face was every bit as good as a fancy sword.

My circle of wards drew power from the crystal core and fed it to the warehouse's outer security. This was it, the last toss of the dice. For a moment I felt faint; I was at my limits and didn't have much more to drag out of my wreck of a body. I sagged, face slick with sweat and my tunic plastered to my back.

Unsure of what to do next, I examined the small sack. Inside were two fluted glass bottles with broken seals, filled with some sort of dirty brown liquid instead of exotic alcohol. I was meant to glass the whoreson and then throw my strongest wind-wall at him. Well, fair enough... if you couldn't trust your past self... and knowing me I'd probably had some vicious surprise in mind.

I was as ready as I was ever going to be, but I didn't fancy dying looking like a penniless drunk who had choked to death on his own vomit so I used a little aeromancy to scour all the sweat, grease and blood from my body with blades of air, ridding me of my unwashed stink. I let the congealed mess slop across the doorway, then straightened out my ragged coat and raked my hair back into some semblance of order.

As I stepped inside the warded circle my skin tingled, pins and needles stabbing. I gripped Dissever tight and faced the doorway. My wicked knife exuded a subdued and nervous hunger. I hefted one of the glass bottles and wondered what kind of deadly magic I'd brewed in such a ridiculously short time.

At least he had the good grace not to keep me waiting. Dust drifted down from the rafters as the building began to shake. A twitch of pain heralded the shattering of the outermost alarm wards. I took a deep breath and nailed an insolent sneer to my face.

The door crumbled at his touch. In my Gift's eye the god blinded like the sun. To my mortal eyes he looked like a wiry little rat-faced shitebag scarred by pox and poverty and the boots of better men, no different from a thousand Docklands scum apart from crimson glistening orbs instead of eyes. He stood at the threshold with blood dripping from clawed fingers and strings of gore drooling down his chin.

The god's gaze slicked across the room. "Ah, yes, Edrin Walker. So good to see you." His mind – so bloody strong! – hammered into my own. The probing was clumsy but the strength behind it was gradually buckling my defences inward, allowing him to catch whiffs of stray thought. I was glad I'd burned away all knowledge of my plan.

"The feeling is not exactly mutual," I replied, struggling to keep the tremble from my voice. "You've always stood for freedom and independence, Nathair, so I beg you to turn back from this madness. Nobody else has to die."

His head cocked to one side. "Freedom and independence? Ridiculous. You mortals have always ascribed meaning where there is none. I care nothing for what the grubbing maggots of this city do beyond providing me amusement. The only freedom that has ever mattered is my own."

Gods, selfish bastards the lot of them. "Well, then, I don't suppose you'd care to piss off and die?"

"Tsk, is that any way to talk to your patron god? Give me the crystal. In exchange I will heal your dying friend. That is your heart's desire is it not?"

He knew it was. Bile seared my throat as his words tortured me. This was Charra's only chance, but as much as I loved her I couldn't doom the world for her. "She's not the sort to choose her life over everybody else's," I said. What was left of her life was hers to spend, not mine to gamble away.

His gaze drifted to the crystal core pulsing in the centre of my circle of wards, its jaundiced light staining the room. An eye ticced. His lips twisted into a snarl and he reached for it, hand passing through the doorway. I squeezed my eyes tight.

The world flashed red and white. An almighty concussion rent the air. Splinters of wood rained down around me. When I opened my eyes again blue spots danced and Nathair stood in a smoking crater where the doorway had been, frowning at his charred arm. Blood dripped from a few tiny wounds to hiss into the floor.

I swallowed. Those wards would have painted the walls with me. "Hey arsehole," I said, every bone in my body screaming to dive out the nearest window and make a run for it. Instead I made him angry. "You helped kill Lynas, you rat-faced imbecile. You will burn for that. When people ask me how you died I'm going to tell them you choked on your own stupidity."

Lips drew back and his jaw yawned unnaturally wide, teeth elongating into fangs. He surged towards me and slammed headfirst into my second web of wards. Only, these were not designed to harm, but to hold. The crystal core flared bright, its obscene power strengthening my defences.

The god's advance slowed, then stopped as the crystal pulsed faster. I smiled. "That's right, you witless scrotum scraping, I made that crystal the keystone of my wards. If you want to break free you'll need to destroy the very thing you want so badly. Suck on that, you muck-snipe!" A god was likely all that could; the plan to use the alchemic bomb had been a long shot at best. It would be a pyrrhic victory if he destroyed it before tearing me limb from limb, but what more could a mere magus possibly do?

He looked from the crystal to me, then shrugged. "I'll acquire another. I have all the time in the world now."

My jaw dropped.

Tentacles of blood, strangely solid, erupted from his back. I ducked as they stabbed towards my face, piercing through layers of my holding weave. They slammed to a stop against another barrier only a hand-span from ripping out my eyes. Wards crackled and hissed as the tentacles inched forward, forcing their way through. The crystal core hummed and pulsed. Unencumbered by any possible warding, the god's mind was free to batter deeper into my own.

I gritted my teeth. *Hold, damn you. Hold!* With him temporarily immobilized, I flung the first of my bottles, then the second. One shattered across his face, the second against his naked chest. They didn't explode. There was no eruption of deadly magic. They just left brown sludge oozing down his body. The room stank of shite.

A scream burst from my lips as I twisted my magic into a wind-wall and blasted him with every fragment of strength I could muster. A howling gale briefly tore at him, shedding droplets of filth like a stinking rain into the night air. The wind dwindled to nothing, the strain too much to continue. I sagged, and we stared at each other in silence for a long moment.

"That was all you had left?" he said. "One last, futile insult?" He laughed, wiping tears of blood from his eyes. "Shit, piss, blood, and soured wine. Ah, Walker, you always did amuse me. It must have been blind, idiot luck that you managed to kill Artha."

He expanded in my mind, magical aura growing until it felt like he would crush me by weight of presence alone. He stepped forward and the crystal core of the Magash Mora shrieked and shattered, instantly overpowered. A hundred dead pieces tinkled across the floor. The warehouse plunged into a gloom filled with a roaring maelstrom of magic that tore at my Gift.

He grabbed for me and I jerked back. Clawed fingers tore a hunk of hair from my head, bringing tears to my eyes.

"Oh," he said. "A magical adaption to sense air movement, most interesting. Very painful to have it ripped out I would imagine." The Thief of Life shook his head with exaggerated sadness and tossed my hair aside. "You could have been so much more, little tyrant. You could have been so useful if you had not fled from me and destroyed what was mine." He pointed a finger and I slammed face-first to the floor, crying out as a rib snapped, Dissever falling from my grasp. He tutted. "Pathetic. You have taken all the fun out of this, but perhaps I can find a use for you, once certain adjustments have been made. A shame it leaves the subjects somewhat devoid of imagination. For you, however, I would consider it an improvement." He leaned down and briefly caressed my scarred cheek with a clawed hand. I winced as a nail gouged a bloody furrow. I heard a sucking of fingers. "Ah, a new flavour of mageblood. A little sour."

I groaned, tried to rise, failed. "You expect me to serve a pathetic god slaved to his foul habit? You are a fool who allowed himself to become addicted to mageblood provided by a self-entitled arsehole of a blood-sorcerer."

The weight pressing down on me doubled. Face-down, struggling to breathe, all I could see was a gory foot as he stroked my throat with long, gnarled toenails.

"I will become the sole God of Setharis, and of this world," he said. "For too long have I been concerned with petty thoughts and limited creatures. And duty, always that dreary duty and the endless task of guarding this realm."

He snarled, bloody saliva dripping onto my cheek, searing a trail across my lips. "You think me addicted to mageblood like that cretin Harailt? Your imagination is far too limited. I intend to give part of myself to every creature that crawls, swims and flies upon this world – a drop of blood swimming in the veins of all creatures, as it already does within my worshippers. All life will become one with me, and all its magic will flow into their One True God. There will be no more Gifted, there will only be Nathair." His eyes burned with all-consuming lust for power. "I will ascend to a new existence beyond that of what you call a god, a great power able to extend my dominion across all realms near and far."

"What of Derrish and Lady Night, the Lord of Bones or the Hooded God?" I groaned. "Won't they stop you?"

Keep him talking, something screamed inside me.

"The gods of Setharis are bound here by enchantments the likes of which you cannot conceive, and which no god can break. The Magash Mora, however, devours all magic." He smirked. "I trapped them below the earth and sacrificed this city to free myself from the chains that bind them still, and I would do so ten times over if needs be. I no longer suckle at the same teat of power as those so-called gods, the very power that binds us to this place. Blood is a stronger source by far. The Scarrabus' art of using mageblood to grow the Magash Mora showed me the path to true power."

I shook my head, not understanding.

He sighed. "I always forget how ignorant you little creatures are. Have you never wondered why the soldiers of Setharis are called wardens? The title has meaning. The gods of Setharis suckle power from the fever dreams of the Imprisoned, that hoary old beast entombed in the heart of the Boneyards, kept slumbering for untold millennia by our constant effort. In ancient days when even the Scarrabus were young, the Imprisoned devoured entire realms, and would again were it to wake. I could not contest the gods of Setharis directly lest our battle wake the beast and doom us all." He cackled. "No more, no more – let those foolish gaolers remain chained to their charge, tortured by the effort of keeping it dormant. Oh blood-blessed freedom, after all this time! Soon I will leave this decrepit city to travel the wide world, and then on to other realms. I will grow in power as worshippers flock to accept my blood, and then in time I shall return to devour those false gods and the ancient beast they guard."

His eyes misted over. "Where shall I go first? What new lands shall I see?" Then he blinked and licked his lips, eyeing me hungrily. "First I must uncover those secrets squirreled away inside your head. You think them secure, but I will have them. Nothing can be hidden from me, not even by the power of false gods. The Arcanum cannot help you and your friends cannot save you. Submit!"

His eyes flared with power. Distilled agony shrieked through my body, pain that nothing living should ever feel. Bones cracked, flesh bulging grotesquely from my torso, organs moving and tearing. His thoughts crashed into me, impossible to resist for long. I screamed, pleading for him to stop.

A shadow flitted into view behind him. He saw it reflected in my eyes and a clawed hand stained with my excrement reached for whoever dared interfere.

A shadow cat tore it off at the elbow. The hulking black beast barrelled past, jaw chomping down on the still-moving hand covered with my scent. The god and I locked gazes for a drawn-out moment, realisation dawning at the same time. My piss, shite, and blood had been in those jars and I had blown a cloud of my scent and magic out into the city. At the moment he smelled more like me than I did.

Hissing filled the air as the rest of the pack slid from the gloom. Nathair growled and grew in height and bulk, defensive tentacles sprouting from his body as five more great daemonic felines leapt from the shadows, claws slashing. His remaining hand tore the face and jaw from one charging shadow cat. Tentacles wrapped around two more and lifted them struggling into the air. The faceless cat slammed into him like a charging horse, trampling him beneath clawed feet before crashing blindly into the wall. The two shadow cats still free of his grip pinned him down and began ripping huge chunks of blood and bone free. Their daemonic fangs and claws proved far more effective than Skallgrim axes.

The crushing weight lifted from my chest. I bit my lip bloody trying to keep the screams in, flailed for Dissever, found it and rolled away from danger. Dissever's rage was the only thing keeping me conscious. I managed to wedge myself against the wall under a rack of shelves as blood and meat rained down all around me. The tentacles holding two shadow cats aloft contracted, snapping thigh-thick spines like dry twigs. Jets of black blood splattered the walls and steamed into dark mist.

A muffled screech to my left drew my eyes to where the first shadow cat had been eating the god's hand. The severed limb had dug its way into the beast's throat, gouging bloody holes as its huge head whipped from side to side trying to dislodge it. The faceless daemon spasmed on the ground nearby, spraying ichor as it busied itself with the task of dying.

My body shuddered at the mere thought of attempting to move, never mind escape. Something popped and twitched inside me, an organ or muscle sliding back into place. Blood filled my mouth as I bit the inside of my cheek. A magus could survive most things, but this...

The god surged upright, throwing two massive corpses at the doorway, smashing gaping holes through the stonework. Half his face was a ruined mess of shattered bone and jellied brain, but it didn't seem to matter. He began a frenzied attack on the other two shadow cats, fang to fang and claw to claw, his terrible ferocity forcing the hulking beasts back.

He laughed off the mortal wounds as his hand plucked a huge feline head from its shoulders like a child picking a flower. Ribbons of pulsing blood wrapped around the other in front of him and pulled the screeching daemon apart one limb at a time.

The cat choking on his other hand rolled and writhed across the floor as the severed appendage savaged its way deeper down the creature's throat. The cat tried to vomit up the hand, struggled until the hand's owner caught up with it and stamped on its head, crushing the skull to a pulp. The faceless shadow cat was the last, its flanks heaving and bloody froth pooling around its throat. The god bent over and buried his fangs in its neck, a nauseating lapping and slurping accompanying the feast. The severed hand crawled out of the other corpse and scurried back home to his wrist while the corpses disintegrated into black mist.

Coughing racked me, my ribs cracking as blood sprayed from my mouth. His expression was utterly bestial as he scurried over on all fours to sniff me. The light of reason returned to his eyes and he reached under the shelves to drag me out by the throat, dangling me in the air like a deranged child holding a puppy.

I plunged Dissever into the arm holding me, but I didn't have the strength to cut deep. Ecstatic power flushed through me as it feasted on god's blood. The Thief of Life winced, slapped my hand away and wrenched Dissever free. The black barbs tore chunks of his flesh out with it.

"What a nasty toy," he said. "You have no idea what sort of horror you formed a pact with. Not that it matters now." His hand squeezed. Dissever resisted for a few seconds, then shattered.

I threw up my right arm to protect my eyes as chaotic magic and metal exploded, needles of black metal piercing my hand. I convulsed as the dark spirit that was Dissever burst free of its prison, and from inside me, with alien glee.

Free! It shrieked in my mind. Dissever was no spirit born from the magic of this world, but was instead some sort of vile daemon. The Shroud between realms tore as its essence surged into the sea of magic that lay beyond the barrier, returning to whatever blood-soaked daemon realm had birthed it. With a small thunderclap, it was gone and the Shroud healed. But not all of Dissever had left me: lurking in the back of my mind remained a small fragment of red hunger and blackest mirth. Our pact was still intact and from elsewhere Dissever watched and waited, expectant, hungry to see what I would do next.

Nathair dropped his jaw like a laughing beast. "If you had known how to play with it properly then you might have posed me more trouble, but never mind, we shall have plenty of time to spend together in the coming days. What fun we will have!" He grinned, exposing jagged teeth like a laughing shark. "I admit that Harailt's little pack of daemons surprised me. I had attributed your previous actions to desperation and now I am forced to admire your base-born cunning. A fine attempt, but futile. Now, back to this secret you possess."

I grimaced and tried not to pass out. "Why are you so interested in what's in my head?" I felt him inside me as an oily slick spreading and seeping into every crack in my defences.

"Somehow you killed Artha, mortal. His death was beyond me and I want to know how the likes of you managed such a feat."

I spat a big glob of blood and mucus into his eye.

He didn't blink or wipe it off. As it slid down his cheek his tongue stretched out to lick and swallow even as his feral mind-probes sliced my thoughts open like a butcher gutting a rotten pig. I was too feeble to resist. "You really don't remember killing a god, do you?" he said, amazement in his voice. "Ah, there is the cause." His power roared through me like a flood. Every part of me screamed in terror as Nathair tore my dire secret free from its prison.

CHAPTER 34

"Artha, uh... m'lord," I say. "Have you gone completely batshite insane?" I scan the inside of his tower, wary of currents of magic that can easily reduce me to ash.

"You test my patience, Edrin Walker," the Setharii god of war says. He lies naked on his back atop the cold and unadorned stone slab that is his most holy of altars. "We have a bargain. Cut deep and cut now, while I can still keep my rage at bay. My will falters. My Gift opens and the Worm of Magic devours more of my self-control each time I succumb. Soon I will become more beast than man."

I don't know where to look. He is impressive, give him that. I avert my eyes and force my shaking hands to press the edge of Dissever to the notch in his chest just below the throat. I pause. "My friends – you've arranged their safety? You will heal Charra?" His promise to kill them if I don't do what he demands still makes me furious, but now I understand the urgent necessity.

He stares up at the vaulted ceiling of twisted golden beams, to where a storm of magic rages above, not blinking as eldritch lightning flashes and arcs down all around us. "Yes. Their transgressions have been wiped from all record and false papers placed so their child need not suffer the Forging. The Lord of Bones and Lady Night will honour our deal and ensure that no magus or god shall ever harm them. They will see to the health of your friends and enforce our secrets." He grits his teeth. "Do it now." His voice brooks no dissent.

As I'd been shown, I open up my Gift and begin to sing, twisting my magic through the words in a very particular way. The words are meaningless, the mental and magical rhythm is the thing. I spit out words fast and sharp, my tune in time with the god's heartbeat. I feel my Gift beginning to resonate with the inner core of his power, enticing layers of arcane protections to open up and accept my presence. I have been handed the secret of killing our gods, a heady and terrifying burden.

I cut deep, blood welling up as Dissever slices through skin. It's tough going, even though Dissever goes through most things as if they are soft butter. The blade jars against bone and I have to brutally wrench it up and down to saw my way through, working the cut down the centre of his chest until a ragged red trench splits it in two. His flesh quivers, trying to heal, but somehow he holds that at bay.

Artha's face is a mask of stoic suffering as he hooks his fingers into the wound and wrenches his ribcage open. It breaks with a crunch of cartilage and snap of bone, splaying open to display organs. His heart pulses with an eerie inner light.

He grimaces, one eye twitching at my hesitation. "Hurry. I can no longer keep the rage in check. My lucid periods grow steadily fewer. Unless you wish a mad god loose in Setharis do it now. Your friends will die first."

I ram Dissever into his heart. The knife sinks a finger-breadth into the muscle. The altar stone shatters beneath us, shards shredding my coat and skin. Jets of hot blood squirt across my face, potent magic searing a path down my chin. The knife point scrapes something solid. I hack away, widening the slick hole. Fire and lightning blasts the tower walls, burning my skin and crisping hair.

Without a weapon like Dissever it would be impossible, but that minor detail wasn't why they needed me – others far more *reliable had spirit-bound weapons. I wrench the knife free and light bleeds from the wound. My hand is poised over the chasm in his chest, sparks of living lightning crackling from the organ to wind around my fingers.*

Blind fury twists one side of the god's face: the Worm of Magic manifesting an animalistic survival instinct all of its own. The other side is a mask of incredible concentration as he fights to keep his body motionless, but he is failing. It seems that the mind of a god is easier to break than the body.

I plunge my hand into his flesh, gagging at the sensation of beating muscle and ascended human blood flowing up my arm. My fingers touch the thrumming crystal, the god-seed at his centre. Light explodes in my mind and I vibrate with unfathomable energy. I wrap my hand around the crystal and pull. His flesh stubbornly resists. I put one foot up on the altar and heave. The god-seed tears free in a fountain of blood. I gag, spitting blood as Artha screams and convulses. The tower shakes. Then he flops down unconscious, his wounds closing. The shaking ceases and the lightning stops. All is silent apart from my terrified panting.

I collapse to the floor, entire body trembling, and try to scrub his blood from my face with a ragged sleeve. Power, absolute blissful power, throbs in my hand, flows into me even as Artha's blood sizzles against my skin. This is the secret to ascension, a false Gift crafted from a flawless crystal of solidified magic, one capable of channelling more raw magic than anything of mere flesh and blood ever could.

I can be a god! I can take this power and do anything I wish, can cast down every bastard who... who... I shake my head groggily. No. That isn't me, and that wasn't the deal. I am human and intent on staying that way. I force my shaking hand to stretch out towards another figure coalescing from the shadows. I drop the source of the god Artha's power into the waiting hands of the Lord of Bones. The old man's white-bearded face is grim and riven by cracks of sorrow. He says nothing, only nods thanks for doing what he couldn't, then dissipates back into the darkness, taking the god-seed to wherever it has to go. Stolen power thrums through me.

Artha's chest rises and falls, his body twitching in the throes of foulest nightmare. I press my hands to either side of his head. He is so diminished, a mere Gifted mortal now, albeit still an ancient magus of such potency that he will stand head and shoulders above even the great Archmagus Byzant himself. As demanded, I begin using my power to wall away his memories. No other living magus is skilled enough to even attempt an act so deep and complex, and the other gods are either unable or unwilling to do it themselves.

I struggle to navigate the roaring floods of mental anguish and turmoil, to hide it all away beneath layer after layer of obfuscating walls, to twist his mental pathways away from the sources of his unreasoning rage. The changes to his Gift wrought by the Worm of Magic blindly resist at every stage but those Worm-wrought changes too are eventually bypassed and isolated from future thought.

When Artha wakes he will have no recollection of being a god or of having any magic beyond a certain innate physical strength and sturdiness impossible to hide. He will be spared memories of fields of rotting flesh picked over by crows and human scavengers, and of devastated tenements filled with the torn corpses of men, women and children slain to assuage his frequent rage. He will finally be free of the blight consuming his mind, instead blessed with a peaceful life tilling the soil of a small farm far to the north. I'm not sure he doesn't deserve to die here, but the Lord of Bones said that thousands of years of service and sacrifice demanded otherwise, and I didn't have a choice: Charra is sick and the Arcanum will burn Layla alive if I don't complete this task.

It is the hardest, most exhausting thing I have ever attempted, hour upon hour of gruelling effort with his Gift fighting my foreign magic every step. Without the stolen power and my absolute need to protect those I love, it would be impossible.

Finally, somehow, it is done, and after a brief rest I begin the

*long descent. Much later I saunter out through the shattered door
of the god's tower and light a soggy blood-stained roll-up from the
flaming wreckage. Artha's "death" cry still echoes weirdly through
the city as my plume of smoke twists into the air. Phantasms drift
through the night and animals all across the city scream and
scrabble in fear-frenzy as the ground shakes underfoot.*

*I flash a grin at the ominous black form of Lady Night, the
god's face a serene silver mask. Thick as thieves, her and the Lord
of Bones. The gods owe me, and I will make sure they honour
the debt. The bargain was struck and only the suicidal welch on
deals with gods. The only one to suffer will be me, but I am fine
with that.*

*"I'm gasping for a drink," I say to her, my throat parched and
my lips burnt and cracked. "You buying? I'm sure you lot can
stretch to that."*

*Icy eyes glare out from behind the mask, silver pupils as broken
as the moon. My grin melts. "It is time for you to leave Setharis,
Edrin Walker," she says, her voice deceptively soft and melodious.
"Forget, and never return."*

I swallow and nod. It was worth it.

Her power sears through my being, locking everything away.

Shock ripped Nathair from my mind. "Alive?" His hand
squeezed my throat harder as he forced his way back into
my mind. I convulsed, choking, blood gushing from my
nose. "Artha lives," he snarled, licking his lips. "He taught
you how to kill us, and those two crusty old liars had a hand
in it. Damn them, how did they know I would betray them
given the chance? What else have you hidden from me?"

He tore my mind wide open, shattering every lock and
door; all except for one, an old barrier of a different nature.
He cursed me, but it wasn't my lock, it wasn't my door, and
I hadn't even known it existed. Somebody else had blocked
off that part of my memory long ago and hidden it from me

– but he didn't care about that. He ignored the burnt-out part of my mind and focused his entire attention on tearing that last barrier apart to bathe in the hidden memories.

Beyond that last locked door lay the great and wonderful Byzant, my friend and mentor. All the times the elder magus had helped me, listened to my worries and soothed my fears – except, now, everything was changed, darkened, and my horror was complete. I now knew what that bastard did to me.

Flashes of Byzant strapping me to his chair flicked through my mind's eye, Nathair watching and laughing voyeuristically as I relived the vile sensation of Byzant being in my head, *adjusting* things to make me into the bitter and contrary bastard that I was – ensuring that I'd build myself an early pyre. It was no wonder that all magi of my sort to appear in the last five hundred years had died young. They were not allowed to live. Those bastard elder magi refused to take the risk and made it look like every one of those poor fools had done it to themselves. Lacking my true Gift for such magics, Byzant utilized a crude but effective alternative to my own techniques, one that exploited my trust in him.

My world rocked, any sense of self torn free. I was not the hard drinking, wild-eyed rebel I thought I was. All I had ever been, Byzant had crafted. Paranoia and self-doubt crippled me, but then came anger. He had made me one thing, but I had burnt that old Walker away.

Nathair lapped it all up from inside my mind, drank in all my secrets and exulted in my utter betrayal and his complete victory. The bastard was distracted, out of his body and far from his home turf. It took a special kind of arrogance to enter the mind of a tyrant, even for a god. It was time to kick him in the balls.

I'd always held back. Always terrified I'd lose control. Lynas had helped steer me right, but he was gone. Byzant had tried to get me killed and Charra was dying. I loosed my rage and savaged the bastard's mind, as brutal as I'd ever feared I would become – one last gasp of power shredding the soft underbelly of his mind. He screamed and squeezed my throat. Everything went black.

I woke sprawled on the floor, blood oozing from burst lips and a broken nose, but that pain was nothing compared to the rest of me. I groaned and flopped over, throat bruised and swollen. The god was still standing, arm outstretched, his face a rictus of horror. I had no idea how much time had passed.

Something was very, very wrong with him. Whatever damage I'd done went beyond the mental, as if his body was merely magical artifice, a glove he wore at whim. The Shroud shuddered and strained as ribbons of emotion burst from his chest in a spray of gore. A multitude of stars and swirling globes of thought drifted through the fabric of his existence. His body deformed, stretching and contracting into impossible angles that transcended physicality. Eyes, jaws, tentacles, wings, claws and other things and feelings I didn't have names for erupted in endless variety.

I dragged myself away, inch by agonizing inch. His eyes flared into blood-red suns, bleeding enough power to turn a village to dust in an instant if it hadn't all been focused on survival. He reconstructed his body like a disassembled blacksmith's puzzle, but his flesh was all wrong: bone jutted from pulsing flesh, gaping wounds oozed blood and fluid and torn veins dangled like branches on a willow. An arm was on backwards.

"What... did... you do... to me?" the god gasped. "I have forgotten... things."

I shook my head and almost blacked out, barely able to think through the pain flooding my body.

I crawled towards the merchant's chair. What pit that thought came from in my fragmented consciousness I didn't know, but I heeded the desperate impulse. I had one last, secret weapon.

Nathair's breath came fast and ragged. Like a wounded beast he turned towards me, air whistling through holes torn in throat and chest.

I wasn't going to make it. The merchant's chair might as well have been leagues of rugged moor and mountains away.

A foot slammed down on my spine. Droplets of blood pitter-pattered onto my back.

"Well played." He laughed, an executioner's mirth. "To think you had that left." His foot pressed harder, grinding down.

I prayed for somebody to save me as he ground his foot down, forcing shrieks of agony from me.

It made him laugh. "Your petty gods cannot help. And ah, such delicious irony, the Hooded God certainly would never help you of all people, for he is your beloved mentor Byzant ascended to take Artha's place." His foot lifted for a few moments, "I know his betrayal hurts, I can feel it's delicious pain in you. It is his forte, however. You have no idea of the number of magi he killed on his path to ascension and the search for Artha's god-seed." The god chuckled and his foot slammed back down. "The ignorant, arrogant fool. He did not understand that to be a god of this accursed place is to be its servant and prisoner. I hope he is enjoying being chained in the darkness below. Now, what shall I do with you, hmm?"

Coughing, I tried to plead for mercy. "I–"

Crack – my spine shattered under his foot. My legs went numb. I blacked out.

Brutal healing ripped through my body.

"Not yet," Nathair growled. His exhaustion was a palpable force emanating from his ruined body. "Let us just make sure we have scoured every shred of knowledge from you, then your indoctrination as my servant can begin." He plunged his fingers into my chest and teased out a rib. I screamed as he snapped it between two fingers. Healing power gushed into me again as he tossed the shards of rib at my face. "You will not need that."

He suddenly wavered, shaking his head groggily. He staggered back and barely caught his balance. "What did you burn from my mind? I will find out one way or another."

Clumsy mental probes battered into me again, deeper and deeper, but I wasn't in any condition to try to resist. It wasn't easy for him. Even without conscious thought, the core of my mind was a devious, cruel creature. I'd long ago taken precautions against the very talent that I knew best. He wouldn't enslave me easily. The weakened god groaned and sagged against the wall as the mental effort of twisting his power into my peculiar path took its toll. I tried to stand, to run, but my shaking legs refused to bear my weight. I flopped to the floor, screaming, arms clamped to butchered side and broken back that hadn't fully healed yet.

"I see a part of your brain has been destroyed to keep the answers from me," he said. "Those memories I cannot obtain, but I am confident we can piece together enough fragments from your dead flesh to grant me some answers."

"Please," I said, defeated and out of options. Whatever last desperate hope I'd stashed in the merchant's chair was out of my reach. I'd failed and he knew it. "No more. I... I'll talk. Tell you everything you want to know. Please..."

"Of course you will," Nathair said, smiling at my abject defeat. Like all gods, he loved to feel superior. "The oh-so-witty little mortal reduced to this quivering slime. Pathetic. But you will still serve me well." He limped over to the fine merchant's chair opposite whilst worrying at the very last bastions of my mind. He collapsed into it, smirking, looking oh-so-regal.

The seat of the chair clicked, metal meeting metal.

Understanding hit us at the same moment. I realized what that burnt-out memory had been, and he was in my head, could see it all in my mind's eye: the seat pressing down on the brass cone, the nose clicking, setting off the alchemic bomb I'd stashed inside.

His hatred stabbed into me. "You little–"

A wall of blood and flesh smashed into me. The world went silent. I bounced across the floor in a cloud of dust and grit, the flesh of my back shredded and burning. The back wall collapsed in eerie silence, stones noiselessly careering across the floor. The entire upper storey and roof of the building was missing.

I blinked away dusty tears, utterly confused that I was still alive. Of the Thief of Life's ravaged body, nothing solid remained. A lightning storm raged in the space where he'd been sitting, bolts of incandescent energy arcing inwards to a single point of blinding light where his heart had been. The storm spun around a shard of glimmering crystal, spiralling ever faster inwards until it met a single point of brilliance that eclipsed that of the Magash Mora's crystal core. His god-seed.

Slowly, sound began to filter back. The building creaked and groaned around me, the cracking of wood and stone, pitter-patter of fragments of ceiling, the drip-drip-drip of blood and minced godflesh, the fizz and crackle of lightning. Fires kindled of their own volition mid-air, churning upwards in spinning vortices.

Blood and god-mush oozed around the floor with a queer life of its own, began blindly flowing back towards the crystal. He was not finished yet and his body yearned to rejoin the god-seed.

My Gift flailed away inside, desperately trying to repair all the damage to my body. I shook, god-blood drenched skin sparking with unfocused power. My body sucked it in like a sponge. Too much power. It filled me, stretched me, threatened to tear me apart. My Gift didn't have a hope of containing it: I wasn't a damn god!

Somehow I managed to sit up and find my voice. I sang, a very particular rhythm vomiting forth as a wail of hatred. What was left of Nathair writhed in agony, but I refused to stop. Artha's gift to me was revenge for the murder of Lynas. I made it to my knees, then after an age up onto my feet. I kept singing as I hobbled towards the incandescent light hanging in the air before me.

I reached the god-seed before Nathair.

The storm of magic ceased. Just for a moment, I wielded all the power of a god. It was mine and mine alone. The remnants of Nathair exploded, motionless puddles dribbling down into the earth. Was he dead? Perhaps; I felt no thought left in it.

I sensed four muted presences far below my feet, buried deep under the black rock of Setharis. They felt familiar, almost like kin. The gods called me to them and my feet began sinking through the rubble. No! Whatever they were, they were no kin of mine. "I hope you are in torment, Byzant." Gritting my teeth, I opened my tattered coat and forced my hand to drop the god-seed into the deep inside pocket, then collapsed like a puppet with its strings severed as strange presences and godly power both cut off.

I wanted to scream and kill, or to curl up and hide, maybe both. The Worm of Magic whispered desperate seductions but my despair was too complete to bother listening.

I was giddy with power and pain, my back crying out in distress. I was a wreck, and despite being full to bursting with stolen power it would take a long time to fully heal, if I ever did. Magical healing was not the same as never having been hurt. It might take years for my shattered bones to knit properly, and missing ribs did not re-grow. Still, I was alive and finally free of my daemons. I could share Charra's last days.

Black shards of Dissever lay half-buried in the debris. I tried to pick one up with my left hand, but it dropped from trembling fingers. I clenched it into a fist and used my right, needles of black iron still buried in the flesh. Nothing but cold and lifeless iron in my hand, but the daemon's presence still lingered at the back of my mind. At the moment it tasted content, with perhaps a smidgeon of pride. *Godslayer*, it whispered.

I limped towards a hole in the wall as the building crumbled around me. It was a strange feeling to be myself again, without disparate parts locked away and hidden in the darkened catacombs of my mind. But there was a hole burnt in my brain that would never heal, and aside from my left hand only time would tell what other problems that would cause. I staggered from the warehouse and it collapsed behind me. Lynas' home crashed down to rubble.

"I got the bastards, Lynas. I got them. You did it, you saved us. If you hadn't burnt down that temple and destroyed all that mageblood we'd all be worse than dead." Tears welled up in my eyes. It was over and Lynas' body was finally at rest, but I couldn't let go. Some of my memories had been damaged or destroyed by the god's brutal invasion of my mind, and more thanks to my own desperation. I felt their loss as much as you can without really knowing what you were missing, but other memories had been fully restored, fresh as ever and swimming about in my head. In a way that was far worse – it was like losing Lynas all over again.

I sat on the rubble, throat cracked and raw from screaming, stomach gnawing and empty, and looked up at the rock of the Old Town, where high up through the pall of smoke the five gods' towers remained silent. With Nathair gone I had half-expected four of them to explode back into life at any moment.

Inside my pocket, power called, and if I wanted, one of those towers could be mine. Honestly, right then I'd have happily traded it for a smoke, a jack of cold ale and a hot roast chicken.

CHAPTER 35

The streets were dead; not just quiet, actually dead. Corpses of cats and dogs and chicken and swine lay eviscerated and drained of blood, piles of feather and bone marking where the god had plucked birds from the sky. Even the tiny husks of flies and beetles littered the ground. Nathair had left nothing alive in his wake. I heard a wail and hobbled back the way I had come on my flight with the crystal with the vague hope of finding survivors trapped under collapsed buildings. Remnants of Skallgrim warriors were scattered across the street, a scrap of scalp and hair there, a finger here, and fragments of shredded armour and broken weapons that had proven useless.

I located the source of the noise and found Harailt still alive, if you could call the state he was in living. His body was a mound of quivering flesh wheezing and bubbling, and his mind a gutted and insane ruin. As I approached he mewled pathetically from a gash in what was left of his throat. Three battered and bloodied Skallgrim surrounded him – lucky stragglers arrived too late to enjoy Nathair's attentions – prodding the mound with weapons. I took their minds without a second thought. They stood motionless, awaiting my orders.

I didn't say anything as I approached the remains of Harailt. His single remaining eye begged me to end the agony. I knew that I should hand him over to the Arcanum, but I didn't have it in me to allow him to live, even in eternal agony. I almost stopped myself, thinking it would be far too quick an end for what he had done. But none of it was Harailt's fault, not really – he had been infested and controlled by Nathair and that Scarrabus parasite. Whatever he had done to me, nobody deserved this. I picked up a discarded Skallgrim axe and chopped, once, twice, a dozen more times to make certain.

He didn't die easily, and it wasn't quick. When he finally breathed his last I didn't feel the satisfaction that I'd expected given our history. I just felt empty.

My three mind-broken thralls followed me as I wandered in a daze back to what was left of Lynas' warehouse and slumped down atop a pile of rubble. I stared at nothing. Thinking. Hurting. Mourning. For what seemed like hours. Eventually footsteps crunching towards me made me look up.

Krandus and Cillian advanced on me through the smoke and dust. Cillian still looked half-dead, but had regained some of her strength since I'd seen her last.

My three Skallgrim thralls closed ranks around me. I wondered how I appeared to the Archmagus: guarded by the enemy, a torn and ragged figure dripping the blood and gore of a god and with a lake of stolen power seething inside me. My coat hung in tatters around my shoulders like a cloak of bloody skin, and at some point amidst the chaos I'd lost my right boot and the little toe with it, leaving just a ragged stump. I didn't feel that pain yet. Funny the trivial details that strike you when imminent death comes knock, knock, knocking at your door. A toe was the least of my worries.

They stopped ten paces from me, power vibrating amongst them like a leashed storm ready to be loosed in the blink of an eye. I waved off my thralls and heaved myself to my feet.

"Magus Edrin Walker," Krandus said, sounding exhausted. "The Arcanum has felt your power used against the populace of Setharis." He calmly eyed my enslaved Skallgrim. "I am required by law to charge you with the ancient crime of tyranny. As of old, we cannot suffer an enslaver to live. How do you plead?"

I lifted a hand to slick gory hair back over my shoulders. The sea of magic in my belly spoke to the wounded animal inside that wanted to lash out, to bring death and ruin to my enemies. It whispered words of victory and assurances of my own might: I had taken three men as my own, and I could take many more if I wanted. It was so difficult to summon the willpower to shove the urges to one side. That was what had defeated Artha in the end: when the god started listening to the corrupting urges of the Worm he began acting on instinct rather than rational thought, and he went too far down that slippery slope to climb back up. Not as he was. I refused to fall as he had – too many innocents would get hurt.

My finger probed at a loose tooth, shoved it back into its socket; it was only a tiny pain compared to my back. I cleared blood and gunk from my throat, spat it out. "The gods as my witness, I am no tyrant, if by tyrant you mean my power was used to enslave people outwith self-defence. What did you expect me to do? Let the Skallgrim tear me to pieces?" I nodded to Cillian. "Let Councillor Cillian be murdered?"

We faced each other down, the Archmagus studying me. The god-seed beat hot against my breast. My hand inched towards it. All I had to do was accept it and ascend, and then they would have to face a tyrant god. Ha, wouldn't the look on their faces be precious then. The Worm of Magic urged me to take the power for my own, but I was beaten down by the world, by pain and death, and didn't much fancy living forever. I imagined being a god with that slimy hooded arsehole Byzant at my side and not being able to kill him. Nathair had spoken of an endless duty and despite everything I didn't think him a liar; me and duty did not see eye to eye at the best of times. No, godhood was not for me. My hand dropped to my side.

Before Krandus could reply, the sky darkened. Feathery, screeching darkness descended. I didn't have the mental energy left to care as a whole flight of corvun alighted on the rubble all around me, dozens of razor claws and vicious beaks between the Arcanum and myself. I chuckled, figuring that it would be just my luck to survive the Magash Mora and the Thief of Life only to be pecked to death by fucking birds. They didn't look at me – bad meat perhaps – instead they cawed and flapped angrily in Krandus' direction.

I looked left and right at the vile creatures, then shrugged. "Ah well, doesn't look like everybody has it in for me."

The Archmagus stared, not at me, but at the birds. His lips twitched into a smile. "It would seem not." I hadn't taken him for one to pay heed to superstitious portents. He hesitantly nodded to them. "I think that clears things up. Do you agree, Councillor?"

Cillian relaxed. "I do."

"Then the law is satisfied," Krandus said. "Magus Edrin Walker is declared innocent."

I blinked. That was it? A charge of tyranny and the two of them dismissed it like it was nothing?

Cillian caught my look. "Martial law, Edrin. Two of the Inner Circle are enough to pass a judgement. The correct one, as it happens."

Every single corvun in the city shrieked and took flight, wheeling above our heads in a vast screeching flock. For the first time in recorded history the great birds ventured beyond the walls of Setharis. Black wings cut through the smoke as they headed out over the docks and across the bay to descend on the surviving Skallgrim wolf-ships fleeing back out to sea. This was no mere murder of crows – this was a carnage of corvun. People watched from rooftops and windows, through destroyed streets and fallen walls, as black death enveloped the ships. When the birds took flight again they left nothing human on those decks.

Krandus glanced at the remains of the Magash Mora, a hill of dead meat made from the corpses of hundreds of thousands of our people and then extended a hand to me. I stared at it for a moment and then clasped it, flesh to flesh. He didn't seem overly worried about a tyrant's touch. It was a display of trust that I had never expected to see. He turned and began the long trudge back up to the Old Town to resume control of his city. Cillian gave me a brief hug before she too left, and I thought my past misdeeds were forgiven as far as she was concerned. I suppose I had saved the city. What more could you ask of a man?

Perhaps the gods, wherever they were trapped, had heard my plea and borne witness after all. The Arcanum weren't all bad, just horribly entitled and not a little arrogant. Sometimes they forgot what it was like to be merely human, not much different from me at times.

As people began to return to the area, staring in shock at the ruins of their homes, I decided to slink off and find a hole to crawl into. I was exhausted and broken and needed to be alone. My thralls stood watch as I curled up in a ruined corner of a building and collapsed into blessedly dreamless sleep.

I woke to a symphony of pains and tried to take the stress off my damaged back and ribs by resting against the wall. Sitting next to the smouldering ruins of the room I had taken only a few days before in the Throne and Fire, it all seemed like an age ago. Another life. The scorched stone was still warm from last night's blaze. Morning mists and drizzle had killed off most of the smaller fires but columns of black smoke still snaked upwards from dozens of sites all across the lower city.

I was a wreck: exhausted, torn up and used up. My right hand itched: I scratched at the black specks, but the iron shards of Dissever were buried too deep to tease out. Every breath hurt and I barely had enough strength to turn my head as somebody slid down the wall next to me.

Dying as she was, face crisscrossed with scabs, Charra's smile was a beautiful thing. I didn't have words good and glorious enough to describe the feeling of being back home with her. In fact, she was my home. My home was people not place. She stifled a cough with a kerchief then wiped the blood from her lips. We sat in silence, watching people wander the streets dazed and smeared with soot, some raking through the debris of their homes on the slim chance of salvaging something of their lives, others weeping and cradling their dead or sitting numb with shock and staring off into the distance. The lucky ones gave shouts of joy and ran to envelop relatives and friends in fierce hugs. Most waited in vain for people to return home, knowing they would likely never see the bodies of their kin. Most of the dead had been melded into the reeking corpse of the Magash Mora.

"I don't have any words for this," Charra said.

I didn't reply, didn't feel there was much point. I couldn't even bring myself to meet her eyes. She was going to die, and far too soon.

Charra sighed. "Not everything in life ends well, Walker. I've tried everything possible to get out of this but I'm at the end of my voyage. At least I had my Layla and a few good friends. I have few regrets."

Despite the outcome, I felt like all I'd done was pointless. Now that I wasn't living under a death sentence I was terrified of the vast and empty gulf of life ahead of me. Now I knew why elder magi kept themselves apart from normal people: they were so short-lived and gut-wrenchingly fragile.

I eased open my tattered coat to show her the god-seed snug in my inside pocket. "How do you fancy being a god?"

"A god?" she asked, raising an eyebrow. "You jest."

I was utterly serious, and she understood that a moment later. She gasped, hand stretching out towards the shining crystal. Her finger stopped a whisker away from touching it.

"A bad idea to offer me so much power," she said. "I'd make an awful god."

I closed over my coat again. I was disappointed but it was as I'd expected. She would have been far better than some. "As would I, but it's your last chance. It might work with an unGifted."

She squeezed my arm. "Thank you, but no. I've made my peace." She looked up at the gods' towers, still dull and lifeless. "Do you know what happened to them?"

I shook my head. "Nathair and these Scarrabus things he was allied with did something to them, something terrible, but I have a feeling we would be in worse straits if they were dead."

A horse and cart drew up and a group of walking wounded clustered around it. A shrivelled up old chirurgeon, two of his apprentices, and a group of helpers hopped off the back to hand out bandages and poultices and wash out wounds with soured wine. They took out needle and thread and began stitching up wounds. People began distributing bread and water, no coin changing hands.

"I've been away so long," I said. "I've missed so much and I can't do a damn thing to help you now." My clenched fist pounded the ground. "Lynas is dead and it's all been for nothing if you die too." All those years away and all I'd had for comfort was the knowledge I was protecting them. What did I have to live for now?

She shook her head. "We can only do what we can do. You're not a god, Walker, and they got the shitty end of the stick too from what you said. Look around. All of this you see before you, all these people still alive – that is not nothing. Lynas did that. You did that. That's what's important. Who gives a damn what those Arcanum pricks think? Layla is fine, and a little piece of Lynas and I will live on in her. He would have called his sacrifice a bargain."

She was right. Charra was always right.

A young girl with a wine-stain birthmark caught my eye, busy splinting and strapping up a man's broken arm. I recognized her and remembered tossing her a handful of silvers outside an inn. She looked half-starved still but did have a new dress, albeit now bloodstained. She busied herself helping the wounded with a determined air, her hands deftly wrapping bandages. One of the chirurgeon's apprentices came over to speak to her. She gave him a shy smile and he flushed a little red. Their body language gave them away, both feeling that unspoken attraction. *Good for you, girl*, I thought; *a worthy profession, and perhaps even a loved one*. There would certainly be a need for healers in the days to come. I sat a little straighter.

Charra gave me a sad smile. "It feels petty to cry over my death amidst all of this. Let's have a going away party instead. I'd get more enjoyment by having it before rather than after. I don't see why everybody else should get all the fun." She slapped me on the back, making me squeak with pain.

"So I'm dying," she said. "Shit happens." She put an arm around my shoulders and pulled me in close. "You saved Layla. I can never thank you enough for that. Now stop being a big, ugly, moody bastard and give me a hug."

Gods help me, I did just that. My tears came thick and fast as I let go of all that bottled up emotion.

Something had changed inside me: all that stolen magic roaring through me, the god blood that soaked into my skin, the emanations of the crystal core and my own tampering… I felt a strange numbness when I thought about the masses of unknown dead. Hopefully it was just shock, but I wasn't holding my breath. All I could do was to hold onto my love for Charra and Lynas, and what was left of my humanity. Just because Lynas was dead didn't mean he was gone.

I pulled back from her and scowled down at myself, "Self-pity never helped anybody."

"It's good to have you back, you big idiot," she said. "I'll get a decent send-off now, hey?" She gave a morbid chuckle, then coughed blood again.

My heart gave a twinge. I couldn't save Charra, but I'd done good. And I'd damn well be around to help Layla – not that an assassin needed much help from anybody. We sat in silence for a while, lost in contemplation.

I couldn't help but absorb the mood of the people. More than ever their thoughts bled into my mind. It was not a hot anger, quick to flare up and swiftly burning out. This was a stone-cold fury that would not stop until cities burned and the shattered bones of our enemies were ground into dust.

This attack had been a very grave error. It was on every face, in every look of shock and loss that was slowly changing to rage. Apathy and in-fighting had been endemic before the horrors of yesterday. We had been a city divided and gnawing on its own rotting innards. If the enemy had bided their time and taken the Free Towns Alliance piece by piece before turning their eyes on us… but no, now that they had roused the serpent from its long slumber there was no lulling it back to sleep. We were a city united by rage and loss.

The Arcanum and the High Houses thought they ruled Setharis with an iron fist, but in reality they too bent to the will of the masses. Magic, wardens, steel and stone – all would be swept away if they dared oppose the unified will of the people of Setharis, and the people demanded war.

Setharis had once had a mighty empire, had callously crushed countless armies and ruthlessly consigned entire peoples to a footnote in history. The Skallgrim tribes would soon learn to regret ever rousing this dark leviathan from its apathetic slumber. And behind them their Scarrabus slavers would learn to fear. We knew they existed now, and we would hunt them with vicious zeal. But all of that would need to wait.

Layla approached us, face drawn and worried, "You found him then?"

Charra opened her arms and Layla flew into them, kneeling in the dirt next to us.

My withered heart gave a lurch, a pang of pure joy.

"So tell me, ladies…"

Charra quirked an eyebrow. "Tell you what?"

"The last ten years," I said. "Tell me everything. Layla, I wish I could have been here to see you grow up."

We talked for hours, and it was just like old times. Lynas was gone, but his daughter was here, safe and telling me silly stories about her beloved father. The hours galloped past until daylight ebbed and night's chill misted our breath.

Eventually Layla helped us old and broken things to rise, and as we limped off I vowed to focus all my efforts on making sure Charra's last days were the best they could be. We were going to lose somebody we loved, somebody who should have had years left to her. With my accursed magic all I could offer was an end to pain and the company of an old friend.

We passed through throngs of the homeless, the wounded

and bereaved. My lot was better than theirs. They'd had far more to lose in the first place.

Charra coughed again, tried to clear her throat with little success. "I could do with a strong drink."

"I'll buy," I said.

She half-laughed, the very best that could be hoped for under the circumstances. "It seems there is a first time for everything. Never thought I'd live to see the day when Edrin Walker bought the rounds. Wait a moment, you cad – I bet you're hoping that you can salvage ale from the ruins!"

As we talked my worry for the future deepened. I was not what anybody could ever call a good man, and soon there would be precious little left in this world that I truly cared about. I feared how deep into darkness I would sink. Other than Layla, what did I have to live for after Charra was gone?

With the gods still missing and the Arcanum wounded, the Skallgrim and their Scarrabus enslavers must have thought their plans successful, at least in part. They thought us defeated. They were so very, blindly wrong. Soon they would experience the pleasure of facing an enraged tyrant with little left to lose. I had run from everything for ten wretched years – no more! It was time to stand and fight. If Nathair had spoken truly then a grand conjunction of realms meant these disgusting parasites were only one of several awakening ancient powers, but none of them had ever seen anything like me. I had bathed in the blood of gods, and my power was growing.

In the back of my head the remnants of Dissever pulsed with pleasure. Images of rivers running red flashed through my mind.

A great war comes.

ACKNOWLEDGMENTS

Hi Mum and Dad! Look, I wrote a book, and it's in bookshops and everything. How very fancy. I guess all those after-school trips to the library for armfuls of books really paid off. Thank you for everything! Billy, thanks for letting me read all your sci-fi and fantasy books as a kid. I would not be a writer at all without my family's support – thanks for introducing me to fantastical worlds beyond number.

To Natasha, *waves* you always said I would make it. You were right, but then you usually are. Thanks to you, Paula and Michael for your constant encouragement and belief in me.

Thanks to the Glasgow Science Fiction Writers' Circle for all the sage advice and honest critique over the years, and especially Hal Duncan and Neil Williamson, without whom this book would not be a patch on what it is now.

Too many friends have given me encouragement and support to name them all here, but you know who you are, and you are awesome.

Thanks to my wonderful agent Amanda Rutter and all at Red Sofa Literary, the amazing team at Angry Robot who have made the publishing process a real joy, and Jan Weßbecher for providing the superb cover art.

Extra-special thanks go to my cat, Misty. Any typos were definitely her doing.

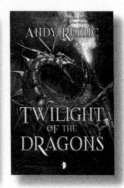

 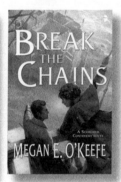 
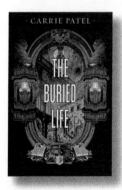 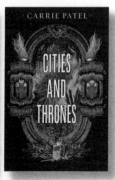 

The Axiom Diamond is a myth...
...and everyone wants to own it